Behind
Palace
Doors

BEHIND PALACE DOORS © 2024 by Harlequin Books S.A.

The publisher acknowledges the copyright holders of the individual works as follows:

UNTOUCHED QUEEN BY ROYAL COMMAND
© 2019 by Kelly Hunter
Philippine Copyright 2019
Australian Copyright 2019
New Zealand Copyright 2019

First Published 2019
Second Australian Paperback Edition 2024
ISBN 978 1 038 91975 5

OFF-LIMITS TO THE CROWN PRINCE
© 2021 by Kali Anthony
Philippine Copyright 2021
Australian Copyright 2021
New Zealand Copyright 2021

First Published 2021
Third Australian Paperback Edition 2024
ISBN 978 1 038 91975 5

STEALING THE PROMISED PRINCESS
© 2020 by Millie Adams
Philippine Copyright 2020
Australian Copyright 2020
New Zealand Copyright 2020

First Published 2020
Second Australian Paperback Edition 2024
ISBN 978 1 038 91975 5

MIX
Paper | Supporting
responsible forestry
FSC® C001695

Published by
Harlequin Mills & Boon
An imprint of Harlequin Enterprises (Australia) Pty Limited
(ABN 47 001 180 918), a subsidiary of HarperCollins
Publishers Australia Pty Limited
(ABN 36 009 913 517)
Level 19, 201 Elizabeth Street
SYDNEY NSW 2000 AUSTRALIA

Printed and bound in Australia by McPherson's Printing Group

Behind Palace Doors

KELLY HUNTER   KALI ANTHONY   MILLIE ADAMS

MILLS & BOON

CONTENTS

Untouched Queen By Royal Command

Kelly Hunter

MILLS & BOON

Books by Kelly Hunter

Harlequin Modern

Claimed by a King

Shock Heir for the Crown Prince
Convenient Bride for the King

Visit the Author Profile page
at millsandboon.com.au for more titles.

Kelly Hunter has always had a weakness for fairy tales, fantasy worlds and losing herself in a good book. She has two children, avoids cooking and cleaning and, despite the best efforts of her family, is no sports fan. Kelly is, however, a keen gardener and has a fondness for roses. Kelly was born in Australia and has travelled extensively. Although she enjoys living and working in different parts of the world, she still calls Australia home.

PROLOGUE

Augustus

THEY WEREN'T SUPPOSED to be in this part of the palace. Fourteen-year-old Augustus, Crown Prince of Arun, had been looking for the round room with the domed glass roof for at least six years. He could see that roof from the helicopter every time they flew in or out, but he'd never been able to find the room and no adult had ever been willing to help him out.

His father said that those quarters had been mothballed over a hundred years ago.

His mother said it was out of bounds because the roof was unsafe.

Didn't stop him and his sister looking for it, even if they never had much luck. It was like a treasure hunt.

They wouldn't have found it this time either, without the help of a map.

The floor was made of moon-coloured marble, and so too were the columns and archways surrounding the central room. The remaining furniture had been covered with dusty drapes that had probably once been white. Above all, it felt warm in a way that the main castle living areas were never warm.

'Why do we not live in *this* part of the palace?' asked his sister from somewhere not far behind him. She'd taken to opening every door of every room that circled the main area. 'These look like bedrooms. I could live here.'

'You want fifty bedrooms all to yourself?'

'I want to curl up like a cat in the sunlight. Show me one other place in the palace where you can do that.'

'Mother would kill you if you took to lounging about in the sun. You'd lose your milky-white complexion.'

'Augustus, I don't *have* a milky-white complexion— no matter what our mother might want. I have black hair, black eyes and olive skin—just like you and Father do. My skin likes the sun. It *needs* the sun, it *craves* the sun. Oh, wow.' She'd disappeared through another marble archway and her voice echoed faintly. 'Indoor pool.'

'What?' He backtracked and headed for the archway, bumping into his sister, who was backing up fast.

'Something rustled in the corner,' she muttered by way of explanation.

'Still want to live here?' He couldn't decide whether the hole in the ground was big enough to be called a pool or small enough to be called a bath. All he knew was that he'd never seen mosaic floor tiles with such elaborate patterns before, and he'd never seen exactly that shade of blue.

'I still want to look around,' his sister offered. 'But you can go first.'

He rolled his eyes, even as pride demanded he take the lead. He'd been born to rule a country one day, after all. A rustling sound would not defeat him. He swaggered past his sister and turned to the right. There was a sink for washing hands carved into the wall beside the archway, and taps that gleamed with a dull silver glow. He reached for one and, with some effort, got it to turn but there was no water. Not a gurgle, a splutter or even the clank of old pipes.

'What is this place? What are all these stone benches and alcoves for?' his sister asked as she followed him into the room. She kept a wary eye on the shadowy corners but eventually turned her attention to other parts of the room.

It was an old map of the palace that had guided them here. That and a history teacher who preferred giving his two royal students books to read so that he could then nap his way through afternoon lessons. Their loss. And sometimes their freedom. If they got caught in here, he could probably even spin it that they were continuing their history lesson hands-on.

'Maybe it was built for a company of warrior

knights who slept in the rooms and came here to bathe. They could have practised sword-fighting in the round room,' his sister suggested.

'Maybe.'

Kings had ruled from this palace stronghold for centuries. It was why the place looked so formidable from the outside and had relatively few creature comforts on the inside, no matter how many generations of royals had tried to make it more liveable. There was something about it that resisted softening. Except for in here. There was something soft and strangely beautiful about this part of the palace. Augustus plucked at a scrap of golden silk hanging from a peg on a wall and watched it fall in rotting pieces to the floor. 'Did knights wear embroidered silk bathrobes?'

His sister glanced over and gasped. 'Did you just destroy that?'

'No, I moved it. Time destroyed it.' Rational argument was his friend.

'Can I have some?'

Without waiting for permission, she scooped the rotting cloth from the floor, bunched it in her hand and began to rub at a nearby tile.

'It's going to take a little more than that to get this place clean.'

'I just want to see the pictures,' his sister grumbled, and then, 'Oh.' She stopped cleaning.

He looked, and…oh. 'Congratulations. You found the ancient tile porn.'

'It's *art*, you moron.'

'Uh-huh.'

'I wish we could see better in here,' his sister said.

'For that we would need electricity. Or burning torches for all the holders in the walls.' He closed his eyes and a picture came to mind, clear as day. Not knights and warriors living in this part of the palace and bathing in this room, but women, bound in service to the reigning King.

Augustus had never read about any of his ancestors having a harem, but then, as their eighty-year-old history teacher was fond of telling them, not all facts made it into their history books. 'So, bedrooms, communal bathing room, big gathering room…what else?'

There were more rooms leading from the centre dome. An ancient kitchen, storage rooms with bare shelves, larger rooms with fireplaces, smaller rooms with candle stubs still sitting in carved-out hollows in the walls. They found chests of drawers and sideboards beneath heavy canvas cloth, long mirrors that his sister swore made her look thinner, and even an old hairbrush.

'I don't think people even know this stuff is here,' Moriana said as she put the brush gently back into place. 'I don't know *why* they're ignoring it. Some of it's really old. Museum-old. The back of this brush looks like ivory, inlaid with silver, and it's just been abandoned. Maybe we should bring the history prof down here. He'd have a ball.'

'No.' His voice came out sharper than he meant it to. 'This is a private place. He doesn't get to come here.'

Moriana glanced at him warily but made no comment as they left the side room they'd been exploring.

All doorways and arches led back to the main room. It was like a mini town square—or town circle. He looked up at the almost magical glass ceiling. 'Maybe our forefathers studied the stars from here. Mapped them.' Perhaps he could come back one night and do the same. And if he took another look at those naked people tiles in the room with the empty pool, so be it. Even future kings had to get their information from somewhere. 'Maybe they hung a big telescope from the ropes up there and moved it around. Maybe if they climbed the stairs over there…' He gestured towards the stairs that ran halfway up the wall and ended in a stone landing with not a railing in sight. 'Maybe they had pulleys and ropes that shifted stuff. Maybe this was a place for astronomers.'

'Augustus, that's a circus trapeze.'

'You think they kept a circus in here?'

'I think this is a harem.'

So much for his innocent little sister not guessing what this place had once been. 'I'm going up the stairs. Coming?'

Moriana followed him. She didn't always agree with him but she could always be counted on to be there for him at the pointy end of things. It didn't help that their mother praised Augustus to the skies for his sharp mind and impeccable self-control, and never failed to criticise Moriana's emotional excesses. As far as Augustus could tell, he was just as fiery as his sister, maybe more so. He was just better at turning hot temper into icy, impenetrable regard.

A king must always put the needs of his people before his own desires.

His father's words. Words to live by. Words to rule by.

A king must never lose control.

Words to *be* ruled by, whether he wanted to be ruled by them or not.

They made it to the ledge and he made his sister sit rather than stand. He sat too, his back to the wall as he looked up to the roof and then down at the intricately patterned marble floor.

'I feel like a bird in a cage,' said Moriana. 'Wonder what the women who once lived here felt like?'

'Sounds about right.' He wasn't a woman but he knew what being trapped by duty felt like.

'We could practise our archery from up here.' Moriana made fists out in front of her and drew back one arm as if pulling back an imaginary arrow. 'Set up targets down below. *Pfft*. Practise our aim.'

'Bloodthirsty. I like it.' Bottled-up anger had to go somewhere. He could use this place at other times too. Get away from the eyes that watched and judged his every move. 'Swear to me you won't tell anyone that we've been here.'

'I swear.' Her eyes gleamed.

'And that you won't come here by yourself.'

'Why not? You're going to.'

Sometimes his sister was a mind-reader.

'What are you going to do here all by yourself?' she wanted to know.

Roar. Weep. Let everything out that he felt compelled to keep in. 'Don't you ever want to be some place where no one's watching and judging your every move? Sit in the sun if you want to sit in the sun. Lose your temper and finally say all those things you want to say, even if no one's listening. Especially because no one's listening.' Strip back the layers of caution and restraint he clothed himself in and see what was underneath. Even if it was all selfish and ugly and wrong. 'I need somewhere to go where I'm free to be myself. This could be that place.'

His sister brought her knees to her chest and wrapped her arms around her legs. The gaze she turned on him was troubled. 'We shouldn't have to hide our real selves from everyone, Augustus. I know we're figureheads but surely we can let *some* people see what's underneath.'

'Yeah, well.' He thought back to the hour-long lecture on selfishness he'd received for daring to tell his father that he didn't want to attend yet another state funeral for a king he'd never met. 'You're not me.'

Sera

Sera wasn't supposed to leave the house when her mother's guest was visiting. Stay in the back room, keep quiet, don't ever be seen. Those were the rules and seven-year-old Sera knew better than to break them. Three times a week, maybe four, the visitor would come to her mother's front door and afterwards there might be food for the table and wine for her mother, although these days there was more wine and less food. Her mother was sick and the wine was like medicine, and her sweet, soft-spoken mother smelled sour now and the visitor never stayed long.

Sera's stomach grumbled as she went to the door between the living room and the rest of the once grand house and put her ear to it. If she got to the bakery before closing time there might be a loaf of bread left and the baker would give it to her for half price, and a sweet bun to go with it. The bread wasn't always fresh but the sweet treat was always free and once there'd even been eggs. The baker always said, 'And wish your mother a good day from me'. Her mother always smiled and said the baker was a Good Man.

Her mother had gone to school with him and they'd played together as children, long before her mother had gone away to learn and train and become something more.

Sera didn't know what her mother meant by *more*; all she knew was that there weren't many things left in their house to sell and her mother was sick all the time now and didn't laugh any more unless there was wine and then she would laugh at nothing at all. Whatever her mother had once been: a dancer, a lady, someone who could make Sera's nightmares go away at the touch of her hand…she wasn't that same person any more.

Every kid in the neighbourhood knew what she was now, including Sera.

Her mother was a whore.

There was no noise coming from the other room. No talking, no laughter, no…other. Surely the visitor would be gone by now? The light was fading outside. The baker would close his shop soon and there would be no chance of bread at all.

She heard a thud, as if someone had bumped into furniture, followed by the tinkle of breaking glass. Her mother had dropped wine glasses before and it was Sera's job to pick up the pieces and try to make her mother sit down instead of dancing around and leaving sticky bloody footprints on the old wooden floor, and all the time telling Sera she was such a good, good girl.

Some of those footprints were still there. Stuck in the wood with no rugs to cover them.

The rugs had all been sold.

No sound at all as Sera inched the door open and put her eye to the crack, and her mother was kneeling and picking up glass, and most importantly she was alone. Sera pushed the door open and was halfway across the room before she saw the other person standing in front of the stone-cold fireplace. She stopped, frozen. Not the man but still a visitor: a woman dressed in fine clothes and it was hard to look away from her. She reminded Sera of what her mother had once been: all smooth and beautiful lines, with clear eyes and a smile that made her feel warm.

Sera looked towards her mother for direction now that the rule had been broken, not daring to speak, not daring to move, even though there was still glass on the floor that her mother had missed.

'We don't need you,' her mother said, standing up and then looking away. 'Go home.'

Home *where*?

'My neighbour's girl,' her mother told the visitor. 'She cleans here.'

'Then you'd best let her do it.'

'I can do it.' Her mother stared coldly at the other woman before turning back to Sera. 'Go. Come back tomorrow.'

'Wait,' said the visitor, and Sera stood, torn, while the visitor came closer and put a gentle hand to Sera's face and turned it towards the light. 'She's yours.'

'No, I—'

'Don't lie. She's yours.'

Her mother said nothing.

'You broke the rules,' the older woman said.

Sera whispered, 'I'm sorry…'

At the same time her mother said, 'I fell in *love*.'

And then her mother laughed harshly and it turned into a sob, and the older woman straightened and turned towards the sound.

'You didn't have to leave,' the older woman said gently. 'There are ways—'

'No.'

'You're one of us. We would have taken care of you.'

Her mother shook her head. No and no. 'Ended us both.'

'*Hidden* you both,' said the older woman. 'Do you really think you're the first courtesan to ever fall in love and beget a child?'

Sera bent to the task of picking up glass shards from the floor, trying to make herself as small as she could, trying to make them forget she was there so she could hear them talk more, never mind that she didn't understand what half the words meant.

'How did you find us?' her mother asked.

'Serendipity.' Another word Sera didn't know. 'I was passing through the town and stopped at the

bakery for a sourdough loaf,' the older woman said
with a faint smile. 'Mainly because in all the world
there's none as good as the ones they make there. The
baker's boy remembered me. He's the baker now, as I
expect you know, and he mentioned you. We talked.
I mean you no harm. I want to help.'

'You can't. I'm beyond help now.'

'Then let me help your daughter.'

'How? By training her to serve and love others
and never ask for anything in return? I will *never*
choose that life for my daughter.'

'You liked it well enough once.'

'I was a fool.'

'And are you still a fool? What do you think will
happen to the child once you poison your body with
drink and starve yourself to death? Who will care for
her, put a roof over her head and food in her mouth,
educate her and give her a sense of self-worth?'

Mama looked close to crying. 'Not you.'

'I don't see many choices left to you.' The woman
glanced around the room. 'Unless I'm mistaken,
you've already sold everything of value. Any jewellery left?'

'No.' Sera could hardly hear her mother's answer.

'Does the house belong to you?'

'No.'

'How long have you been ill?'

'A year. Maybe more. I'm not—it's not—catching.
It's cancer.'

The older woman bowed her head. 'And how much longer do you think you can last, selling your favours to the lowest bidder? How long before he looks towards the girl and wants her instead of you? Yuna, please. I can give you a home again. *Treatment* if there's treatment to be had. Comfort and clothing befitting your status and hers. Complete discretion when it comes to *whose* child she is—don't think I don't know.'

'He won't want her.'

'You're right, he won't. But I do. The Order of the Kite will always look after its own. From the fiercest hawk to the fallen sparrow. How can you not know this?'

A tear slipped beneath her mother's closed lashes. 'I thought I'd be better off away from it all. For a while it was good. It can be good again.'

'Do you really believe that?' The older woman crossed to her mother and took hold of her hands. 'Let me help you.'

'Promise me she won't be trained as a courtesan,' her mother begged. 'Lianthe, *please.*'

'I promise to give her the same choice I gave you.'

'You'll dazzle her.'

'You'll counter that.' The older woman drew Sera's mother towards the couch, not letting go of her hands, even after they were both seated. Sera edged closer, scared of letting the hem of the woman's gown get in the puddle of wine on the floor, and loving the sweet, clean smell that surrounded her. The woman smiled. 'Leave it, child. Come, let me look at you.'

Sera withstood the other woman's gaze for as long as she could. *Stand tall, chin up, don't fidget.* Her mother's words ringing in her mind. *No need to look like a street urchin.*

Fidget, fidget, beneath the woman's quiet gaze.

'My name's Lianthe,' the woman said finally. 'And I want you and your mother to come to my home in the mountains so that I can take care of you both until your mother is well again. Would you like that?'

'Would there be visitors for Mama?'

'What kind of visitors?'

'The man.'

Her mother and the lady shared a long glance.

'He would not visit. I would be taking you too far away for that.'

'Would there be wine for her?' Because wine was important. 'Wine's like medicine.'

'Then there will be wine until we find better medicine. Tell me, child, are you hungry?'

So, so hungry but she'd learned long ago that sometimes it was better to say nothing than to give the wrong answer. Her stomach grumbled the answer for her anyway.

'When did you last eat?' the lady asked next.

Same question. Trick question. 'Would you like some tea?' Sera asked anxiously. There was tea in the cupboard and Mama always offered visitors a drink. Tea was a warm drink. She knew how to make it and what cups to use. There was a tray. 'I could bring you some tea.'

The lady looked towards her mother as if she'd done something wrong. Something far worse than forgetting to lock the door or not turn off the bedroom lamp at night. 'Yuna, what are you doing? You're already training her in the ways of self-sacrifice and denial. It's too soon for that. You know it is.'

Another tear slipped silently down her mother's face. Lianthe's gaze hardened.

'And now she looks to you for guidance and approval. Yuna, you *must* see what you're doing here. This isn't freedom. This isn't childhood as it's meant to be lived. This is abuse and, of all the things we taught you, no member of the Order ever taught you that.'

'He's not to know,' her mother said raggedly. 'He's not to take her.'

'He will never know. This I promise.'

'She's not to be sent anywhere near him.'

'You have my word.'

'She gets to choose. If she doesn't want to be a companion, you set her up to succeed elsewhere.'

'Agreed.'

'Sera?' Her mother asked her name as a question but Sera stayed quiet and paid attention because she didn't yet know what the question was. 'Should we go to the mountains with the Lady Lianthe? Would you like that?'

Away from here and the baker who was a Good Man and the kids who called her names and the men who looked at her with eyes that burned hot and hungry. Away from the fear that her mother would one day go to sleep on a belly full of wine and never wake up. 'Would there be food? And someone to take care of us?'

Her mother buried her face in her hands.

'Yes, there will be food and people who will care for you both,' the Lady Lianthe said. 'Sera. Is that your name?'

Sera nodded.

'Pretty name.' The woman's smile wrapped around her like a blanket. 'Pretty girl.'

CHAPTER ONE

SHE WAS A gift from her people to the King of Arun. An unwanted gift if the King's expression spoke true, but one he couldn't refuse. Not without breaking the laws of his country and severing seven centuries of tradition between his people and hers. Sera observed him through a veil of lashes and the protection afforded by her hooded travelling cloak. He could not refuse her.

Although he seemed to be considering it.

She was a courtesan, born, bred and shaped for the King's entertainment. Pledged into service at the age of seven in return for the finest food, shelter and an education second to none. Chosen for the beauty she possessed and the quickness of her mind. Taught to serve, to soothe, and how to dance, fight and dress. One for every King of Arun and only one. A possession to be treasured.

She stood before him, ready to serve. She wasn't unwilling. She'd already received far more from the bargain than she'd ever given and if it was time to pay up, so be it.

He was a handsome man if a tall, lean frame, firm lips, a stern jaw and wayward dark hair appealed—which it did. He had a reputation for fair and thoughtful leadership.

She definitely wasn't unwilling.

He looked relaxed as his gaze swept over her party. Two warriors stood to attention either side of her and another watched her back. The Lady Lianthe, elder spokeswoman for the High Reaches, preceded her. A party of five—with her in the centre, protected—they faced the Arunian King, who stood beside a tall leather chair in a room too cold and bleak for general living.

The old courtier who had guided them to the reception room finally spoke. 'Your Majesty, the Lady Lianthe, elder stateswoman of the High Reaches. And party.'

He knew who they were for they'd applied for this audience days ago. His office had been sent a copy of the accord. Sera wondered whether he'd spent the past two days poring over old diaries and history books in an effort to understand what none of his forefathers had seen fit to teach him.

He had a softness for women, this King, for all that he had taken no wife. He'd held his mother in high regard when she was alive, although she'd been dead now for many years. He held his recently married sister, Queen Consort of Liesendaach, in high esteem still. His name had been linked to several eligible women, although nothing had ever come of it.

'So it's time,' he said, and Sera almost smiled. She'd studied his speeches and knew that voice well. The cultured baritone weight of it and the occasional icy edge that could burn deeper than flame. There was no ice in it yet.

Lianthe rose from her curtsey and inclined her head. 'Your Majesty, as per the accord afforded our people by the Crown in the year thirteen twelve—'

'I don't want her.'

Lianthe's composure never wavered. They'd practised for this moment and every variation of it. At the King's interruption, the elder stateswoman merely started again. 'As per the accord, and in the event the King of Arun remains unmarried into his majority, the people of the High Reaches shall provide unto him a concubine of noble birth—'

'I cannot accept.'

'A concubine of noble birth, charged with attending the King's needs and demands until such time as he acquires a wife and produces an heir. Thereafter, and at the King's discretion—'

'She cannot stay here.' Finally, the ice had entered his voice. Not that it would do him any good. The people of the High Reaches had a duty to fulfil.

'Thereafter, and at the King's discretion, she shall

be released from service, gifted her weight in gold and returned to her people.'

There it was, the accord read in full, a concubine presented and a duty discharged. Sera watched, from within the shadows her travelling hood afforded her, as Lianthe clasped her bony hands in front of her and tried to look less irritated and more accommodating.

'The accord stands, Your Majesty,' Lianthe reminded him quietly. 'It has never been dissolved.'

The King's black gaze swept from the older woman to rest broodingly on Sera's cloaked form. She could feel the weight of his regard and the displeasure in it. 'Lady Lianthe, with all due respect to the people of the High Reaches, I have no intention of being bound by this arrangement. Concubines have no place here. Not in this day and age.'

'With all due respect, you know nothing of concubines.' Fact and reprimand all rolled into one. 'By all means petition the court, your parliament and the church. Many have tried. All have failed. We can wait. Meanwhile, we all do what we must. Your Majesty, it is my duty and honour to present to you the Lady Sera Boreas, daughter of Yuna, Courtesan of the High Reaches and valued member of the Order of the Kite. Our gift to you.' Lianthe paused delicately. 'In your time of need.'

Sera hid her smile and sank to the floor in a curtsey, her head lowered and her cloak pooling around her like a black stain. Lianthe was not amused by their welcome, that much was clear to anyone with ears. This new King knew nothing of the role Sera might occupy if given the chance. What she could do for him. How best he might harness her skills. He didn't want her.

More fool him.

He didn't bid her to rise so she stayed down until he did. Cold, this grey stone hall with its too-righteous King. Pettiness did not become him.

'Up,' he said finally and Sera risked a glance at Lianthe as she rose. The older woman's eyes flashed silver and her lips thinned.

'Your Majesty, you appear to be mistaking the Lady Sera for a pet.'

'Probably because you insist on giving her away as if she is one,' he countered drily. 'I've read the housing requirements traditionally afforded the con-cubines of the north. I do hope you can supply your own eunuchs. I'm afraid I don't have any to hand.' His gaze swept over the warriors of the High Reaches and they stared back, eyes hard and unmoving. 'No eunuchs accompany you at the moment, I'd wager,' he said quietly.

He wasn't wrong. 'I can make do without if you can, Your Majesty.' Sera let warm amusement coat her voice. 'However, I do look forward to occupying the living quarters traditionally offered the concu-bines from the north. I've read a lot about the space.'

'Is there a face to match that honeyed voice?' he

asked, after a pause that spanned a measured breath or four.

She raised her hands and pushed her travelling hood from her face. His eyes narrowed. Reluctant amusement teased at his lips. 'You might want to lead with that face, next time,' he said.

Sera had not been chosen for her plainness of form. 'As long as it pleases you, Your Majesty.'

'I'm sure it pleases everyone.' There might just be a sense of humour in there somewhere. 'Lady Sera, how exactly do you expect to be of use to me?'

'It depends what you need.'

'I need you gone.'

'Ah.' The man was decidedly single-minded. Sera inclined her head in tacit agreement. 'In that case you need a wife, Your Majesty. Would you like me to find you one?'

Augustus, King of Arun, was no stranger to the machinations of women, but he'd never—in all his years—encountered women like these. One cloaked in a rich, regal red, her beauty still a force to be reckoned with, never mind her elder status. The other cloaked in deepest black from the neck down, her every feature perfect and her eyes a clear and bitter grey. Neither woman seemed at all perturbed by his displeasure or by the words spilling from their lips.

He was used to having people around who did his bidding, but he called them employees, not servants, and there were rules and guidelines governing what he expected of them and what they could expect from him.

There were no clear rules for this.

He and his aides had spent the last two days in the palace record rooms, scouring the stacks for anything that mentioned the concubines of the High Reaches and the laws governing them. So far, he'd found plenty of information about their grace, beauty and unrivalled manners. So far, he'd found nothing to help him get rid of them.

A concubine of the High Reaches was a gift to be unwrapped with the care one might afford a poisoned chalice, one of his ancestor Kings had written. Not exactly reassuring.

'These living quarters you've read about…' He shook his head and allowed a frown. 'They've been mothballed for over a hundred and twenty years.' As children, he and his sister had been fascinated by the huge round room with the ribbed glass ceiling. Right up until his mother had caught them in there one day, staging a mock aerial war on a dozen vicious pumpkins. She'd had that place locked down so fast and put a guard detail on the passageway into it and that had been the end of his secret retreat. 'There's no modern heating, no electricity, and the water that used to run into the pools there has long since been diverted. The space is not fit for use.'

'The people of the High Reaches are not without

resources,' said the elder stateswoman regally. 'It would be our honour to restore the living area to its former glory.'

They had an answer for everything. 'Don't get too comfortable,' he warned and looked towards his executive secretary. 'Let all bear witness that the terms of the accord have been satisfied. Let it also be recorded that my intention is to see the Lady Sera honourably discharged from her duty as quickly as possible. I'll find my own wife in my own good time and have no need of a concubine.' He was only thirty. Wasn't as if he was *that* remiss when it came to be-getting an heir and securing the throne. His sister could rule if it ever came to that. Her children could rule, although her husband, Theo, would doubtless object. Neighbouring Liesendaach needed an heir too, perhaps even more so than Arun did. He nod-ded towards his secretary. 'Show them the hospital-ity they've requested.'

If the abandoned round room didn't make them flinch, nothing would.

The guards bowed and the women curtseyed, all of it effortlessly choreographed as they turned and swept from the room, leaving only silence behind. Silence and the lingering scent of violets.

Sera waited just outside the door for Lianthe to fall into step with her. Two guards and their guide up ahead and another guard behind them, a familiar routine in an unfamiliar place.

'That could have gone better,' Sera murmured.

'Insolent whelp,' said the older woman with enough bite to make the stone walls crumble.

'Me?'

'Him. No wonder he isn't wed.'

The King's secretary coughed, up ahead.

'Yes, it's extremely damp down here,' offered Lianthe. 'Although I dare say the rats enjoy it.'

'We're taking a short cut, milady. Largely unused,' the man offered. 'As for the rooms issued for the Lady Sera's use, I know not what to say. You'll find no comfort there. The palace has many other suites available for guests. You have but to ask for different quarters and they'll be provided.'

He opened a door and there was sunshine and a small walled courtyard stuffed with large pots of neatly kept kitchen herbs. Whoever tended this garden knew what they were about. Another door on the other side of the little courtyard plunged them into dankness once more before the corridor widened enough to allow for half a dozen people to walk comfortably side by side. At the end of the corridor stood a pair of huge doors wrought in black wood with iron hinges. Two thick wooden beams barred the door closed.

The old guide stood aside and looked to the High Reaches guards. 'Well? What are you waiting for?'

'*Very* welcoming,' murmured Sera as the guards pushed against the bindings and ancient wood and metal groaned. 'Perhaps some plinths and flowers either side might brighten this entrance hall? Discreet lighting. Scented roses.'

With another strangled cough from their guide, the bars slid to the side and the doors were pushed open. A soaring glass-domed space the size of a cathedral apse greeted them, encircled by grey marble columns and shadowy alcoves. What furniture remained lay shrouded beneath dust sheets and if rugs had once graced the vast expanse of grey stone floor they certainly weren't in evidence now. Dust motes danced in the air at the disturbance from the opening of the doors, and was that a dovecote in one of the alcoves or a postbox for fifty? Another alcove contained the bathing pool, empty but for dirt, but the plumbing had worked once and would work again—it was her job to see to it. There were faded frescoes on the walls and a second floor with a cloistered walkway that looked down on the central area. Chandeliers still hung in place, struggling to shine beneath decades of dust. There was even a circus trapeze roped carelessly to a tiny balcony set one floor above the rest. Illustrations in the journals of the courtesans of old had not done the place justice.

'Well, now.' Sera sent a fleeting smile in Lianthe's direction. 'Nothing like a challenge.'

The older woman nodded and turned to their

guide. 'Can you offer us cleaners?' The man looked unsure. 'No? Then we shall invite our own, and tradespeople too. I suppose we should thank the monarchy for preserving the space in all its historical glory. At least there are no rats.'

'And I think I know why.' Sera stared up at the domed glass ceiling to where several lumpy shapes sat, nestled into the framework. 'Are they owls?'

Lianthe looked up and smiled. 'Why, yes. A good omen, don't you think? Would you like to keep them?'

'Depends on the rats.' Call her difficult but if the rats were gone Sera was all for providing alternative living space—and hunting options—for the raptors. 'We may need the assistance of a falconer. I don't suppose King Augustus keeps one of those any more either?'

'No, Lady Sera. But King Casimir of Byzenmaach does,' said their guide.

'Ah, yes.' Lianthe nodded. 'The falconers of Byzenmaach are men of legend and steeped in the old ways. Tomas-the-Tongue-Tied is head falconer there these days is he not? How is the boy?'

'Grown, milady, although still somewhat tongue-tied,' said the old guide and won a rare smile from Lianthe. 'But ever devoted to his winged beasts. If you need him here, we can get him here.'

'Wonderful,' said Sera. Eyes on the prize, or, in this case, the speedy removal of hunting birds from her future living quarters. 'Let's aim for that. Unless by "Don't get too comfortable" King Augustus meant for me to sleep with the wildlife? Perhaps I should go back and ask.'

'You must definitely ask,' said Lianthe.

It was decided. Sera shed her travelling cloak and watched the old courtier blink and then raise his hand as if to shade his eyes from the glare. Granted her dainty six-inch heels were a burnt orange colour and her slimline ankle-length trousers were only one shade darker, but her tunic was a meek ivory chiffon and the gold metal bustier beneath it covered far more than usual and ran all the way up and around her neck.

'Something wrong?' she asked the old guide.

'Headache,' he said, and touched two fingers to his temple.

'I know massage techniques for that,' she began. 'Very effective. Would you like me to—'

'*No*, milady. No! You just…' He waved his arm in the air ineffectually. 'Go and see Augustus. The King. King Augustus.'

'I know who you mean,' she said gently, sharing a concerned glance with Lianthe. 'Are you quite well? I'd offer you a seat if I could find one. Or a drink. Would you like me to call for water?'

'No, milady. I'm quite recovered.'

But he still looked painfully pinched and long-suffering. 'Is it the jewels? Because the bustier isn't quite my normal attire. It's part of the courtesan's chest.'

'It certainly seems that way, milady. I must confess, I wasn't expecting the bejewelled wrist and ankle cuffs either.'

Ah. 'Well, they are very beautiful. And surprisingly light given all the bronze and amber inlays and gold filigree. There are chains to go with them,' she said.

'Of course there are.' The man's fingers went to massage his temple again.

'Will I find the King in the same place we left him?' asked Sera, because sometimes it paid to be practical.

'He may be back in his office by now. Two doors to the left of the room you met him in. The outer area houses the secretary's desk. The secretary's not there because that would be me and I am here. The inner room is his, and the door to it may or may not be open. Either way, knock.'

Sera found the King exactly where the old courtier said he would be; the door through to his office was open and she paused to check her posture before knocking gently on the door frame. He lifted his gaze from the papers on the big black table in front of him and blinked. And blinked again.

She curtseyed again, all but kissing the floor, because this man was her King and protocol demanded it.

'Up,' he said, with a slight tinge of weariness. 'What is it?'

Not *Come in*, so she stayed in the doorway. 'I want to invite Tomas the Byzenmaach falconer to call on me.'

'Tired of me already?' He arched an eyebrow, even as he studied her intently, starting with her shoes and seeming to get stuck in the general vicinity of her chest. The golden bustier was quite arresting but not the most comfortable item of clothing she owned. 'That was quick.'

'I need him here so he can remove the raptors from my quarters.'

'Raptors as in dinosaurs? Because it's been that kind of day.'

'Raptors as in owls.'

'I'm almost disappointed,' he said, and there was humour in him, sharp and slippery. 'What is that you're wearing, exactly? Apart from the clothes. Which I appreciate, by the way. Clothes are useful. You'll get cold here if you don't wear more of them.'

'You mean the jewellery? Your secretary seemed very taken by it as well. It's ceremonial, for the most part, although practical too.'

'Practical?'

'D-rings and everything.' She held up one wrist and showed him the loop and then pointed to another where the bustier came together at the back of her neck. 'So do I have your permission to call in the falconer?'

'Is this a plea for different living quarters? Because I'm being as clear as I can be here. I don't want to give you *any* quarters, but, given that I *must*, you are welcome to more suitable living arrangements than the ones you have requested. I would not deny you that.'

'It's not a plea for new quarters.' He tested her patience, this King with the giant stick up his rear. 'And, yes, you're being very clear. Perhaps I should be equally clear.' Save herself a few meetings with him in the process. 'I want your permission to clean and ready my living quarters for use. I will call in experts, when necessary. I will see the courtesan's lodgings restored and it will cost you and the palace nothing. I will take all care to preserve the history of the rooms—more care than you or your people would. I will submit names, on a daily basis, of each and every craftsperson or cleaning person that I bring in. By your leave, and provided I have free rein to do so, I can have those rooms fit to live in within a week. Do I have your permission?'

'You argue like a politician. All fine words, sketchy rationale and promises you'll never keep.'

'I'll keep this promise, Your Majesty. Consider this a test if you need a reason to say yes.'

'And when you leave again? What happens to all these home improvements then?'

'I expect the next courtesan will benefit from them.'

'Sera.' He spoke quietly but with an authority that ran bone-deep, and it got to her in a way the authority of her teachers never had. 'There's not going to be another courtesan delivered to a King of Arun. This I promise.'

'Then turn the place into a museum,' she snapped, defiant in the face of extinction. 'You don't value me. I get it. You don't need my help, you don't want my help, and you don't understand the *backing* you've just been blessed with. So be it. Meanwhile, we're both bound by tradition and moreover I have dues to pay. Do I have your permission to engage the help I need to make my living quarters habitable?'

'And here I thought courtesans were meant to be compliant.'

'I am compliant.' She could be so meekly compliant his head would spin. 'I can be whatever you want me to be. All I need is direction.'

His face did not betray his thoughts. Not by the flicker of an eye or the twitching of a muscle.

'You have my permission to make your living quarters habitable,' he said finally. 'And Sera?'

She waited.

'Don't ever walk the halls of my palace in your ancient slave uniform again.'

The King's secretary had gone by the time Sera arrived back in the quarters she'd claimed as her own. She held her head high as she entered, never mind that the chill in the air and the ice in the King's eyes had turned her skin to gooseflesh. She wouldn't cry, she never had- -not even at her mother's funeral—

but the gigantic task of readying this space for use and earning Augustus of Arun's trust, and, yes, finding him a wife, was daunting enough to make her smile falter and her shoulders droop as she stared around at her new home.

Lianthe and the guards had already begun pulling covers off the furnishings and for that she would be grateful. She wasn't alone in this. Other people had faith in her abilities.

'I've already sent for cleaning equipment and linens,' Lianthe said when she saw her. 'Did you find him again?'

'I did.'

'And?'

'He's a funny guy. He's also hard as nails underneath, doesn't like not getting his own way and he's going to be hell on my sense of self-worth.'

'We knew this wasn't going to be an easy sell. I'm sure you'll come to a greater understanding of each other eventually.'

'I'm glad someone's sure,' she murmured.

'And what did he have to say about securing a falconer to help get rid of our feathered friends?'

'Oh, that?' She'd forgotten about that. 'He said yes.'

CHAPTER TWO

SIX DAYS LATER, Augustus was no closer to a solution when it came to removing his unwanted gift from the palace. He'd kept his distance, stuck to his routine and tried to stay immune to the whispers of the staff as word got around that the palace's pleasure rooms were being refurbished. Ladies Sera and Lianthe had engaged cleaning staff and craftspeople to help with the repairs. Stonemasons had been brought in. Electricity had been restored. Structural engineers had been and gone, proclaiming the glass-domed roof still fit for purpose, with only minor repair required.

Tomas the falconer had come for the owls and brought King Casimir of Byzenmaach's sister Claudia with him. Apparently Sera and Claudia had gone to school together. Sera had prepared a lavish dinner for them that had gone on for hours. They'd caught up on each other's lives. Swapped stories. Augustus had been invited.

He hadn't attended.

Whispers turned into rumours, each one more fanciful than the rest.

The Lady Sera was a sorceress, a witch, an enchantress and his apparent downfall. Her eyes were, variously, the softest dove-grey and as kind as an angel's or as bleak as the winter sky and hard as stone. She and her guards danced with swords beneath the dome, and splattered reflected sunlight across the walls with uncanny precision, so the cleaners said. She'd had the trapeze taken down only to replace it with another, and this time the trapeze fluttered with silks that fell to the floor, his secretary told him.

Silks she climbed up and down as if they were steps.

Yesterday, a convoy of heavily guarded trucks had arrived from the north and requested entry, sending palace security into a spin and Augustus into a rare temper. *Don't get too comfortable*, he'd said. He would find a way to undo this, he'd said. They *knew* he was working on it. They had no need for deliveries full of priceless artworks only ever revealed when a courtesan of the High Reaches was in residence at the palace.

Even the palace *walls* were buzzing.

Augustus's father, former King and still an advisor to the throne, had been no help. He'd been married with two young children by the time he'd reached thirty and no courtesan of the High Reaches had ever come to him. There was no *precedent* for getting rid of one that didn't directly relate to the rules of the accord. A courtesan, once bestowed, could be removed once a wife and heir had been secured and not before. She could be sent elsewhere at the King's bidding but would still retain full ownership…no, not ownership, access…full access to her quarters in the palace.

She had the right to refuse entrance to all but him. She had the right to entertain there but the guest list had to be approved by him. He'd asked for more details when it came to Sera Boreas's background and education and an information file had landed on his desk this morning. She'd studied philosophy, politics and economics at Oxford. She'd taken music lessons in St Petersburg. Dance lessons with members of the National Ballet company of China. Learned martial arts from the monks of the High Reaches. Her origins were shrouded in mystery. Her mother had kept the company of high ranking politicians and dignitaries the world over. Her mother had been a companion, a facilitator, often providing neutral ground where those from opposing political persuasions could meet. Lianthe of the High Reaches might just be her grandmother but that had yet to be verified. The more he read, the less real she became to him.

For all her contacts and endless qualifications, he still didn't know what she *did* except in the vaguest terms.

In the last year alone, and as the youngest representative of the Order of the Kite, she'd graced the dining tables of dozens of world leaders and people of influence. Her reach was truly astonishing.

And he was currently keeping her in the equivalent of his basement.

He needed to talk with her at the very least.

And damn but he needed another woman's opinion.

And then his intercom flashed.

'Your sister's on the phone,' his well-worn secretary said.

'Put her through,' he murmured. Problem solved.

'Augustus, I know you're pining for me, but did you seriously buy a cat?'

'I—what?' Not exactly where his head had been at. Augustus scowled, and not just because his sister's recent marriage had left his palace without a social organiser and him with no clue as to how to find a replacement equally dedicated to the role. 'Who told you that? Theo?'

'He told me I needed to phone you because he'd heard rumours you were all lonely and had acquired a pet. He also mentioned something about a cat. Is it fluffy? Does it pounce? Has it conquered cucumbers yet?'

Theo, King of Liesendaach and neighbouring monarch, was Moriana's new husband. Theo, King of sly manoeuvres, knew exactly what kind of cat Augustus had bought. 'Moriana, let's get something clear. I am not a lonely cat king. I bought a catamaran. An oceangoing, racing catamaran.'

'Ah,' she said. 'Figures. In that case, I have no idea why Theo was so insistent I phone you this morning. We've just returned from visiting Cas and Ana in the Byzenmaach mountains and, by the way, I will *never* tire of the views from that stronghold. More to the point, I got on well with Cas's new bride and his newfound daughter. There's hope for me yet. They did ask me why they hadn't received an invite to your Winter Solstice ball. Strangely, I haven't received my invitation yet either. I left very comprehensive instructions.'

Moriana was the Queen of Checklists. He had no doubt there would be a binder full of colour-coded instructions sitting on a table somewhere. 'Why isn't Marguerite on top of this?' his sister scolded.

'She didn't work out.'

Silence from his sister, the kind of silence that meant she was valiantly trying to keep her opinions to herself. He gave it three, two, one…

'Augustus, you can't keep firing social secretaries after they've been in the role for two weeks!'

'I can if they're selling palace information to the press,' he said grimly.

'Oh.'

'Yes. Oh. There's a new assistant starting Monday. Meanwhile, what do you know about the Order of the Kite?'

'You mean the courtesans?'

'So you do know something about them.'

'I know they existed centuries ago. They were kept in our round room. Like pets.' Moriana paused, and Augustus waited for her to put Theo's comment about him having a pet together with his question and come up with a clue, but she didn't. 'There are some costumes in the collection here that were reputedly worn by them.' Moriana was warming to her theme. 'Gorgeous things. I wouldn't call them gowns exactly— more like adventurous bedwear. The leather one came with a collection of whips.'

'Whips.' No guesses needed as to how some of those courtesans of old acquired their exalted levels of influence. Augustus put two fingers to his temple and closed his eyes, a habit he'd picked up from his secretary, or maybe the old man had picked it up from him. 'So what else do you know about them? Anything from this day and age?'

'These days they're the stuff of legend. There's a children's book in the nursery about them, assuming it's still there. Seven-year-old girl, clever and pretty, gets ripped from the arms of her unloving family and taken to a palace in the sky to learn how to dance and fight and be a spy. Then she meets a King from the Lower Reaches and spies for him and he falls in love with her and they live happily ever after. Ignore the bit where she poisons his barren wife. You should never believe everything you read.'

'Does this book have a name?'

'*The King's Assassin.* It was one of my favourites. Why?'

No one had ever read it to *him*. 'I currently have the Lady Sera Boreas, daughter of Yuna, Order of the Kite, staying in the round room. She arrived last week, as a *gift* from the people of the High Reaches.'

Silence from Moriana the Red, whose temper, once roused, was also the stuff of legend, and then, 'Say that again?'

'There is a courtesan here in the palace and at my service. Yesterday, six truckloads of priceless antiquities turned up. They belong to the Order of the Kite and can only be seen when a courtesan is in residence here. *Now* do I have your attention?'

'Did you say *priceless antiquities*?'

'*Focus*, Moriana. There is a pet concubine in the round room. No—did you just squeal? Don't squeal. Invite her to stay with you. Keep her. Show her the whips. No! Don't show her the whips. I take that back. But find out what she's doing here. Can you do that?'

'Does she have books?' his sister asked. 'I bet she has history books with her as well. Do you know what this means?'

It probably meant Moriana was about to try and organise an exhibition of antiquities native to courtesans. 'It means I have a problem that I don't know how to solve yet. What exactly am I supposed to do with this woman?'

'Is she beautiful? They were reputedly all rare beauties.'

'That bit's true.'

'Is she smart?'

'I would say so, yes. Also cunning and completely unfathomable.' Keeping her distance and rousing his curiosity, making her presence felt all the more keenly by the simple act of staying out of his way. 'I need you to come here and see what she wants. Befriend her. Gain her confidence. Tell me what she wants.'

'I can be there in a week.'

'I meant today,' he countered.

'Can't. I have a luncheon at twelve, a charity meeting at two, hospital tour at three and then I'm having a private dinner with my beloved husband who I've barely seen all week.'

'Absence makes the heart grow fonder. I'll send the helicopter for you.'

'Or you could talk to her yourself and find out exactly what this woman can do for you. Can she act as a social secretary, for example? Can she organise the Winter Solstice ball? Courtesans of old were muses, strategists, women of great influence. Think Madame de Pompadour or Theodora from the Byzantine empire. She might be one of those. Give her something to do. Apart from you, obviously.'

'She is not doing me,' he ground out.

'Has she offered?'

She'd arrived wearing a collar and manacles, amongst other things. She'd called herself a courtesan and then she'd ignored him. 'Who the hell knows?'

'Do you—okay, you know what? Never mind, because there are some things sisters simply shouldn't know. Give her the Winter Solstice ball to oversee. I'm serious. Put her to work. See if she truly wants to be of use to you.'

'I'd rather she left.'

'But why? You need a social secretary who wants to do a good job and isn't inclined to sell us out. Talk to her. See what she wants from her role and from you. Your goals might align.'

'What if she doesn't want to be here at all?'

'Then you'll work together to find a way out of this. But not before I've seen all the art and persuaded her to let us photograph and document it, where possible. I can't wait to see it.'

Augustus sighed. Theo really was a bad influence on his sister, who'd once dutifully dedicated herself to serving the Arunian monarchy. These days she shone a light on the already glittering Liesendaach crown and Augustus sorely missed her attention. He did need someone to replace his sister. Someone with a personal stake in taking on the role and making it their own. A wife…he'd been thinking of it. Not doing anything about it, mind, but thinking that soon he would start looking in earnest. Meanwhile, he had a…courtesan…at his disposal. Whatever that meant. Maybe they could renegotiate her job description.

'All right.' There was nothing else for it. 'I'll talk to her.'

It took until mid-afternoon before Augustus made his way to the round room in search of the elusive Sera of the High Reaches. Ignoring her presence and hoping she'd miraculously go away wasn't working for him. Answers on how best to get rid of her were not forthcoming. Moriana thought she might be of use to him and he trusted his sister's judgement in most things. Sera's CV would make any power broker salivate. To have those kind of contacts at his disposal…

And yet he wasn't the type to share power and he didn't trust her motivations one little bit.

So here he was, foul of temper and distinctly lacking in patience as he stood at the closed doors to the round room and eyed the profusion of damask roses and soft greenery with distaste, even as the scent of them conjured memories of cloistered gardens and all things feminine. His mother had enjoyed overseeing the floral arrangements throughout the palace, but she'd not have allowed this flat-out challenge to grim austerity. This tease to stop and sniff and feast the eyes on such unrepentantly fleeting beauty.

With one last scathing glare, Augustus stood firm against the temptation to lean forward and let the scent of the roses envelop him. Instead, he pulled the dangling cord that would announce his arrival at the doors. He heard the faint chime of bells and then nothing. Ten seconds later, he reached for the cord again, and then the door opened and the roses were forgotten.

Never mind the creamy skin and the perfection of her lips, the delicate curve of her cheekbones, the raven-black hair that fell in a thick plait to her waist or those eyes that glistened dove-grey. Today his courtesan wore low-slung loose trousers and a cropped fitted top that clung to her curves like a greedy lover's hand. She was lean and lithe in all the right places, and generously voluptuous in others.

It was a body designed to bring a man to his knees and keep him there for eternity.

She stepped back and dropped her gaze demurely, even as she opened the door wider and sank to the floor in a curtsey, and he might have felt a heel for causing such an action except that she moved like a dancer, fluid and graceful, and he wanted to watch her do it all over again.

'Don't do that.' It was a curt reminder, mostly to himself, that she shouldn't be on her knees in front of him. It gave him too many ideas, all of them sexual.

'My mistake.' She rose as gracefully as she'd gone down in the first place. 'Welcome, Your Majesty. Please forgive my appearance. I wasn't expecting company.'

'What were you doing?' Her skin glowed with a faint sheen of exertion.

'Forms,' she said. 'Martial arts patterns.'

'Don't stop on my account.'

'I can do them any time,' she murmured. 'I'd rather have company.'

He looked around, taking in the now spotless round room, its stone walls and floors covered in tapestries and carpets, oil paintings and silver-edged mirrors. A huge round sofa had been placed in the centre of the room, beneath the domed glass ceiling. The seats faced inwards and there were openings at all four points of the compass. 'Where is everyone?'

'The tradespeople and artisans have gone and the Lady Lianthe with them. My guards are currently in a meeting with your guards about how best to utilise their services, given that standing outside a door that no one ever knocks on is a waste of their time and expertise. The maids have been and gone. There is only me.'

Holding her own in a round room built for hundreds to gather in and bedrooms enough for fifty. 'It's you I've come to see.'

She turned her back on him and led him towards the sofa at the centre of the room. It was leather and studded and looked comfortably soft with age. Pillows and throws had been placed on it at intervals, and the circular floor tapestry framed by the sofa had a stained-glass quality about it, with different scenes to look at depending on where a person sat. 'What is that?'

'On the floor?'

He nodded.

'It's a communication device. Each scene depicts an action: a need or desire, if you will. In older times a visitor to this place—or even another courtesan— would approach this area and in choosing where to sit would telegraph their needs. Those needs would be seen to.'

'Just like that?'

'So they say.'

'And is that the way it's going to work for me?'

'Why don't you sit somewhere and see?'

'Maybe I will.' Maybe he wouldn't. Better all round if he didn't engage, no matter how fascinating the history she brought with her. 'I've been trying to get rid of you.'

'I know that, Your Majesty.' She glanced towards the tapestry. 'Take your time looking at it. Even if you don't plan to use it as directed it's an amazing piece of artistry. I'll make tea.'

He watched as she walked away from him, tracking every curve as if it would somehow allow him to see inside her skin. Only once she had withdrawn from sight did he turn his attention back to the mood-gauging tapestry on the floor in front of him. He'd never seen such a thing.

Some of the panels were easy enough to figure

out. There was an orgy scene, with bodies entwined in the throes of ecstasy. A gentler scene in which a man reclined while a woman read to him. Another scene depicted people eating from a table covered in delicacies. A bathing scene. A sword-fighting scene. Another showing a reclining man being entertained by dancers holding fans. A dozen men and women stood around a table, deep in sombre discussion. A sleeping couple filled another panel. With every step another mood or need satisfied. A man lashed to a wooden X, his back a mass of welts as he writhed beneath the whip. A beautiful woman holding that whip, her expression one of complete control and focus. Punishment delivered, but not in anger, and the man on the cross looked…grateful.

His courtesan had returned with tea; he could hear her off to one side and see her in his peripheral vision.

'You do all this?' he asked, keeping his gaze fixed on the whipping scene. 'Put a man to the lash and strip the guilt from his soul before putting him back together again?' The next scene showed the same woman tending the man's wounds.

'I've been trained to, yes.' She approached from his left and held out a porcelain cup filled with pale amber tea. 'Will you sit?'

He took the tea and let his fingers brush hers. She stilled, and so did he.

He didn't believe in instant attraction. He'd never

been a slave to his body's baser demands. But if one tiny touch could send this much heat and awareness coursing through him, imagine what she could do with full body contact?

'It's a trap,' he said at last.

'How so?' Her gaze was steady, her features as smooth as marble.

He gestured towards the depictions of service laid out before him, and it was all very tempting, except that beneath the surface pleasures lay a darker truth altogether. Mind, body and soul. She wasn't here to serve. She was here to own him. 'What wife could ever compete if I had this at my disposal? Where else would I go but here, where every whim would be served up to me on a gilded plate? By the time I'd satisfied every corrupt thought lying dormant in my soul it would be too late for either of us to escape. I'd *own* you, in ways you've never dreamed of. And you'd own me.'

'Well, that's one interpretation,' she said. 'There are others.'

'Tell me some others.'

'Ignore the sexual element and take advantage of my political prowess instead. Arun is a stabilising force in this region. Many would like to keep it that way, including those I answer to. Including you.'

'Am I not doing that already?' Because he thought he was.

'Your plans to unify water resources across four

neighbouring nations haven't gone unnoticed. This region will grow to become a power bloc—provided you can hold it together.'

He had Theo, Casimir and Valentine right there with him, a shared vision for their region. 'I can hold it together.'

'Indeed, we think so,' she said. 'But who will explain your ambitions to a wider world that might fear such a power shift?'

'And I suppose you can help me there.'

She couldn't fail to pick up on the sarcasm in his voice but she paid no heed to it. 'The Order of the Kite has contacts you don't yet have. I can make introductions, facilitate communication channels that you will then keep open when I leave.'

'And what's in it for you?'

A tiny smile graced her lips. 'World peace?'

'You're a saint,' he said. 'But I still want to know—what's in it for you personally? I don't understand why a modern-minded woman with your kind of looks and education would choose such a role. I don't know what your angle is. Do you want to marry a man of power and gain power and status through him? What happens after me? Do they send you onto the next visionary King in need? And the next after that?'

'I only need to do this once,' she replied quietly. 'I serve you until you release me, at which point my debt will have been repaid. Then I'm free to choose my own way.'

'What debt?'

'The Order cared for my mother through a long and arduous decline and she died with peace and dignity. They saved me from a life in the gutter.'

'And how old were you when this happened?'

'Does that matter? Others turned away from us. They didn't.'

'It matters.'

A small frown appeared between her eyes. 'I was seven.'

Seven years old and taken and trained and made to feel beholden to her rescuers. 'So basically you've had no choice but to do what they ask of you.'

'Have you ever had a choice but to serve the monarchy?' she asked, and he glared at her. 'I think not. We are not so different, you and I. You were born into service. In a way, so was I.'

Except that for her it wasn't a lifetime commitment. 'I'm releasing you from your duty. Soon as I can.'

She nodded. 'I'd like that. But at least make use of me first.'

His gaze slid to that cursed wheel of desire on the floor.

'You don't have to take advantage of all that's on offer.' She barely knew him and already she was reading him like a book. That didn't happen to Augustus. Ever. 'But you could take advantage of some of it without surrendering your mortal soul.'

'There's an opening on my staff for a social sec-

retary. I need someone to organise a ball and other
smaller events.' He handed the teacup back to her,
still full. Not a drop had passed his lips. 'Can we
start with that?'

Sera nodded as she set the tea aside. 'Of course.'

'I think fixed boundaries between us would be
best. Meanwhile, is there something I can do to make
your stay here more comfortable? Anything you need
that you haven't already seen to?' She wasn't a sorceress. He wasn't a lovesick fool, but he could still
offer common courtesy.

'If you and I are to be observing fixed boundaries,
there is something I'd like to discuss.'

He waited.

It was the first time he'd ever seen her looking
nervous.

'Am I free to seek sexual satisfaction elsewhere?'

Continued silence was often a tactic he used to
force the other person to speak. This time, pure
shock stilled his lips.

Sera of the High Reaches squared her delicate
shoulders and fixed him with pleading kitten eyes.
'I've never truly been intimate with another person.
That was reserved for you. I'd be lying if I said I
wasn't looking forward to it. And seeing you're not
of a mind to…'

He wasn't a complete stranger to women becoming impatient for sexual experience. His sister, dear
Lord, had been quite adamant about partying up a

storm at one point. But not under his roof, and she'd never actually gone through with it. Theo had seen to that, with Augustus's full blessing. Now this.

'You're a *virgin* courtesan?'

'Yes. Do you seriously think they would send someone *used*?'

'Oh, pardon my ignorance. Forgive me that I assumed some small measure of *experience* from a trained *courtesan*!' Never mind the beast in his belly that flicked a scaly tail and roared because she'd been kept pure so that *he* could be her teacher. It wasn't *right* for him to want that, and it certainly wasn't right that she'd had no say in her own sexual enlightenment.

He had a courtesan. A virgin courtesan. Standing there beneath the dome, her midriff bare, hair pulled back and no make-up on her face. 'Do you have someone in mind to be intimate with?'

He had the sudden reckless desire to strangle them.

'I had you in mind,' she said as her gaze briefly dropped to his lips. 'I do know what to do in theory.'

'Theory isn't *doing*. What if I wanted to use you roughly? Tie you down, take away all your control and self-respect and make you beg for release? Take away your ability to reason? Take every slight ever dealt me and transfer them to your flesh? Did your illustrious tutors ever teach you how to deal with sadistic madmen?'

She had no answer for him.

'You know *nothing*,' he challenged.

Her first kiss was his if he wanted it, not to mention the second. All of it. He headed for the door before he lost his mind and took what she offered so freely. He had his hand on the door before something made him look back. She'd fallen to a curtsey facing him and the door, her body placed right in the centre of that cursed carpet depicting every sin and pleasure known to man.

'Get up.' He didn't want this. He didn't dare take it. 'Come here.'

He waited until she stood before him, her eyes betraying uncertainty as he leaned down until their lips almost touched. 'Lord knows I didn't ask for you, but you've come here labelled as *my* courtesan and I will cut the hand off anyone who touches you. No kissing. No sex. No flirting with any of my employees. Are we clear?'

'Clear. Very clear,' she whispered with a tell-tale tremor in her voice. He was scaring her.

And then he got caught in the whirling vortex of her expressive grey eyes, and maybe he wasn't scaring her at all. Because that look right there looked a whole lot like surrender.

'Do the work I ask of you,' he grated. 'Put me in contact with the power brokers you think I need to cultivate. Find me a suitable wife if you can.' He could claim those perfect lips if he wanted to, tease the bow of the upper one with the tip of his tongue, slide in easy and experienced and lay her mouth to waste. She wasn't unwilling. She definitely wasn't unwilling.

'Above all…don't tempt me.'

Sera shut the door behind him and leaned against it, still reeling beneath the weight of his words and that brief brush of his lips against hers. It had barely qualified as a kiss but she could still feel the burn of his palm against her chin and the rough stroke of his thumb against her cheekbone. His breath caressing her lips and the swift charge of desire when their eyes caught and held.

She'd wanted him to kiss her properly. Lay claim or lay to waste; either would have been acceptable. She slid to the floor, both hands between her legs, pressing down hard against the feelings he'd ignited inside her. She was so ready for a physical awakening. All the theory in the world and exploration with her own hands could only get her so far. She wanted *his* hands where her hands were, driving her higher until she broke all over him.

It wouldn't have to be all give on her part and all take on his, even if she did want to read and respond to every nuanced muscle twitch he made. She *had* been trained to please, no matter what he might think. The physical arrangement between courtesan and

King didn't have to be the bad thing he was making it out to be. Did it?

Closing her eyes, she pressed up into her hand, seeking release, sharp and swift, as she allowed herself to imagine his kiss. Not the tease he'd left her with.

A proper kiss.

She ran her tongue over the spot where his lips had just been and came moments later, imagining it.

CHAPTER THREE

IT TOOK SERA two days to organise the midwinter
ball. The guest list had already been prepared by
Moriana, formerly of Arun and now Queen Consort
to the King of Liesendaach. Her Royal Highness
Moriana had returned Sera's call promptly and approved the additional guests Sera had put forward for
the express purpose of finding Augustus a wife. In-
vitations had gone out. The palace staff were happy
for someone—anyone—to take the helm and direct
the preparations. The ball was an annual event and
they were well trained and competent.

After that, there was a dinner for twelve to organise, and then an informal supper for thirty in one
of the smaller palace libraries. Moriana had phoned
Sera about the library event guest list several times
already and once to discuss what books would go on
display in the library given the handful of historians
on the guest list. Moriana had asked if there were
any books belonging to the courtesans of the High
Reaches that Sera could put on display.

At that, Sera had hesitated. Some books could be displayed without controversy, but not all. The journals of the courtesans of old were fascinating, but they weren't for public viewing.

Augustus had not been back. No other visitors had called on her and her guards had been incorporated into the regular ranks of the palace, although she still met with them for morning exercise. They met in the horse yard behind the stables, where the sawdust on the ground was sweet and soft. They'd thought it out of the way enough that they wouldn't bother anyone. Three days in and already they had a growing audience for the martial arts patterns they completed in unison and the sparring that came afterwards. Give it another week and the requests for lessons would start. She could see the hunger for more in the eyes of those watching. The curiosity, reluctant admiration, and sometimes the heat.

Always the heat.

Aware of the restlessness riding her, Sera pushed her body hard during morning exercise, as comfortable as she could be with the hot eyes of the crowd, the sun weak and watery and a chill in the air that reminded her of the mountains.

When she met the ground for the third time because of inattention, Ari, the guardsman who'd put her there, stepped back and disengaged from their sparring. She wasn't easy to take down, and this time the kick to her sternum would have broken bones if she hadn't deflected the blow at the last minute. Ari had expected far better from her. She wasn't concentrating.

She lay there, eyes closed and reluctant to take a breath because when she did it was going to hurt. She felt rather than saw someone crouch down beside her and, quick as a snake, she clamped her hand around their wrist as they went to touch her torso.

'Easy.'

She opened her eyes to slits and studied the forearm she'd captured. It was tanned and corded with muscle, the hand looked strong and the fingernails blunt. She looked for a face to match the hand but the sun was directly in her line of sight. It wouldn't be Ari or Tun; they knew better than to offer to help her up. It might be someone from the audience who didn't understand the limits she lived by.

She moved just enough to let the man's body block the sun, the better to see his face.

Augustus.

She took in a breath and pain didn't slice at her. She eased into a sitting position and didn't pass out. Good news.

'You went down pretty hard,' he said gruffly.

'My own fault,' she murmured, and let go of his arm. He had the right to touch her. She could not refuse.

He stood and held out his hand and slowly, carefully, she put her hand in his and let him help her up.

His hand was more calloused than she'd been

expecting from a man who did no physical work. Her hand looked tiny clasped in his. His dark eyes showed no emotion.

'Why are you here?' she asked.

'I live here. And when rumour reaches me that half my security force is turning up on their days off to watch the northerners beat the living daylights out of each other I get curious.'

Fair enough. She took back her hand and spared a glance for her guards. Only two were here with her; the third was on duty. Neither stepped forward, although Ari's fingers flickered a message that hopefully only she could read. Had he injured her?

No.

A silent conversation, meant to set her guardsman at ease.

He didn't seem convinced.

'What may we do for you, Your Majesty?'

'Find somewhere else to practise, for starters. You have half my men-at-arms gagging for a glimpse of you. The other half have already seen you fight and now have a new erotic fantasy to be going on with.'

He wasn't being fair. 'Sawdust is soft and the floors in my quarters are too hard for serious sparring. Where else might we practise? We are also open to teaching those of your court who wish to learn the forms and uses they might be put to. Ari is a master. Tun a champion who will soon retreat to the mountains for his final year of meditation before he too becomes a high practitioner of the art.'

'What grade do you hold?'

'I hold my own.'

'You didn't today.'

'I lost focus. If there's some other place you'd rather we practise we'll take it, Your Majesty. We practise daily, together and alone. It's not just exercise. It's a way of life for those who guard the temples of the High Reaches. It's contact and communication. Learning how to read a person's movements. It's non-sexual. Instructional. There's no harm in it,' she said in the face of his continued silence.

He gave Tun and Ari a glare far sharper than any knife. 'Then why are you hurt?'

'I'm wiser in the face of Ari's takedown. It won't happen again.'

'What did the older one say to you with his sign language?'

She hadn't thought he'd been in any position to see that. 'He wanted to know if I was injured.'

'He could have asked.'

'You were there and seeing to me. Discretion was best.'

'Tell them not to use sign language again in front of my men. It breeds suspicion and there's already far too much of that around here because of you and the old ways you've brought with you.'

It was true; the people here continued to see her as *other*. 'People fear what they don't understand.'

'They also fear rare beauty, overt displays of power and influence and those who never stay down, even when beaten. Especially when beaten. Tone it down, Sera, or I'll shut you in your room full of temptation and beautiful things and leave you there.'

'I'm never going to please you, am I? You give me functions to organise and I organise them. I come meekly when called. I've stacked the midwinter ball full of accomplished single women for you to meet. I've set up introductions with people of influence. What else do you want?'

'I want sweet dreams,' he grated. 'I'd prefer them not to be about you. My sister has just flown in. She says she's already been in contact with you by phone. She wants to meet you.'

Sera wasn't ready for guests, sweaty and aching as she was. She wanted to ask more about his dreams. 'I'll need half an hour before I'm properly presentable.'

'You don't have it,' he said, and opened a half-hidden door in the castle wall. 'After you.'

She had sawdust in her hair and on her sleeve and down the leg of her loose cotton trousers. 'Are you always this petty?' she asked, and watched his eyes narrow.

'It's an impromptu visit and my sister schedules herself so tightly that she never has much time,' he

KELLY HUNTER   73

countered. 'Believe me, I like spontaneity less than you do but she's here now and you look fine as you are. Through this door and keep walking for a minute or two. After you.'

She stepped inside and kept to a brisk pace. The corridor was narrow but well lit. The next door he bade her to walk through opened into a large sitting room with a wall full of windows overlooking palace gardens. An elegant woman in a tangerine sundress rose from a chair as they entered. Sera took note of her poise and careful smile before dropping to the floor in a curtsey, suddenly light-headed at the piercing pain coming from somewhere near her ribs. Maybe she had taken some damage after all.

'Moriana, meet Lady Sera, Courtesan of the High Reaches,' Augustus said from somewhere beside her. 'Sera, get up.'

'Augustus, she's not a hound,' Moriana protested.

'If I don't tell her to get up she stays down.' Augustus scowled as he bent forward and curled his hand around her upper arm and drew her to her feet. 'You *are* injured. Don't lie to me again.'

'I'm okay.' If he would stop looking at her as if she were a stain on his shoe she might feel less dizzy and disoriented.

'Have I caught you at a bad time?' his elegant, well-mannered sister asked as Sera swayed and tried to find her centre and her balance. Augustus's hand tightened vicelike around her arm. 'I hope Augustus hasn't had you cleaning out the stables.'

'No, Your Highness.'

'I found her engaged in hand-to-hand combat with two of her guards.'

'For exercise,' Sera stressed.

'Find another form of exercise.' His eyes burned black.

'I've been doing martial arts for fifteen years. If you tell me to give it up I will because I'm duty bound to obey you, so here's a thought. Don't ask me to.'

The quiet clearing of a throat reminded Sera that they weren't alone and she bowed her head in shame. She wasn't presentable or amiable enough for guests. 'I can do better,' she offered quietly, and it was a blanket statement that covered a multitude of sins. 'I will do better.'

'Oh, for f—I'm trying to *protect* you.' He turned to his sister. 'She's here. She's all yours. I have other things to do. If she collapses, leave her where she falls.'

'Augustus!'

Sera watched from beneath lowered lashes as Augustus stalked from the room, leaving thick silence behind him and no even ground to stand on.

'Well, that was…unexpected,' the King's sister said with no little bemusement. 'What *have* you done with my courteous, by-the-book brother?'

'Barely anything.' And wasn't that the truth. 'He

doesn't want me here, Your Highness. That's all.' It underscored their every interaction.

'And how old are you?' Augustus's sister asked next.

'Twenty-three.'

'You look about sixteen. Maybe that's what's bothering him.'

Sera couldn't say.

'Are you here of your own free will?'

'I am.' Perhaps this woman, out of everyone here, would understand. 'I undertake my role willingly and with honour.'

'I'm glad to hear it. But it's been over a hundred years since this court has seen a courtesan of the High Reaches. We are, as a rule, a suspicious lot and fiercely independent. How can you serve my brother? What is it you bring?'

'Political backing and access to people of influence. You saw the additions to the most recent guest list for the library evening?'

'A diplomat, a peacekeeper and a historian from well beyond our northern borders. Not people we usually deal with.'

'Yet their voices are heard elsewhere, where others have concerns over the grand water plans for this region. What better way to begin conversation than with a casual evening of books, fine food and access to one of the monarchs at the heart of those plans?'

'Are you saying that my brother can't find his own way through the political mire?'

'I'm saying that the Order of the Kite has influence far beyond Arun's reckoning, and beyond Liesendaach's too, never mind your husband's dealings. Should your brother ever ask for access to people who can aid him in his vision, he shall receive.'

'And has he asked?'

'No.' There was the not so small matter of his pride, not to mention his innate suspicion. Trust did not come easily to the royals of Arun. 'There's also the issue of your country needing an heir to the throne.'

'I fail to see how a courtesan can help with that.'

'And yet courtesans throughout the centuries have brokered marriages and more. Something is holding your brother back from making a commitment. Once we understand what it is we can address the issue and find someone who can give him what he needs. I can encourage him to explore or even simply to voice those…needs…in a safe and confidential environment.'

The elegant Queen Consort suddenly looked supremely uncomfortable. 'What makes you think my brother has particular needs?'

'The fact that he's not yet married, perhaps?' There was no delicate way to put this. 'Look, everyone explores their inner desires given the right opportunity. My job is to give the man a non-judgemental space to do it in. Some of the preferences of former Kings of Arun have been quite specific.'

Moriana blinked. 'Do I really want to know?'

'There are journals, milady. As a direct member of Arun's royal family, you have the right to view them.'

'May I see them now?'

'Of course. I have some in my quarters.'

'The rumours surrounding your quarters are quite…elaborate.'

'The rumours are true. Would you like to take tea with me there? Your brother has yet to put a cup of mine to his lips but I assure you there's no poison involved. That would be counterproductive.'

'You do know that I can't tell whether you're joking or not?'

Sera smiled. The King's sister stared.

'I'm beginning to realise the extent of my brother's problem,' Moriana said drily. 'Yes, I'd like to see the journals and what you've done with the round room. I'll cancel the rest of my morning engagements.'

'Wonderful.' Sera thought about curtseying again, but the memory of the pain involved gave her pause. She turned and headed for the door instead, opening it for her companion.

'So you've been working with Augustus and his assistant. Have you met our head of household staff yet?'

Sera nodded. 'And the chefs, function waiting staff, and the head gardener.'

'Have you met my father?'

'Only briefly, Your Highness. He came to view the work of the stonemasons. He didn't stay long.

'He tends to leave things to Augustus these days. Do you have family?' Moriana asked.

'No, Your Highness. My mother died in my early teens and I have no brothers or sisters.'

'And your father?'

Sera paused. 'He is unknown to me.'

'It's just…the accord says you are of noble blood-lines.'

'My mother's ancestry,' said Sera. 'The Order traces its bloodlines through the female.'

'How unusual,' murmured the other woman. 'And when you leave here, once Augustus marries and gives the country an heir, what will you do? More courtesan work? Or do you get to become something else then?'

'There are many forks in my road. Some of them lead to high places and some of them don't. I have contacts the world over and a good education. The opportunities available to me after I've discharged my duty here are truly limitless.'

They'd reached the round room doors. Sera opened them and stood back to allow Moriana to enter. Augustus had not cared for the artwork on display or the comforts on offer; he'd barely glanced at them. Perhaps his sister would show more interest.

Moriana stepped inside, her gaze instantly drawn upward towards the sunlit glass dome. 'It's still stunning, that roof. But the sun doesn't always shine in Arun. I grew up here and I should know. Are you warm enough in here?'

'There's oil heating in the side rooms and alcoves for when the sun doesn't shine and warm the stone in the central dome. It's enough.'

'And far too big for just one person,' murmured Moriana. 'In times of old, how many others would have attended you here?'

'Dozens, Your Highness. But the Lady Lianthe will visit on occasion. And others might also venture here, with your brother's permission. Friends and tutors, other members of the Order.'

'How many members of the Order are there?'

'That I couldn't say. But I'll show you where the journals are. By your leave, I'll make myself presentable while you look at them.' Sera was very aware of the sweat on her skin and the sawdust still clinging to her trousers.

Moriana nodded. 'Shall I ring for tea?'

'I don't ring for service, Your High—'

'Call me Moriana.'

'I don't ring for service, Lady Moriana. I'm the one who serves.'

'Then we shall both serve ourselves,' said Moriana easily. 'You get clean; I'll make the tea. Shall I sit in the middle of the room once I've explored the art on the walls and discovered your journals? Is that appropriate?'

'Of course. The journals are in the glass case in the library alcove. They can't leave here, nor can they be copied. You'll understand why once you begin to read them. Of the other books in the library, I've left some on the table that might be suitable to place on display in the palace reading rooms and libraries. I haven't forgotten your earlier request.'

A visitor, finally, and an important one. Sera shed her clothes and combed out her hair. Not as swiftly as she would have liked, but it couldn't be helped given the state of her ribs. Nothing broken, no, but there was bruising already and had she been alone she'd have iced the area. As it was, she took a soft cotton scarf and wrapped her torso tightly and wished for pain-killers. Maybe she'd find some later, but right now she had Moriana of Liesendaach to make welcome.

Sera chose a simple linen tunic and stretchy leggings to wear over her makeshift bandage. Loose enough to hide the torso wrap, embroidered enough to show her respect. She wound her hair into a bun, slipped her feet into backless high heeled sandals and swiftly applied eyeliner, mascara and soft, moist lipstick.

By the time Sera returned, almost ten minutes later, Moriana was standing at the edge of the floor tapestry that had so captivated Augustus, a fragile porcelain cup in her hand.

'This is quite something,' she said as Sera approached. 'Does it tell a story?'

'It's a request wheel, my Lady Moriana. You arrive and sit where you will, according to need, and I will see to that need.'

Moriana froze, her cup of tea halfway to her lips.

'Your brother doesn't like it,' Sera added. 'I think he found the whipping scene somewhat confronting.'

'Uh-huh,' his well-spoken sister said with a blush. 'So he's supposed to come in and choose his…'

'Fix,' suggested Sera. 'Yes. Having said that, he's been here exactly once and refused a seat. Perhaps he just needs to get used to it. It saves quite a lot of time.'

'Uh-huh.' No more tea for Lady Moriana. She returned her cup to the saucer she held in her other hand and walked a slow, rapt circle around the tapestry. 'There's an orgy scene.'

'Yes. If you don't mind me saying so, you Arunians do seem a little repressed.'

Moriana smiled faintly. 'Perhaps. Do you have a favourite scene?'

'I like reading aloud to people.' She'd learned that particular skill while tending to the children of the High Reaches. 'I like spirited intellectual debate and reasoned argument, so I quite like the conversation scenes too. As for the sex scenes…' Chances were she'd like those too if she ever got a chance to indulge in them. 'Each to his own, no?'

Moriana hadn't yet fled the room screaming. This

was a good thing. 'What's the one with the people standing around the table covered with maps?'

'Strategy sessions for weighty subjects like war and succession. There is a book to accompany the carpet. I've set it aside for your brother, assuming he ever wants to see it.'

'I could take it to him when I leave here,' Moriana offered. 'It might be better presented to him as a curious artefact rather than a working guide to your services.'

Sera nodded. 'Please do. Would you like to sit?'

'This…circle…works for me too?'

'Of course.'

'So if I wanted to sit and discuss my brother's marriage options with you, which panel would I choose?'

'You might choose the panel with the maps. Strategy session,' Sera offered. 'I'd get my computer and take a seat within that area also and we'd discuss options. I'd provide refreshments. More tea or cold drinks, stuffed dates or something savoury. We'd plot and plan and consider what we already know when it comes to the monarchy's needs and preferences. We'd come up with a list I would then consult whenever I have to plan another function or dinner and I would make sure to get the women on that list in front of him.'

Moriana sat where suggested and the world did not end. She took a deep breath and then looked up at Sera with a smile. 'I love stuffed dates.'

'Tell me…' Sera was wholly prepared to woo the King's sister to within an inch of her life. 'Do you like them dipped in chocolate?'

CHAPTER FOUR

IT WAS A TRAP. Even as Augustus stood at the door to Sera's quarters at half eight the following evening and pulled on the bell to signal his presence, he knew he should have stayed away or at the very least had her brought to his office earlier in the day. He wanted to talk about this list of potential brides she and Moriana had cooked up between them. The first three on the list would be presented to him at the Winter Solstice ball, Moriana had said. Sera would not be present.

What good was a matchmaker if she wasn't even going to be present?

The door in front of him opened, and this time the menace from the High Reaches stood ready to serve him. He'd told her he was coming. He'd given her a time frame and ample opportunity to get ready for him. Nothing was going to happen except conversation. Moriana had navigated that blasted courtesan's carpet wheel successfully enough, and there was

even a training manual to go with it. He'd browsed
through it during his lunch break.

He was getting more used to the physical effect Sera of the High Reaches seemed to have on
him. Eyes soft and inviting, lips curved in welcome.
Her over-tunic a flowing drape of gossamer moss-
coloured silk, then underneath a plum-coloured bodice and straight skirt that finished an inch or so below
the tunic. Her hair had been pulled back into a high
ponytail yet still reached her waist. Delicate silver
fans with tassels fell from her ears and swung gently
as she moved. Matching tassels fell from the place
where she'd gathered her hair. Her make-up was subtle rather than overwhelming.

She was breathtaking.

Wordlessly, she invited him to enter and he did.

'May I take your jacket?' she asked. He thought
Why not? and let her ease it from his shoulders and
hang it on a wooden clothes dummy in the alcove
beside the door. She closed the door behind him and
studied his face intently. 'I haven't curtseyed,' she
said.

And for that he was grateful. Every time she did
she fed a demon that demanded he take advantage
of her willingness to grant him anything he wanted.
'How are your ribs?'

'Perfectly fine, thank you.'

There was a new table in the round room. A small
round table with room enough for three people to

sit around comfortably or four people at a squeeze. There was a new sofa as well, although the round one and the cursed floor tapestry still took pride of place. This new sofa had been placed against a wall. A stack of reading books sat next to it and two wing-back leather library chairs had been positioned to either side. The carpet in between looked thick and plush and was a deep and solid red. She saw him looking at the set-up and extended a graceful arm in its direction.

'I took the liberty of setting up another seating area. Your sister thought it might encourage more visitors, or, at the very least, make them less suspicious once they got here.'

His sister was a genius when it came to putting people at ease.

'You must miss her,' Sera said next.

'We all do.' He'd once thought Moriana neurotic and highly strung. He'd thought his palace would run just as smoothly without her incessant attention to detail. It hadn't. A fact which had surprised him and approximately no one else in the palace. 'My sister used to manage the monarchy's social obligations. There can be two or sometimes even three social functions a day here. And then there are the balls and state dinners. She left comprehensive instructions for every event, but even so I miss her judgement when it comes to who to seat where and what alliances are to be encouraged. It's all in her head, and in mine, and neither of us have time to download a lifetime's worth of observations into someone else's brain. Especially when that someone is just as likely to go to the press with tasty gossip at the first opportunity.' He was tired and irritable and what was it about this woman that had him spilling confidences like an overwrought teenager?

Moving on.

Moriana had sat in the strategy section yesterday morning, she'd told him. It had worked for her. It would work for him. He strode to the central sofa and sat in the area with the people and the table and the maps. Strategy session.

Sera smiled at him, really smiled, as if he'd made her happy, and—oh, *crap*.

Could he order her not to smile at him like that?

'Would you like water, wine, coffee or tea?' she asked.

'None of it. Go get the list of potential wives you and my sister cooked up between you and then take a seat. I have some amendments to make.' He hoped he sounded rigidly officious rather than downright surly but he didn't like his chances. Neither option was a good example of confident, competent leadership.

'I'll get my computer,' she said, and when she came back she sat beside him easy as you please and earnest in her role as matchmaker. For his part, he found himself moving closer, well and truly enmeshed by her delicate perfume and perfect profile and the little fan earrings that brushed the skin of her neck.

All of it was captivating and it took all the willpower he had to turn his attention to the database full of potential brides. A database full of not just names but lineages, occupations, hobbies and… 'Is that a character assessment column?'

'Subjective, of course, and predominantly based on their public personas. They may be quite different underneath. We can adjust it as we go. It would be helpful if you could give me some indication as to what you admire most in a woman,' she said. 'Do you want someone with a calm disposition or are you after more fire than that? Someone fun-loving and easy-going or someone more highly strung and demanding? A pliable companion or someone you might on occasion have to work to placate?'

'Meekness bores me. Theatrics annoy me. And stupidity is an unpardonable sin.'

Sera's fingers flew across the keyboard and several names disappeared. 'Any hair, eye or skin colour preferences?'

'None.' He hadn't known he had a preference for grey eyes, raven-dark hair and skin the colour of pale rose petals until a few days ago. Hopefully his current obsession would be short-lived.

'Will you entertain marriage to a woman whose religion is different to yours?' she asked.

'No. She would have to convert.' The demands of the Crown overrode all else in that regard.

More names disappeared from the list.

'Would you like a virgin?' she asked.

'Are you serious?'

Her fingers paused over the keyboard. 'Ah…yes? Historically—'

'Let's keep it modern day.'

'The question stands,' she offered quietly. 'Some things are best left to those who enjoy initiating others. Do you want a virgin or would you prefer someone who brings adequate experience to sexual matters?'

'It's not important!' Said no scaly possessive alpha beast ever.

'Okay.' Another pause. 'Thank you for answering.'

'You're blushing,' he told her darkly. 'All virgin brides aside, how can you possibly think yourself ready to do some of the things in these pictures when you've never been touched?'

His virgin courtesan. The idea was ridiculous.

Beyond ridiculous.

No wonder it kept him awake at night.

'Bodies can be prepared in advance for just about anything. It's the endorphins.' Sera stared at the screen, delicate colour still filling her cheeks. 'More specifically, increased levels of oxytocin can act as a natural pain inhibitor. Additionally, minds can be manipulated to respond with pleasure to dominance, submission or many other…things.'

All of a sudden the idea of a virgin concubine wasn't ridiculous at all, and it was burning hot in this room built for pleasure. 'So you think you're ready for anything?'

'I hope I am. To be otherwise would be unaccept-able. Disgraceful.'

'On what planet is not being ready to partake in an orgy or whip a man bloody disgraceful?' She had a flawless knack for rousing his temper. 'Dammit, Sera. I have no idea who you're answering to!'

'I answer to you.'

'The hell you do! Otherwise you'd be gone from here, as requested! Do you even understand the Pandora's box of problems you bring with you? That I'm trying to *work* through while keeping you pro-tected?'

'I don't need protecting.'

'You say you're innocent. The innocent *always* need protecting.' He stood abruptly and stepped away from temptation before he did something unforgiv-able. 'Read out the remaining names,' he ordered, and she did, her voice becoming steadier as she went. He had her remove several more names from the list, because he'd met those women before and they weren't for him. He found himself circling the sofa, and then moving further afield, looking at other tapestries and sculptures, other furniture sent to grace a courtesan's workplace.

Over and over, his feet returned him to the centre of the room where she sat, his gaze drawn to the pleasure wheel at her feet. Where would a virgin trained as a courtesan even want to start when it came to serving someone sexually?

Finally the names stopped coming and his reason for being there ended.

'It would help if you could give me some additional ideas of what you're looking for in a wife,' she said.

Good question, but he didn't really have an answer for himself, let alone one he'd ever voiced to anyone else. He was so used to *not* voicing his innermost thoughts. 'Why? So you can sell a list of my private wants and needs to the highest bidder?'

'I would never do that. No courtesan of the High Reaches would ever betray your confidence. Above all else, it is the rule that governs us.'

He wanted to believe her. And really, what would it matter if people knew what he was looking for in a wife? The basics, at any rate.

'Resilience is important,' he offered, and wondered why it was easier to talk to her than just about anyone. 'There's no point choosing a wife who'll crumble beneath the pressures and constrictions placed on her. She'll be bound by duty to Crown and country. She'll have to cope with extensive press coverage wherever she goes. I want her at the centre of things, right by my side, and she needs to be stubborn and curious, observant, intuitive and good with people she barely knows.'

Now that he'd started, he didn't know how to stop confiding in her, because he *had* thought about this. He'd thought about this long and hard and it was good to finally say some of it out loud. 'Above all I want to know what's going to keep her at my side when the going gets tough. Because it will. My mother loved my father above all else and he loved her. This country benefitted greatly from their love match. My sister loves Theo and he loves her. Liesendaach wins. Sometimes I doubt I have the capacity to *be* in love with another person in that same way. And yet I can see the benefits. The strength in it. I'm not against it.'

Too much.

Too much revealed.

He turned away to study yet another tapestry that hung on a nearby wall. She had no comment for him other than the tapping of computer keys.

'Okay,' she said finally. 'And, forgive me the intrusion, but do you find sex satisfactory?'

'What are you now? My virgin sex therapist?'

'Do you need one?'

He barked a laugh. Better than a growl for this confidante with a sharply honed wit. 'I get by.'

'Some of your ancestors have preferred men.

They've required wives who could accommodate those preferences. Turn a blind eye at times.'

'I prefer women.' Truth.

'What of fidelity?' she asked. 'Will you practise it?'

'Yes.'

'Do you require fidelity from your wife?'

'Yes.' Surely she knew this already? He'd already banned her from taking her kisses elsewhere and had almost punished her guard the other morning for daring to spar with her. 'I don't share.'

More typing and no comment whatsoever.

'I'm thirty years old. I prefer women to men. I've never been in love. And I thought I had more time in which to marry before the courtesans of old descended from a mystical mountain to help me do my duty,' he offered curtly. 'I can find my own wife, regardless of what you, your Order or my sister might think. The only reason I'm here is because I refuse to let you conspire behind my back. You may as well conspire with me. It'll go much faster if we work together on this.'

'Yes, I know,' she offered quietly.

'I also want to be able to explain your role here without calling into question my sanity, my morals or yours. From here on in when you're dealing with my staff or handling guest lists you'll be known as Lady Sera Boreas, Executive Function Manager for the Royal Palace of Arun. You'll answer to me or my executive secretary. You will oversee the functions in person but not be in attendance as a guest. I want you in corporate clothing. Smart suits, modest jewellery, tidy hair. No shackles or manacles, no golden bustiers, no six-inch heels while you're on duty in public.'

'And in private?'

'I can't tell you what to do once you're in the privacy of your own quarters.'

'Actually, you ca—'

'Don't say those words.'

It occurred to him that he was already telling her what to do in the privacy of her quarters, and he smiled without humour. It was an impossible situation and he saw no way out of it other than to make her leave or turn her into a respectable employee of the palace. He waved his hand around the room. 'All that you've brought to my palace works against me in the wider world. The rebirth of these quarters is all my staff can talk about. Word has spread. King Augustus of Arun keeps a courtesan hidden in a round room, built like a birdcage. He's been bewitched, his needs are dark, he's not a modern-day king. You're a sorceress, a temptress, a creature of myth. That's what they're saying about you, me and this situation. It's time to take control of this narrative.'

'You want to reframe me.'

He nodded. 'Minimise the mystery. Modernise the mythology. I need you to arrange for one piece of art to be displayed in the palace's grand entrance hall. I want notes to accompany it, emphasising its historical significance. I want a dozen books from your collection showcased in the state library, several pieces of art or treasures of historical significance in circulation throughout our galleries. I want a narrative built around the Order of the Kite that starts with it being supportive, historically complex, non-political, culturally significant and ends with the information about your current non-sexual role in my administration. I want you to give history talks in university lecture halls and libraries. I want you to be the guest of honour as each treasure on display is unveiled. I want you to talk about the Order of old and then I want you to talk about the roles women have traditionally played in government, the roles open to them today and your own education.'

'Your Majesty, the Order does *not* seek publicity.'

'Then they shouldn't have sent you here.' His gaze clashed with hers, storm clouds meeting a bleak black sea. 'I'm asking you to be a modern-day woman for a modern-day audience. One who embraces the history and power of your Order and can competently explain your presence here. One who shines a favourable light on us both. Do it or I'll do it for you.'

Augustus shoved his hands in his pockets and turned away. Looking at her never ended well. He always grew resentful of his body's instinctive response and his brain lost its way. 'You're not stupid,

Sera. Philosophy, politics and economics—those are
your degree subjects and you only ever earned dis-
tinction marks or higher. If you want power here I'm
challenging you to take it openly. Carve out a place
for yourself that the public will accept. That *I* can
accept.' He spared a glance for the pleasure wheel.
'Because there are too many elements here that I
dare not accept.'

'Your Majesty—'

He wanted to hear her say his name. Not *Your
Majesty* or *milord* or *sire*. Only his mother and
sometimes his sister had managed to make his name
sound anything more than an unwieldy mouthful.
They'd laced it with affection and love. Exaspera-
tion too, for his cool and calculating deliberations.
His father didn't call him by name all that often.
His father called him *Son* and it was a reminder of
his role in the continuation of their line more than
anything.

He wanted to hear her say his name but there was
no picture in the carpet for that. 'The only words I
want to hear out of your mouth are "I accept your
challenge and this amazing opportunity to become
a relevant member of your court".'

Silence filled the room as he looked up to the
soaring ceiling, anywhere but at the woman seated
somewhere to his left. There were other ways he
could deal with this. Send her away on a quest, take
his case to parliament and the high courts and dis-

solve the accord and make an enemy of a secret Order with tentacles everywhere. The way he'd outlined— dealing openly with a modern interpretation of her position here—was by far the best. But he needed her co-operation.

'I accept your challenge.'

He closed his eyes as her soft words slid through him and with them came relief. 'Your owls have returned,' he said by way of acknowledgement. 'Two of them. Are they inside or out?'

'In. But I don't think they've returned. I think these ones were merely absent when Tomas came for the rest. I'm glad they were both away and not just one of them. I think they're a mated pair.'

'Do you know what kind they are?'

'Tomas tells me they're Great Horned Owls. I sent him photos. Lianthe would say it's a good omen.'

'And what do you say?'

'As long as they stay up there and I stay down here, I say we can probably come to some kind of mutual living arrangement. The bathing pool was filled today.' It was a change of topic, a change of voice—lighter now, with a faint undercurrent of enthusiasm. He risked a backwards glance and found her standing and somehow changed. More hopeful, perhaps. More relaxed. 'It really has been a pleasure to see this place come alive again. It's been over a hundred and twenty years since anyone's lived here. Don't you find that just a little bit fascinating?'

Memory conjured up the marble pool room, with fancy tiles, private alcoves and exposed stone benches. He did want to see the transformation; there was no denying it. 'Show me.'

The dirty grey colours he remembered now glowed ivory, each marble vein shining beneath layers of polish. Sera flicked a switch and lit the area, contemporary lighting, all of it, but it felt as if flame flickered and shadows danced.

'What are the alcoves full of pillows for?' he asked.

'Massage, body treatments, sex. There's a steam room here too. I know you'll not use any of it but we went with authenticity. This was its function.'

She had such an easy way of saying *sex*. As if it was nothing. Just another function of the body. He'd never found it so, endorphins or otherwise. Sex was revealing, and he far preferred to keep his own counsel. 'And the main pool is heated?'

'To three degrees above body temperature. Three hundred years ago your forebears and mine used fire to heat the pool. Yesterday, engineers from the High Reaches laid solar strips to the framework of the dome. This part of your palace now powers itself, and then some.'

Her face had lit up and her pleasure at the improvements seemed real.

He'd agreed to modifications to the rooms Sera occupied. He hadn't specifically agreed to *any* of this. Under the guise of honouring tradition, it felt as if the power here had been quite deftly wrested from his grasp.

She watched him from the shadows while he struggled with what to do with her in private as well as in public.

'Would you like to bathe?' she asked at last—she had to know he wanted more than that. She'd been taught to read people, had she not? Surely she could see the tension and the want in him and not just for warm water. He wanted what the cursed pleasure wheel had told him he could have. He wanted her hands on him, undressing him, washing his hair as he reclined. All those things the bathing picture showed and more, while the light from the wall sconces threw puppet shadows on the walls.

'I shouldn't.'

'Seems a shame to let it go to waste.'

'Don't tempt me.'

'Sometimes a bath can be just a bath.'

'Say my name.' He needed to hear it fall from those perfect lips.

She looked at him, as if trying to read his mood and good luck with that.

'That was an order.'

'Augustus.'

She made it sound like welcome and desire all rolled into one and he tried not to curse as he shoved his hand through his hair and tried to make sense of both his demands and his resistance. 'Did they make you practise that?'

They had. Sera knew better than many how to modulate her voice to convey different feelings. But the breathlessness in her voice this time was all hers. She gestured towards a stack of towels and potions, trying to get back on track. 'Augustus, would you like to bathe? The pool is ready and I've had lessons in how to make the experience a relaxing one. I could wash your hair. Oils to soothe, invigorate and everything in between. What is your mood?'

'You mean you can't tell?'

'You're hard to read.' She hadn't been expecting the way forward for her that he'd proposed. A public image to craft and shape. A role beyond those already identified by the tapestry. And nothing but strict hands-off in private. It was the keeping-distance-in-private request she would have the most trouble with. 'Or you could bathe alone and I can go and read a book in another room. This pool is for *your* use, Augustus. In any way you see fit.'

She turned away, left him to his thoughts, and approached a small side table groaning with essential oils and liquid soaps. She reached for the sandalwood, bergamot and orange and mixed them in a hand bowl, taking her time. 'I find ritual soothing,' she murmured, still not looking at him as she took the bowl to the water's edge and poured the fragrant oil mix into it, rinsing the bowl three times before setting it aside and rising. 'But if you prefer less ritual and more distance, perhaps you might cast me in the role of pool attendant. I can pile towels by the side of the pool and leave you to it.'

She didn't want to shatter the fragile peace they'd created this evening. She wanted it to continue.

'What does the ritual involve?' he rasped.

'I would remove your clothes, provide your soap, wash your hair, towel you dry, moisturise your skin and dress you again. It can take up to an hour of your time.'

'And what's in it for you?'

'Ritual soothes me. And also...'

'Also what?'

'You're not going to like it.' He wasn't going to *accept* it. 'I want to serve here, the way I've been trained to serve. It doesn't have to be sexual. It doesn't have to be complicated. You could find refuge and relaxation here if you wanted to.'

'Do it.'

His words didn't come from a place of acceptance. They came at her twisted and wrapped in loathing. Not a good start but at least she had permission to try to bathe him properly.

She ventured closer, until she was standing in front of him. Undressing a man wasn't a hard thing to do. There was an order to the releasing of buttons and the removal of clothes. She knew what to do. Only her trembling fingertips betrayed her as she reached for one of his wrists, turned his forearm towards her and fumbled with the tiny cufflink there. She bit her lip, intent on her task, and wondered if the crazy throb of the pulse point at his wrist was for her.

She slowed her breathing and got on with her task, undoing first one cufflink and then the other. She stepped in closer as she undid his tie, and his eyes never left her face and hers never left his. Buttons, so many buttons on his shirt, tracking a path down his chest, the last of them hidden beneath his trousers as she pulled the shirt free and dealt with them too. Buttons and knuckles and air that had suddenly grown too thin for breathing.

'This isn't going to end well,' he rasped.

'Relax. I'm a professional.' She pushed the front of his shirt aside and slid her hands up and over his shoulders, taking his shirt with her. By the time she'd smoothed her hands down his arms the shirt was on the floor.

She knelt at his feet, removing his shoes and socks and running her hands up his legs and over his thighs as if soothing a savage beast. She kept her hands on him as she undid his trousers, slid her hands beneath his waistband and down over his buttocks, taking the fabric with her, all the way down his legs. 'Put your hand on my shoulder or my head for balance,' she said, as she lifted first one foot from the puddle of his trousers and then the next.

His boxers were stretched tight over his manhood,

plumper now than it had been moments ago but not yet at full stretch. If she removed his underwear in the same manner she'd removed his trousers she was going to get an eyeful.

And then she leaned in, her hands high on his thighs, and breathed him in.

Hours of video instruction had done nothing to prepare Sera for the impact of the man standing before her. The heat coming from his skin and the scent of him. The glittering black eyes and his complete attention.

She didn't know where or how he exercised but he did, his body lean and his belly ridged with muscle. He had body hair but not a lot. His manhood looked thick beneath the thin stretch of cotton, and she wondered if her mouth would fit around it. Not just thick but long as well. The stretch for her mouth and throat would be considerable.

He took a ragged breath and stepped away from her touch and shed his boxers. He was beautiful naked. He was beautiful everywhere.

'I'll take that bath now.' His voice whispered over her, making promises not kept by his retreating body. She felt the loss of his regard as he stepped into the water and submerged himself completely. The bathing rituals went unobserved as she knelt on a cushion and waited for him to need something more from her, hands clasped in her lap, back straight, head bowed. Still and silent until needed. Ritual.

She watched from beneath her lashes as he selected soap and started washing, his touch far rougher
than hers would have been. She watched him rinse
off, water running in rivulets down the hard planes of
his chest, dripping from his elbows as he pushed dark
tendrils of hair away from his face. He caught her
watching him and stilled. Did he want to get out now?
Should she anticipate his need for a towel? Would
he accept one from her hand? Bathing rituals shot
to hell by him, leaving her untethered and wanting.

'Sera.'

Surely she could look her fill now that he'd called
her name. She lifted her head.

'Will you wash my hair?'

Finally, something she had previous experience
with. She almost fell over herself in her haste to fetch
the water jug and shampoo selection. Ritual, as he
watched her prepare the edge of the pool and gesture for him to lie back with his head in the shallow
dip. She leaned over and filled the jug, wetting his
hair all over again, her hand firm on his forehead to
prevent water trickling down his face.

She opted for a firmer touch than the one she'd
used on the children of the High Reaches, massag-
ing his scalp once the conditioner had gone on and
drawing from him a groan that made her smile her
relief.

'Harder,' he rasped, so she increased the pressure from her fingertips and leaned into it. With his

eyes closed she could study his profile more closely. Inevitably, her gaze moved on from his lips to his chest, then his stomach and onto lower depths. His legs were slightly parted. His manhood looked erect.

When she finally turned her attention back to his face, he was watching her through narrowed eyes.

Hot-faced, she filled the water jug again and began to rinse his hair.

He let her finish, he gave her that, and then he was underwater again, and again, and then standing and heading for the steps.

To ogle his sharply defined muscles and the proud jut of his arousal or pick up a towel and have it ready for him? Sera knew what she ought to be doing. She'd trained for this.

By the time she reached the side of the pool and handed him a towel and he'd taken it and wiped his face and dropped it and stood naked before her, she met his gaze unflinchingly. He had nothing to be ashamed of.

Neither did she.

'If you could kiss me in one place and one place only, where would you kiss?' he demanded.

She'd seen so much sex in the guise of instruction. She knew the psychology and physiology behind each and every action, but knowing wasn't doing and she'd never done any of it. His lips beckoned, the fierce cut of his cheekbones. The curve of his shoulder appealed, the water droplet sliding down his neck—she could lap it up and find the pulse point.

But his hand moved to curl around his erection and it drew her gaze like a lodestone. More than anything else, she wanted to know more of *that*. For some reason, kissing his lips seemed like more of an intrusion than kissing him *there*.

He looked so good naked and wanting, almost vibrating with tension as he waited for her to choose which part of him to kiss. He might not even allow it. Maybe all he wanted to know was her preference so he could destroy her with wanting and never having any of it.

She dropped to her knees and his eyes flared a heated warning.

'Really?' he rasped.

'I want to know what it's like,' she replied. 'Do you?'

'I already know.'

She kept her gaze on his face, willing him to let her have this. 'I want to know too.'

'Brave,' he rasped. 'Did they teach you how to do this?'

'Yes.' With toys and tutorials but it was nothing compared to the soft warmth of his shaft as she leaned forward and placed her moist and parted lips against the most sensitive area just beneath the tip.

She tongued him carefully and he tasted of nothing but water. Not until she ran her tongue across the slit did she get a sense of his essence. The skin was slick and smooth. His hiss was hopefully one of pleasure. She knew not to use her teeth. She sucked, ever so gently, and received a fresh burst of flavour for her efforts.

'That's it,' he murmured. 'How much can you take?'

All of it. She closed her eyes and opened her throat and took him deep, down to where her lips met his testicles and she had to breathe through her nose. His hand came to cover her head, not pushing, just keeping her there, then he slowly withdrew until only the tip of him touched her lips.

'Breathe,' he ordered, even as his hand reversed its pressure and he drew her back down onto him. 'Again.'

She lost herself in the rhythm of his slow and measured thrusts.

'Put your hands on me,' he said, and she did, first his thighs while her thumbs brushed the swell of his balls, and then more boldly while he simultaneously thrusted and cursed.

'Look at me,' he ordered on his next withdrawal and she opened her eyes while he searched her face as if studying a puzzle he had no answer for. 'You like this,' he muttered finally. 'Heaven help us both.'

Yes, she liked it. The careful thrusting, his innate gentleness and iron control. The satisfaction that came of knowing that she was the cause of his arousal. She knew how to finish a man, theoretically. Suck and swallow, throat muscles working him over, but when she tried he withdrew so fast and roughly he left her blinking up at him. What had she done? Or not done? 'I'm sorry, I—'

'Don't apologise,' he said, but she still felt as if she'd failed and he must have seen some of that thought written on her face, because he groaned and hauled her up and into his arms and crashed his mouth down over hers, hard and hungry, all power and unrestrained passion, and she responded in kind because this kiss was better than anything she'd ever felt.

He groaned into her mouth and she swallowed it down and opened for more. He tilted her head and consumed her and she fisted her hand in his hair and worked her lips down his neck, nipping and sucking, because she could do that to him here, and skating the edge of violence suited her, suited them both.

She had too many clothes on and he had none. They were ignoring so many steps in the sex-making process. Or maybe they weren't.

'Take me in hand,' he muttered. 'Touch me.' He lifted her bodily and she curled her legs around him. He put her back to a column and rocked against her as his mouth claimed hers again.

He came with layers of silk clothing still between them, grinding down hard against her core and tipping her over into orgasm moments after his own release, strong hands to her buttocks, wet hair at odds with the harsh heat of his breath and the still scorching feel of his mouth on hers. She'd always known about the fire deep down inside her. It was the reason they'd chosen her.

She'd suspected from the beginning that there was a matching fire in him.

After a dozen more harsh breaths, both his and hers, he set her gently on her feet and turned away, not looking at her once as he found his clothes, put them on. He didn't speak, didn't look her way as he headed for the main room and swiftly strode towards the door. He didn't speak as he opened it and let himself out. He left, that was all.

And then the emptiness crashed down on her.

CHAPTER FIVE

AUGUSTUS, RULER OF ARUN, had always kept himself tightly under control. Born to inherit his father's throne, raised to think before he spoke, to weigh and qualify every action. His sister had been the unruly one, governed by her emotions, and only careful tutelage and cultivation of a serene public persona had ever contained her. For Augustus it had been easy. Not for him the pitfalls of adolescent crushes or fierce bursts of anger. He was the cool-headed one, the old soul, the stuffy one. No unexpected or unplanned behaviour from Augustus of Arun. He knew what he had to do at all times and he did it, all childhood resistance to his lot in life long since diminished.

So what the ever-loving hell had just happened in there?

Because he'd never done that before in his life. Taken his own pleasure and given nothing back in return. Leave a woman, *any woman*, let alone a virgin, leaning against a wall for support, her clothes stained and her eyes blown wide with shock, her lips…

Her lips…

What she'd done with them.

He could write an incoherent ode to them.

What had he done? Where was all his rigid moral certainty now?

No one should be made to serve the way she had been groomed to serve him. Even kings needed barriers. Free rein and ultimate power was never a good combination. That was how despots were created.

He hadn't even given her pleasure.

Augustus stopped to lean against the cold stone of the corridor wall. He closed his eyes and bowed his head and tried to make sense of what he'd done. He was attracted to Sera—had been from the moment he'd laid eyes on her. He'd wanted to set her free from the duty bestowed on her and he'd tried. He'd combed every old text and obscure law journal he could find for ways to release her. It was the honourable thing to do. So far, so good. And while that was still happening he'd allowed her to settle into those dusty old quarters and revive a tradition long dead, and legitimise it with artwork and furnishings, and he'd left her alone to get on with it. He'd given her a secretarial role to be going on with because he'd needed a social organiser and she'd needed to serve.

He'd let her draw up a list of potential brides, not because he wanted to get married but because if he did marry she would surely go away. A stupid reason to marry but he needed to marry sooner or later and he wasn't complaining.

He'd behaved.

Right up until he hadn't.

He'd left her standing there, wide-eyed and mute, her mouth a wreck and her body trembling.

He heard a slight sound, a shuffle, and opened his eyes and met the shadowy gaze of one of her guards, half hidden in a recess. The man wanted him to know he was there, that much was obvious. Would he check on Sera once Augustus had gone? Would he comfort her and curse his King?

When had all reason and rational good sense deserted him?

Augustus pushed away from the wall and turned back towards the double doors that kept people out and Sera in. He rang the bell and stared at the flowers and waited.

Nothing happened.

He rang the bell again, and this time, after several more impatient seconds, a peephole opened and he moved to stand in front of it.

She opened the door to him in silence, a towel wrapped around her otherwise wet and naked body.

Washing the stench of him away, he thought grimly, and his heart clenched.

'Your Majesty,' she said, and her voice was huskier than it had been earlier, and he certainly knew why.

'You know my name.'

Only she didn't say it.

'May I come in?'

She stood aside and opened the door and glanced behind him and so did Augustus. The guard stood there watching them, fully visible now, arms crossed in front of his chest and his eyes sharp. Augustus didn't know what she did—more of that silent communication business—but the guard nodded slightly and faded from view.

'You told him you had everything under control?' he asked.

'Yes.'

'Is that what you really think?'

'I think you're conflicted.'

'I think I'm a monster,' he said.

'Because you gave me what I asked for?'

'You didn't ask for that.' She looked at him sharply and then glanced towards the big circular sofa. 'I don't want to sit at your cursed wheel,' he muttered. 'You were bathing. Do you need to continue with that?' She might as well be clean. God knew no amount of water was going to wash him clean of this sin.

With the grace of a dancer and no inhibitions whatsoever, she walked towards the pool and shed her towel before stepping lightly into the water, deeper and deeper still, until she was shoulders deep and her hair billowed about her like tendrils of ink.

'I'm sorry.' She'd never know how much. 'The way I treated you earlier was unacceptable.'

She watched him pace and then reached for the soap. 'You fear passion,' she said.

'No.'

She raised an elegant eyebrow.

'I lost control. I took without thinking. I hurt you.' The way she'd taken him in her mouth, letting him push deeper than he'd ever pushed before—all animal instinct. 'I can hear the damage in your voice.'

She looked at him, her thoughts her own, and then swam to a tap and turned it on and pushed her face beneath it and opened her mouth and drank. He wanted to look away from the innocent abandon in even that small act. The open mouth and the eyes that never stopped watching him, cataloguing every tiny twitch—or so he imagined. She swallowed and so did he, remembering, and the deep ache of desire that should have been sated sputtered to life again.

She swallowed more and then turned the tap off and cleared her throat. 'How do I sound now?'

A little less rough. 'Your lips are still swollen.' The make-up was off but the lush redness remained.

'I can't tell.' She was at the side of the pool again, closest to him, all graceful hands and arms, breasts with the nipples puckered up tight, but she wasn't self-conscious—not one little bit—and he looked away and kept right on pacing, wondering why he'd turned around and come back because he was unravelling all over again. 'Have you finished bathing?' she asked solemnly.

He'd finished undressing in front of her, full-stop. At least one of them should be clothed at all times. It was his new motto when dealing with her. 'I didn't—'

She waited for him to continue.

'You didn't—'

She was still waiting for him to finish a damn sentence.

'First times should involve satisfaction for all concerned,' he muttered finally. 'I should have made it so. I can still show you what it can be like.'

'By taking control?'

'Yes.' By taking control and keeping it and pasting over the last twenty minutes with something infinitely more palatable.

'You do realise that my satisfaction isn't the goal here?' she asked, and that, more than anything else in this crazy set-up, made his temper spike.

'Because your teachers say so? Because you're here to serve and my satisfaction comes before yours? Because you don't deserve a first kiss that's gentle and respectful? Because, believe me, Sera of the High Reaches, everyone deserves that.'

'It wasn't gentle, true.' She was getting out of the bath now and walking towards him, water caressing her skin. 'But my self-respect is intact, even if yours is not.' She tilted her head back to look at him. 'Your ego is bruised because you think I didn't like your taste or touch? I can assure you I did.'

How could she have?

Her eyes seemed to soften as she stared at him. 'Would you like to try again?' she invited softly. 'Bolster your ego, dilute your guilt—whatever it is that brought you back here to apologise? Because you can kiss me again if you like.'

It wasn't *about* him. 'What would *you* like? From me?'

'Right now?'

'Right now.' Because he'd do it. 'This isn't about me.'

'Do you really believe that?' She picked up a towel and patted her face and wrapped it around her small frame and tucked it in. She pushed her hair to one side and combed through it with her fingers before wrapping slender fists around the dark mass and stripping the water from it in one smooth movement. 'I'd like to kiss you again,' she said at last. 'I'd like for you to kiss me, gently and respectfully, whatever it is you think I need, and we'll see how that goes. I might like it more than our earlier kisses. I might not. I'll let you know.'

She would like it more. She had to—for his sanity. He didn't know what he'd do if she liked it greedy and rough, because that wasn't him. He wasn't drawn to explore the darker sides of desire, those places where control bled away and chaos slipped in. Regardless of whether she was willing to accommodate him.

One kiss, and this time he'd do right by her, ease in slow with the barest touch of his lips against hers. Plenty of room for her sigh and his relief as her eyes fluttered closed as he slanted his head and fitted his lips more firmly against hers. Waiting rather than demanding her compliance, and there it was, the tip of her tongue skating along the edge of his upper lip, and he was careful, so careful to follow her cues and keep his hands to himself. Easy, never mind the want that pushed up from those places he always kept hidden. Sweet, because first kisses should be savoured, not driven into someone with the force of a fist.

He pulled back slowly, letting the space between their lips grow, watching her face come back into focus, pale and perfect, and her eyes open to regard him steadily.

'Better?' he asked and she smiled ever so slightly.

'Different.'

He could do better. Another kiss, this time with the reins less tightly held. Letting slip, just a little, to allow for a response that wasn't so carefully composed. She responded beautifully, so willing to follow where he led, so open to whatever he wanted to bestow. Enough to make a blush light her cheeks and her eyes look unfocused. Enough to risk his thumb against her lips when his mouth wasn't there, smoothing them, learning them, setting everything back in order because he couldn't have it any other way. 'Better?'

'Is this what you want from a wife? Someone

who'll never truly know your heart because you're too busy hiding beneath all that delicious self-control?'

'Don't push me.' Even as he pressed her bottom lip lightly against her teeth. Not hurting her, no. And yet. 'Rule number one of the Arunian monarchs: don't ever lose control.'

'And what's rule number two?'

'An eye for an eye.'

He dropped to his knees in front of her and tugged the towel from her body. He pressed his lips to a bead of water that sat at the junction of her perfectly toned thighs. She gasped, and it was all the encouragement he needed. Hands sliding up her thighs to part them. The taste of her sweet on his tongue, and just like that he was ravenous again, licking and striking, flicking and sucking, listening and responding to every sound and twitch she gifted him with. He was good at this.

And she was so utterly, gloriously responsive.

Virgin.

A virgin he should have left alone or, failing that, someone whose pleasure should have very definitely come before his own. His shaft twitched, only this time he ignored it. He'd taken his pleasure. Now it was her turn.

Her fingers came up to guide his head with more force than expected. But then, this slip of a woman knew exactly how to wield swords and knives and even sharper words.

A ragged curse that felt like an endearment. A trembling 'oh' when he redoubled his efforts.

He wanted her to say his name again as she came.

Words that seemed lost beneath her quiet gasps and his growls when he grew greedy and still couldn't get enough.

She came on his tongue, tense and trembling, and he could swear he felt the ripples of her body beneath his hand, and he should have withdrawn then, done and done, but there was always one more taste he had to have, even if he did avoid her most sensitive areas, and then she was dropping to her knees to face him and her hands were on his shoulders, and she said, 'Kiss me again and mean it, Augustus,' and his name on her lips was like a promise, so he did as she asked and knew himself for lost.

'Don't,' he whispered, when he finally found the will to pull away from her. 'Don't tempt me.'

This time, when he left, he made it all the way back to his quarters before shedding his clothes and stepping beneath a scalding shower in a futile effort to cleanse his soul.

Don't make me lose control.

Physical activity was the only thing that prevented Augustus from climbing the walls in the days that followed. He swam until he either had to get out of the pool or drown, he ran on the treadmill in his private gym until he bent double and emptied his stomach. He put his recently purchased catamaran through its paces until he found its tipping point and it still didn't take the edge off.

He tried burying himself in work, which worked until his put-upon secretary demanded an assistant.

He went on a date with a perfectly eligible woman who was charming and accomplished and didn't challenge his self-control one little bit. He hated every awkward, stilted moment of it.

He visited Theo's cousin Benedict to look at horse-flesh and met the long-term mistress of Theo's father, who just so happened to own the horses they were looking at, and he'd stood in the stables and wanted to ask her what it was like to own the heart of a king but never to hold his hand in public. In the end he didn't ask because he didn't have the right to pry and he probably wouldn't have liked the answer anyway.

Benedict, after spending half a day with him, dropped all pretence of pleasantries the minute they left the stables and brought out the bolt-cutters in an attempt to prise Augustus open.

'What on earth is wrong with you?' he demanded bluntly. 'I've seen junkies desperate for their next fix in better shape than you.'

And Benedict would know. Even though he'd settled down and returned to the family fold after his father's death, there wasn't much Benedict of Liesendaach didn't know about the darker side of sex, drugs and reckless self-indulgence.

'I'm not on drugs.' He'd never followed that road.

'And yet you're radiating barely concealed angst all over my calm. Are you having an existential crisis? You'd be surprised how many people invite me to tea and then proceed to come undone. As if I give a damn.' Benedict was eyeing him speculatively. 'Although for you I might show minor concern. I owe your sister a favour. She gave me my cousin back.'

'Whatever debt you think you owe Moriana, leave me out of it.' He didn't need saving or fixing or whatever else Benedict thought he was doing. He just wanted a distraction from the woman in his birdcage who was messing with his head. The woman who this morning had put a tapestry illustrating one of his ancestors feasting in the round room on show in the main entry hall. The accompanying plaque named every nobleman in the picture, the names of every courtesan and the date. On a plinth beside the tapestry sat an open recipe book, written in a language of old. Beside it, she'd offered a printed translation of *Feast Number Six for Midwinter Dining*.

Augustus scowled afresh. Sera of the High Reaches was doing exactly what he'd told her to do and, what was more, she was doing it well.

'No sexual identity crisis?'

What the hell was it with these questions lately? 'I'm male. I'm straight. I sincerely don't know what else to say to that question.'

'Not a problem,' said Benedict blithely. 'But if

that *had* been your problem I would have helped. I take my role seriously when it comes to being a guiding light for same sex relationships of the royal variety.'

'You buried yourself in vice, became estranged from your family and then downplayed your most important romantic relationship for years.'

'And now I'm back. Like I said: guiding light. I'm a veritable lighthouse.'

Augustus snorted.

'Besides, there are other existential crises to be had,' continued Benedict. 'No unexpected desire to be tied, gagged and at someone's mercy?'

'No.'

'Bootlicking, public sex, voyeurism…'

'I worry about you occasionally,' said Augustus.

'I'm worried for you right now, in spite of my self-proclaimed indifference. It appears I'm getting soft.'

'Worry about something else.'

'I hear you have a courtesan in residence. Moriana thinks it's wonderful. A revelation, rich in art, history and cultural significance. Which, while I embrace your sister's enthusiasm for all things cultural, rather seems to be missing the point. You have a woman who has been trained to indulge your every sexual whim living in your birdcage. How's that working out for you?'

Trust Benedict to get straight to the sexual point.

'The Lady Sera has now retired from her former

role as courtesan and has taken on an events management and PR position.'

Benedict had his head down and his hands in his pockets as they headed for the car that would take them on to future engagements, but at this he looked up. 'No special services at all?'

'She's finding me a wife.'

When Benedict laughed, he did it body, heart and soul. He was laughing now, near bent double, and all Augustus could do was scowl.

'That's the worst idea you've ever had,' offered Benedict when his amusement no longer threatened his ability to talk.

'Thank you for your enduring support. Moriana's helping her.'

'Good heavens, you're serious.'

'When am I not?'

'Says he who threatened Theo with a procession of elephants after he proposed to your sister.'

'I reiterate—when am I not serious?' Elephants too had been part of Arun's lore of old. His courtesan could probably tell him all about them. 'I need a wife in order to make the courtesan in the birdcage go away. I also need an heir and Arun could use a Queen. They seem like good enough reasons to make marrying a priority.'

'I understand your need for a wife. I even understand your desire to canvass other royal opinions as part of your decision-making process. But why's the courtesan helping you choose one?'

'She's not helping me choose, she's simply helping to organise the parade of eligible women.'

'Giving her ample opportunity to manipulate the parade itself,' Benedict offered with a hefty helping of sarcasm.

'If I don't like what I see I can always look elsewhere.' Augustus was famously picky when it came to choosing women to keep company with. 'It's not as if I haven't already looked. I need to broaden my horizons. This is one way to do it.'

'Are you intending to bed your former courtesan while you wait for your potential Queen to amble by?'

'No.' But his brain conjured the image of Sera on her knees before him and then another one of her naked beneath him, a writhing, pleading mess as he sent her soaring, those expressive grey eyes blind to everything but the feel of him. 'That would be potentially off-putting to said future wife.'

'Tempting, though.'

'Very,' he admitted through gritted teeth.

Benedict smirked. 'I see your dilemma. Fewer scruples would help.'

'A king leads by example. Sera of the High Reaches needs to leave my employment in the same state in which she entered it.'

'Right. And meanwhile you…'

'Go slowly round the twist, yes.'

* * *

Sera knew Augustus was avoiding her and, frankly, that suited her just fine. Courtesans weren't meant to blush at the memory of a man's mouth on her. She wasn't supposed to crave Augustus's attention the way she did. Anything would do. A touch, a glance, the merest shred of his attention. Anything to feed the bubbling cauldron of emotion he'd awakened in her. The desperate need to satisfy his desires and hers. The things they could *do*, and *feel*. They could be fearless together…

She read texts on controlling sexual situations, because that was his way, was it not? She read texts on how best to stay safe while surrendering control. She did everything he asked of her. Put artwork from the High Reaches on display in his palace and the libraries and galleries of Arun. Arranged speaking engagements for herself and spent hours crafting speeches to fit various target audiences. She set about reinventing her role here and part of her relished the challenge even as another part mourned the loss of tradition. She purchased clothes more suitable to a corporate banker than a courtesan, and when the Winter Solstice ball came along she attended it as the events co-ordinator, dressed fully in nondescript black. Black boots, black trousers, fitted black blazer and her black hair pulled back in a high ponytail. Communication pack at her waist and an earphone in her ear, she was quite clearly working the event and not there as a guest.

It didn't stop people—mostly men—from staring at her regardless or luring her to their side under the guise of making a complaint and then asking for her phone number or simply asking her what she was doing later. No finesse, but most accepted her polite brush-offs with equal civility. Those who pressed their suit met Ari and Tun. Augustus might have requested her presence here tonight but he hadn't been stupid enough to leave her unprotected.

Small mercies.

Just because he had no desire for a courtesan, didn't mean others were equally restrained. Augustus had relinquished his claim on her in the most public way possible—by putting her to work, very visibly, in another role. Others were singularly inclined to pick her up where he'd left off.

It made it extremely difficult for her to competently do her job.

When Augustus's long-suffering secretary caught her eye and wordlessly directed her to the service doors, Sera made her way towards them. He met her there, his face impassive.

'The King respectfully requests that from this point onwards you leave all requests for your personal attention for either me or your guards to deal with,' he began.

'With pleasure.'

'He also requests that you stop deliberately attracting attention.'

Deliberately attracting attention? 'Are my black clothes not modest enough?'

The older man hitched his shoulders in a wordless gesture signifying who knew what.

'Shall I overcome years of comportment training and walk with a slouch?'

Another shrug. 'I'm just the messenger.'

'Then you can tell the King that this is no more and no less attention than I ever receive. People look and people want. There is no "off" switch. The relationship between King and courtesan is often mutually beneficial in that once he stakes his claim the unwanted attention afforded a courtesan will *stop*. Of course, *this* King is far too enlightened to understand that the course of action he insists I follow has consequences he knows nothing about.'

'I'll let him know,' the older man said, and strode off.

The next time a guest beckoned her forward, she sent Ari to deal with him.

The next time the King's secretary approached she summoned her gentlest smile.

'The King suggests you supervise the event from the upper west balcony,' he said. 'From behind the lights.'

'Of course.' There were two ways to reach the suggested balcony. By the servants' entrance or by the central staircase. She chose the stairs. Head held high and the six-inch heels of her boots very much on show, she made her way straight up the middle with Tun and Ari falling into place on either side of her and two steps behind. She didn't bother looking back.

She knew damn well she had almost everyone's attention. Including Augustus's.

He found her two hours later, after the remains of the meal had been cleared away and guests had gravitated towards the dance floor, some to dance, some to stand and mingle at the edges. He'd mingled too, for as long as his patience would allow, and then he'd slipped away through a side door and taken the back way to the balcony. She had her back to him as one of her guards opened the door so he could enter. The second guard appraised him coolly before apparently making some kind of decision and silently taking his leave and closing the balcony door behind them and plunging them into near darkness.

'Why are you up here when you should be down there?' she asked without even turning around.

Why indeed? 'How did you know it was me?'

'Ari gave us privacy. There's only one person in this palace he'd do that for without waiting for my command.' She turned to face him. 'Your Majesty.'

He didn't make the mistake of thinking Sera's guards were under his control. According to his Head of Security, they were compliant to a point.

Co-operating when they could, fitting unobtrusively into whatever protection detail was in place. Beyond that, they were hers. 'Lucky me.'

Her shuttered glance mocked him.

'Would you prefer I call him back in?' she offered, dry as dust.

'No. The evening didn't go quite to plan, as far as you were concerned.'

'Didn't it?' She sounded wholly unconcerned. 'I thought it went well. You mingled. Ate well. Met the women you wanted to meet. I gather Katerina DeLitt is a pleasant enough conversationalist.'

'She is.' One of his sister's additions to the potential brides list. A noblewoman with strong trade connections. 'She's titled, well-read, entertaining and perfectly pleasing to the eye. And yet no one here this evening seemed to be able to see past you.'

'It happens.'

'Why?' His knew his voice sounded tight with frustration. 'You were supposed to blend in as an employee, shatter the myth of the courtesans of old. Instead you—'

'Instead I what?' He really should have taken note of the sharp note in her voice. He hadn't grown up with a temperamental sister for nothing. 'Did I not dress appropriately and make sure the evening ran smoothly? Was I not available to troubleshoot guest issues as they arose? Did I not do what you asked of me?'

'You drew too much attention.'

She leaned back against the balcony and crossed her arms in front of her, wholly unconcerned by the low balustrade and the significant drop to the floor below. 'I've been drawing that kind of attention since childhood. They say I have too much presence, that my beauty serves to make others insecure. Some people want to tear me down before I've ever said a word to them. Others would own me for their own ego enhancement. I don't blend in. I never have. My beauty will always be both celebrated and de-monised, sometimes both at once, because beauty is power, and never more dangerous than in the hands of someone who knows how to use it.' She cocked her head to one side, her face in shadows and the spotlights behind her shining out across the ball-room below. 'You want me to craft a new persona while I live beneath your roof and I have no objec-tion to doing so. But the response of others to power such as mine is always going to be part of it. *Your* response to me is always going to be part of it. So what's it to be? Are you here to work with me? Ask me to set up another meeting for you with the pleas-ant enough Katerina DeLitt? Perhaps you'd also like to tell me to make a note to never invite Peter Saville and Ricardo Anguissey to the same event again lest their wives and everyone else discover that they're in each other's pants? Or are you here to condemn me because my mere presence makes others behave badly?'

He'd been about to do that last one. He hadn't liked the attention his guests had bestowed on his new events co-ordinator. The predatory nature of some of it. His instinctive desire to protect her from it. He'd wanted to claim her, to own her, to tear into anyone who dared covet her. Berate her for using the same stairs dozens of his other employees had used throughout the evening.

He wanted to step away from the door and look into her face, the better to try and interpret her every thought. He wanted to see her eyes darken with desire not hurt, and then he wanted to turn her around to face the ballroom and tell her that none of the people down there mattered; only his elemental desire to claim her mattered. And then he would step up behind her, open her trousers and bring her to quivering arousal with his fingers while his mouth ravaged hers and smothered her soft gasps of completion. She'd let him.

He knew damn well she'd let him.

And the next time he saw her she'd have drawn up a new list of candidates eligible to become his Queen—women with a knack for surrendering to exhibitionism or possessiveness or whatever this was that he wanted from her.

From *her*, not them.

'Is my Minister for Trade really having an affair

with our Liesendaach Ambassador?' he said instead. 'I'll have to tell Theo.'

'You're assuming he doesn't already know.'

Augustus lowered his head and bit down a snort. She had a point. 'In that case, I'll ask my sister why I shouldn't simply send Liesendaach's diplomatic representative home and get them to send a new one.'

She smiled ever so slightly, and dropped her arms to her sides and then curled her hands around the railing behind her. 'That would be one way of opening dialogue about the conflict of many interests, yes.'

He liked seeing her less defensive when she looked at him. 'What else did you see?'

'Your Transport Minister's wife is pregnant and not coping well with the demands of his job and her first trimester sickness. One of the Cordova twins of Liesendaach will be going home this evening with your Horse Master, although I'm not sure which one. And Prince Benedict of Liesendaach enjoys winding you up more than you can possibly imagine. If he wasn't so enamoured of his partner I'd think him desperate for your attention.'

'Benedict enjoys cultivating other people's low opinion of him. It prevents them from noticing how ruthlessly cunning he is until it's too late. At which point he usually has enough dirt on them to make them beholden to him for life. Never underestimate him.'

'I like him already,' she murmured.

'He collects art. I'm sure he'd like to see some of the treasures that now reside in the round room.' Benedict would go nuts over the tapestry wheel on the floor. 'You might want to be careful about where he wants to sit on that round sofa of yours. Because he'll doubtless want to sit in every damn section, just to see what happens.'

She smiled and for a moment his breath caught in his throat. It didn't matter what they'd just been talking about because that smile was one he hadn't seen before—openly conspiratorial and at the same time unguarded. As if gossiping about guests and trusting her to deal with Benedict however she saw fit made her happy.

He looked away, trying desperately not to be one of those men who looked at her and wanted her for all the wrong reasons. Nor did he want to be among the masses who became putty in her hands with just one smile. He wanted to do right by this woman who'd been placed in his care regardless of whether he wanted her there or not. Set her up to succeed. Give her a way out of the lifestyle she'd had thrust upon her when she was seven years old.

No judgement. No slaking his desires. Just common human decency. 'Make sure Katerina DeLitt is invited to the next palace function, along with the next set of candidates,' he said gruffly. 'I like her.'

And then he left.

CHAPTER SIX

THREE DAYS LATER Sera stepped naked into the bathing pool and kept going until every part of her was underwater from the neck down. The pool had been getting warmer by the day and now it ran hot, day in and day out. No one used it but her. Augustus had declined, ever since that first time. Her guards declined the use of it—even if they knew she'd be out all day giving a talk at one gallery or another or being interviewed by journalists or overseeing this function or that. Augustus kept her busy and if he wasn't in residence, his secretary kept her busy. TV show hosts loved her because the cameras loved her face and she could string two words together.

She was compliant, carving out a place for herself in his world that had nothing to do with the sexual aspects of a courtesan's role and everything to do with social outreach and celebration of history and letting people get a behind-the-scenes glimpse of the day-to-day running of the palace.

She was an ambassador. Making connections, building a web, consolidating power that didn't belong to her, and the role suited her to perfection. She was good at it.

Augustus was managing her, piling on the work, keeping her so busy in her dual roles of palace PR and events management that there was barely time for thought, and far too little time for herself.

This morning she'd requested of his secretary that down time be built into her weekly schedule and that if she was obliged to work weekends she wanted the following Tuesday kept free for her own use.

'Finally,' she thought she'd heard the old man mutter beneath his breath, and then he'd pulled a file drawer open and moments later handed her a bunch of papers on workplace rights. 'Read these, sign these, hand them back in and I can most assuredly do something about that, Lady Sera. Not everyone here is willing to work like a dog for no apparent reason.'

She'd read through the employment conditions, signed them and handed them back in and now had every full Tuesday, Wednesday and Thursday morning off.

Much to Augustus's displeasure.

Sera ducked beneath the water, wetting her hair and holding her breath until the need to breathe forced her to rise.

Tomorrow was Tuesday, her first full day off, and

Ari had invited her to spar with him during tomorrow's six a.m. lesson. She hadn't sparred with anyone since Ari had dropped her to the ground and Augustus had helped her back up. She'd taken on a tutor's role instead, helping those who'd taken up the invitation to practise the forms, and she enjoyed her role, but maybe tomorrow she *would* spar with Ari again.

Take back some of her own identity.

If Augustus objected she would tell him she was a tutor now and call it a demonstration.

As for the charities she'd been working for so tirelessly, maybe it was time to invest some of her own identity into that too.

And see what good and noble King Augustus would do.

'What do you mean she wants to take a courtesan's clothing collection on the road, starting with viewings at city brothels?'

Augustus knew he was glaring at his personal secretary but the idea was preposterous. He was doing everything in his power to *remove* her courtesan status. He was trying, above all, to render her role here respectable. The very *least* she could do was appreciate it.

'Lady Sera's guards put forward the security arrangement plans this morning,' his secretary informed him placidly. 'There's a fifty-page report justifying the social benefits involved, including col-

laboration with community welfare groups and backing from your police commissioner and city mayor.
Two of the brothels are extremely prestigious. Others
are less so. I have it on good advice that several are
for…acquired tastes. They're all registered and legal.'

Silence was one response to situations out of his
control. It wasn't the only response available to him.
'Get her in here. Now.'

'Lady Sera's schedule for the day puts her at the
state library attending a history lecture until one. This
afternoon she'll be overseeing the botanists' picnic on
the lawn surrounding the royal glasshouses.'

Roses. Good grief. Roses and social welfare. Just
what he needed.

'Ask the Lady Sera if she's available for dinner this
evening. Put us in the blue dining room with several
dishes for sharing, a small selection of sweets and
let us serve ourselves.' It wasn't an unusual request,
although it was one he usually reserved for family.

'Does next week's costume tour have your approval?' His secretary reminded him of the matter
in hand.

'No. Have you read the proposal?'

'It makes for interesting reading. I particularly
enjoyed Chapter Two.'

'Fifty pages, you say?'

'With references, footnotes and a reading list,' the
older man said, handing it over. 'She's also written
you a report outlining new initiatives for education

reform, particularly with regard to non-academic children. She confirms a substantial donation from the temples of the High Reaches to set up a pilot project. You want to see that proposal too?'

'Give it over.' He didn't have time for this. He truly didn't.

'Additionally, Lady Sera has been restructuring the fund-raising portfolio related to education. The one your grandmother, mother and Moriana have toiled over for generations.'

'What for? What part of "It's a good one" doesn't she understand?'

'I'll leave that for you to judge. I'll warn you though, she's already engaged your sister's co-operation and they're looking at some quite sweeping reforms.'

'They'll still have to go through me.' He wasn't looking forward to being the voice of reason. He could already name a dozen education initiatives that Moriana had wanted to support that had been shut down by various committees full of education experts. 'Let's dig deeper into Sera's background and education qualifications. Personal history too. I want no surprises when it comes to what kind of reforms she's likely to advance.'

'You have a dossier on her.'

'I have a CV. I want to expedite that full investigative report I ordered. Whatever has been collected, get them to send it.'

The older man nodded.

'As for education reform—'

'It's been on your agenda for the last six months,' the older man offered drily. 'You keep shuffling it to the bottom of your pile while you concentrate on regional water plans. I gave the portfolio to Lady Sera a week ago on a whim. So if you want to blame somebody for that particular report, blame me.'

'I will.' Augustus looked at the folder in his hand and scowled.

'Children are our future,' the older man said serenely. 'I so look forward to yours.'

'Alas, that will require a wife.' And, at last glance, he still didn't have one in mind.

He already gave careful consideration to the charities and initiatives he supported.

'Will you be requiring casual dress for dinner this evening or something more formal?' his secretary asked.

'Casual.' Even if the image of Sera in a formal evening gown made him momentarily lose focus. What would a courtesan of the High Reaches regard as formal clothing? What would she regard as casual? He hadn't forgotten the collar and the manacles she'd worn upon her arrival. 'Definitely casual.'

Sera arrived at the door to the blue dining room at precisely thirty seconds past seven. The door was open and Augustus was already within. She entered and he looked up, a dark-haired devil with classically handsome features and black eyes that knew how to drill deep.

She pushed back the hood of her travelling cloak and met those eyes with polite composure, before dropping to a curtsey and rising again before he could tell her to get up. He could add *Doesn't take orders* to her list of sins. There were bigger sins.

'You wear a travelling cloak to walk down a corridor?' Augustus asked as she reached for the tie at her neck and stepped aside so that Ari could wheel a covered rack of clothes into the room and set it to one side. She waited until Ari had stationed himself outside the door before closing it behind him and turning to face her host.

'You ordered me never to appear in front of your court wearing the clothing of my profession,' she reminded him gently. 'Remember?'

The cloak came off. Her tunic was sheer and the bodice beneath it was more beautiful and intricate than he had ever seen before. Fitted trousers, high heels, no jewellery but for the pearls in her hair. Modesty for the most part, enticement if anyone was so inclined. She draped the cloak over the back of a nearby chair and turned to face him again.

'You call that casual dress?' he asked.

'Yes. Also, you're wearing a hand-tailored suit, a fifty-thousand-dollar vintage watch, and the only concession you've made to dressing casually is that the top button of your shirt's undone and you've loosened your tie.' She arched an elegant eyebrow. 'Did you expect me to wear shorts?'

'I'm pretty sure the watch wasn't worth fifty thousand when my grandfather bought it,' he offered mildly. 'But point taken. You look lovely.' She always did, no matter what she wore.

He ought to be used to it by now.

'I know your interest in historical gowns and clothing is limited,' she said, turning towards the clothes rack. 'But I took the liberty of bringing a few along for show and tell. They'll form part of the costume collection I'd like to take on the road to various places, should you give the go-ahead.'

Which sounded all well and good, but he'd read the proposal—all fifty pages of it and the appendices—and by *various places* she meant brothels.

Augustus would have reprimanded her for being so blatantly obvious about her political agenda, only she'd turned her back on him and his attention had been firmly caught and held by the dazzling dragon-shaped embroidery that wove through the material at her back, leaving pockets of nothing but creamy skin showing through the delicate gaps. Shimmery scales collected from heaven only knew what kind of beast highlighted various dips and curves, and as for those forest-green stilettoes that matched one of the dragon's main colours, how did she even balance on those things?

'Would you like a drink?' he asked, rather than

engage with the topic she'd introduced. He was no novice when it came to directing conversation where he wanted it. Or keeping people off-balance, if he wanted to.

Movement was good. Movement meant he could leave the dragon at her back behind. The sideboard was stacked with a selection of beverages. 'Wine?'

'Thank you.' Sera smiled, her movements quick and effortless as she removed one particular gown from the rack and twirled it around on its hanger, the better to make the skirt flare. 'Take this gown, for example.'

'No. Sera, you're not taking it anywhere.'

Her eyes turned stormy. 'You haven't heard me out.'

'Red or white?'

'White.'

He poured some into a wine glass and took it to her and their fingers touched.

Her gaze met his and the outside world as he knew it skidded to a halt as a kaleidoscope of memories flashed through his brain. Sera on her knees in front of him, swallowing him down. Sera rising naked from the bathing pool and wringing water from her hair. Sera pushing back the hood of her travelling cloak. Sera, all too tempting, no matter what she said or did.

Perfect posture, regal bearing. He wondered if it came naturally to her or whether it had been drummed into her by her elders, the way Moriana's had been ground into her. The way cool analysis and never letting anyone get close enough to truly know him had been drummed into him.

'Is there a reason you don't trust me to do a good job with this?' she asked. 'Have I not been pitch-perfect in my presentation of the courtesans of old so far?'

'You have.' He had to give her that. 'Different audience.'

'You mean you'd rather not put me in front of an audience that might actually *benefit* from their profession being acknowledged and treated with respect?'

'You can reach them without prioritising them. You already are.'

'But I want to prioritise them.'

'Why?'

'You've never lived at the edge of poverty and violence and hopelessness, have you?' She waved a careless hand in his direction. 'No need to answer; I know you haven't. But I have. And every day I thank my looks and my luck and the training someone saw fit to grace me with that I'm not still there.'

'I can't imagine you there.' He just couldn't.

'My mother was once a courtesan to a high-born man. She loved him, and in many ways that precipitated her downfall because I don't believe he ever loved her at all. He just wanted her at his beck and call. He certainly didn't want me to ever draw breath.

My mother fled, but his reach was long. She tried to start over, but he always found her. She hid, and once I was born she hid us both, over and over again, always moving, always one step ahead. The houses got smaller. The cupboards got barer. Her sponsors meaner.'

He didn't like this history she was telling him, but he listened while she paced.

'I don't remember all that much of the very early years but, by the time I was seven, my mother was lost in the bottle and dying of cancer and I was so skinny and malnourished that I couldn't even sit at a table and eat the first meal Lianthe ever put in front of me. I ate a quarter of it, and even that was too much for me. To this day I still prefer to snack rather than sit down to a three-course meal.' She spared a glance for the dinner table. 'I trust it's simply an eating preference by now but it was born of necessity.'

'Why are you telling me this?' About the food. Her mother and the bottle.

'You ask me why I proposed the costume tour of the brothels and this is part of it. It's personal for me. This lavish, glittering history of the Kings' courtesans is their history too, and you have no idea what simple acknowledgement can mean to those who are outcast. Those who live on the fringes of society and who are so often overlooked. I'm already reaching out and talking to your noble art curators and librarians about the history of courtesans—at your request. Why *not* reach out to the people who identify with that history the most?'

She was warming to her theme and he couldn't take his eyes off the glittering, shimmering dragon which writhed on her back.

'Education and learning. Physical and mental health. Those are causes the Arunian royal family has supported for centuries.' Irony tinged her voice. 'Causes you continue to endorse and pour money and resources into. My costume tour proposal should have made sense to you. I designed it to fit within your broader mission statements.'

Too smart by half. Too bold with her plans. And defiantly, unapologetically idealistic. He wondered if he'd ever been like that when it came to what causes to support. He rather thought not. 'It fits to a point,' he said carefully. 'I applaud your…passion for outreach.'

'No, you don't. You'd rather bury it. Turn me into a perfect puppet who performs whatever tasks you deem suitable for someone like me.'

'What I'd rather do is protect you,' he argued. 'Keep the press off your back and your reputation spotless by only giving you certain roles to play. If I send you to brothels the press will draw comparisons to what you do here, for me. They'll dig up your history, make front page news out of you.'

'So? I'm not ashamed of my pathway through life. I am who I am. You think you're protecting me— you're not. You think that by carving away at the unsavoury parts of me you're reshaping me into something better. You're not. All you're doing is carving me up.'

Sera's hands trembled as she cupped her wine glass and brought it to her lips. She made a good show of wetting those lips but he'd bet his kingdom on the fact that she didn't swallow so much as a drop. He strode to the sideboard, poured her a glass of water and exchanged it for the wine before she could protest.

'Why say yes to wine when you don't even drink?' he snapped.

She took the water and drank it down, not stopping until she'd finished, and then set the glass on the table. 'Is that a no to taking the costumes on tour throughout your city brothels?'

'Yes, it's a no. You're not doing it. It's a bad idea.'

She looked strangely shattered as she collected her cloak and fastened it around her neck. 'As always, I am bound to your will and will abide by your command. Now, if you'll excuse me, I'll take my leave.'

'Sera.' Her compliance should have pleased him. Instead, it left him strangely bereft. 'You could stay and eat.'

Not that she ate in the same way he did, apparently. She'd already told him that.

'And talk about what?' she asked coolly. 'Adding perfection to the list of things you require in a wife? No supporting those lost causes, right? No acknowledging the seething, need-ridden underbelly of humanity from that pedestal she'll be standing on, right? Consider it done.'

'I didn't say that.' She could get under his skin faster than any woman he'd ever known. Call up a temper he took a great deal of care to conceal. He still had her glass of wine in his hand. The temptation to drink it was strong. His fingers tightened on the stem. That tiny insignificant tell did not go unnoticed by his courtesan.

'Go on.' She drew closer and closer still until her breath fanned his ear and the scent of tea roses teased his nose. 'Throw it.'

'Why would I do that?' He set the glass on the table gently, never mind that the temptation to hurl it at the nearest wall was strong. 'I'm not a savage.'

'I guess they carved that out of you as a child.' She drew closer and closer still until her lips touched his ear. He shuddered and not with disgust. She didn't miss that tell either. 'Who needs passion? Who needs compassion? Not a king.'

'There's nothing wrong with cool calculation,' he argued. It was what he'd been raised to believe. 'Passion's overrated.'

'If you truly believe that, I pity you.' Her hand snaked up to fist in his hair and he made no move to stop her. 'You should have just thrown the glass.'

'The world might have ended if I had.'

'It wouldn't have.'

The kiss, when she dragged his head down and

lifted her lips to his, was searingly hot and decidedly angry. It brought him to full and throbbing hardness in the space of thirty seconds. If this was punishment for his refusal to accommodate her wishes, he'd take it. If it was a thirst she couldn't control, he'd slake it. If this was her way of trying to make him change his mind, good luck with that.

She drew back all too soon as far as he was concerned, but he wasn't the one running this little power play; she was. He'd figure out what that kiss meant soon enough.

'You're a good king, Augustus. No one can deny it.' She let go of his hair, took a breath, stepped back. 'I hope one day you get to be human too.'

He waited until she and her dragon and her rack full of courtesans' clothing had left the room. He shut the door behind her and counted to ten, and then ten again, before striding across to the table and draining her wine glass.

He let anger, frustration for all the things he could not do, and aching desire for all the things he could not have fill him. He flung the wine glass at the fireplace, where it smashed into glittering pieces.

And the world did not end.

The following day didn't begin well for Augustus of Arun. He'd slept poorly and risen with the sun. He'd gone to the kitchen to find his own breakfast, only to overhear two of his catering staff talking about how Sera's guards had put on a fighting display with long sticks yesterday morning, apparently, and the hits had come thick and fast and left everyone who watched in awe. They fought in the covered stable area these days, not because he'd given his tacit approval but because of the sawdust on the ground and the space and relative privacy it afforded them. Augustus wondered if they fought there because any gathered crowd could melt away into the shadows fast if they were discovered.

He grabbed a bread roll straight from the oven, ripped it open and cut the end from a length of resting roast beef, and knew for a fact that he wouldn't have got away with either action had he still been a child.

He cut through the back door and headed for the stables. He found the crowd easily enough and it looked like a regular martial arts lesson to him, with Ari leading and Tun and Sera helping the trainees with the movements. Sera still practised the forms with her guards on a daily basis, so he'd been informed, but she hadn't sparred since that day he'd hauled her off the ground.

Two men standing in front of him sent him startled looks and shuffled to the side but he shook his head and gestured for them to stay where they were. He didn't want to be noticed this morning. He just wanted to watch.

When Ari told the class they would be doing the

form one last time from start to finish, Sera and Tun fell into step with him, making it look effortless. And when that was done and everyone had bowed and the class had been dismissed, Ari and Sera moved over to a canvas holdall and unzipped it and rolled it out along the ground—it was like no holdall he'd ever seen. More like a portable armoury.

Ari selected two wickedly curved short swords with black handle grips, while Sera selected similar, only her grips were red. They sat in her hands as if they'd been made for her. Maybe they had. The form they practised next had its origins in the one they'd practised in class, that much he could see, the lines of their bodies extended by glittering curved knives.

They made it look as if they'd been born holding knives and cutting patterns in the air.

And then Sera said something to Ari and he frowned, and she smiled back at him sharp and sure and broke from her pattern and moved to face him, not quite head-on, a little to one side. They bowed to each other, plenty of space between them. Tun came to stand between them as a referee would in a boxing ring. At his word he stepped back and they began to fight.

If anyone thought they'd hold back because of the lethal weapons in their hands, they thought wrong.

The fighting was fast and vicious, with Sera on the attack and Ari defending, and Augustus felt his breath lodge somewhere in his throat. Ari was bigger, stronger and his reach was longer and still Sera came at him, even when he began to strike back. The clash of swords rang in his ears, broken only by the occasional murmur from those watching.

He thought about stopping the fight. Demonstration. Whatever it was, he thought about stopping it, but there was no way he wanted to break their concentration. Absolute focus and unearthly skill was all that stood between them and a potentially fatal blow.

And then, between one moment and the next, Ari was on his back on the ground and Sera was on top of him, the curve of one blade at his neck and the other poised to take his upraised hand off at the wrist.

The man in front of Augustus swore silently beneath his breath, and Augustus knew that by lunchtime the palace would be buzzing with the news that the courtesan of the High Reaches was some kind of mystical warrior in addition to being the Devil's temptress.

Surely she'd been sitting on the fallen sword master for far too long.

He watched her roll off and to her feet as if she'd heard him. Tun clapped once and she and Ari moved close for quick smiles and quiet conversation as they released their fighting grips on the blades and began to examine the edges of them. All in a day's work. Nothing unusual about what they'd just demonstrated.

Who were these people?

She saw him out of the corner of her eye and started to walk towards him. People melted away as if sensing conflict. All except for her guards, who stayed right where they were, neither courting conflict nor avoiding it.

'Is that your way of blowing off steam?' he asked.

'It works.'

He'd been thinking about her words from last night. Her scorn for his cool calculation and his need to control what he could. 'You want to know what I see when you're out there passionately blowing off steam?' He didn't wait for an answer. 'Absolute control.' His gaze skipped towards Ari. 'And lives utterly dedicated to the quest for it.'

'Why are you here?' she asked next.

'I've been thinking about what you said last night and all the things I didn't say. The personal things that might have helped you understand my reluctance to have you reach out to a bunch of brothels.'

She waited for him to speak, and he didn't want to, he really didn't, but she'd shown him her heart last night and her passion and maybe they would understand each other a little better if she knew his.

'When I was fifteen I had my first kiss. She was a stable girl, several years older than me, and she'd been lobbying for that kiss for at least three years. It was pretty chaste, as far as kisses went, but she sold her story to the papers that afternoon and we all read about it at breakfast the following morning.'

The lecture his father had given him still had the power to make him wince.

'The woman I finally lost my virginity to was an older woman as well—a woman with enough money and power and sheer front to withstand the hounding of the press for months. Just long enough for me to feel safe in her arms. And then she turned around and finally granted that press interview and laid me bare.

'She called me an accomplished lover—and I was by then—and then added that I could also be a little too passionately intense for some tastes. She told them she envied me my brilliant mind and in the same breath warned of sweeping social and economic reforms once I took the throne. I'd made the mistake of talking to her about the causes I was passionate about, you see. I'd talked big bold plans that didn't have a hope of seeing the light of day—not then. Not without years of careful planning. The press called me an ignorant, idealistic fool and I was—I was a fool to think I could confide in her or trust her. She praised my protective nature, especially when it came to those I consider family, and then casually mentioned how rigidly impenetrable I could be when it came to letting other people in.'

None of it true. All of it true.

'Which was quite the complaint because, as far as I was concerned, I *had* let her in. Like a fool.'

Sera opened her mouth to speak but he put his hand up to stop her.

'And now you, a courtesan sent here specifically to serve me, wants to go into the brothels and talk job descriptions, and they're going to have questions art curators and librarians would never dare ask you. Questions about me and what I want and need and think and who's to say you won't expose me?'

'I would never do that.' She drew herself up and still didn't manage to reach his shoulder. Bare feet. A face flushed with exercise. 'I am a courtesan of the High Reaches. Confidentiality is the key to our *existence*, and beyond that...' She shook her head. 'Augustus, I will never betray your confidences. Not sexual, emotional or intellectual. You have my word. My oath. That's what you *get* when you get me. A safe space in which to simply be human.'

'I want to believe you.' He looked away from those earnest grey eyes. Experience suggested he shouldn't.

'I can't make that decision for you,' she offered quietly.

He nodded. He'd think on it. 'There was another reason I came out here this morning,' he said, while in the distance a stablehand worked on a horse's hoof with a file.

'What is it?'

He couldn't even bring himself to look at her while he was saying it. 'I love the way you move.' It was as simple and as complicated as that. 'I envy the fierce blend of passion and control you bring to everything you do and it's never more evident than when you're out there, facing an opponent. It's beautiful.'

It was the first thought he'd shared in years without analysing the pros and cons of doing so.

And it was met with complete and utter silence.

He glanced back, just in time to see a softly startled smile cross her face.

'I…thank you,' she said.

And the world did not end.

'What do you want done with the costume tour proposal?' Augustus's secretary asked him two hours later.

Augustus ran a hand across his face and memories flashed before him. Sera with a blade in each hand and total concentration on her face. Sera with a dragon on her back and her face alight with pleasure. Sera, who never failed to stand out, no matter what kind of company she was in, and who had yet to set a foot wrong in public.

Sera as a child, with a plate full of food in front of her that she could not eat. A plate that was only there in the first place because someone had *seen* her plight rather than turn away from an outcast child struggling for existence.

Sera's proposal to reach out to her sisters in service had healthcare and educational elements, but first and foremost it was about acknowledging their existence.

She could have been one of them. *Was* one of them, for all her finery and expensive education, and he'd never met a woman more accomplished.

Her mother had been one of them. A broken one.

This was no soulless, rudderless outreach programme. Sera had this one covered. He could trust her not to make this all about him. Couldn't he?

He dropped his hand and searched his heart and not his head.

'Green-light it,' he said.

CHAPTER SEVEN

THE INAUGURAL COURTESAN costumes tour, starting at a seedy but legal downtown brothel and finishing at the National Art gallery of Arun, received some of the best press Augustus had ever seen. It brought together six health and education outreach programmes already in place and cemented Arun's reputation as a progressive nation with the welfare and education of *all* its people at heart. Far from damaging his personal reputation, he was being hailed as a saviour. A man that any woman, courtesan or not, would be proud to have in their corner. He'd even accompanied Sera on one of the tours, to watch her in action and lend his support, and there'd been not one single, solitary crack about him partaking of her sexual services.

It was a God-given miracle.

Suffice to say, the fund-raising dinner he was currently attending suffered a little in comparison, even if Sera had organised it. The dinner helped raise funds for cancer research and had been on his social calendar for the past seven years running. He was seated next to Katerina DeLitt at his request and the lady was well aware of it. To her credit, she was socially adept and inclusive of the others around them. She had a charming smile and the kind of effortless poise he was used to. She had yet to hold his attention for long but maybe that was his fault for having Sera oversee the event.

Sera, with her tailored black suit and sky-high stilettos. Sera, with her hair coiled tightly into a bun at the nape of her neck and a face practically devoid of make-up. She didn't need make-up. She was quite beautiful enough.

He'd corner her afterwards for a crowd report and she'd tell him whom was currently at war with whom and other minor matters of interest. Her powers of observation kept his sharp too. Being able to one-up her in the observation stakes was wholly satisfying. Not to mention hard to do.

'She's very beautiful,' said Katerina DeLitt from somewhere beside him.

'Excuse me?'

Could be his attention had been somewhere it shouldn't be, but he trusted Katerina DeLitt's manners to prevail and doubted she would repeat such a confronting statement.

'Lady Sera Boreas. She's very beautiful.'

'Ah.' Guess he was wrong. He eyed the woman seated to his left with renewed interest. She smiled wryly, diamond earrings dangling as she tilted her head the better to observe him.

'And talented too, assuming even half the things I hear about her are true,' she said next.

He knew full well he should steer the conversation elsewhere. Hard to court one woman when seemingly fixated on another. He could talk about the weather. The charity. Or horses—he had a fleeting memory of Katerina talking animatedly about horses.

Or he could succumb to curiosity. 'What kind of things do you hear?'

Katerina shrugged. 'She has great skill with knives, she can dance like a dream. She has a mind trained towards observation and is bound to you in ways no one can quite explain. You were forced by ancient laws to open your home to her. You can't get rid of her until you find a future wife and take steps to secure the throne. Even then, you might not let her go.'

'Sounds about right.' Katerina's information was good. 'Although I will let her go.'

'They say she has your ear, among other things. That she is your muse.'

Augustus frowned.

'Your Majesty, if I may be bold—and that does seem to be the best way to deal with you—what is it you want from me, when your attention is so obviously elsewhere?'

He appreciated her bluntness and returned it in full. 'I need a wife who will give me children and occupy the role of Queen Consort with all due diligence. Your name came up and I enjoy your company. I'm getting to know you.'

'I see. And what of love?' Katerina asked drily.

'Love can grow.'

'Your Ma—'

'Call me Augustus,' he interrupted.

'Augustus.' She said it nicely but not the way Sera did. 'Your Majesty, I know it's not fashionable, but let us be even more frank. As honoured as I am to have your attention, I'm in no hurry to put my heart on the line for you, knowing what else is available to you at any given time.'

'Meaning?'

She inclined her head towards Sera.

'That is not an option,' he grated. 'Sera will leave once the terms of the accord have been satisfied. She may well leave before that if I can find a workaround.'

'But will your chosen Queen Consort ever be able to take her place? I have my doubts. Ask yourself this, my King in need of a Queen. When you walked in here this evening, who was the first person you looked for? Who did you *keep* looking for until she appeared?' Katerina smiled again, and it was a gentle smile, without malice. 'Be honest. Because it surely wasn't me.'

Another event, another debrief afterwards. That was the routine Sera and Augustus fell into over the weeks that followed. Sometimes they talked in his office and sometimes they used a small parlour in the west wing that he favoured, and sometimes, if he'd been held up after the event, he came to her quarters and sat within her sofa circle, always requesting a strategy session. Sera didn't mind it. She took quiet satisfaction in her ability to be of use to him, and if he kept his hands and his kisses carefully to himself while in her presence, so be it.

She didn't want to think about her growing need for his attention. The way her body craved his touch and her mind constantly circled back to him and what he was doing, how he was feeling. Whether he'd ever touch her again with the sole purpose of giving and taking pleasure.

She didn't want to admit she might be falling for him.

Nothing good had ever come of a courtesan falling for a king.

Tonight, Augustus's behaviour was different in that he stood staring at the request wheel at his feet for a good long while before turning to look at her. She'd been expecting him—maybe—and had changed out of her workwear into casual trousers and her customary tunic top. Nothing too sheer or revealing. No jewellery or make-up embellishment. The only concession she'd made to vanity was to let her hair down after she'd showered and not put it back up before opening her door to him. She liked the way he looked at it. The way he jammed his hands in his pockets as if to stop himself from reaching out to touch it.

The sexual attraction between them hadn't gone away, for all their business-based interactions. It simmered between them, thick and syrupy. Every glance, every pause, a study in denial.

For both of them.

'You know what I really want tonight?' he asked, and her brain helpfully supplied the perfect answer.

Me! You want me! Please take me!

'A toasted cheese sandwich.'

Or—or she could feed him. He wasn't even looking at her. 'That can be arranged,' she offered hospitably. 'Anything else?'

Me! Pick me!

'I wouldn't mind if it came with a glass of wine and some background music that I don't have to listen to as if it's the finest thing I've ever heard.'

'You didn't like the music gala this evening?'

'I liked it well enough but I was tired. Maintaining the fiction that I wanted to be there took more effort than usual.'

An honest response that painted him in a less than perfect light. A rare occurrence for this man who'd been trained from childhood to never show weakness or reveal any thoughts that could be used against him.

'Sit. Please.' She had music, food, and an excellent

cellar full of wine on hand. 'I can feed you.' Cross off another scene on the pleasure wheel as done. It wasn't the sex scene she craved, granted, but it was progress.

'We can call for food,' he said.

'No!' Just…no. 'Does it matter who prepares it? I have a fully stocked kitchen. Why not let me put supper together?'

'You don't have to. That's not your role.'

'Always so hung up on roles.' He had no idea how much it pleased her when she was able to put her training to use and serve him. It wasn't a hardship. It was her pleasure. 'Many people take great pride and pleasure in being able to put food on the table and invite others to share it. It happens I'm one of them. Sit. Please.'

Please.

Sera didn't wait to see if he did her bidding, but when she returned he was sitting on the sofa in a different place to usual and the picture at his feet was that of people sharing a meal.

The wine she returned with was the best in the cellar and she knelt at his feet to pour it, faltering only when she went to hand it to him and found him watching her with hooded eyes that burned with a hunger that had nothing to do with food.

But he took it from her with a quiet, 'Thank you,' and if his fingertips touched hers, well, he'd said he was tired and it wasn't exactly light in here tonight with the moon behind a sky full of clouds. It wasn't warm in here either, beneath the glass dome, but he didn't seem to notice. Sera wanted to pretend that the tremble in her fingers as she released the wine was because of the cold, but self-deception had never been her friend. She'd shivered at the merest touch of his hand.

He said nothing more as she rose and turned some music on, soft and soothing.

He had his eyes closed and his head resting against the back of the sofa when she returned with the food. She'd brought extra: a small plate of honeyed pastries and a bowl of nuts. Sliced melon. Not a lot. Not a feast to make a person groan at the thought of eating it all.

'I hope some of that's for you too,' he murmured.

'It is.'

'Don't kneel at my feet, Sera. It might be what the picture shows and your courtesan training demands but I couldn't stand it.'

More weakness from him tonight, and he was deliberately letting her see it. She didn't know what to do with it. How to process it. So she sat and helped herself to some melon and then a glass of wine and sipped.

'You don't drink.' He was watching her, eyes still half closed.

'It's not that I don't drink at all. Sometimes when the vintage is very fine, I do.' She lifted her glass to

the light and hid behind the poise the Order had in-
stilled in her. Her relationship with alcohol was complicated. There was the way her mother had abused
it. The way it lowered inhibitions and let devils in,
false confidence in. But there were other things about
it that deserved consideration. 'I learned about wine
as part of my training. If you were to ask me to rank
different areas of study, I'd put my study of wines
and winemaking somewhere near the top, mainly
because it's proven surprisingly useful. Everything
from making small-talk with the high-flying wine
aficionados of the world to tweaking wine selections
for different charity functions so that the chefs are
happy, the drinkers are happy and the hosts are not
paying a fortune for it.'

He smiled and she wished he wouldn't, because
it made her glow on the inside. Such a whore for his
attention.

'And is there a wine to go with toasted cheese
sandwiches?'

'There is, and we're drinking it.'

His smile widened. The glow inside her ignited
and morphed into an open fire surrounded by a
hearth.

In a family room.

'How are the owls?' he asked as he reached for
a sandwich.

'They have names now,' she told him, taking on
the mantle of conversation while he ate. 'Tomas and

Claudia had lunch with me on Wednesday and we chose names then. I did notify your secretary Claudia was coming, and Tomas with her. I always ask permission to have visitors and provide details.' No exceptions.

Augustus shrugged, seemingly unconcerned. 'Some details stop at my secretary, especially if they're of no concern. How is Claudia?'

'She misses the freedom she had in the mountains.'

'Is that why she spends so much time with the falconer?'

'There could be another reason for that.' Augustus raised an eyebrow and this time it was Sera's turn to shrug. Far be it for her to lay Claudia's heart bare, although she had a fair idea where it lay. 'So, the smaller of the two owls is the male. His name is Orion. His larger companion is Ara, his mate, and he indulges her shamelessly. Their enemies are other owls of the same species and the occasional falcon. They're very adaptable and tend not to make their own nests, preferring instead to use nests abandoned by others, or make do with a man-made structure. Orion will fly down and perch on the trapeze on occasion, the better to see what I'm up to. He then reports back to Ara, who likes to pretend my activities are beneath her notice.'

'But they're not?'

'I've seen her watching me. She's more interested than she lets on.'

He'd finished the sandwich and was washing it down with wine. He looked more closely at the label on the bottle and then back at her.

'From the cellars of the Order of the Kite,' she said in answer to his question. 'They have quite the collection.'

'So I see. I know so little about this Order of yours. I have historians researching it, of course, but there are no experts to be found. Not amongst anyone I can get hold of.'

'What would you like to know?'

He snorted softly. 'Start at the beginning.'

'Of the history of the Order? It's over two thousand years old and began as a way for women in positions of power, or women close to men in positions of power, to connect and share journeys. They created a mountain retreat, a place of learning. Alliances were forged. Daughters were positioned for particular roles within the world order of the day. Was a particular ruling court strong in trade but weak when it came to the comforts of its people? Who, from the pool of women available, was best placed to effect change? Occasionally, a ruler would reach out and request someone with particular connections and skills. If the Order could accommodate them, and it was perceived as being in their best interest to do so, they would.'

'Did the women of the Order ever have individual agendas or did they serve a higher cause?'

'I'm sure many have had their own agendas over

the years. Politics is everywhere, and the Order is not immune. But on the whole I'd say the quest for balance, peace and prosperity guides all our members. I think of us as a benevolent force rather than a disruptive one.'

'I hate to break it to you, Sera, but taking up residence here in my palace and worming your way into my life and my thoughts…it's disruptive.'

'Am I not helping?' Pain lanced through her chest and she clamped her lips shut on a barrage of protest.

'In some ways you are. In other ways you're not helping at all.'

She didn't know what to say to that, and he didn't seem inclined to elaborate. Instead, he leaned back with his head against the back of the sofa and stared at the stars as if they had failed him.

'I was fourteen when I finally found this room,' he offered quietly. 'I'd been looking for it for years. I could see the dome from the sky, but the passageway to get here was boarded up and the room was out of bounds. Forgotten, until Moriana and I found it again and made it our own.' He pointed with his wine glass towards the platform halfway up the wall. 'We used to sit up there and shoot arrows into pumpkins down below. We damaged so many arrows when they struck stone instead of the target. I don't think we had a straight arrow left between us by the end of it all. I know we damaged the walls and the floors but I didn't care. Told myself I was striking back at the source of my discontent. The palace. The Crown. The expectations that rode me like a second skin. *Be worthy. Don't fail. Perform.* I was the Crown Prince—I had to perform. Everywhere except for here. There was no judgement here. I could curse and roar and take risks I could never take elsewhere. When I was in here, I could fly.'

Suspicion bloomed swiftly. 'You used the trapeze?'

'It's just a swing,' he offered mildly.

No safety net, half-rotted rope. No training. Dear God. 'And the adrenaline rush the first time you used it?'

'Pretty big.' He snorted softly. 'I thought this room would no longer feel like sanctuary once you claimed it. Figured if I stayed away my problem with you would go away, only I keep turning up at your door and you keep welcoming me in, offering me anything. You've no idea how much I want to claim you, and to hell with self-restraint and leading by example and kings not having courtesans in this day and age.'

'You could.' Her hands shook with the force of her need as she set her wine on the small side table. 'You could do that.'

'I'd make it so good for you.' He had a voice tailored for sin and seduction and lips that beckoned, even when his words were cruel. 'Treat you like a queen.'

'I don't want to be a queen,' she said, but he was drawing closer and she wasn't moving away.

'We all do things we don't particularly want to do.'
He brushed his lips against hers and she opened for
him instinctively, her tongue coming out to meet his.
He slid a gentle hand beneath her hair and cupped
the back of her neck, his thumb brushing the skin
just behind her ear as he tilted her head where he
wanted it and claimed her lips once more. Her eyes
fluttered closed.

It was a kiss to get lost in.

When they broke it several years later, he rested
his forehead against hers and drew a ragged breath.
He ran his hand across her shoulder and down her
arm to tangle her fingers in his. 'Last chance to tell
me you don't want my hands on you, Sera. Because
this is going to complicate things.'

'I want this.' She'd never for one moment not
wanted this, from the moment she'd laid eyes on
him. 'I crave this,' she whispered, and took the initiative and straddled him, a knee either side of his
hips, and slid her hand from his the better to bury
both of her hands in his hair. 'I can make it good for
you too. So good.'

His shirt had to go. Hers too, and he helped her
with that, in between a dozen deep and drugging
kisses. Breathing was overrated. His tongue curled
around her puckered nipple was not overrated, and
then he closed his mouth around it and sucked and
she nearly came from that alone. His hands dug into
the globes of her behind as he ground up against her,

and she gave herself over to sensation and arched into the hardness of his erection and let her head fall back and her hands guide his head towards her other breast.

A soft grunt punched out of her, and he groaned and his hands tightened on her.

Moments later, she was on her back and seeing stars, real ones shining through the glass-domed roof, and Augustus was lifting her legs and removing her shoes and stripping her naked.

She'd been taught what to do, how to please, but she was too caught up in sensation to do any of it.

He started with kisses and gifted them everywhere. The tender curve of her shoulder, the hollow of her armpit and the curve of her breast. Her ribs, the jut of her hip. And then he lifted her leg and started again at her instep and worked his way up. The back of her knee—who knew that would be a go-to zone for squirming? The flesh of her inner thigh. Higher. Black eyes glittering as bold fingers paved the way for his mouth.

She was gone the minute his lips closed over her and his tongue flicked. Whatever this was had been weeks in the making. Every fight, every glance, every moment of pregnant silence between them had been a stroke towards this, and it was wingless flight and fall without a safety net and utterly overwhelming.

It still wasn't enough.

'I need—'

'I know what you need,' he growled. 'And I need a condom.'

'I'm protected.' She opened hazy, glazed grey eyes and caught his face between both hands. 'But there's physical protection to hand if you want to be sure. Be sure.'

She slid out beneath him and crawled naked towards the orgy picture of the pleasure wheel offerings, reaching down to push at something that snapped open, a formerly hidden drawer at the very bottom of that part of the sofa. 'What size?'

What *size*? His brain struggled for clarity until she held up several packets.

'Not that one, not that one, probably this one,' she said, reaching down and plucking a packet from a well-ordered tray. 'You seem rather well formed.'

'You seem rather well stocked.'

He had to laugh. He had to stalk, and push her down on her stomach and start kissing her all over again, even as he reached for the packet in her hand. He hadn't kissed his way down her back yet and that was an oversight he aimed to correct. She was so responsive, so very ready to melt into his touch and give herself over to him. And his need to take was so very big.

He took his time, calling on every bit of the control that had been drilled into him since birth. *Don't lose it. Don't let go. See to the other person's need first because that was service and above all a king served his people. Don't be greedy or entitled.*

Give.

So he gave and gave but she gave it all back and they fed off each other and when he finally breached her, slow and sure, it felt like sliding his soul home.

He stilled, murmuring nonsense against her lips, and she surrendered, eyes never leaving his face as she asked for more.

He took her to the edge, time and time again.

And then he ruthlessly tipped her over the ledge and followed and gave her everything.

CHAPTER EIGHT

'DOES IT HURT?'

Sera couldn't believe how gentle Augustus was being as he bathed her, every stroke of the wash cloth a caress, the water soothing on her skin and the low-lights in the sconces making shadows dance on the walls. He'd been born to care for people, this King, even if he did it from behind self-imposed walls. Get behind the walls of the man and he was overwhelmingly responsive to passion and possession and taking overwhelmingly good care of the woman in his arms.

'It doesn't hurt,' she assured him as he dragged the wash cloth slowly over her centre folds. She'd been a virgin, yes, but her life to date had been an active one and penetration hadn't hurt her the way she'd been warned it might. If the lover was careless or in too much of a hurry.

Augustus had been neither.

'I liked it very much,' she offered and thought to win a smile from him, but he didn't smile.

'Guess you're in the right profession, then.'

Her smile faltered. 'I guess so.'

'Sera—'

But she didn't want to hear what that roughened, sex-soaked voice had to say next. Didn't want to spoil this night with politics or reality or the sure knowledge that she was never going to get to keep this man on a permanent basis. She told herself she didn't want to keep him. That what he'd given her was enough. That she could still walk away from him with her heart intact.

She tried to believe it.

She put her finger to his mouth to silence him, and when he put his hand to her wrist and drew her finger away, she replaced it with her mouth. 'There's more we could do,' she whispered against his lips. He'd been tender with her but she knew there was more. The fingers at her wrist tightened. 'You know there's more you could teach me.'

'Eager.'

'I've been waiting a long time.'

'For me?' This time when he caressed her folds the wash cloth was gone. 'Or for sex?'

'All of it. I didn't expect to want you as much as I do. I could kiss you for hours.' No one had ever told her she'd feel like this. 'Soft and gentle.' Because he had been so very, very gentle with her. Taking care of her pleasure before his own. Reining himself in. 'Or not. Let's try not.'

He claimed her lips with his in a punishing kiss that she returned in full measure. Slick-scraping and filthy, it sent a lightning arc straight through her. And the passion grew.

With a rough fist in his wet hair, she dragged his lips from hers. 'You've seen me dance with swords. You know I'm not going to break.' She knew where she was going with this and it was like stepping off a ledge with a trapeze swing in hand and no knowledge at all of where they might land. 'You know we're not going to be able to have this for ever, but we do have tonight and I want you inside me again, cursing me because you've never had it so good. Ride me till you scream. Or I scream. Take me apart and put me back together again with a piece of you in me.' He was on board with every loaded word, if his glittering, hooded gaze and his iron-hard erection was any indication. 'So do me a favour and this time don't hold back.'

He carried her, wet and wanting, to an alcove filled with pillows and throw rugs and all manner of oils and unguents.

And this time he didn't hold back.

CHAPTER NINE

Augustus strode into his office in a mood that ran blacker than usual. He'd woken alone in Sera's quarters, with a breakfast tray beside him and a blanket draped over his nakedness. They'd finally made it to her bed during the night. Sleep had overtaken him at some point after that. There'd been a note on the pillow next to his head. *Exercising*, was all the note said. A morning ritual for his courtesan of the High Reaches. No matter what.

He'd left a similar note on the pillow requesting her company mid-morning. He had a lunch date he couldn't get out of. With Katerina DeLitt.

He stalked to the coffee corner in the outer office and poured a cup for himself in silence. Lukewarm coffee was his friend.

His secretary cleared his throat and Augustus spared him a glance and there was something off in the older man's gaze—but how could he know?

Granted, the man knew practically everything, but still…

Did he have *I lost my mind and my heart last night* written on his forehead?

'Morning,' he muttered.

'You're late,' the older man said.

Augustus nodded. Instead of taking a quick morning shower, he'd lingered in that damned bathing pool of Sera's, working the kinks out of his body and hoping she'd turn up. She hadn't.

The older man handed him a file and Augustus took it. 'What's this?'

'The investigative report on Lady Sera's mother arrived last night, hand-delivered.'

'Sounds ominous.'

'My investigator judged the information to be of extreme sensitivity so he went old school, helped by the fact that he's seventy years old and *is* old school. The report is hand-written; no digital copies exist and he cleaned up as he went.'

'Meaning?'

'Meaning no one's ever going to find that information again unless they read the file you're holding. You've paid handsomely for the information and that service, by the way. Enough to send an old military-hero-turned-investigator into welcome retirement.'

'I live to serve.' Augustus took the folder from the other man with a frown. He dealt with classified information on a daily basis. He'd never read a hand-written report before. 'Is the information really that sensitive?'

'I doubt it'll start a war. I suspect it'd come as a shock to some of the people involved. Perhaps not all.'

'Be cryptic, then. What do I have on at eleven? Can we clear some space for a meeting with Sera?'

'Another costume tour of the brothels? Circus arts for children? Tortoise races?'

Augustus allowed himself a smile. 'Not yet. And I'm going to need more coffee. Double shot. Hot.'

He went to his office and shut the door behind him, slapped the file down on his desk. His desk was big, black and imposing and his chair was fit for a king and significantly more comfortable. The room was cold, his sister was always complaining of it, but he found it stopped people from lingering overlong and the less they lingered, the more work he got done.

The first half hour of his day was always dedicated to reading. Daily reports sat waiting for him in a tidy pile, arranged in order of importance. He could have read them on his computer just as easily, but there was something about the ritual of paper copies and the pile getting smaller as he worked his way through them that appealed to him. There was an end to that pile of papers, whereas digital news was never-ending. Even if he was deluding himself, he liked to think that his workload had an end-point.

Sera's mother had loved a man, an abusive man, and had a child by him. Sera had already told him this. But she'd never mentioned names, and if he was contemplating marriage to her—which, God help him, he was—he wanted no surprises.

Sera didn't know what to expect when she walked into Augustus's office at exactly eleven a.m. She'd left him sleeping soundly in her quarters because she hadn't known how to deal with him after a night like the one they'd just shared. She still didn't know how to deal with him. But she crossed the cold room and took a seat in the chair placed strategically on the opposite side of his gleaming black desk and tried not to fidget beneath his impenetrable black-eyed gaze.

Gone was his openness of last night and the defencelessness he'd exposed in his sleep. The tousled hair and the boneless weight of his body in her bed. The long, dark lashes fanning delicately over the skin beneath his eyes. He'd been beautiful in his sleep. Softer and more boyish and she'd looked her fill in case she never got to see it again. Some of the things they'd done last night... Skin to skin with heaven in between.

She'd asked for it. She had asked for it. And she had received. 'Morning.'

He quirked a brow and returned her greeting and asked if she wanted some coffee.

She didn't. 'You wanted to see me?'

'For several reasons, not all of them concerning business.' A crack appeared in his regal regard. A flicker of something that might have been concern. 'How are you this morning?'

She felt as if she'd been skewered with a hot buttered sword, had begged for more and been given it. Should she say that? She might have said it to the man. Not to the King.

'So-so,' she said instead. 'Ari chose not to call on me to spar with him this morning. He tells me my concentration's off.'

'Does he know I stayed the night?'

'He's head of my security detail. Of course he knows. Are you worried he'll gossip?'

'No.' Augustus didn't look worried. 'If there's one thing I'm learning about the Order of the Kite, it's how well they can keep secrets. If I wasn't increasingly wary of the lot of you I'd be impressed.'

'If you want to know more about the Order, ask.' She was serious. She'd been handing out historical information ever since she'd got here. 'There's not a lot more left to tell.'

'Really?' The huffing sound he made was an irritated one. 'I had two reports cross my desk this morning, both of them concerning you. One of them informs me that before you came here you were the Chief Financial Officer for a global not-for-profit organisation that distributes over half a billion dollars each year to charities. Lady Lianthe controls the company—which I assume is connected to the Order of the Kite.'

Sera nodded. All of this was public knowledge, or at least accessible knowledge if you knew where to look.

'You were being groomed to replace her,' he said next.

'I was, yes.' She squared her shoulders and avoided glancing at the report beneath his hand in favour of studying the hand itself. Long fingers, broad base and a signet ring with the royal crest on his middle finger. A kernel of need began to heat deep inside her. Those fingers were magic.

'And here I was trying to turn you into a humble employee so you'd have something more than courtesan to show on your résumé when you left here. More fool me.'

He was angry this morning. Clipped vowels, exact pronunciation. Sera eyed him warily.

'I have no complaints about the work I do here,' she said. 'The charity programme here has been honed over centuries, much like the one the Order oversees, and it's been illuminating to compare and contrast the similarities and differences. They're both good. Different, but good. Besides, you know why I'm here. There is no secret. I didn't come here to court business opportunities. I came here to honour an ancient accord between my people and yours and repay a personal debt I've been accruing since I was seven. I win, Augustus. You keep implying I'm here under duress. You're wrong. I'm here because I choose to be.'

He had the best sexy brooding face she'd ever seen. 'And where does last night factor into all this winning?'

'Last night can be whatever you want it to be. Forgotten. Repeated. Picked apart until it bleeds.' She was predicting the latter and sought to head him off. 'I enjoyed it.'

'You were a virgin.'

'And?'

'And now you're not.'

Apparently she wasn't the only one with slow brain cells this morning. 'I'll celebrate later. First let me reassure you that I have no regrets, no inclination to tell anyone else what transpired between us and no plans to force you to marry me now that you've claimed my precious virginity.' He looked highly sceptical and Sera bit back a sigh. She had no wish to trap him. That had never been the goal here. Helping him address his needs had been the goal and she was doing that, wasn't she?

Frustration looked remarkably like arousal on him. 'So you *don't* want to marry me?'

Panic hit her hard and fast. 'That's not even on the table. Marriage isn't for the likes of me. Courtesans don't marry.'

'Don't they?' He was getting colder by the second. 'Is it formally not allowed or is it something you personally just don't want to do?'

'You're angry with me.'

'Sharp as ever,' he clipped. 'Answer the question.'

'I've never considered marrying you.' She kept her voice even but it was a near thing. 'Courtesans and kings can be intimate, no question. They often grow quite fond of each other. I'm fond of you.' *Liar—you're in love with him.* 'But a wife's role is very different to that of a courtesan.'

'Really?' She hated his mockery. He did it so well. 'How so? You're already bound to me and under my protection.'

'For a time,' she injected.

'You take on hostess roles, offer me counsel and share my bed.' His lips twisted. 'And you're fond of me.'

She was. Very. 'Augustus, you're a king. I'm nobody. A trained companion.'

'You have connections worldwide and a powerful political faction behind you. You're not nobody.'

She searched for another excuse. 'Your people would never accept me.'

'Wouldn't they? Because, given the press you receive, I'd say you have a better than fair chance they're going to love you.'

'Because I'm an oddity. A throwback curiosity with a sharp brain, a pretty face and interesting clothes.'

'You're making my argument for me.'

She had other arguments. 'You want love. That's why you've stayed single so long. I can't give you that.' Her mother had loved deeply and paid a dreadful price. Sera had paid that price too and had no wish to repeat the experience. 'I won't.'

'What exactly is it you think we did last night, Sera?'

'It was good, I don't deny it. But I've been trained to please.'

Last night...what you did with him? That was love, a little voice told her helpfully. *Are you really going to deny that?*

'My mother loved and look where it got her,' she said doggedly. 'Even when she left him she couldn't escape him. She was never *free*. One day I'm going to be free. If I were to marry you I'd never be free. That other role—'

'Wife,' he offered, not at all helpfully. 'Queen Consort. Mother of Kings. Or Queens. Princes and Princesses.' His eyes slayed her with his intensity. 'Heart of a nation.'

Yeah. That. 'I'd never be free.' She retreated into silence. So did he. While the tension in the room threatened to choke her completely.

'Right.' Bitterness tinged his voice. 'Not as if you want to be royal. Which brings me to the second report on my desk. If you wanted to be royal, all you'd have to do is tell people who your father is.'

Sera swallowed hard, her mouth suddenly dry. 'What do you mean?'

He tapped at the folder and her gaze was inevitably drawn to it. 'I mean you're a king's daughter by blood. You simply choose not to acknowledge it.'

He couldn't know that. No one knew that.

'The only time my late mother spoke of my father, she spoke fearfully and never by name,' she offered steadily. 'She said he was a monster who had no time for daughters and I believed her. I don't know who he is but, even if I did, why would I want to acknowledge a man such as that as my father, high-born or not?'

Augustus leaned forward, elbows on the table. 'You know exactly who I'm talking about.'

She'd pieced it together over the years, yes, and then *held her tongue*. Confiding in no one. She wondered if ants felt like this when put beneath a microscope and burned. 'My birth certificate says *father unknown*.'

'Your father died recently. Your half-brother is a king and as a child you went to school with your half-sister. *If* she's a half-sister. Who sired *her* is a matter of speculation. It could have been the King's brother rather than the King. The point is, you have family. A royal family.'

And she wanted no part of it. 'You have *no proof* of any of this.'

'Haven't I?'

'Augustus, please. Leave it alone. It benefits no one.'

'You know who he is.'

Yes. 'I know nothing.'

'You're lying. You're a royal daughter of Byzenmaach. Does Cas's sister know who you are?'

'Claudia is my *friend*.' Sera stood, incapable of sitting still any longer. 'If my father is who you say he is, then you know he had no use for daughters. The *world* knows this. Yes, my mother was sent to contain him when he began to mistreat his wife. She was to offer other activities for him to focus on, less damaging ways to vent his anger, and she did but he was beyond her control. She failed, and fled and hid and I'm *glad*. I take no pride in the blood running through my veins—and you're only assuming it's his. The man was a tyrant and a murderer. His son, bless us all, is a far better man than he ever was and Byzenmaach is now in good hands. What would I add to that? What could possibly be gained?'

'Power,' he offered.

'I *have* power.'

'Royal status.'

'A noose around my neck.'

'Family,' he said softly, and at this she broke years of deportment training to wrap her arms around her waist and hunch forward as if preventing her stomach from falling out.

'I already have a family,' she whispered, and tried not to think of the pictures in the paper she'd seen recently. Casimir of Byzenmaach, half-brother, wholly in love with his new bride and bastard daughter. A king whose sister had recently returned from exile to claim her rightful place. 'I am Sera Boreas of the High Reaches, daughter of Yuna, pupil of Lianthe, member of the Order of the Kite, and courtesan until you release me. I need no royal titles. I want no royal duties.'

'Not even for me?'

I don't know what you want from me!' she cried.

'Yes, you do. I've been saying it all along. I don't need a courtesan, Sera, I need a wife. And you, for all that you'll service me while I'm looking for one, aren't interested in the position. For what it's worth, I don't blame you. You have the world at your feet. Why take on royal duties when you don't have to?' His face hardened. 'But you can't stay here any more. I won't look elsewhere while you're here. And it appears I do need to look elsewhere.'

She stood immobile. 'I can't leave. The accord—'

'You can leave. In fact, I insist.'

He sat so still and silent. She couldn't read him. She didn't know what to say to him. 'By the terms of the accord—'

'I have the right leverage now to do whatever the hell I want. And, believe me, Sera, and with no disrespect to you or your secret Order, I've had enough.'

If anyone had ever asked Augustus of Arun what it felt like to be in love, he couldn't have told them. He'd never been in love before, not once. Not until

Sera Boreas walked out of his office and took his beaten, bleeding heart with her.

He put his hands to his face and took a couple of deep breaths. It didn't hurt any less but breathing was a function of living and he still had to do that.

Sera had chosen freedom over duty. Freedom over *him*, and it was a fair call. Last night had been brilliant but he'd been reading too much into it. Passion did that. Wanting something too much did that. So they'd made love. So what? Courtesans did that. Didn't mean she wanted to stay and be his wife.

He reached for the phone.

'Get my lawyers in here. I'm drafting a written offer of marriage to Katerina DeLitt.' Another proposal that was likely to be rejected but it would serve a purpose and he didn't have to present it to Katerina yet. 'I also need you to find out what Sera weighs, double it, and I want that weight in gold removed from the vaults. I want a copy of my offer of marriage to the Baroness DeLitt and the gold delivered to Lianthe of the High Reaches and I want it done today.' He needed to stitch up the gaping hole where his heart had once been and he didn't need an audience. 'And then I want Sera and her guards escorted from my *goddamn home*. Today.'

CHAPTER TEN

SERA STARED UNCOMPREHENDINGLY at the letter Augustus's private secretary had just handed her. It hadn't taken long to read.

'Lady Sera, you are free to leave,' Augustus's secretary said firmly. 'The terms of the accord have been satisfied, or close enough. I've made arrangements for you and your retinue to stay at a hotel in the city.'

Ari stood beside her, arms crossed and his face impassive. 'It's eleven at night.'

'It's a five-star hotel with round-the-clock check-in,' the older man countered. 'Organised and paid for until the end of the month, should you wish to delay your return to the mountains. They're expecting you.'

'How? How has he satisfied the terms of the accord?' asked Sera.

'The King has an offer of marriage on the table and believes the terms of the accord have been satisfied in principle, milady. Lady Lianthe agrees. *Double* your weight in gold has already been delivered to her.'

'I—' She needed to call Lianthe. She needed to speak to Augustus. 'Is His Majesty in? May I speak with him?' Not that she had any idea what she was going to say. *Thank you? How did you do it? Are you really going to cut me loose, just like that?*

'He's not in.'

There'd been no evening event written into his schedule this morning. Sera knew this because the man standing in front of her had been emailing her Augustus's daily schedule every morning for several weeks.

'May I see him in the morning?'

'His Majesty has a full schedule tomorrow. He needs to finish everything he put on hold today in order to accommodate your wishes.'

'My wishes?'

'Your wish to leave.'

'Right,' she said faintly. 'That wish. The owls—'

'Will be taken care of. Your belongings packed and returned to the High Reaches. There's a palace vehicle at your disposal. It's waiting for you at the south wall entrance.'

Funny how freedom felt a lot like dismissal.

Sera nodded. Manners before breakdown. Discretion over protest. 'I'll leave a letter for His Majesty on my desk. Will you see that he gets it?'

'He'll get it.' The older man seemed to soften and sag. 'The question you should be asking is: will he read it?'

* * *

Ari waited until the King's secretary had left the room before turning silently towards her, eyebrow raised.

'I need to ring Lianthe,' she told him. 'Alert the others that we might be on our way.'

He nodded and reached for his phone, heading over towards the entrance doors but staying inside the room where once he might have stood outside the doors to give her more privacy. Sera walked in the opposite direction and made her call from the bedroom.

Lianthe picked up on the second ring.

'Is it true? Have the terms of the accord been satisfied?' Sera asked without preamble.

'Well, he doesn't have a wife and he doesn't have an heir but he does have a valid wedding proposal in play and I have no reason to believe it will be rejected. He also informs me that your presence is no longer required and has threatened to expose your connection to the Byzenmaach throne if I don't agree with him.' Lianthe drew a heavy breath. 'So I agreed with him. I'm not sure where he got his information from. I can't imagine you told him.'

'I didn't.' Sera closed her eyes and tilted her head towards the sky, only the sky wasn't there; it was only the ceiling. 'He had us investigated.'

'That information's not available.'

'Nonetheless, he got it from somewhere.' The sudden sting of hot tears welled beneath her eyelids. 'He asked me to marry him. And I didn't know what to say.'

'I suspect that says it all.' The other woman's voice was soft and soothing. 'What a pity. I find his utter ruthlessness on your behalf quite admirable. He must be very much in love with you.'

'He's trapped, that's all. He's being forced to take a wife and his heart's not engaged with any of the available candidates. I've watched him. He can drum up polite friendliness towards them if pressed.'

'And what does he drum up for you?'

Stories from his childhood and an insatiable sexual hunger that had left her wrung out and panting. Challenge and temper and unexpected moments of understanding. 'More. But Lianthe, I'm not cut out for love. Courtesans don't love. They serve, willingly, and I have. We were doing well. No one ever said anything about *love*.'

'You have something against it?'

Yes. 'I don't believe it brings happiness.'

'Your mother was an extreme case. She had a soft heart and the man she fell for, he wasn't soft at all.'

'Neither's this one. He's difficult and demanding.' And passionate and protective and a demon in bed. 'And petty and powerful and…' Gorgeous and supportive of her charity schemes and… 'He's a king in need of a queen. There'd be oaths to Crown and country. I'd be accountable for every minute of every day. Who would want that?'

'Who indeed?'

'It's a lifetime sentence of duty and reckoning and being judged. And usually being judged wanting.'

'Indeed.'

'Who'd want that?' she repeated.

'Not you, clearly. You probably wouldn't rise to the occasion at all, even if you loved him. Which you don't.'

'I don't.'

'Well, then.' Lianthe sounded disturbingly cheerful. 'When are you coming home?'

'Want to talk about it?'

Augustus scowled at his sister and wondered, not for the first time, why he'd allowed her to invite herself to dinner. She said she'd missed him—which he very much doubted, given how busy she was. She'd wanted a catch-up—which usually meant pumping him for information or delicately *revealing* information that might be of interest to him. The fact that he'd banished the only other woman who'd ever come close to providing him with this type of relaxed political conversation was not lost on him. 'Talk about what?'

'The rumour that you've proposed, or are about to propose, to Katerina DeLitt. The abrupt midnight departure of your courtesan.' Moriana waved an airy hand towards him from across the dining room table. 'You choose.'

Sera had left four nights ago. The people of the High Reaches would be coming to collect everything that belonged to them, Lianthe had said, but she hadn't mentioned when. Stepping into the round room only to find Sera not there was driving him insane. The soft hoot of owls mocked him. The tapestry wheel of pleasure haunted him. So many things they hadn't done yet. Perhaps he should be thankful.

'I choose silence.'

Moriana allowed him that silence for all of thirty seconds, and that was only because she had a mouthful of food.

'You want to talk to Theo about it?' she asked when her mouth was empty again. 'Or Benedict? Benedict's surprisingly insightful when it comes to matters of the heart.'

It stood to reason he would be, what with all that practice. 'Thank God he's not here,' Augustus offered drily. 'Sera Boreas has gone, the accord has been honoured to everyone's satisfaction, and I'll be married by the end of the year.'

'So you say. But to whom? And please don't tell me you're madly in love with Katerina. I know you. And you're not.'

'Since when has love ever been a prerequisite for marriage?'

'Since when has love ever *not* been a prerequisite for you?'

'Not everyone is cut out for the kind of love you and Theo share.'

'You're not so different from me.' Moriana raised her chin and regarded him haughtily. 'You want that kind of love—you always have.'

He offered up a careless shrug and cut into his meal, ignoring his sister's scowl. She hated it when he refused to engage. Said it was a stalling tactic that had no place in open conversation.

'Augustus, I love you. You know this.'

Uh-oh.

'But I've had a dozen calls this week from people here in your palace, begging me to come and strangle you. At which point I would become their ever so reasonable Queen.'

Augustus snorted.

'I'd probably have to renounce Theo to do it, of course, and this baby currently in my belly would probably be kidnapped back and forward between palaces until he ran away and joined the circus, but at least your palace employees wouldn't be suffering.'

'You're pregnant?' She didn't look pregnant, even if she did look more vibrant than usual. He'd put that down to their argument, or the wine she…wasn't drinking. So much for his keen powers of observation. Sera would have caught that one within five minutes of being in the room.

Moriana nodded and offered up a tiny but self-satisfied smile. 'I'm barely nine weeks in. We're keeping it quiet until I'm a little further along, but I wanted to tell you now and in person.'

'Congratulations.' He meant it. 'Are you well?' Was she happy about it?

Theo would be ecstatic with an heir on the way.

'I'm as well as can be, given that I can barely keep dry toast in my stomach before lunchtime. Augustus, I'm so happy. A mother. Me!'

Envy had no place in his heart. His sister was happy and deserved to be. He could wait, and one day it would be his turn to puff with pride and joy because his wife was pregnant. But there was only one woman's face he could see in that particular daydream. Sera, with her slender frame, luminous grey eyes and flawless skin.

The same woman that had chosen freedom over a life spent with him.

He didn't blame her.

He'd done everything in his power to set her free.

'You could go after her now that the accord has been satisfied,' said Moriana, and he blinked because he thought they weren't having this conversation, only apparently they were. 'You always did have trouble with the *she was duty bound to serve you* part.'

'If we're using the argument that Sera's now a free woman, she could come back at any time. Do you see her here?' He didn't need Moriana's answer. 'Neither do I.'

'She hasn't returned to the High Reaches,' Moriana said tentatively.

'Perhaps she's sick of serving them too.'

'I have it on good authority that she's in Byzenmaach, at Cas's Winter fortress.'

'She's *where*?'

'Visiting Cas's sister.' Moriana eyed him with blatant curiosity. 'They know each other. Studied together in the mountains as kids.'

He hadn't told Moriana about Sera's parentage. He hadn't told anyone. He'd tried telling himself that such effective leverage could be used over and over again if he kept it to himself but the truth was he'd never go against Sera's wishes to keep her father's identity a secret and he'd never use that particular leverage again. He was done with it. He was done with *her*.

'So what are you going to name this baby? Have you given it any thought?'

'I've given it no thought at all yet.' Her eyes glinted with sharp humour.

'And the due date is when?'

'Thirty-one weeks from now, apparently. You could drop in on Claudia or go see Tomas about how to get rid of the remaining owls in the round room. They shouldn't be too hard to catch, seeing as I have it on good authority that you're feeding them.'

'Lies.' All lies. 'And the baby's health? How's the

baby's health?' Why couldn't she be one of those expectant mothers that talked of nothing else?

'Good try, brother.' Moriana outright smirked. 'Should you be fortunate enough to be invited to see beyond the veil of Theo's outright terror at the thought of becoming a father, I should warn you he will talk of nothing else but baby names, giving birth and raising children. Honestly, I think it broke his brain.'

It was Augustus's turn to grin outright. 'Really? Theo's gone gaga? I'd like to see that.'

'You have no idea.'

'I'm thrilled for you both.'

Moriana looked positively tearful as she set her cutlery down and reached for her napkin to dab at her eyes. Their late lamented mother would have scolded her twice over. First for her unseemly display of emotion, and then for inappropriate use of tableware. Such scolding would have once sent his sister spinning into the depths of despair but the new, improved Moriana didn't seem to care.

'Have you really proposed to Katerina DeLitt?' she asked, because she was a sneaky, *sneaky* woman, not above using tears to disarm him.

'I've drawn up an offer, yes.'

'Have you sent it?'

It was still sitting on his desk. 'Do you have anything against her?'

'Nothing at all, apart from the fact that you're in

love with someone else. As a woman who's been in Katerina DeLitt's position before, she has my utmost sympathy. If you had any sense, you wouldn't even consider proposing to her in your current condition. If she had any sense she'd refuse you.'

'Maybe she will.'

Sera had refused him.

His sister regarded him solemnly. 'Will you at least meet with Sera again before you take such an irrevocable step with someone else?'

He gathered up the icy reserve he rarely wore around his sister and pinned her with his gaze. As dear as she was to him, and pregnant along with it, her interference was unwelcome.

'I didn't want to talk about any of this with you, but I heard you out and now it's your turn to hear me. No, I will not seek out Sera again. I've had my say already and her ambitions do not include becoming my Queen. I will not discuss this with you or anyone else ever again. And if you don't like my answer, feel free to leave.'

CHAPTER ELEVEN

CASIMIR OF BYZENMAACH'S Winter fortress perched atop a mountain pass. Sera had reached out to Claudia and asked if she knew of a place where she could exercise and clear her head and it was a measure of their friendship that the other woman had instantly invited her to stay.

Accepting that invitation without disclosing the secret of her parentage made Sera the worst friend in the world, but up here in the mountain pass, with Tomas's falcons soaring overhead and dawn breaking softly over the horizon, she felt a peace steal over her that she hadn't felt in days.

She finished her forms and bowed to the valley below and the rising sun and turned to find her hostess sitting silently on a rock behind her, watching. So she bowed to her too and watched the other woman smile.

'That was beautiful,' said Claudia. 'But then, you always have been very beautiful.'

'My lot to bear.' Always making waves, being

coveted or even despised for no other reason than she'd drawn someone's eye. Glazed stares, suspicious glares and people wanting to possess her.

Augustus had wanted to possess her from the beginning.

It was a miracle, really, that he'd withstood that urge for as long as he had.

'Whose heart have you broken this time?' Claudia asked.

'One does not kiss and tell,' she replied quietly and picked up the towel she'd brought with her and put it to her face.

King Casimir and his family were at their Summer palace in the city, not here. She'd wanted to meet him. She hadn't wanted to meet him. Those two thoughts did not coexist peacefully.

She didn't know what she wanted any more.

Lowering the towel, she closed her eyes and drew fresh breath, feeling at home here, in a way that had everything to do with cool mountain air and not having to view the sky from beneath a web of steel and glass.

No endless dinners, galas and fund-raisers to oversee.

No severely tailored work clothes.

No king to serve.

No duty.

'I don't know what to do any more,' she confessed. 'I have no plans, no direction, no thoughts for the future. I'm finally free and all I'm doing is looking over my shoulder at what I left behind.'

Claudia nodded. 'I know that feeling. Here.' She opened a small basket at her feet. 'I brought breakfast. The food here is amazing.'

Sera spread her towel on the ground and sat cross-legged, and for a time they feasted on meat pastries and sweet milky tea. But Sera wasn't quite ready to let go of her friend's earlier comment. 'Do you ever think you should have stayed in the mountains?'

'I'm of more use to the people of the High Reaches if I'm advocating for them here, so no. I shouldn't have stayed in the mountains.'

'But do you like it here?' Sera watched as the other woman's gaze tracked a falcon in full flight. 'Do they treat you well?'

'They treat me like a princess, because that's what I am. Some treat me like a newfound friend and confidante and I like that. Some can barely look at me but dream of the day I was taken from them, nonetheless. It's not always easy but I'm making my home here.' Claudia reached for a paper napkin. 'I wanted you to meet my niece. Face of an angel and an absolute terror. Wants to be a Samurai this week. I thought you two could bond.'

'I'd like to meet her.' A niece. She blinked back sudden tears.

'Hey.' A warm palm snaked out to cover her forearm. 'What is it?'

'Nothing, I—nothing. I'd like to meet her some day.'

'Hardly a thought to induce tears—although some of the guards here may beg to differ.'

Sera smiled, as she was meant to smile. 'Thank you for inviting me here.'

'Stay as long as you dare.'

'Another day, perhaps. After that I don't know. I need to keep moving.' Searching, so that she didn't keep remembering nights full of politicking and quiet confidences and one night in particular when she and Augustus had forgotten their roles and let honesty rule them.

'May I do a visualisation exercise with you?' Claudia reached out and took both of Sera's hands in hers. 'It's one I've found useful whenever I find myself adrift. Close your eyes.'

Sera nodded and closed her eyes.

'You're standing at a crossroads. Seven paths to choose from, radiating out in all directions. Some safe, because you know where they lead. Some bright and beckoning and full of new adventures. Others dark and seductively forbidding. On some paths you can see family in the distance and maybe you're not sure of your welcome because they look so happy. What else could they possibly need?'

Sera opened her eyes and searched the other woman's face for some sign that she *knew*.

And found nothing.

'Close your eyes.' Claudia moved her thumbs in

soothing circles over Sera's skin. 'Someone stands beside you at that crossroads. Someone you'll never leave behind because you carry them in your heart like a talisman. Someone whose path was chosen for them the minute they were born. They couldn't follow you even if they wanted to. All they can do is be there at the crossroads where your lives intersect and watch you make your choice and let you go. They'll fight for your right to do that, you see. Of all the gifts they can give you, it's the most expensive.'

Sera trembled. 'I know who you're talking about.'

'Do you? Because it could be anyone. It could be me.'

Sera snapped her eyes open and saw nothing but love and gentle understanding.

'It could be me saying I'm right here and ready to be whatever you need me to be,' Claudia repeated quietly. 'Close your eyes and breathe.'

Sera closed her eyes and breathed.

'Whenever I do this exercise I see Tomas beside me. Whoever heard of a princess and a falconer? He won't even lay a hand on me, can hardly bear to look at me, but I swear to you I'm laying down a new path for us, brick by brick, just in case he ever wants to walk my way. It's not so easy to live a royal life, you see, and those already there will never force the issue. You don't need to mention my regard for Tomas to him, by the way, unless it comes up in conversation. At which point, go for it and use embellishments.'

Sera opened one eye and arched her brow.

'Shut it. No winking,' her sister of the heart replied with a tiny grin. 'I'm trying so hard not to make this about me. Close your eyes and open your heart.'

Sera obeyed.

'I know there's someone there beside you at your crossroads. I know you can't move forward without resolving your feelings for them. Doing that is your next step and it might be the most important step you ever take.' Claudia moved forward; Sera could feel it even if she couldn't see it. The other woman's cheek brushed hers, comfort, solidarity and warmth, as she whispered, 'You know who you see.'

They walked back down the mountain in the crisp morning air, Claudia looking skyward more than once and smiling softly when a falcon appeared and circled above. 'They questioned Tomas for days after I disappeared,' Claudia told Sera. 'He was eight years old and the last person to see me and they grilled him over and over again, with no mercy given for the fact that he too was a child.'

'And now he uses falcons to track your every movement?'

'Not my every movement.' Claudia sprang from one step to the next, her feet sure as they made their way down the rocky path. 'He's been training himself to wait longer and longer each time I come up here before flying one of his hunting hawks to find out where I am. We're up to almost an hour.'

'And do you help him with the birds?'

'You know I do.' Claudia had skills of her own in that area. 'Watching that man work is a pleasure I have no words for.'

'And how will you manage to steer him towards romance if you're the Princess in the castle and he's but a mere falconer?'

'By putting my own spin on this Princess gig and getting out of the castle a lot,' Claudia offered drily. 'It helps that Cas is so utterly overcome by my return that he lets me do whatever I want.'

'He didn't reprimand you for staying away?'

Claudia might have been kidnapped as a child—for her own good, as it turned out—but she'd had chances to return over the years and had never done so. Not until her father had died and her brother had taken the throne.

'It wasn't safe for me here. You know that.'

'But it is now.'

Claudia nodded and looked to the sky and let the early morning light caress her face. 'It is now.'

Coffee was served on their return, set up on a little table on a balcony overlooking a walled garden. There was also fresh fruit and bread, and an array of northern delicacies to tempt them.

'Is this all for us?' asked Sera because, frankly,

half a dozen more people could have joined them and it still would have been too much food for one sitting.

'They're making up for all the years I was gone. It's what people do around here.'

'Every day?'

'Every damn day.' Claudia reached for a royal blue folder sitting on the table. 'Mind if I look through my morning mail? The palace keeps me informed as to the news of the day.'

'And you trust this information?'

Claudia laughed. 'Oh, Sera. The look on your face. If something of interest comes up I look into it. Did you not rely on the Arunian palace for information?'

'Not really. I have my own sources.'

'I find these ones useful and I don't have to go looking for them. They even present them in order of palace importance. Very informative in itself, would you not say? Take this one, for example: it's item one and it's a note from the desk of Moriana of Liesendaach, formerly of Arun, telling Cas that there's been an assassination attempt on her brother but rumour of his death is a gross exaggeration. Is that not good to know?'

'What?'

Claudia passed the sheet of paper over without further comment, and picked up the next item. 'And here's what the tabloids have to say. Hmm. Your good King was in a bad part of the city last night.

Two people in custody, Augustus and a minor in intensive care.'

'A minor?' Sera wasn't tracking too well any more. Hadn't been since the words *Augustus* and *death* had been mentioned in the same breath.

'Here.' Claudia passed that one to Sera too before picking up her coffee in one hand and sifting quickly through the others. 'That's all the information I have. Do you have anyone you can get more information from?'

'Not at this hour.' It was still too early for regular workday hours, and for all that Augustus's executive secretary often stayed late, he rarely began his day before nine. 'Unless the entire communications team has been called in to deal with this. Then there might be someone there willing to give me more information.'

'Would you like to use one of our phones?' Sera asked.

'They'll think the call is coming from the Byzenmaach King.'

Claudia raised a dark brow. 'And? Not as if there aren't advantages to that approach.'

The woman had a point.

She found a phone and made the call to Augustus's office number and waited impatiently for someone to pick up.

The call appeared to get diverted and Augustus's

secretary answered on the sixth ring, his voice curtly polite and the strain in it evident.

'It's Sera,' she said.

Silence.

'I'm staying at the Winter fortress in Byzenmaach and heard the news this morning.'

More silence.

Don't hang up... 'How is he?' She cleared her throat. 'Please.'

Claudia was watching her from the doorway. Ari stood sentry on the other side of the room, silently watching them both.

'He's in intensive care,' the older man said finally and Sera let her head droop so her hair curtained her face.

'And his condition?'

'He needs someone to fight for him.'

'I can fight,' she said, blinking back tears. 'I know how to fight.'

'Yes, I know. We all know that. But, if I may be so bold, don't come back if you're not planning to stay. He let you go once because that's what you said you wanted and it nearly destroyed him. Don't make him go through that again.'

'I won't.'

'Would you like to put that in writing?'

'If you tell me where he is, I'll put it on a billboard.'

'He's at the Sisters of Mercy Hospital in the capital. They have a helipad, and I assume you have access to a helicopter and a pilot. Tell them to go through me and I'll clear your way for landing.'

It was more welcome than she'd ever hoped for. 'You're probably going to get into trouble for this.'

'I probably am,' he countered drily.

'That's a debt you'll be able to collect on, should you ever need something from me in the future.'

'Do you still have your guards with you?'

'Yes.'

'Then I'm calling that debt in right now. Bring them. The King's head of security quit this morning in a fit of temper. There's an opening.'

'I'll bring them.' She couldn't resist the next question. 'What happened?'

'Which version would you like, milady?'

'Your version.' She trusted the older man's take on palace events.

'In that case, the answer's very simple. Most people have a healthy sense of self-preservation. My King has lost his.'

It took three tries to put the phone back in its cradle and the third time Claudia's hand was guiding her. 'I need a helicopter,' she said.

'Then you shall have one.'

'And a pilot.'

'I shall fly you myself.'

Which was how Sera managed to get from Byzenmaach's Winter fortress to the Sisters of Mercy Hospital in just over an hour, her guards flanking her as she strode from the helipad towards the building. She had her travelling cloak on but didn't bother with the hood. Memorable entries were her speciality, and she had every intention of brazening this one out.

Augustus's secretary stood waiting for her and opened the door as she approached.

'How is he?' A question that carried with it everything her world had narrowed down to. Because there was only one person she wanted to walk beside in this world and if he wasn't alive...

If she never got that chance...

All the colours of the world would be gone.

'Please. How is he?'

'Follow me,' he said. He avoided her gaze and supplied no other answer. Maybe he had no answer for her. 'Is his sister here? His father?' Had Augustus's next of kin been gathered?

'They're about.' The older man swept them through a long hallway with security guards at either end. Guards who nodded and straightened to attention as they passed by. She thought Ari's barely leashed displeasure at their carelessness in letting an assassin get close enough to their King to do damage might have something to do with it. That or her own scathing, stormy gaze.

'Ari and Tun will relieve the guard detail on the door to the critical care unit,' she said, and smiled tightly when the old courtier blinked at her sheer hide. 'You were the one who wanted them here. No one said anything about you commanding them.'

'Perhaps you will allow His Majesty's guards to brief your men on what actually happened last night before you sweep them aside,' the older man advised. 'The King occasionally goes into the city by himself and in disguise. He did this last night.'

'And you *let* him?'

'Freedom's irresistible to those who've never had it.' They'd reached the end of yet another long corridor with guards stationed at either end. 'You can go in.'

'Is anyone in there with him?' It wasn't that she was putting off walking through those doors. She simply wanted to be prepared for whoever she might find.

'His sister's just stepped out.'

There was never going to be a better time.

There was one bed in the room she entered and it was empty, machines switched off and the bottom sheet rumpled, the top sheet pushed aside. Augustus stood to one side of the window on the opposite side of the room, his face pale and wan, his chest bare, his shoulder bandaged and his left arm strapped tightly to his chest.

His eyes widened at the sight of her.

'Hello,' she said awkwardly, caught completely off guard. Not that the sight of him standing there didn't fill her heart to overflowing, but this really

wasn't the kind of intensive care she'd imagined. 'I...
Ah, you can stand.'

He raised a quizzical eyebrow.

'And...uh...walk. That's good. Brilliant recovery.' She'd been had, but right now she didn't give a damn. 'So good.'

'What are you doing here?' If she was drinking him in with her eyes, he was doing much the same to her.

'I was—'

In the area and just thought she'd drop by? Hardly.

'That is to say—'

He was waiting for her to say.

'I was visiting Claudia, my friend who is not my sister, and she has this mountain...'

He looked sceptical. 'Of course it's not her mountain, but it's a mountain nonetheless, and I was up there thinking about you, and me, and whether there could ever be a "you *and* me" that wasn't all about honour and duty and sacrifice. A you and me that *does* involve those things, sure,' she said, and contradicted herself completely and stumbled on regardless. 'Because you're you and there's no getting away from your duty as King, but above all that, or maybe underneath it, I was wondering if there might be a "*you and me*" who could be together and we could make a point of building some freedom into our lives, keeping the courtesan's quarters open as a place where you can be you and I can be me, and there could be holidays in the mountains and I could show you things you've never seen. And maybe at some point, if you haven't already proposed to Katerina DeLitt, that is, we could talk about you marrying me.' She tailed off, wishing he'd say something. 'Because of love.'

'Was that supposed to make sense?'

Yes, yes, it was, and if it hadn't she'd try again. 'I'm in love with you.'

'Why?' The tiniest tilt of his lips gave her the courage she needed to keep going.

'Because you let me in, even though you knew this was going to get messy. Because you let me try and be all those dozen different things I was taught to be, no matter the cost to yourself. Because you put my needs before yours and fought for my right to be free in a way you can never be. And I *am* free now and I'm still being selfish, because when I heard you'd been hurt there was only one place I wanted to be. So here I am.'

And there he stood.

'Of course, you might not have much use any more for the love of a former courtesan and that's okay too.'

'No reciprocation required?' he asked softly.

'No. That's not love. Love is standing here and feeling so much relief and joy that you *are* okay. And then turning around and walking out that door if you ask me to.'

She wanted to stay. She so badly wanted to touch him. But she didn't have the right to.

'Come here,' he said and she walked closer and fought every twitchy bit of muscle memory not to sink to the floor at his feet. He'd never wanted that from her.

'If there's such a thing as love at first sight, I felt it the first time I ever saw you.' He touched his fingers to the tie at her neck and tugged it loose and then used both hands to push her travelling cloak from her shoulders until it pooled in a puddle at her feet. 'First time you ever curtseyed for me, I was torn between wanting to keep you there for ever and never wanting you to lower yourself in front of me again because I wanted an equal. I *needed* an equal. And you stayed and triumphed, no matter what I threw at you, and I realised I'd finally found one.' He traced the line of her cheek with the backs of his fingers. 'Always knew I'd have to let you go.'

'You did.'

'And yet here you are.' He threaded his fingers through her hair. 'And I think you should know that I have no intention of ever letting you go again.' He kissed her gently at first and then somehow it became all-consuming.

They were both breathing raggedly when finally he broke the kiss. He rested his forehead against hers and huffed a laugh before taking a determined step back. 'I had a plan for if you ever came back. It involved rather more clothes and no bullet wounds on my part, and there was possibly a fantasy moment of you wearing ancient slave jewellery mixed up in there somehow, but I did have a plan and it went something like this. I love you. I want you by my side from this day forward and not as my courtesan or employee.'

He got down on bended knee and tugged his ring from his finger and held it out to her. It was a dark blue cabochon sapphire with the royal insignia of Arun overlaid in diamonds. 'This one's heavy, I know, but it's yours if you'll take it. There'll be other rings, I promise. Sera, will you marry me?'

'Yes.' A lifetime of royal duty in exchange for the opportunity to walk beside the man she loved and who loved her in return. 'Yes, I will.'

He put the ring on her finger and she looked at it and then at him. 'I know what you mean now about having someone kneel at your feet. It's very disconcerting having all sorts of thoughts running through your mind about what they might do while they're there.'

'Tell me about it,' he said with a glint in his eye that promised exploration. 'And don't spare the details.'

'Another time, perhaps. Once you've fully recovered from your...did you say *bullet wounds*?'

'I may have been an idiot in your absence. You're likely to hear about it at some point. I believe there's a *Bring Sera Back* petition circulating through the palace as we speak. Or perhaps everybody's signed it by now. There was a jar circulating too. People were putting gold jewellery into it, trying to raise your bodyweight in gold as an incentive to woo you back.'

Sera blinked. 'They what?'

'Good thing there's not much of you.'

A knock on the door preceded the entry of Moriana of Liesendaach, formerly of Arun. She took one look at Sera and her brother, still on bended knee, and said, 'Oh, now that's a pretty look.'

'Do you *mind*?' Augustus asked her.

'Oh, no. Not at all. Please. Continue. Don't mind me.' Moriana waved away his concerns. 'Hi, Sera.'

Sera waved and the ring on her finger glinted.

Moriana's smile broadened. 'Does this mean I can have my six gold bracelets and Theo's two golden goblets back? Because Theo did, in fact, get into trouble for donating those goblets to the cause. Not only are they insanely heavy, apparently they're two thousand years old.'

Sera leaned forward and put her lips to Augustus's ear. 'I think you should get up now,' she whispered. 'I promise to make it worth your while later.'

The smile of unfiltered joy he bestowed on her was one she wanted to see at least once every day for the rest of her life.

'We're getting married,' Augustus said.

Moriana rolled her eyes but her smile almost rivalled her brother's. 'I never would have guessed.'

'And I need to speak with my future wife about

exactly how quickly we can make that happen,' he continued regally and pointed towards the door.

'I can help you there.' Moriana was enjoying herself way too much. 'Royal weddings take time. Months. Years! And involve processions.'

'Out!' He sounded so commanding.

'In the mountains of the High Reaches there's a ceremony called a binding,' Sera offered quietly. 'It involves two people pledging their hearts into the other's safe keeping. There are four witnesses, one for each point of the compass. It's very simple. Will you do it with me?'

'I'll do it today and every day for the rest of my life,' he promised, and touched his lips to hers.

When Sera finally surfaced, Moriana was gone and the door to the room was firmly closed.

'How soon can we break you out of here?' she asked, and placed a gentle hand to his shoulder and then to his heart.

'They're being overly cautious,' he grumbled. 'I can be out of here tonight.'

Uh-huh. She'd like to see him try.

'One week,' she promised. 'One week today and with the mountains as our witness I will bind my heart to you.'

EPILOGUE

AUGUSTUS STOOD DRAPED in the ceremonial black furs that also served to keep the bitter cold at bay. He wore his royal uniform beneath the borrowed cloak because, for all that he was standing on a mountain with a blizzard closing in, he was still the King of Arun and carried the hopes of his people with him.

He'd been in the mountains for two days and had stayed in a sprawling fortress every bit as grand as any he'd ever stayed in. Sera had shown him the horses, the falcons, the temples and the steps carved into a mountain path that wove its way ever skyward in suicidal fashion. Only for her had he risen and bathed and dressed before dawn and climbed those icy steps, grateful for the burning torches carried by others and the chain ropes beaten into the rock centuries ago and the heavy-duty gloves lent to him by Ari this morning.

A High Reaches binding was not for those who lacked courage and the journey there was part of the process.

His sister and her unborn babe were here, swathed in ceremonial garb and red-gold furs. She would take the East point on the compass, the new dawn. The Lady Lianthe stood to the North, a guiding light, the voice of experience. His father stood to the South, the foundation stone for all that would grow. Princess Claudia of Byzenmaach took the West point and, while darkness and betrayal rode with her as part of her past, she wore love like a shield and had cloaked herself in purest white.

The sky overhead was a vivid blue, a perfect complement to the snowy white and the occasional slash of rocky grey.

There were the four points of the compass, an invisible circle connecting them, and only two sets of footprints within that circle.

They met at the centre, where a goblet of melted snow sat on a stony plinth, and if Theo thought his goblets were heavy they had nothing on this one.

Sera wore a cloak of grey to match her eyes and he couldn't wait to see what was under it. Something similar to bridal wear, she'd told him demurely. Beyond that, he'd have to wait and see.

Her hair had been coiled atop her head and dressed with diamonds.

She wore a fine platinum necklace, matching earrings and the royal ring he'd given her one week earlier in lieu of an engagement ring.

She was loving and giving and his and he'd never felt more blessed.

There would be a wedding, of course. A royal one with cavalries and balconies and a kiss in full view of the people. It was expected. It was tradition. But this…this moment here was deeply, emphatically personal. Simple words meant for no one but the one receiving them.

Four witnesses, a sacred mountain, a cup full of water and a vivid blue sky.

And then Sera spoke.

'My heart is pure and true and yours,' she told him. 'I offer it from a position of knowledge, power and freedom.'

It was all he'd ever hoped for.

'I accept this priceless gift and I will never let you down,' he promised and drank from the goblet.

And then it was his turn to say the words. 'My heart is steadfast and often guarded because it carries with it the weight of a nation but to you I offer it freely and without reservation. It's yours.'

'I accept this priceless gift,' she said, and drained her goblet. 'And, let all here bear witness, I will never let you down.'

* * * * *

Off-Limits To The Crown Prince

Kali Anthony

MILLS & BOON

When **Kali Anthony** read her first romance novel at fourteen, she realised a few truths: there can never be too many happy endings, and one day she would write them herself. After marrying her own tall, dark and handsome hero in a perfect friends-to-lovers romance, Kali took the plunge and penned her first story. Writing has been a love affair ever since. If she isn't battling her cat for access to the keyboard, you can find Kali playing dress-up in vintage clothes, gardening, or bushwhacking with her husband and three children in the rain forests of South East Queensland.

DEDICATION

To my beloved editorcat. Our last book together.
I miss your paws on my keyboard every day.
Nineteen years was not enough.

CHAPTER ONE

HANNAH STOOD IN a shaft of bright sunlight at the rear of her studio. A sickening pulse beat in her chest. The dizzying smell of paint and solvent, usually a reminder of everything she loved, threatened to overpower her. She hurried to the window and threw it wide open onto the rambling tangle of a cottage garden. Gulped in the warm, summer's air.

The hollyhocks were in bloom.

Her mother had loved the hollyhocks best of all the flowers growing here.

'Miss Barrington?' A bodyguard. One of three mountains of men who'd arrived minutes before. Two of whom were now stalking through the place, assessing her home for any risk. The one staying with her frowned, no doubt concerned she might be letting in an assailant to harm their employer, whose arrival was imminent. As if she could organise anything like that with the half-hour's warning of his impending visit her agent had given.

'The smell of paint.' She waved her hand about like

she was shooing away any offending scents. 'It might irritate His Highness.'

The man nodded, likely satisfied she was thinking of his employer's comfort. They probably wouldn't care about hers, or that in this moment it was like a hand had grabbed round her throat and squeezed. She took another deep breath. The bodyguard stationed himself at the doorway separating her studio from the rest of the house and crossed his arms as though he were guarding *her*. Did she look as if she were about to run?

Tempting, but there was nowhere else to go.

Her country cottage, the family home. Her safe place and haven was all she had left of her parents. She looked around the bright room she'd made her studio when she'd been old enough to move out on her own. People said she was crazy to come back here, away from the city, to a place tired from nine years of tenants. But people didn't understand. Even though there'd been a fresh lick of paint, no one had covered over the marks on the wall in the laundry where her parents had notched her height over the years. The low-ceilinged kitchen remained unrenovated, a place where they'd sat to eat their meals and laughed. The whole place sang with those memories. The happy and the devastating.

The burn of tears pricked her eyes. Now all this was at risk. Her aunt and uncle had been her guardians. Looked after her inheritance when her parents had died. Taken in the broken teenager she'd become. Sure, they'd been distant rather than cruel, never having wanted children of their own and not knowing how to deal with her. But she'd trusted them, and her uncle's betrayal still cut deep and jagged. An investment she hadn't wanted gone terribly wrong. Almost everything, lost. Her father would be trying to claw his way out of the grave over the way his brother had behaved towards his only niece.

Everything seemed tenuous in this moment. Nothing else had broken her. Not her parents' death in the accident, not the loss of her horse and everything she loved. She'd clambered out of the well of grief on her own. Sure, her fingertips might have been bloody, nails torn, the scars carved into the soul of her waiting to open at any given moment. But to have to sell this, the little farm where she'd lived some of the best days of her life? That would crack her open and no king's horses or men would ever be able to put those pieces back together again.

Perspiration pricked at the back of her head, a droplet sliding beyond the neck of her shirt, itching her skin. She moved closer to the window. Fished a hair tie from her jeans pocket, scraped her hair back and tied it up in a rough topknot.

The bodyguard looked down at her. Crossed his arms. 'You seem nervous.'

How could she tell him that his employer's past and her own were inextricably bound? That his employer was the last person she wanted to see, because he was a reminder of the worst day of her life? Of teenage dreams destroyed?

'I've never met a prince before.' It wasn't *exactly* a lie. 'And I haven't had time to tidy up.'

The bodyguard's gaze roved over her in a disapproving kind of way. She looked down at her hands. Nails short and blunt. Cuticles ingrained with paint. She grabbed an old rag and wet it with solvent, rubbing at her fingers in a vain effort to clean them. Perfect princes probably wouldn't admire commoners with filthy hands. Not that she was seeking admiration, but still. She supposed she had to keep up some kind of an appearance. After a short effort she dropped the now dirty rag on the tabletop and sniffed at her fingers, which smelled like pine.

She held them up. 'Better?'

The bodyguard grunted.

Hannah checked her phone. Still some time. She picked out a slender paintbrush and stood back from her easel. Her art usually calmed her, a way to lose herself in colour and light. Nothing could touch her when she was in the flow of a portrait. She tried to loosen the death grip of her fingers. Dipped her brush into some paint. A swipe of Tasman blue, a touch of titanium white. She frowned. The eyes in this portrait gave her trouble. Too much sadness, not enough twinkle. She reached out her brush to add a dash of colour near the pupil, trying to ignore the tremor in her hand.

The cheery tinkle of a doorbell rang through the room. Hannah's paintbrush slipped from her fingers and clattered to the floor, leaving smudges of blue paint on the old boards.

The burn of bile rose to her throat. He was early. She left the portrait and wiped her damp palms on her jeans.

'Remember to curtsey,' the bodyguard said.

The teeth of anger bit her then, at this man's disdain

when she was the one being imposed upon today. She'd said no to this commission when it had first been proposed months ago, before she had had any idea how bad her finances were. His employer had ignored her refusal. It was just like saying no to her uncle when presented with a speculative investment. He'd ignored her too. She gritted her teeth, hating that these people hadn't listened to her, as if her opinion were meaningless. But even though things were bad it didn't mean she had to grin and bear it.

Hannah stalked up to the man guarding the doorway and glared. He towered over her but she didn't care. She wasn't going to be pushed around, by anyone. Looming bodyguard *or* prince.

'I do have a concept of manners. And I understand how to behave around royalty.'

The man didn't move, but his eyes widened a fraction as if in surprise. Good.

A murmur of voices drifted down the hall. The tap of fine leather on floorboards grew louder. She backed further into the room, tried to swallow the knot rising in her throat but her mouth was dry.

A shadow appeared in the hall behind more security. Grew and grew till it took human shape, striding through the doorway.

'His Royal Highness, Crown Prince of Lasserno,' the bodyguard announced.

Alessio Arcuri.

More beautiful than she'd remembered, though the recollection was coloured by her youth at the time. Then, she'd only caught thrilling glimpses of the handsome, fairy-tale prince, a rider on the showjumping circuit. The young man her teenage heart had crushed over with a terrifying ferocity. Now, she could fully appreciate the height and breadth of him. His severe yet tantalising and lush mouth. The perfection of his aquiline nose. The caramel of his sun-bronzed skin. The shock of his thick, dark hair. She could pretend her admiration was one of an artist surveying his commanding masculine shape. But who was she kidding? This was a distinctly female attraction to a male in his absolute prime.

After nine years, she still felt like that giddy teenager.

It made her prickly all over. Too big for her skin. She wanted to shed parts of herself like a husk, and come out more sparkling, more polished. Just *more*. Because she didn't need a mirror to realise she looked like some ruffian and he looked as if he'd walked straight from a red carpet.

She resented his perfection, when his snap visit with little warning meant she'd had no time to tidy her own appearance. His exquisitely cut suit in the deepest of navy, a pristine white shirt. Red and blue tie in the finest of glowing silk. She was sure she stared before remembering her manners, dipping into a curtsey. 'Your Highness.'

'Signorina Barrington.' He canted his head in a way that suggested she was *adequate*, then motioned to the man standing behind him. 'This is my private secretary, Stefano Moretti. He's been communicating with your agent.'

The other man was almost as perfectly attired and

presented as his employer. Attractive, but without the indefinable presence of the Prince. She nodded to him. He smiled back.

'Welcome to my home and studio. It's a surprise and I'm underprepared. I didn't expect royalty to drop by today. Would you like a tea?' She motioned to a battered table in the corner of her studio, the ancient electric kettle, some chipped cups.

Alessio looked to where she'd indicated, gaze sliding over the table as though viewing a sad still life. No one came here—this was her private space—so there was no one to bother about damaged crockery. Personal sittings took place in her public studio on the outskirts of London. The one she'd only recently given up, her uncle's actions meaning it was an extravagance she couldn't afford. Yet seeing the room with Alessio in it reminded her how tattered and worn it seemed. She'd never worried before. This was her home. But all it took was a perfectly pressed prince to bring into screamingly sharp relief how threadbare her life had become.

'Tea? No. I was in the area purchasing some horses, and, since you've been ignoring my secretary's requests...' His voice had the musical lilt of Italian spoken in a glorious baritone. Honeyed tones she could listen to for hours. The voice of a leader that would echo on castle walls. One whose dictates would invariably be followed by most.

Not by her. She wasn't this prince's subject.

'I haven't been ignoring them. My answer was clear.'

He hesitated for a second, cocked his head as if he

were thinking. She had the curious sensation of being a specimen under glass.

'Have we met before?'

The high slash of his cheekbones, the strong brows. The sharply etched curve of his tempting lips. Eyes of burnt umber framed by the elegant curl of lamp black lashes. Hannah had never formally met him, but she'd never forgotten him from the showjumping circuit. Alessio Arcuri was the kind of man to leave you breathless. The fearlessness as he rode. The sheer arrogance that he would make every jump successfully. And he did. Horse and rider the embodiment of perfection.

It was why she and her friend had been chattering away in the back of the car on that terrible day. Gossiping about why he'd retired from competition at the age of twenty-two, much to their teenage devastation. Now, it seemed so young. Back then, he'd been the epitome of an adult and everything a clueless sixteen-year-old craved to be. How he appeared to know, in a way that was absolute, his place in the world. The utter confidence of him, when Hannah was still trying to find her bearings. Then she dropped out of riding too, the deaths of her parents and her horse too much to bear. And she'd tried not to think about Prince Alessio Arcuri since.

At least, until her agent's call a little over half an hour ago, when all the memories she'd bottled up had come flooding back.

'No. We haven't met.' Not exactly. He'd been handing out the first prize at a showjumping event she'd competed in after his retirement had been announced. Her friend had won that day, Hannah a close second. Unusual for her but Beau had been off, as if her horse were foreshadowing the devastating events of only hours later. She'd been so envious of that first-prize ribbon. How she'd coveted the handshake Alessio had given to her friend. Craved for him to acknowledge her. Then their eyes had met. Held. And for one perfect, blinding second her world had stopped turning.

After what had come later in the afternoon, those desires seemed childish. It had taken another terrible moment on that day for the world to stop turning a second time. It hadn't restarted.

His being here brought back too many memories of a split second when all her innocence and faith in the good of the world had ended. Riding passenger in the car driven by her friend's parents. Rounding a corner, littered debris…the…carnage. Car and horsebox destroyed. Everything she'd loved, gone. A freak accident. A tractor in the wrong place on a narrow country road. Hannah flinched. Shut her eyes tight against the horrible vision running like a stuttering film reel in her head.

'Are you all right, Signorina Barrington?'

She opened her eyes again. Nodded. Breathed. Stitched up the pain in her heart where it would stay for ever. Hannah didn't want to go back to that time, and if Alessio truly remembered he might start asking questions. She couldn't deal with them, not now.

Alessio looked at his bodyguards, standing as a brooding presence in the corner. Said something in rapid Italian and they bowed and left the room. The atmosphere relaxed a fraction.

'I'm here to discuss you painting my portrait.'

Hannah clasped her hands behind her back. 'As my agent would have told you, I have a number of commissions…'

Alessio stepped towards her and she was forced to look up because, whilst she wasn't tiny, he dwarfed her. He was even more astonishing up close. Nothing marred his features. It was as if no part of the man would deign to be anything less than polished and perfect. He held her transfixed with those velvety brown eyes of his. Till looking at him any more left her head spinning.

He must have taken her silence as reticence.

'Your fee. I'll double it. And I'm a prince, so…'

She stepped back. It was either that or lean into him and all his solidity in a moment when she felt a little broken. 'I know what you are.'

What was she doing? Crucifying herself, that was what. She needed this commission, but she couldn't help herself. She'd made a promise when she first started painting, that she'd only take the jobs she wanted. Trying to establish a connection with your subject could prove taxing some days. In the early stages after her parents died she'd drawn them incessantly, terrified that the memory of how they looked would fade. Day and night she sketched, to perfect them so she could never forget. It had exhausted her, the obsession. Made her ill. Sometimes it still did when she became engrossed with a commission. It was why she chose so carefully.

Alessio Arcuri would never be a careful choice. Any connection with him could break her.

'Then I promise if you paint my portrait I'll ensure everyone knows who *you* are. So far those you've painted have been…inconsequential.'

Portraiture had never been about accolades, but about preserving memories. The minutiae, the nuance of a person. Sure, she was paid well for what she did, but it was *never* about simply being paid. It was about ensuring people weren't forgotten.

She looked at the portrait of the older woman currently on her easel. A believer in justice, lover of barley sugar and Yorkshire tea. 'I wouldn't say a judge is *nobody*. The law's important, as is doing the right thing. But I mostly like painting pictures of people the world overlooks. They deserve their moment to be seen, to be remembered. You're seen all the time.'

Alessio shrugged. That movement seemed out of place on a man who appeared only to move when absolutely necessary. 'Is anyone truly seen? The press often tries to paint pictures of me and they're rarely right.'

'What picture do they try to paint?' The cool command? The lack of emotion? She could imagine they'd claim he was more automaton than real and relish finding the tiniest chink in his gleaming armour to take him down.

Alessio raised an eyebrow. 'You haven't looked me up on the internet? I thought you were renowned for knowing your subjects.'

'You're not my subject so I haven't needed to know you.'

'The judge.' He inspected the painting, eyes narrowing as he stared at the woman on the canvas. 'That portrait tells stories. I want you to tell mine. You're the best. No one could see me like you could.'

Part of her wanted to mine the essence of him, because people fascinated her. But doing so had a cost and she wasn't sure she was prepared to pay it when Alessio reminded her of everything she'd lost.

'"The best" is subjective. I have terms for everyone I paint. My agent tells me you refused mine.'

Sue had been clear. You didn't say *no* to a prince. Hannah had to keep her options open... She knew what those ominous words meant. Once her uncle's duplicity had been discovered, this meeting with the Prince had become necessary. Resented, but necessary none the less.

'I'm here now,' Alessio said. The hard, uncompromising set of his jaw told her he might register what she said but he wasn't really listening.

She turned her back on him and walked to a paint-splattered desk on which her palette and scattered half-used tubes of oil paint were strewn in the haphazard way of this whole room. She opened a drawer and pulled out a few papers, then walked back to where he stood and thrust them in his direction. He took them from her paint-ingrained fingers. Flicked through.

'Am I a cat or dog person?' His eyebrows rose in disbelief. 'What is this?'

She took time with her subjects. The questionnaire was one small part. There were personal sittings, the live sketching. She'd been comfortable with each person she'd painted so far. Had liked them and their quirks in their own way. But Alessio Arcuri? She wasn't sure she could. A person's eccentricities, no matter how small, gave them personality. How could she do justice to this man, who didn't seem to have a quirk about him? He dazzled like a flawless gemstone.

'Those questions are the reason I'm so good at what I do. I get to know my subjects. Intimately.'

At the last word his eyes widened a fraction. Surely he wouldn't think… Heat rushed to her cheeks. The corner of his mouth kicked up a minute fraction. The moment counted in milliseconds and then it was gone, before his attention returned to the paper in his hands. But even those seconds had her heart racing in an attempted getaway.

"What is your best childhood memory?" "Your worst?"' A frown marred his forehead. He thrust the pages back at her. 'No. If the press got hold of this—'

'They won't.' She ignored his outstretched arm. 'I read it, then destroy it. I also sign non-disclosure agreements for those who want them. No information has *ever* reached any press outlet from me. You could take some time and fill out my questions right here.'

He seemed to stand even taller now, imposing like the prince he was. She could even imagine the gleaming crown on his head.

'All these people you paint. The press has no interest in them. Me? I'm royalty. You know how tabloids clamour for stories. I give them none. But this?' He waved his hands over the offending document as if he were trying to bat away some pestilential bug set on biting him. 'I don't answer twenty questions, for anyone.'

'There are eighteen questions. But the number isn't important. You can *tell* me the answers.'

He dropped the papers on the table next to him. 'You're a stranger.'

And that was the way it would stay for ever, even though there was something about this tussle Hannah began to enjoy. A tiny thrill that his interest still held, no matter how she pushed. It told her he *really* wanted her to paint him, stroking an ego she didn't realise needed attention. What would her sixteen-year-old self think now?

That young girl would think all her dreams had come true.

'Here's the thing. Doing this allows me to paint at my best. The type of picture you seem to desire, seeing as you're still standing in my studio. You want me to paint your portrait, then…double my fee and answer my questions.' She rose up, stiffening her spine to match him. If he was playing the prince card then she'd pull a queen on him, because this studio was *her* domain and she ruled here exclusively. 'You can take it or leave it.'

Alessio hadn't expected a warm welcome, but he'd expected something more polite than this. Certainly, she'd curtseyed as expected. A seemingly respectful bow of the head when he was sure none was meant, because her eyes had flashed a kind of warning, the whole of her bristling like some disapproving hedgehog. Cute, but all spike and prickle. Right now, she stood framed by the light from the windows behind her. Dark hair mussed in an unruly topknot. Dressed in a blue and white striped men's shirt with a frayed collar, cuffs pushed back on her forearms, smeared and smudged with paint. Loose, ripped jeans. Trainers as paint-spattered as the rest of her.

Dishevelled and all the more enticing for it.

'I tend not to accede to ultimatums,' he said. Though he admired hers more than he'd admit. She'd hold her own with some of the best of his courtiers, this woman.

She glared at him, no respect meant there at all, and their eyes truly met. Hers were green, perhaps. Arresting. Their depth and swirls of colour transfixed him. She carried the world in that luminous gaze and something drove him to discover what lay behind it, when discovering anything about her other than whether she was prepared to paint his portrait was impossible. He pushed the interest aside.

Ruthlessly.

'I tend not to *give* ultimatums.' Her voice was deeper than he'd expected. Almost…aristocratic in its tone. It feathered his spine the way a stroke of her paint-ingrained fingers might. And in these moments he couldn't avoid the pressing sense of déjà vu, as if he was missing something. Everything about her seemed… strangely familiar.

She claimed not to know him but was as skittish as a colt in spring when he'd first mentioned it. Perhaps it had something to do with his security detail. They tended to suck the air out of the place with their professional brand of malevolence, which was why he'd asked them to leave. Stefano stayed, of course. Alessio didn't spend time alone with women he didn't know, not any more. There would be no ugly rumours. Everyone who surrounded him was carefully vetted and explicitly trusted. He'd learned lessons about putting faith in the wrong person. His father might have courted the press with his outrageous behaviour but Alessio gave them nothing.

'We seem to be at a stalemate,' he said.

She cocked her head. Raised her eyebrows. 'Yet you're *still* here.'

Perhaps there was an answer which could accommodate everybody. His life had been spent trying to find solutions to every problem, mostly regarding his father. He'd become an expert at it, spending his hours working to silence hints at his father's worst excesses, the rumours about the missing gems from the crown jewels. As for Hannah Barrington—when he'd asked Stefano to find the best portrait artist in the world he hadn't expected it to be a reclusive young woman of twenty-five, whose paintings looked as if they contained the experience and insight of a life long-lived. On viewing her portfolio of work, he knew he'd found the person for his portrait.

He turned to his secretary. As he did so, Hannah seemed to start towards him, then checked herself. Interesting. Did she think he was about to leave? Perhaps she wanted this commission more than she was prepared to admit? If so, everyone had their price. And he was prepared to pay a high price for her. Hannah Barrington was the best, and he'd have nothing less. *'Start as you mean to finish,'* his English nanny had used to say, teaching him her language as a young boy and what it meant to be leader of his principality. Better a foreigner who knew the value of royalty and duty, than his father, who valued none of those things. The lessons Alessio had learned at his knee were all about excess, indulgence and infidelity. Not the qualities of the leader Alessio wished to aspire to be.

Stefano raised an eyebrow as Alessio approached looking far too entertained at developments. His friend, partner in crime in the years gone by and now private secretary remained his most trusted confidant.

'It gives me great satisfaction that there's one woman in the world who's immune to your charms,' Stefano said in their native Italian, presumably so Signorina Barrington couldn't understand. 'Although you're not being charming today.'

Whilst he knew it was rude, Alessio didn't switch to English, and wouldn't until he had his solution. 'I need to know the state of my diary. I've *no* need to charm anyone.'

He'd set aside that reputation years ago. Alessio would admit in his youth he had relished in the position his birth gave him. He wasn't proud of those things now, especially the string of women who had cemented his playboy reputation. *Like father, like son*, the press used to say. A creep of disgust curled inside him. Not now. An advantageous marriage to a perfect princess was next on his agenda. To give Lasserno the stability it had lacked since his mother's death. Some heirs to continue his line. The royalty in Lasserno would soon be feted in its perfection, not mocked for its all too human failings. That was his mission, and he would succeed.

Stefano pulled up Alessio's diary, showed it to him. Busy, but not impossible.

'Your problem is that you don't like people saying "no" to you,' Stefano murmured. In English this time.

How many times had he tried to stop his father? Curb his behaviour? It was what he'd ostensibly been brought home to do, ripped out of his life showjumping and studying in the UK when his mother had fallen ill, because at least when she was well she'd formed some sort of brake on his father's worst excesses. And yet when he'd brought up ideas to reinvigorate the economy and tourism in a country whose beauty and natural riches were equal to anywhere in their close neighbour, Italy, he'd been met with disparaging refusal. No answers as to why his ideas wouldn't work. Nothing at all.

Stefano was correct. Alessio didn't like being told *no* on things he was right about. Not without a sensible reason. Since his father's abdication he'd not heard that cursed word from one of his government or advisors. It was…gratifying in a way he could never have imagined. A vindication of all he'd been trying to achieve over the years.

Alessio turned his attention to Hannah. Checked his watch. 'I will not write answers to your questionnaire, but I do have some limited time in my schedule.'

Time he could control. Leaking of information he couldn't.

A slight frown creased her brow and he wasn't sure whether the disapproval was back, or whether something else was at play.

'Then I can't—'

'My calendar is free of more onerous engagements. You wish to know me to paint my portrait? You'll travel to Lasserno. Become my official artist for two weeks. Follow me and learn about me. It should be enough.'

He could almost *sense* the weight of Stefano's incredulous stare but he didn't much care what his best friend thought at this moment. The woman in front of him had his complete focus. The plump, perfect peach colour of her mouth. The rockpool-green of her eyes. Eyes which stared deep inside as if they saw the heart of him. Eyes a man could drown in and die happy if he allowed himself, which Alessio could never do. It was no matter. He was used to compartmentalising that side of himself. There would be *no* rumours of improper behaviour on his part. His life was one of supreme control, Lasserno his only mistress.

She planted her paint-stained hands on her hips. 'Now, look. That's—'

'Not your process. I'm aware. This will be better.'

He could get anyone else to paint him. Most people would climb over themselves to take the commission and the accolades it would afford. In coming to his decision he'd been shown the work of many artists who were all superb and could acquit themselves admirably. The minute he saw Hannah Barrington's work, he knew. It was her he must have. No one else would do. And yet here she stood, utterly uncompromising. As if she were still intent on *refusing* him. The challenge of it set his pulse beating hard. He'd not felt anything like it since the last time he'd taken his stallion, Apollo, over the high fence behind the vineyards on the castle grounds.

'I have other clients.' Whilst her hands were still firmly on her hips, her teeth worried furiously at her bottom lip.

'You have an agent. She can tell clients you're painting a portrait of a prince. They'll understand, because my patronage will increase the value of their own pictures. I promise, this commission will be the *making* of you.'

'It's *two weeks* away from my home. You're not the only busy person in the room.' All the glorious fire in her, such a contrast to the cool mint of her eyes. For a moment he wished he were an ordinary man who could explore these ordinary desires, but that was a folly he would not indulge in.

This portrait, the *perfect* portrait, would show the world exactly how he meant to carry on his role as a leader. It would be the best. *He* would be the best prince Lasserno had seen in its long and proud history. He would write over his father's legacy, scratching it out in a neat and perfect script till it disappeared and was forgotten.

Hannah was the first piece in a larger puzzle. Time to sweeten the deal. To make it irresistible.

'I'll offer you *five* times your normal fee for the inconvenience.'

Her nostrils flared, and her eyes sparked at the mention of increasing her fee. Avarice was something he understood, a common currency, and he was happy to fuel it so long as it was legal and he got his way in the end. His former girlfriend, Allegra, was a perfect study in how money won over loyalty. Luckily he had more than the reporter had offered for a story on how his father had been picking gems from the crown jewels and giving them away as favours. Replacing them with paste. He'd never forgotten the lessons learned in that episode about unburdening yourself to the wrong person.

Hannah opened her mouth to speak. Alessio held up his hand, because there was more.

'*But* you accompany me as official palace artist in residence. You won't receive a better offer from any other client,' he said with a smile which felt like victory. 'Take it…or leave it.'

CHAPTER TWO

HANNAH SQUIRMED, TRYING to get comfortable in the chair on which she'd been directed to sit by Alessio's secretary. Who'd have thought something so ornate, with all its carved wood and brocade upholstery, could be so hard and uncompromising? A bit like its owner, and maybe that was the point. Being left like this to await *His Highness* held all the appeal of that one time she'd been sent to the headmaster at her austere boarding school for *'having your head in the clouds rather than in reality, Miss Barrington'*. No sympathy for the plight of a teenager who'd been ripped from everything she knew and loved.

She'd received a detention that day for telling him that reality sucked. After losing her parents, her imagination was a safer place to reside. Drawing obsessively. Trying to remember every line of their faces as the memories faded. The love she saw when they'd looked at her, rather than the feigned interest of her uncle and aunt.

She shut those thoughts down. They had no place here. Hannah stared at the looming oak doors of what she'd been told was the Prince's office. Everything seemed to loom in an ominous way here, in this imposing castle which rose from a landscape of olive groves and vineyards in turreted glory. Hannah worried at a tiny thread which dared to loosen itself from the chair's rich brocade. Her imagination didn't seem safe now, with Hannah spending far too much time dreading the shape of the next fortnight. Alessio was a reminder of that day, of all she'd lost. She took a deep breath, chased away old memories of her time before the accident when her reality had allowed her to dream of princes who set her heart fluttering complicated rhythms. Of a time when her parents had said she could have anything she wanted if she dared to dream, such as one day riding for her country as Alessio did. Thoughts of a time *before* had started nipping her heels with her arrival in Lasserno polished, primped and plucked. Sue had taken to Prince Arcuri's invitation with an unhealthy enthusiasm, seeing it as her only chance to turn Hannah into something she was not—a woman of the world.

Hannah looked down at her hands. They were almost as unrecognisable as the rest of her with manicured nails, moisturised cuticles and not a stain of paint to be seen. Her hair had been stylishly trimmed, and brows sculpted to perfection. At home in England Hannah never needed much. No fancy dresses or make-up. Simple food on the table. She didn't go out. Her life was paint and canvas, palette and brush. Her art was her work and her work was her life, but Alessio's commission dictated there were some things she required.

New clothes to suit the list of occasions he'd sent

were packed in a large suitcase. Well, not exactly new.
Her uncle's duplicity meant haunting charity shops, but
with a bit of inventive tailoring she'd come up with a
wardrobe that would satisfy the eyewatering requirements of His Royal Highness, the proverbial pain in her
backside. But, standing in front of a mirror this morning in her jeans and boots, tailored navy jacket with
crisp white blouse, she'd been unrecognisable. Hannah
didn't know who the person was, staring back at her.
She wasn't sure she liked it.

One of the oak doors glided open. Her stomach
twisted into sharp, complicated knots as Stefano
stepped into the hall. She'd come to know him a little
over the past week when she'd been getting everything
in order to come here. His missives had been polite, his
manner on the phone efficient, sympathetic and kind,
but she'd been able to glean nothing about his employer
from him. All she'd discovered had been found online.

That the press believed the man's austere demeanour hid greater sins.

'His Highness will see you now.'

She walked through the open door and it thudded
shut behind her. She took a few steps over the plush
crimson carpet then stopped, overwhelmed by the sheer
scale of the room.

Magnificent frescoes covered the ceiling. Adorning the walls were paintings of what must have been
former rulers. Uniformed and striking a pose, warriors
on horseback with swords drawn, all staring down in
their own princely kind of way from their vast gilded
frames. But more magnificent than anything else in the

opulent space was a man lit up in a shaft of sunlight like a god. Standing behind an expansive antique desk, he outshone any of his forebears, more regal than all of them put together in his dark suit and ultramarine tie.

She almost forgot herself as she stared, Alessio's black hair gleaming, his intense eyes hooded and assessing, the slash of one aristocratic eyebrow raised quizzically. What were all those rules she had to remember again? Sensible thought had fled. Before she made a total fool of herself, she gave a hasty curtsey because it seemed the thing to do, then hurried towards the desk. He made some dismissive waving kind of motion which she took to mean, *Have a seat*, and sank into the armchair opposite. Just in time, because her legs seemed like overcooked noodles in their inability to hold her up. The corner of his mouth threatened an almost smile, and her heart skipped a few beats, its rhythm constantly out of synch in his presence.

'You had a good flight?'

'The royal jet was an extravagance.' With all its buttery leather and plush carpets. She'd been treated like a princess by the efficient flight crew. 'I could have flown commercial.'

'Think of it as a reward for uprooting your life over the next fortnight. I trust your other clients weren't too disappointed about your upcoming absence.'

She noticed it wasn't spoken as a question.

Positively enthusiastic had been the general response. The Prince had been irritatingly right. They all saw the value of their own portraits increasing because she'd agreed to take on the commission. She'd been surprised they hadn't met her at the airport and thrown streamers in a grand farewell as she boarded the aircraft. She shook her head, which earned her another tilt of his mouth in what she suspected was Alessio's version of a smile. Her silly little heart tripped over itself at how the tiny move softened every harsh feature on his face to something more. More handsome, more vital, more… human.

But this man wasn't human, he was a prince. Unattainable. Untouchable. As a young girl she dreamed of princes, but dreams didn't make reality. She could never forget it.

He sat in the leather chair at his desk. Even that move was perfectly executed. 'I thought we would have a brief discussion about expectations whilst you're here.'

'You mean, in addition to the indexed folder I was given on the plane?' There seemed to be so many dizzying rules and requirements, how to address staff, what to wear. An agenda for almost every minute of the day. It was no wonder the man in front of her looked so serious. There didn't seem to be a moment when he sat still, apart from when he was asleep, because the time he 'retired' had been scheduled in as well. When was there ever space to simply *be*? Sit on a comfortable couch, with a warm drink in hand, and stare out of a window at a view. Imagine…a different life.

She looked at him, sitting straight and perfect and still. Not a hair out of place. Not a wrinkle in his shirt. As if he were carved out of painted stone. It seemed he was more statue than flesh and blood.

How exhausting.

'At all times, your behaviour reflects on me. I ask you to recognise that and adjust your manner accordingly.'

She sat up a little straighter in her seat, the heat flaming in her cheeks. A slice of something hot and potent cutting through her. 'I might not be aristocracy but I wasn't brought up in a shoebox. I know how to behave in civilised society.'

He cocked his head. Those umber eyes of his fixed on her with an almost otherworldly intensity. 'How gratifying to hear. When we're in public together, you'll walk behind me. The only woman who will ever walk at my side is my princess.'

'So where is this princess now? Do I get to meet her too?'

'There is no princess yet.'

'Shame. I thought she might be able to give me some tips. Juicy gossip even.'

The perfect Prince's eyes narrowed. His lips tightened.

'There is no *juicy gossip*. My life is my country. My country is my life. That is all you need to know.' His voice was ice. The cold blast of a winter gale. A tremor shuddered through her at the chill of his tone. She almost believed there was nothing more to him than this and didn't know why that thought left an ache deep inside, because it struck her as sad.

'Duly noted,' she said. Her answer seemed to mollify him. He gave a curt nod in reply.

'When we are in public you will refer to me as Your Highness or Sir.'

'I've read the rulebook, though there was one thing

it didn't address.' She leaned back into the soft upholstery of the armchair and tried to relax, though nothing
about the man sitting opposite encouraged her to do so.
'What about when we're in private?'

'There will be no *"in private".'*

Hannah looked about the vast room, through the windows that gave a view of rolling hills and olive groves
beyond. Pencil pines spearing upwards from a garden
like dark green sentinels. 'We're alone now.'

'Stefano.'

'Si?'

Hannah whipped round. Stefano stood just inside
the closed doors of the room. He gave her a wry smile.
She turned back to Alessio. Crossed her legs. Clasped
her hands over her knee. He followed her every move,
almost as if he were cataloguing her.

'Where were you hiding the poor man—in a cupboard?'

'There is a chair, in an alcove, inside the door. However, where Stefano sits is immaterial. What is material
is that we will not be alone.'

'Then how am I meant to begin the process of painting your portrait?'

'I would have thought it quite easy. Brush, canvas.'

She shook her head. 'I can't work with strangers…
loitering about. Portrait painting is a contract between
two people. The artist and the subject. Of its nature
it's…intimate. I—'

'So you have said before. You don't get to dictate
terms, Signorina Barrington.'

No. There was a way she worked and, although she

tried to be a little flexible, the way he spoke to her rankled. She clenched her hands a bit harder round her knees.

'It's a wonder you don't pick up a brush and paint yourself...*Your Highness*.'

Everything about him seemed impassive, inscrutable. Having barely any expression, his face was marked only by a cool, regal kind of presence. She could get the measure of most people, but never the measure of him. Even as a far younger man, there'd been nothing on his face to tell what he might be thinking. Like a blank canvas waiting for the first, defining brushstroke.

'If I could, I would.' Alessio sat back in his leather chair, which creaked as his weight shifted. Steepled his fingers. 'However, there's a reason I engaged you and that's because you're reputedly the best. I will have *nothing* but the best.'

A vice of tightness crushed her chest. Right now, she wasn't at her best. What her uncle had done had floored her. She had thought she could at least trust her family. Now she was being forced to take this commission due to circumstance, which was not the way she'd ever worked. What would her parents have thought of all this? They believed they'd ensured the security and comfort of their only daughter and she'd let it slip away by being too absorbed in her art and not keeping a close enough eye on things, till it was too late and the money gone. The threat of tears burned the back of her nose. Even after nine years the grief still hovered close. All these things had weighed on her and right now her thoughts were not about colour and light, or the gentle tilt of someone's almost smile, but on survival again.

Though that might suit a painting of this man. The expressionless quality. She could try losing herself in that, a simplicity which meant she didn't need to fight the canvas to find the heart of him. Because there was nothing in his face she could grasp, apart from the impact of his sheer masculine beauty. Like the statue of David. Exquisite, perfect, coldly etched. She doubted he had a warm, beating heart. But in the end to do her best, to paint what critics said she was renowned for, she needed *something* curious for her brushstroke to shape. Some expression to show the person before her was man, not marble. Because sadly she was a portrait artist, not a sculptor.

She stood and walked towards a wall on which one portrait hung, of a man sitting on a golden chair. Old. Imposing.

'I didn't invite you to leave your seat.' Alessio's voice was cool as the blast of air-conditioning on a hot summer's day. She wheeled round. He was still seated himself. Was there something in that dossier she'd been given to read about this? She couldn't remember, though the man probably wasn't used to having anyone turn their back on him. Still, whilst he was a prince, she was a grown woman. She'd accord him the respect required because of the quirk of his birth, but asking for permission to stand?

Ridiculous.

'That's going to make things difficult if I need to ask you for permission whenever I have to do something.

Your Highness, may I drink my glass of water? Your Highness, may I use the bathroom? Your Highness, may I apply this charcoal to paper?'

He swivelled his chair to face her, gazing at her with an intriguing intensity, as if she were an olive he was about to skewer in the tines of a martini fork.

'There are rules by which the palace and my country is run. Those rules keep chaos away from the door. In this place, you follow mine.'

'That's not going to work when I'm trying to draw or paint you.'

'We'll see.'

'So let me ask.' She swept her hand across the room, taking in all the ancestors hanging on his walls, staring out at them disapprovingly. 'Given you have an opinion on all things, what do you want your portrait to look like?'

He frowned, making the merest of creases in his perfectly smooth forehead, but she saw it none the less. 'Isn't it your job to decide?'

'How about that one?' She pointed to a man on horseback in a grand uniform braided with gold. There was no emotion on his face at all, nor in the way he watched the room impassively, with dark eyes. All the emotion was contained in the wild eyes of the rearing bay on which he sat, as if it were nothing but a plump little pony and he was going for a quiet afternoon ride. 'He looks suitably warrior-like.'

She could imagine Alessio that way. She'd seen him ride, the fearlessness which made everyone hold their breath. The memory was like a stab at her heart, a constant reminder of everything she'd lost. Because she'd loved flying over jumps too. Encouraging herself and her horse to go hard, be better.

'Since we're not at war, no.'

Relief crashed over her like waves in a storm. Not on horseback, then.

'What about him?' She pointed to another grand portrait. The man on the gilded seat. With distant eyes and a hard mouth. His demeanour stern, looking like a disapproving relative. One hand clasping a gleaming sceptre. The other gripping the arm of the chair on which he sat. A large, bejewelled ring adorning his finger. Not a relaxed pose, even though you couldn't tell from his face. The face told her nothing. 'He's sitting on a throne. Very regal and proper.'

'The throne is…no.'

Alessio stood and walked towards her. His flawless grey suit gripping the masculine angles of his body. Every movement long and fluid. It was clear this was his domain and he was comfortable in it. He moved next to her. Not too close, but any distance was not far enough. He had a presence. Not threatening, but overwhelming, as if everything gravitated towards him. She swallowed, her mouth dry, her heart tripping over itself.

'Then who do you want to be? How do you want to be seen?'

He stared down at her. Like a ruler lording over his subject. Except she'd *never* be that. But still, he radiated such authority she almost wanted to prostrate herself in front of him and beg forgiveness for some minor and imagined infraction.

'I *will* be the greatest prince Lasserno has ever had. That is how I will be seen. Nothing less will do.'

As she looked into his coldly beautiful face, Hannah had no doubts he'd achieve it. Her only problem was, how on earth was she going to paint it?

He should have remained seated. He shouldn't be standing anywhere near her, but he was sucked into Hannah's orbit like a galaxy falling to its doom in a black hole. He still couldn't overcome the niggling sensation that he knew her. That alone should have sounded some kind of warning, but he was too enthralled by the way she fought him to worry about a creeping sense of *déjà vu*. Most people bowed or curtseyed. Pandered to his every whim. She didn't seem inclined to do any of those things. She treated him as if he were nobody at all.

It should annoy him, and there was a thread of cool irritation pricking through his veins, but it tangled with something far hotter and more potent. Especially now. When he had last seen her she had been sweetly dishevelled. All mussed up and messy. Somehow completely unattainable because of it. She had looked as if she had no place in his world since there was nothing messy about his life. Not any more. Not since his mother died and he had had to grow up fast, pulling things together because his father had made enough mess for a hundred men.

Yet Hannah today...

Her hair wasn't some tangle of a bird's nest knotted carelessly on top of her head. It swung past her shoulders in a fall of sleek dark chocolate. Soft layers framed her face. Standing this close, he was captivated by her hypnotic green eyes, a wash of deep gold surrounding her pupils, which made them gleam as mysteriously as a cat's. She wasn't paint-spattered, as if that had been some kind of barrier separating them. Her shoes weren't trainers, but polished black knee-high boots which wrapped round her slim calves. Dark jeans hugged her gentle curves. A crisp white shirt was unbuttoned enough to interest, but too high to give anything but a frustrating hint of her cleavage. Somehow, in this moment she looked more woman and less...waif.

What the hell was he doing? It was as if without the paint she'd been stripped of her armour as his artist and become someone attainable. She could never be that. She couldn't be *anything* to him. He was on a quest for his bride, to join him on the throne. A professional matchmaker was putting a list together at this very moment. And now he'd set down that path, his behaviour must be impeccable. No casual liaisons to report to the press in a tell-all that sought to bring him down to his father's level where Alessio would *never* go.

This woman, whilst beautiful and challenging, was effectively his employee. Someone to be afforded appropriate distance and dutiful respect. Not to be the subject of carnal thoughts about her mysterious eyes, or how luscious and kissable her mouth appeared when smoothed with a little gloss...

He stepped away. She'd travelled many hours to be here, and yet he'd brought her to his office and not even offered her refreshments. No doubt she'd need her room and a rest. He'd ask Stefano to take her there and he'd work to regain his equilibrium.

She took a step towards him, hands on her hips. Eyes intent. A picture of defiance. Nothing like the behaviour dictated to her by the dossier he'd asked Stefano to put together, which was as much about his protection as hers.

'If I'm going to paint the *greatest* prince Lasserno has ever had, I need to see where I'm going to work.'

'Of course, follow me.' He said the words without thinking, before his brain engaged to remind him the less time spent in her presence the better. But it didn't matter as his feet carried him towards the door of his office with her following behind. Past Stefano, who simply looked at him with a quizzically raised brow that had become all too familiar since Hannah had entered his life, rose, and followed as well. Against all better judgement, Alessio almost stood him down. Told him to get back to whatever he was doing on his phone and he would handle this, but his better judgement won.

Nowadays, it always did.

'Your home is beautiful,' Hannah said in a breathless kind of voice better suited to quiet, candlelit dinners aimed at seduction than a stroll through the palace halls, but this place inspired similar reactions in those who'd never seen it before. There was nothing special about her.

'Thank you.' He supposed it was the polite thing to say, but he always felt more of a custodian than anything else. It was all a workplace to him. 'My ancestors built it as a fortress in the Renaissance. However, they

refused to eschew comfort and style over practicality
on the inside. It was designed to intimidate those who
sought to intrude, and delight those invited in.'

Which is what the tour guides parroted, through the
public areas. He'd learned their script. It was easier that
way, because his view of the place was tainted by the
memories of a childhood where even as a young boy
he had recognised the chilly dysfunction between his
parents, which had soon descended into a fully blown
cold war. Before his innocence and any belief his father could be a good man had been shattered for ever in
the throne room he would only sit in once, to take the
crown. Then he would never enter it again.

'What was it like living here? In all of this? Did you
ever break anything precious?'

The only precious thing broken here was trust.
'Never broken anything, no. I was the perfect child.'

'Of course you were. Striding the halls with purpose,
even as a ten-year-old.'

No, he'd been playing hide-and-seek with Stefano
in places he should not be, when he'd sneaked into the
forbidden throne room. Seen his father, with a woman
bent over the arm of the throne. Alessio's stride faltered.
Hannah almost crashed into him but pulled up close.
He knew. He could almost feel her enticing warmth. He
turned to the window overlooking a garden.

'I thought you might enjoy the view. Stefano's ancestors designed the garden in the formal Italian style.
I'm sure he'd like to tell you about it.'

Any more quizzical looks from his best friend and
Stefano's brows would end with a permanent home in

his hairline. Alessio allowed him to tell the story of the famous garden with its clipped hedges and fountains. He stood back, letting the chatter wash over him. Taking slow breaths. *'You will not tell your mother. This is our secret.'* Both his father's cold eyes and the glassy ones of the woman had been on him that day. He could barely understand why his father's hands twisted into her hair as if it had to hurt, though the look on her face spoke nothing of pain, even to his young brain. He hadn't known why their clothes were in disarray, or why his father's free hand had seemed to be in places it shouldn't on a woman, or so he'd thought as a child.

All he knew was that what he was seeing was *wrong*. He'd come to realise later what had been going on in the throne room. How his father had been defiling it. Each day he felt tainted by the creeping guilt at keeping his father's dirty secrets, because the man had made him party to more than one young boy should know. It was as if he'd been trying to mould Alessio into his own, dissolute image to spite his mother.

Lost in his own thoughts, Alessio had failed to realise Stefano and Hannah were now silent.

'Enough of gardens?' he asked, trying to sound suitably composed and regal. He hadn't been assailed by that memory for years and couldn't fathom why it would creep out of its dark, muddy hole to ambush him now.

'It's very beautiful and…ordered.'

'That's the way I like it.' His own thoughts right now were a messy jumble of memories that should never have seen daylight again.

'Do you ever walk in it? Take time to, I don't know, smell the flowers?'

'I… There are no flowers.' Where was all this uncertainty coming from? His role and what was required of him was *all* about certainty. He straightened, remembered exactly who he was. 'As for aimless wandering, I don't have time.'

Stefano had stepped back to his position three paces behind, but Hannah stood right next to him. Looking up with her entrancing green eyes. Lips slightly parted as though there was something always on the tip of her tongue to say.

He had no doubt she'd say it.

'Important prince and all, I know. That's something I need to talk to you about. The time you've allowed for me.'

He'd asked Stefano to schedule the barest minimum for formal sittings. She was following him about like a shadow for the next fourteen days. What more did she need?

'I'm a busy man.'

'Places to be. Country to run. I've seen your diary, but I need more. And I'm talking hours, not minutes.'

They neared the door of her rooms and the adjoining parlour which he had thought would be the perfect place for her to work. Like her studio in England. He'd searched the palace for somewhere with the same alignment. A similar light to fill the room, although here the sun streamed in a bit more brightly than in her own studio. There was no rambling garden outside, but the view was pleasant enough, he supposed. He never really looked any more, too occupied with briefings from his government to gaze at the horizon and contemplate the landscape.

'I can find more, if it's what you require. Perhaps you could accompany His Highness on some...unofficial engagements.' Stefano this time. It was as if both were conspiring against him. 'There's a hospital visit, to see children.'

Those visits were *private*, never made for accolades. 'The children aren't some circus where you watch them perform.'

Hannah frowned. 'I'd never treat sick children that way. But I need to see all aspects of you, not just the official ones. That's what will make my portrait the best.'

Before he could protest, she turned to Stefano and smiled. Wide, warm, generous. The type of smile which sent a lick of heat right to his core. One you could bask in. It had no agenda or artifice at all to add a chill to the edges of it. 'Thank you. Any extra time you can find me would help my work.'

Better her smile be for his friend than him. There was no place for it in his ordered, planned life. One where everything was cool and clinical. That was the way he preferred things to be. Like the hedge garden, clipped and precise. Even though he now felt inclined to take to the palace gym and hit a punching bag, hours earlier than his normal training session, rather than speak to the finance minister about fiscal policy and Lasserno's deficit.

The doors of the room where Hannah would live

loomed large. 'Stefano will show you where everything is. I'll leave you to him.'

A gracious host would escort his personal guest in, ensure she was settled. That she was happy with everything, so she'd gift him some genuine smiles which chased away the cold. Instead Alessio strode down the corridor away from Stefano and Hannah, protocol and graciousness be damned. The temptation snapped at him like a whip and he never gave in to temptation.

Smiles like Hannah's were dangerous, because they chased away common sense.

CHAPTER THREE

HANNAH STOOD IN what was best described as an expansive parlour, in the suite of her rooms. It was if she had been dropped into a fairy tale, except she didn't feel like a princess, but an impostor.

Everything here was too magnificent to touch. Her canopied bed with its silks and embroidery in the palest cerulean blues. Magnificent tapestries of pastoral scenes with shepherdesses and frolicking lambs adorning the golden walls. The deepest of carpets she stood on and wiggled her toes into, as if she were walking on a cloud. It reminded her of how threadbare her life back in England seemed to have become, because there was never a time here that anything would be hard or cold. In this palace, nothing would deign to be anything other than perfect. As perfect as the man who ruled here.

The man she was now waiting for, because her equipment had been unpacked and set up in this room to catch the best light. She'd only brought the bare necessities to Lasserno, pencils and charcoal so she could study and sketch, learn about the Prince who would be taking up her next few months of waking thought. She'd set up what she needed on a small side table next to a chair, ready for when His Highness deigned to grace her with his lofty presence.

A sickening knot tightened in her stomach. As if she needed to run rather than be faced with a blank canvas, her empty sketchbook. Hannah ground her teeth against the rising queasiness. She usually loved the challenge of getting to know a new subject. Finding the key to a person, the one that unlocked every brushstroke she'd put down in the time it took to perfect the essence of them on a canvas. But a lot was riding on this commission. Her future. Her home. It wasn't that she was afraid of doing a job she knew so well, afraid of the thrill of knowing a person, of finding the man Alessio hid. Not at all. It was what she stood to lose if she couldn't fulfil it.

She checked the time on her phone. For a man who wanted his portrait painted, he really didn't want to spend much time anywhere near her. Most people enjoyed their sessions, or so she'd been told. She did. She loved learning someone's nuances, the privilege of being allowed to glimpse a private part of a person that many never saw. Alessio seemed to think she could paint him from memory alone. He probably believed that he was unforgettable, so one glance would be all she needed.

He might not be entirely wrong about that.

Enough. She grabbed her sketch pad and watercolour pencils. There was a pretty desk with a view from large windows, overlooking fields of grapes and olives out towards Lasserno's capital. In a copse of ancient olives there peeked a small, domed structure. Like a chapel, or perhaps a folly, although Hannah didn't think Alessio would allow anything so whimsical as that on the palace grounds. The whole scene shimmered with the warmth of a Mediterranean summer. She sat at the fragile-looking desk and sketched, losing herself in perfecting the cobalt blue of the sky, the ochres, umbers and greens of the landscape glowing in the sunshine.

The muffled noise of a well-oiled door handle and hinges made her turn, spring from her chair as if the seat burned her.

Alessio strode into the room, all of him pressed into hard lines with a flawlessly cut suit and pristine white shirt. A tie of carmine sat at his throat with its fat knot, looking tight enough to strangle. Except she was the one who couldn't get any air, as if he'd sucked it all from the room. He glanced at the gleaming gold watch at his wrist then to her as she wobbled in an uncertain half-dip because she wasn't sure of the protocol if she was going to see him multiple times a day. He flicked his hand in a dismissive kind of way.

'No curtseying unless we are in public.'

'We sort of are, since your secretary's here.' She gave Stefano a little wave. He smiled back in his own handsome kind of way, though it was nothing like the glowering magnificence of his imposing boss.

Alessio looked at her, then to Stefano, and his eyes narrowed. 'You don't strike me as someone who's obtuse, Signorina Barrington.'

'I'm not. You're the one who sent me a volume of rules to follow.'

'So you're prepared.'

'They make me nervous I'm going to get something wrong.' Everything about this made her nervous, particularly him. It was as if all common sense and the need for self-preservation fled in his presence. 'I'm painting your portrait, not stepping out as your significant other. Will you give your princess the same sort of list?'

'No, because, being a princess, she'll know the rules already.'

'Rigidity and protocol don't fit in well with my work. How about we throw away the rules when we're in here?'

He raised one dark, imperious brow. Tugged at the cuffs of his shirt. Checked the time again.

'Who am I to stop you, since it appears you already have?' Alessio stalked towards her where she stood frozen in front of the spindly, gilded desk. She had that sensation again, that she was an insect under a magnifying glass. Alessio loomed close. He wasn't threatening at all. It's that he had a presence. An aura that crammed the space full, till there was no room for anything else. Especially not sensible thought.

'What are you doing there?' He motioned over the sketch she'd started, of the view outside.

'In nine years I've barely gone a day without my art.' There'd been only a few. The anniversaries, where sometimes the grief would steal upon her with a more vicious attack than usual. Sapping her will to do anything but curl up in bed and weep. 'In the last week, I've missed three with all the planning and preparing and I needed to *do* something. It helps me—'

'Relax. I'm like it with horse-riding, yet I rarely get a chance any more.' She froze. The freedom of the ride. Soaring over the jumps in partnership with her horse. She used to revel in that joy too, until the day it represented everything she'd lost. She hadn't ridden since.

Alessio wasn't looking at her unfinished artwork right now, but out of the window, his eyes distant and unfocused. That small offering of something private about himself was a gift and she doubted he realised he'd given it to her. Then the distance in his eyes faded, and they narrowed. As if he'd come back to himself, was pulling himself into reality rather than some faded memories. The whole of him stiffened, and he became the ruler of Lasserno again, rather than a simple man.

'You're drawing with coloured pencils? It seems beneath your reported talents.'

She let out a slow breath, the precious moment lost. 'I use these because they're a challenge for me. Watch.'

She dipped a brush into a small glass of water which was probably crystal and not designed for this task. Alessio didn't seem to mind. He'd probably drunk from crystal since birth. Nothing as common as plain glass would deign to touch his perfect lips. She took the brush and swiped it gently over a part of the sketched scene. The pencil bled to paint in a wash of colour.

'Magic,' he said.

'Oil paints are forgiving. These, not so much. They're unpredictable, and it's harder to cover up your mistakes.'

'Like life,' Alessio murmured, or at least that was what she thought he said as he moved closer, leaning over the picture. She was sure there was something in that fat instruction booklet about not standing too near him, but for the life of her she couldn't remember what it might have said. Not with all the *proximity*. His height, his magnetic presence. The teasing scent of him, something masculine and fresh like the aftermath of a summer's storm. The warmth he radiated, almost better than morning sunshine. She wanted to lean into it and bask. But she was here to do a job. Having poetic thoughts about unattainable princes was not part of it.

She stood back. Put a respectable distance between them. Likewise, he seemed to shake himself out of the fascination for her simple artwork. He straightened, adjusted his tie. Checked his watch *again*.

'I have limited time. We should start. What do you need from me?'

She needed him to stop being so…him. Instead she pointed to a chair she'd manhandled into better light. He looked at it, at the scuffed carpet where she'd half dragged it across the room. Frowned, but said nothing, instead unbuttoning his jacket and lowering himself into the armchair. Watching her as his secretary watched them both.

'I need fewer people in the room. I can't concentrate like this.'

There were too many eyes on her. She took a slow breath to try and ease the weight of expectation in their stares.

'Stefano stays.'

So imperious. Hannah blew out a huff of breath, grabbed a fresh sketch pad and some sharp-as-a-needle pencils, then sat opposite him. His rich brown eyes fixed on her. There was something addictive about all that focus, as if she were the only person on earth.

Yet even though he sat in a comfortable armchair, he didn't look comfortable. There was nothing relaxed about him, as if he were on edge. *Waiting* for something to happen. Which seemed strange because the man ruled a country. She assumed anything that happened to him was entirely his choice and at his whim. Yet, for all the breathtaking perfection of him, he was still a human and she reminded herself that not all the people she painted were relaxed in the beginning.

'Today, I'll be doing a few sketches. All for reference.' He nodded as she opened her sketchbook. Alessio sat upright, not even his legs crossed. Impossibly formal. She didn't want to focus on his face, nor on those eyes which seemed to barely blink. The rest of him was stitched tight into his suit. But his hands... Veins and tendons corded under his golden skin.

She began to lightly sketch the shape. The elegant, blunt-cut nails. Ignored the slight dusting of dark hair over his metacarpals, hinting around the wrist from under the pure and flawless white cuffs of his shirt. She'd leave those details till later, but for now she marvelled in his long, strong fingers, curled tight over the arms of the chair.

'What have you been doing today?' she asked. The sun streamed through the mullioned windows, brightening the room. A light breeze drifted through one she'd opened earlier.

His jaw tightened. 'Ruling my country.'

'And that involves?'

'Making many important decisions.'

Which was no kind of answer at all. She snorted, looked up at him. His fingers flexed a little. Relaxed, but still not enough. 'Okay, you've been very...princely. Let's take a step back. What time did you get out of bed?'

'Four.'

'A morning person, then.'

His eyes narrowed the merest fraction. 'I'm a busy person.'

'No rest for the wicked?'

A muscle in his strong, square jaw ticked. 'You'll have to ask my father about that maxim.'

She hesitated for a second, the pencil no longer slipping so easily over the paper. When researching Alessio, as she did with every client, she'd read about his father. The man who'd abdicated under the cloud of some scandal. It was all a bit murky. As for the man in front of her, apart from his official website and carefully curated online presence, there was really nothing. Alessio Arcuri presented to the world like the perfect prince.

The press wondered whether Alessio was like his father, and only hid it better.

'Can you take a deep breath in and let it out slowly?'

The tips of Alessio's fingers seemed a little whiter on the arms of the chair, his fingertips denting the fine fabric.

'I don't know what you're asking of me.'

'You seem a bit...' she waved her left hand with the pencil in it, as if drawing in thin air '...rigid.'

'Signorina Barrington, I learned protocol and deportment in classes from the time I could speak.'

He leaned forward, his voice low and cool. Eyes flashing tiger-gold in something like a warning. His forearms now resting on his knees, hands in front. Such a compelling picture. She held her breath and waited for more.

'From the age of five, I could sit perfectly still and silent for well over an hour. Never once moving. If I did move, my tutor's dog had a habit of nipping my ankles. I didn't like getting bitten. So this is how I sit.'

She started another sketch of his hands now, with fingers clasped before him as if in some kind of fervent prayer.

'You can't position yourself like that all the time. What about when you're relaxing? Men, they slouch in a…manly kind of way. Lounging with intent.'

Not that she really had much experience in the way men sat, other than those whose portraits she'd painted, but at least they'd looked at home in the chair she'd placed them in. Alessio's secretary seemed to have relaxation down to an art, having perfected a kind of indolence in the back corner of the room. Or her father, who had always looked comfortable in front of the television with her mother, holding hands. She blinked away the tears her memory wrought. All she knew was that the Prince before her looked as if he were about to order someone's execution.

Perhaps her own. He raised a supercilious brow, his normally full and transfixing lips now a tight line. 'Are you accusing me of not being *masculine* enough?'

'No.' Not a single woman on the planet could ever accuse him of that. She stared at the dark shading of stubble on his jaw, even though it was mid-morning and he must have shaved, at the broadness of his shoulders, the narrow taper of his waist. She was almost suffocated by how masculine he was. All that testosterone made her quite giddy. 'You're the epitome of masculinity. That suit. The bold red tie saying *leader*. Does your valet choose the colour based on what duties you have to attend to? Red for ruling, blue for official visits, yellow for meeting children...'

'Now you're questioning my sartorial choices? What makes you assume I keep a valet?'

'I'm sure all princes have them. To...darn your socks if they get holes in?'

'My socks do not require darning.'

'No, they're probably woven from magical thread by some goddess. I imagine that's your style, impeccable as it is.'

Behind Alessio, his secretary jumped from his chair. He might have looked stricken, but instead he appeared to be choking.

Alessio stood too, and she was forced to look up at his imposing form, the energy around him almost palpable. Not so impassive now, with his jaw hard, nostrils flaring. Even if he wasn't a prince, this man could rule any room he entered.

'Stefano. Please attend the oracle and request the goddess weave me more socks whilst I deal with Signorina Barrington's mocking of me.'

'Any particular colour, Your Highness?'

'Black.' He turned and speared Hannah with a hot glare. 'The colour of my righteous anger.'

Alessio began to pace, something blazing and unfamiliar bubbling in his chest. After years of attempting to inject calm and order into the palace and his life, this woman seemed intent on destroying it in the space of a day. He could not allow anyone to witness it, sending Stefano away before the man fell about laughing, which would have led to jokes at his expense for weeks.

'Alizarin Crimson,' Hannah said.

'What?' He didn't understand her, not at all.

'That would be the colour of righteous anger. It's a deeper colour than simple red…solid, less flash. Now, if you were plain angry, the light version of cadmium red would suit better. So I suggest you should have sent Stefano for red socks rather than black.'

Alessio kept up his pacing, unable to sit still. No one questioned him any more, no one mocked him, or disagreed with what he said. After years of chaos in the palace, his rule was absolute. That was by his design, and his demand. People knew what he expected of them and complied. No arguments. Gone was the frustration at ideas cast aside, attempts to thwart his father ignored by those who sought to profit from Lasserno's losses. Graft, corruption and sheer negligence had been rooted out ruthlessly. Stefano argued he should release the reins, relax a little. Allow people to see the man rather than the Crown Prince. But that was the way to chaos, no matter what the press made up about him. The standards he set were highest for himself. His recent life was about calm and control. This? Hannah Barrington seemed designed to torment him.

'I don't want to speak about socks. What's the point of these ridiculous questions?'

All the while she'd sat there in her own chair. Wearing black leggings, and some kind of soft grey top which clung to her slender form, sheer enough so he could see the trace of a bra. No colour on her, yet she was the most vibrant thing in the room, and he couldn't look away. Right now she wasn't looking at him, instead gently sweeping an infernal pencil over the page as he wore a path through the carpet, burning through his frustration. She didn't seem to notice. Nibbling on her plum-coloured bottom lip. A slight frown on her brow. Such focus on a piece of paper, not on him.

'I'm trying to engage in conversation,' she said, 'which would be easier if you participated by conversing back.'

'I am speaking to you.'

She glanced up at him briefly, her gaze searching. Flickering over him as if in a quick and efficient study, then back down at the page in front of her. 'Conversation is a different thing entirely. It's an exchange. You're not exchanging, you're…dictating.'

He stopped behind the armchair in which she'd placed him. Gripped the back till his fingers crushed the exquisite fabric. He'd not sat all day, but had been solving a thousand small problems, and a few large ones, on the move. Reviewed the longlist of candidates for Lasserno's new princess. Whilst he'd wished to be anywhere but here, the thought of stopping for the brief hour he'd allocated to her today had been almost pleasant. Yet she'd kept talking, and those questions had dredged up memories and feelings he hadn't experienced in years. It was as though, if he let her speak any more, he might tell her everything that had plagued him since his mother's death.

'So you converse by asking about a valet? What other staff will you be enquiring about? Whether I have my own personal fingernail-buffer?'

He couldn't see what she was doing, the book in which she drew tilted the wrong way. She looked up again from her page. Cocked her head. Fixed her attention to his hands again. Her lips parted, then she went back to drawing.

'That *would* tell me a lot about you, but you strike me as…assured rather than vain.'

He couldn't help a bitter laugh. At least there he hadn't taken after his father. A man always seeking approval, adoration. Being feted for his looks. Searching out women to worship him. His wife's love had never been enough. In the end coldness and hatred was all that had fuelled their doomed marriage.

'So long as my suits fit, I have little interest. I don't need to appear on best-dressed lists year after year.' Unlike his father, who'd eschewed the court-appointed royal tailor for Savile Row. Almost putting the man and his family out of business, when they'd tended royalty in Lasserno for over a century. Alessio had rectified that slight, supporting locals who had a long and proud tradition rather than looking outside the country for what was easily supplied here.

Anyhow, what did a suit matter when all he wanted to do was spend the limited time available to him on horseback, as if to outride the weight of responsibility that some days seemed as if it could crush him? His suit was a mere costume he wore, the trappings of a leader. It said nothing about the man at all.

Hannah stopped drawing, looked at him again. Long, slow. Her gaze drifting over his face, lower. To his hands. Fixing itself there. The way she studied him took on a life of its own. His heart beat a little faster. An odd sensation stirring in his gut, almost like excitement. He released his grip on the chair in front of him and stood straighter. Was her assessment of him an artist's, or a woman's? Did she like what she saw? He didn't know why that last question was so important to answer, because the answer was meaningless and changed nothing.

'Your suit fits…exquisitely.' Her voice was soft, breathy, almost as if what she said surprised her. The tone of it stroked over his skin, touching him everywhere. Alessio relished the sensation. It was like being handed an unexpected gift.

Hannah placed her sketch pad and pencil face down on the carpet. Stood, pursed her lips. 'And I think that's half the problem. Let's start again. Your Highness, could you please take off your suit jacket and have a seat?'

Your Highness. Said with her perfect rounded vowels. A slight huskiness to it. He hesitated, almost as if being asked to remove his jacket were stripping him naked. As she waited for him she tucked an unruly strand of dark hair, that had escaped her efforts to secure it, behind her ear. Alessio peeled the jacket from his body, the air of the room cooling him as he did.

Hannah walked towards him, left hand outstretched. He handed her his jacket. She took it and hung it over the back of a small dining chair, running her hands over the shoulders. A stunning flash of heat tore through him as he imagined those hands stroking over his own shoulders. Something that could never, ever happen. He sat in the armchair again. Settling in to get comfortable when all of him was on edge. Tried to *lounge with intent*, whatever that meant.

'You should take off the tie.' Alessio didn't think. He moved his hands to the red silk. Loosened it, and only had a fleeting moment where he could finally breathe before his chest tightened again. He held out his hand with the tie and she took it, the minutest brush of her fingertips on his, and the world could have stopped turning, on the precipice of tempting desires he must ignore.

Was she affected too? Her hands caressed the tie, gently smoothing the fabric, wrapping it round her palm to create a perfect spiral and placing it on a side table. Then she faced him. Perhaps the colour was higher on her cheeks? Or perhaps he was projecting his own torrid desires onto her.

It had been a long time since he'd been with a woman. When he realised the extent of his father's profligate behaviour, he'd seen no choice but for his own to be exemplary. All his waking hours had been taken up with trying to draw attention from his father, hiding his ultimate disgrace, rebuilding Lasserno's reputation. He would not let his people suffer at the hands of his family. These things required him to be better. He shouldn't crave the softness of a touch. He'd inured himself to such things because of the job he must do. It required toughness, no distractions. He'd risen above it before. He would again.

But how for a few bright, blinding moments did he wish he could fall.

She moved closer again, looking down on him. A strange and discomfiting position to be in. As if for the first time he was at some kind of disadvantage, when his whole life had been full of the advantages of his position. Her eyes were luminous in the late-morning light. A mysterious wash of green and gold, like the ocean close to the shore. Hannah cocked her head. Pointed, waggling her finger at him. He shouldn't have tolerated that. It was a breach of protocol, but protocol be damned. He didn't care.

'The top two buttons as well.'

Dio, in this moment she could have him completely naked if she asked. The thrill of that thought was intoxicating. The whole atmosphere in the room thickened, time slowing to these perfectly innocent words weighted with his illicit imaginings. Alessio didn't even think. He undid the two buttons on his shirt. More slowly than he ought, since she kept her gaze on every move of his fingers, almost as if hoping he didn't stop, that he undid all of them.

Or that was what he imagined. In his fantasies he could allow it. Never in reality.

She moved her hand, as if she were reaching out

again. Hesitated. Checking herself. Her lips parted. Then she dropped her arm and stepped back. Shook her head.

'What?' His voice was rough as it ground out of him. Frustrated at the things he could not have.

Hannah went back to her chair. Grabbed her sketch pad and pencil. 'I thought you might run your hands through your hair. Make it a little untidy.'

Their gazes clashed and held. He'd look as if he'd rolled out of bed if he did that. Did she want him messy? As though they'd spent a night together? His hands involuntarily gripped the satiny fabric of the chair again, to hold on to something.

'But then I realise that untidy wouldn't be you… Your Highness.'

He almost shouted to her that yes, it was. He could be that man. He had been in the past, when life had been freer and he'd thought only of riding for his country, not taking the throne too soon and repairing the disaster wrought by his father. But she'd reminded them both, with his title, that he was born to a job and would not deviate. He clenched his teeth. Swallowed down the bitter taint of disappointment as she began her drawing again, with deft moves of her pencil that felt as if she were inscribing on his skin. He wondered what else she saw of him, with her artist's eyes.

'Could you answer a question for me?' she asked. 'One question, honestly, with no equivocation?'

Alessio gritted his teeth. He'd kept so much of himself private for so long, particularly after Allegra's attempts at courting the press, that agreeing to any question he didn't vet beforehand was unnatural to him. Most respectable journalists in Lasserno knew this and played the game with the rules he'd set. The tabloids made up what they wanted in the absence of a story. He didn't like this stranger, this young, almost guileless woman, demanding parts of him he rarely granted to anyone.

'Yes.' She didn't look up. Showed no reaction to his agreement at all. But he wasn't giving away everything without exacting a price. 'So long as you answer one of mine.'

Her head whipped up from the page. She was paying attention to him now, and something hot and potent thrummed through him. He liked it far too much.

'That's not how this works. It's all about you.'

'You want to know so much of others yet give none of yourself.' She nibbled on her bottom lip again, drawing his attention to her distracting mouth. The way her teeth worked on the soft flesh. He craved to soothe away the sting of her teeth, see if her lips were as soft as they looked.

'It's my job.'

'People might accuse you of having something to hide.'

He wasn't sure she had secrets. She'd been investigated before the commission for his portrait was requested. In his life now, that was a given. But in some perverse way he enjoyed her discomfort, since she was causing him so many inconvenient and uncomfortable thoughts of his own.

'I don't have any secrets. I just find people prefer

to talk about themselves. I'm not that interesting. But if you answer my question, you can ask one of yours.'

She shrugged, and the soft shirt she wore sagged a little, exposing the hint of a bra strap before she pushed it back onto her shoulder. But he didn't miss the slice of pale blue, and he firmly shut down imaginings of whether her underwear was lace or something practical. Instead, he checked his watch. Their hour had almost ended, and yet he didn't want to leave. How long could he wait here, sitting in the chair, before someone would come to find him?

'Then ask what you wish.'

'If you want to escape from it all, what do you do?'

He could have laughed, the answer so easy it required no effort at all. 'I ride my horses.'

Her look softened a fraction, or perhaps it was his imagination. The corners of her mouth turning up, her gaze seeming far away. It almost appeared wistful, but the moment was lost as she went back to her drawing. He could have asked her any question at all, but that fleeting look on her face spoke to him in some way.

'Do you ride, Signorina Barrington?'

Her pencil dragged to a stop on the page. Her eyes a little wider as she paled, looking almost...fearful.

'I—I haven't...not for a long time.'

He wondered whether she would answer more questions if he asked them, but a respectful knock sounded at the door. He let out a long, slow breath. The knock reminded Alessio of his real life, not the fantasy that he could do what he wished, without all the responsibilities he had. He rose from his chair as the door opened and

Stefano walked inside. Holding a pair of black socks. An eyebrow raised, meaning he would ask questions about what went on in this room whilst he was away, which Alessio would not deign to answer. He needed to go now, but his decision was simple. She wanted to get to know the man? He had the perfect answer.

'Prepare yourself. Tomorrow, meet me at the stables. Then we'll ride.'

CHAPTER FOUR

HANNAH HESITATED AT the door of the magnificent stables on the lower reaches of the palace grounds. Assailed by the earthy scents she'd once loved, of lucerne, hay and straw. In the past that smell had signalled her happiest moments. Spending time with her precious horse, Beau. The hours brushing him, mucking out the stables, never a chore. She'd dreamed of owning stables like this back then. Such fleeting, futile fantasies before everything had turned to dust.

The awe of the space mingled with a heaviness in her chest, making it hard to breathe. She didn't want the memories now. This stable, riding, were symbols of a life lost to her. There was no escaping it here. The glint of crushed metal, the tick of a hot, broken engine. The dread silence from her parents. The terrified whinnies of her mortally injured horse. It all came back with a sickening rush. She faltered for a second. Stood to take it in, work it through. For a moment, the pain of that day was as sharp and bright as if it had just happened. But she had no choice other than to be here. Hannah took a deep breath. This was simply a job. Though it didn't stop the sense of regret and loss almost overwhelming her.

She walked to where she'd been told to go. Where two horses now stood saddled, with a person she assumed was the groom. Their tack was shiny and perfect.

That sick feeling intensified…the roar of blood surging in her ears, her heart pounding against her ribcage. Everything was swirling in a dizzying attack to her senses of a day when life as she knew it had ended. She'd lost her hopes and dreams in the accident. Her whole life had changed. She'd rebuilt it, but some days the foundations seemed a little unstable. As if everything could fall apart again. Which was more truth than a lie, after what her uncle had done. A sense of betrayal sliced through her again, that the people she should have been able to trust had failed her. It all came down to work in the end, yet right now if she could turn around and flee, leave handsome princes and shattered dreams behind, she would. But her choices ended with her uncle's embezzlement. Hannah faltered, stopped for a second. Took some steadying breaths as her legs trembled.

How was she going to get on a horse's back, when she could barely walk to where they stood?

'Signorina Barrington?'

That voice from behind. Deep, with a lilting accent. Smoothing over her like some balm to her troubled soul. The prickling sensation of someone close. Alessio's presence penetrating the cold grief threatening to overwhelm her.

She turned. He crowded out everything else in the space, not as close as she'd thought, but it didn't matter how far away he stood, she was sure she'd still feel him. It was as if he had an aura a mile wide, obliterating her awareness of anything else. And if she'd been faltering before, right now she was paralysed.

She'd glimpsed him a few times at a distance when she'd been competing, dressed for competition himself. He'd been overwhelming then, to a young girl with hormones making themselves known in confusing ways, like a fairy tale brought to life. But nothing prepared her for this, Alessio in a short-sleeved polo shirt which showed off his tanned skin, the swell of his impressive biceps, the strength of his forearms. His legs, encased in buff breeches and riding boots, caused her mouth to dry. Because, whilst all of him was only hinted at under a suit, this figure before her wasn't the young man she'd pined over, whose riding she'd watched obsessively whenever she could find it. He was a thirty-one year old in his prime and it showed in every inch of him. His broad chest, muscular thighs. Which she probably shouldn't be staring at, and…was her mouth open? She closed it. She was only trying to get air, that was all. Trying to stop her heart pounding. But it wasn't the sickening rhythm of before, instead morphing into something harder, more insistent. The drumbeat of a pulse that spoke of a sultry type of rhythm she tried hard to ignore.

As she looked up from how well his breeches fitted and into his face, he frowned, the merest of creases in his otherwise unmarred forehead. Probably judging the worn old jeans she'd sneaked into her bag almost out of spite, because she was sure nothing that much past their prime would ever grace the palace walls.

'Are you all right?' Something about his question made everything inside her still. It was as if he saw her. 'You look pale. You're not afraid of horses, are you?'

She shook her head. The fear was not of the animals, but of the memories. 'No. Probably a little late to sleep, a little early to wake.' It wasn't exactly a lie. The thought of riding with him today had left her tossing and turning, with dreams of running after things she couldn't catch, of accidents she couldn't prevent. 'As I said, I haven't ridden for a while.'

Still, his gaze searched her. As if he realised she wasn't telling the truth. 'Come. Meet your horse. If you have any fears, she should allay them.'

He walked ahead of her, and for once she was happy to follow as his rule book dictated. It was no chore to watch his long, assured stride, taking in her fill of the broad shoulders tapering to his narrow waist. She shouldn't look, really, but what woman wouldn't stare at that backside? Her cheeks burned hot at the prickling awareness of him, and how magnificent he was. They arrived at the groom, and Alessio turned, the corner of his mouth quirking in a smile which told her he *knew* she'd been staring and didn't really mind.

Typical.

He reached out and rubbed the silky nose of an impossibly pretty dapple grey. 'This is Kestia. She's a placid mare who knows what she's doing. You'll have no trouble with her. I promise.' Alessio stared at Hannah as he said it, narrowed his eyes. Cocked his head a fraction.

She didn't like that look. It was as if he was contemplating things he didn't want to say. Hannah narrowed her own eyes back at him.

'You're not thinking that I'm a...troublesome mare, are you?'

His full and perfect mouth curled into something of a wry grin. Her breath caught. When he wasn't so stern and forbidding, he was the type of man who could cleave a woman's heart in two if she allowed it. Which was risky, when there were so few pieces of her heart left to break. Alessio placed a hand flat over his chest. 'I'd never think such a thing.'

She needed a distraction from him so she reached out and stroked down her horse's side with her flat hand. The coat was smooth and warm to the touch. Alessio watched the gentle move, before his umber eyes held her gaze for a heartbeat. Then it was as if he came to himself and stepped back, his face cool and impassive again. He moved to his own horse. A dark bay stallion. Tall. Clipped mane. Gleaming coat. His ears were pricked high and his eyes were alert. Nostrils flaring. The sort of horse she would have given anything to ride.

'He's magnificent,' she said, as Alessio took his mount's reins.

'Apollo's special. However, I've been ignoring him lately and if I don't take him out soon he'll punish me. His groom rides him but for some reason he prefers me. It seems we have an affinity.'

'You're both hot-blooded?' She didn't know where

those words had come from. They blurted out of her but both Alessio and his horse seemed tense, as if they were bristling to break into a run and never stop.

'He was inclined in the past to be more reckless than is good for him. He's fearless when sometimes he should be cautious.' Alessio stroked his horse's nose. 'He's settled since I've owned him. Is a champion in all ways.'

Alessio had been fearless too, once. She wondered what had happened to him and his showjumping. The reasons he'd stopped had been lost in the annals of history, the internet only briefly mentioning his riding. It was as though that part of him had been scrubbed away. But she remembered him. He'd left her breathless, even then. She had scoured the internet for videos of his events. Watching him over and over. Why give it all away when he was rising to the top of an elite field with everything ahead of him?

'Would you compete again? With Apollo?'

'I have a country to rule. There is no time for anything else.' Alessio's eyes were bleak and distant. He cleared his throat, nodded to the little grey. 'We should ride. We don't have much time, and a dinner tonight to ready ourselves for.'

The dinner. Of course. Though she wondered how much time he thought she needed to get ready, because it was hours away yet.

They mounted their horses with the assistance of the groom, and she settled herself into the saddle, the warmth of the animal's body seeping into her. Familiar and heartbreaking in so many ways but exhilarating in others. The sensation washed over her again, here, up high. Of being capable of anything. That was how she'd felt once. As if life were full of promise rather than weighed down by reality.

How she wished she could be that sixteen-year-old girl again. To have the freedom and belief that everything would always be okay. To have the hope for life and love, rather than the inevitability that loss was always the risk when you loved another. She had taken years to contemplate dating, at Sue's encouragement. She'd been introduced to someone who might not have made her heart race but seemed kind. Solid and safe. She had thought there was something there, allowed herself the tiniest shred of hope that there was a future worth waiting for. Only to have it crushed when he had said art took up too much of her time. He had wanted some fun, and that it was painting or him. As if she could stop something that was intrinsic to her being. And with his words, any hope had died too. It was an unacceptable risk now. The prickle in her eyes and sting in the back of her nose warned of tears. The grief bubbling close, especially here. Of what she'd lost, sure, but also of what might have been. She took a deep breath, steadied herself. Loosened her grip on the reins and tried to relax a bit.

This fortnight was a job. This moment, a simple ride on a sweet mare with a subject she was supposed to paint. Nothing more. And that subject looked incomparable astride his horse, Apollo prancing in anticipation of leaving the stables, Alessio's control light, brilliant.

'He's impatient to get going,' she said.

'Always.' Hannah wondered if he was talking about

his horse or himself—both looked outside the stable doors as if they wanted to bolt and never return. 'Are you ready?'

She nodded, the unsettled queasiness still rumbling around her stomach. Alessio walked them out of the stables and she rode beside him, the rhythm of it all familiar and as comforting as it was heartbreaking.

'I'm surprised Stefano isn't here with us.'

Alessio snorted and his horse flicked and twisted his ears, as attuned to his rider as his rider was to him. 'You'd never see him on the back of a horse. I think he's afraid of them, but he denies it. Are you comfortable riding faster than a walk? Apollo needs to move.'

She nodded and Alessio nudged his horse into a trot. She followed, settling into the rise and fall of it. She pulled in beside him, keeping up easily. He'd been right. She might be a little rusty, taking a while to learn her horse's stride whereas once it would have almost been instinctive, but she hadn't forgotten, even after all these years.

'Where are we going?' she asked. They curved along a path, the sound of the horses' hooves thumping on the ground in a soothing rhythm. If she had her bearings right, they were riding out into the view she saw from her window each day.

'Through the vines, out past the olive grove, then circling back. It should take about an hour and there's space if you feel confident enough to let the horses gallop.'

She felt almost confident enough now, sitting up on her beautiful grey, feeling that familiar thrum of excitement, the desire to take off and be free. But she didn't want Alessio asking questions about her experience. About why she had stopped riding too. It was so hard to hold back, when all she wanted to do was lose herself in the speed of her mount to feel as if she were flying again.

'From the window of my room there's an interesting little domed building amongst some trees. Can we go and see it?'

She didn't miss the slight tightening of his hands on the reins. The way his horse became restive and tossed his head. Broke his even stride. Alessio murmured softly in Italian. Almost like an apology to Apollo for disturbing him. Then he glanced back at her.

'The pavilion. *Ovviamente*. Of course.'

He led the way past some low fences, towards the grapevines burgeoning with fruit where a few people worked.

'Do you ever jump these?' She nodded to some little gates obstructing the gravel path to the stables. Alessio gave an almost smile. The merest tilt of his lips. Something distant and somehow...wistful.

He turned to her, and her fingers itched for the scratch of pencil on paper, to catch the question in his eyes, the curve of his mouth. The certainty in the way he held himself, that this was his rightful place and destiny. Whilst the idea of a blank canvas had terrified her before, she could see this. How she'd shape the paint to fit him, his body owning the canvas as he owned this land.

'*Sì*. My horses are all able.' The people in the vines

ahead of them raised their hands and waved. He waved back. 'I may need to speak to my vigneron later. About the harvest.'

'Everything going well?'

'It looks to be a good vintage. A perfect show-piece for our country's wine industry, and what it can achieve.' He said the words with steel-edged pride, as if it was a personal achievement.

They rode on into the shade of some glorious old olives, gnarled and ancient, the dappled sun warm on her skin, the scent of earth and horse everywhere. She'd forgotten the joy of this, the simple pleasures of riding in nature.

'The countryside is beautiful here,' she said. 'I'm surprised Lasserno's not more popular. There isn't much advertising about its tourism.'

His shoulders stiffened. 'It's a hidden treasure but people think we're a poor cousin of Italy, no matter the natural beauty and riches. We've been undervalued for too long, not enough made of our assets. Industries like winemaking have been left to crumble and waste away. I sought to change that the minute my father left the throne.'

'Was he keen to retire?'

'The only thing he was keen to do was plunder the country's riches for himself. People suffered...the treasury was emptied. I feared nothing would be safe.' Alessio's jaw clenched. 'Had he not abdicated the role I would have taken it from him.'

Even though the temperature was warm, the breeze cool, it was as if she'd been plunged into midwinter. She didn't know what to say. Alessio talked about making war with his own father, and that added another layer to the complex picture he painted for her. This man was the one you'd commit to canvas wielding a sword on horseback, like the imposing portraits of his ancestors.

They rode in silence for a little longer. It was as if he'd said too much and she guessed he had, being normally so self-possessed.

'Are we going to the pavilion?'

He turned to her, his eyes bleak and cold. 'You still wish to see it?'

She nodded. Anything to break the terrible chill that had fallen over them. His shoulders slumped a fraction, and it seemed almost like a defeat. Then he straightened again as if steeling himself.

'Come this way.'

Alessio wheeled his horse around and encouraged him into a canter, as if he'd forgotten she hadn't ridden for years. And all she could do was try to follow in his wake.

Alessio didn't know what it was about Hannah, how when she asked a question it was as if he'd been injected with a truth serum. He said what he wanted, what he'd bottled up, like purging his soul. In that way she was dangerous, non-disclosure agreement aside. People might have tried guessing things about his father, the reasons why he had stepped down, but the truth had been well hidden. Alessio had ensured it. Lasserno's former prince had been all about laziness and destruction. However, *no one* should ever know the extent to which Alessio had investigated removing him. Perhaps his father had had an inkling before his abdication. The palace had been full of spies and sycophants before Alessio had rid the place of them. That could be why his father had jumped before being given an unceremonious push, because Alessio had been ready to give him a final shove if it meant saving the country.

But this was a secret the world could never know, because it signalled instability. Let everyone believe the lie his father had done it for the good of the country. Yet today Alessio had put everything at risk, all because of the gentle questions of the woman riding with him.

Hannah followed close behind him as they approached the pavilion. He wasn't surprised she'd asked to see it, such a quaint building peeking out of the olive grove. A folly to something that would never last. He wondered what Hannah would see here. Whether she'd sense the tragedy or only see the fantasy of the place. Alessio wasn't sure why her opinion on these things mattered.

He pulled up Apollo and dismounted, the curdle of dread filling his stomach. Here sat a tribute by his mother to a love that had burned brightly and exploded in a supernova-like cataclysm, before imploding into darkness, cold and endless. So many hopes and dreams had been built into this little structure. A testament to the dismal failure of relationships. His father, unwilling to be faithful. His mother, unable to forgive. Their country the ultimate loser. Alessio curled his loose reins around an ancient olive tree. Hannah dismounted with a practised ease that belied her supposed inexperience and

did the same, her boots crunching in the fallen leaves
on the ground as she approached him.

'This is such a beautiful spot.' Her voice was a little
breathy as she looked around, her cheeks with a healthy
pink glow.

Yes, it was a pretty spot in the dappled sunshine.
The whitewashed pavilion with a domed terracotta roof
tucked away in the shade. But it had nothing on her. In
her worn jeans and buttoned shirt which clung to her
elegant curves she glowed as if from the inside out, with
something that looked a lot like joy.

'Can we go inside?'

He nodded. 'It's never locked.'

He walked up some small stairs, turned a latch and
entered the place he hadn't visited in years. Not since
the death of his mother when he had come here and
raged at the universe for stealing the wrong parent. But
demons needed to be conquered, especially for him now
the country was his to rule. There was no place he could
fear to tread, not now.

The pavilion had been kept pristine. No leaf or dust
dared grace any surface. The floor was an exquisite
mosaic of the goddess Venus rising from the waves.
Fluted columns against the walls supported the roof,
decorated in between with leadlight windows and pan-
theons of gods staring down at them. A few wooden
benches sat inside. Once they'd been covered with plush
cushions, this structure designed as an opulent meeting
place, away from the strictures and rules of the palace.

Hannah followed him inside, stood in the middle
of the room looking up at the ceiling with the painted

plaster like a summer's sky. She turned on the spot, her lips parted, face alive as if in wonder.

'What is this place used for? The light's gorgeous. It would be a beautiful space to paint in.'

Alessio shrugged. 'Nothing now. Once it was a retreat. A place to be alone. To contemplate.'

The lies…all the lies. They threatened to choke him even though they needed to be told. He wouldn't betray his mother's memory at the way his parents had debased themselves in their horror of a marriage towards the end.

'It seems almost like it was built for… I don't know. Lovers.'

So close to the truth, this woman. Always probing and finding the right answers. She could be a danger to his equilibrium if he didn't proceed with care.

'It was built by my mother on the second anniversary of her marriage, as a gift to my father.'

'That's so romantic.' Her voice was the merest whisper, the brush of a cool breeze through the olive trees surrounding them.

'Yes, isn't it? Romance is all around us.' His voice in response sounded hard, cynical. Even to his own ears. Echoing in this little space with nothing soft to absorb it.

In truth, this building was a testament to a failed marriage. His parents' relationship had been reported as one of great passion, until his father became bored after Alessio was born. This building hinted at something grand and consuming. Love perhaps. Obsession more likely. Or a desperate, clinging hope of keeping something that was already slipping away. He had no memory of his parents' love, only what cold, black coals were left when the flame had burned out.

'You say that like romance isn't a good thing.'

A slight frown marred her brow, those eyes of hers watching him. Assessing all the time. The sense of it prickled down his spine. A warning that he was transparent as glass and she could see all his cracks and flaws underneath. She was an artist after all. She was programmed to look for those things. He didn't want her to see them. They were secrets he kept from the world. The face he projected was the one he wanted her to paint, not the man he hid.

'If not reciprocated, it's a disaster.' The shouts, the fights. The priceless porcelain hurled across rooms, smashing against walls. His mother's cry. *'You loved me once!'* His father's reply. *'I hate you now.'* That was where romance ended. In rage and recrimination.

'What about you?' he asked. 'Would you build such a lofty monument to romance yourself?'

Hannah looked around the space. Tucked an unruly strand of hair behind her ear. She nibbled at her plump, peach lips. But she wouldn't look at him.

'My art takes up all of my time and emotion.' She appeared to have hunched in on herself, as if she were trying to tuck herself in, fold herself away till she was hidden. 'And that's enough.'

He understood his own attitude all too well. Love was a lie. Romance a folly as real and palpable as the building in which they stood. He wondered what led a young woman like her to reject it, when most had their heads in the clouds.

'So cynical for one so young,' he murmured. And something of a kindred spirit, but he didn't want to think of that. Of the way she stood there. Her cheeks coloured a beautiful pink from the warmth of the day and the mild exertion. How her eyes were the translucent green of Lasserno's coastline, where the water met the rocky shore. How they were alone, where the only thing he could hear were the birds and the whisper of a summer's breeze through the trees outside. The beat of his heart thudding in his ears. Then she looked up at him, a flash in her eyes like sun on the sea. Her gaze casting down his body, then back to meet his. Her lips parted.

This, between them, was nothing about romance but something more primal—though no less destructive. An awareness like a match freshly struck and flaring to life. If he were another man he would have taken the few steps forward to close the space between them, wrapped her in his arms, kissed her and explored this attraction. The heat of desire coursed through his veins, settled down low. Snapping at his heels to prompt him into action. He took a deep breath against the immediacy of this craving. Something he didn't want or need.

The only thing he had to rule his life by was the desire to serve his country. To be better. The best. And nothing else would do, particularly not following this desire running between them when nothing could ever come of it.

'We should move on,' he said. 'The horses need exercise. But if the light appeals, you may come here and paint.'

At least it might help keep her away from him and his incendiary desires with no outlet.

'Thank you.' Hannah's voice was low and husky, the sensation of it scoring over his skin.

They left the small pavilion and he shut the door behind them, on the past. He was all for moving forward, the only direction for him now. They approached the horses, happily nibbling on some grass under the trees, heads lifting and ears pricking as they approached.

'I'll give you assistance to mount Kestia.' He didn't want his horse's back hurt by an inexperienced rider struggling to get on. It had nothing to do with a need to move close, where he could smell the scent of her like the apple trees which graced the sheltered orchards of the palace gardens. It most certainly was not an excuse to touch Hannah in any way, to feel the warmth of her body through her jeans as he assisted her onto the horse, but he needn't have worried. She was graceful, assured. Almost as if she'd been born in the saddle on which she sat. Looking perfect on the horse he'd bought for his future princess, whoever she might ultimately be from the list of candidates now sitting in the top drawer of his desk. After Hannah left, after his coronation, then he'd decide that part of his future. He still had time.

Alessio shoved those thoughts aside. He swung himself onto Apollo's back and led through the olives into the heat of the day, pointing out landmarks as he saw them. Anything to keep his mind off the way her cheeks glowed pink in the warm sunshine, the way soft strands of her dark brown hair escaped the riding helmet, curling round the base of her neck.

He'd rather encourage Apollo into a gallop and keep riding till both were exhausted and covered in sweat, to burn away these sensations that were so foreign to him. And he couldn't sit here any longer, taking this sedate pace. He needed more, to outrun the crushing in his chest. The feeling of being trapped in a way he couldn't explain.

Reprieve came from a man walking through the grapevines in the distance.

'Do you feel confident enough to ride back to the stables yourself? As I said, I need to speak with my vigneron.' It wasn't far and Kestia was quiet and sound.

Hannah hesitated for a second, then nodded. 'I'll be fine. You go ahead.'

It didn't take a moment to encourage Apollo to move. Alessio clicked his tongue and the horse knew what he wanted, accelerating into a gallop and giving them both the freedom they craved.

Hannah watched Alessio ride out. The magnificence of it as he took off over the landscape. She settled Kestia, the little horse becoming impatient seeing the big bay streak away into the distance. Hannah patted her neck as they walked a short way. Out of Alessio's presence it was almost as if she could let out a long-held breath, those moments in the pavilion, built as a tribute to love and romance, filling her with something she barely understood. An awareness that took root and grew unchecked and uncontrolled in that little space, and for the briefest, blinding flash she craved to explore it for herself. But those feelings led nowhere. They were remnants of childish fantasies and nothing more.

Now she was firmly grounded in reality, sitting on the back of a beautiful horse for the first time in nine years. That was a thrill of its own, and with Alessio occupied she could ride as she wanted with no one to ask questions of her.

'Okay, little girl, let's see what you can do.' She encouraged her horse into a trot through the vibrant landscape, the sun high in a cobalt sky, a cool breeze making the afternoon comfortably warm rather than oppressive. They broke out onto the path, towards the castle rising majestically from the landscape. Like a fantasy picture made real.

She spurred her horse on a little faster now, settling into the rhythm, the quiver in her belly all about excitement. How had she forgotten how alive this made her feel? It was as if a switch had been flicked, a light turned on, illuminating all the dark and missing corners in her life. Ahead lay the low gate they'd passed on the way out on their ride and Kestia's ears pricked. Hannah's heart thrummed in her chest, the excited beat of it because this jump was *easy* and she was going to take it. As they approached the obstacle Hannah checked the length of her mount's stride, preparing them for the jump. Adjusted her position and they flew, for the briefest of moments, before safely landing on the other side.

All those things she'd suppressed, forced herself to forget, coalesced into that bright, brilliant moment soaring over the fence. The jump hadn't been difficult for either of them, but still she patted her little horse, whispered words of praise as the tears stung in her eyes. The memories of competition, her parents' pride at her success... There was joy in this moment, but it was also suffused with a deep ache which never really went away.

She rode on, not slowing her horse. They entered the stable area and she dismounted with a smile which might not leave her for hours, rubbing Kestia's mane, smoothing her hands over her soft coat. The thud of hooves in the distance caught her attention and she glanced outside to see Alessio galloping towards them like a warrior. He rode into the stables with a flash and clatter of hooves and pulled up his horse, leaping from Apollo and stalking towards her, reins in hand.

'What the hell do you think you were doing?' His eyes glittered like black diamonds. Jaw clenched hard enough to shatter teeth.

'Riding?' She stroked her horse's velvety nose, trying to ignore the man crackling next to her with the energy of a summer storm. 'She's wonderful. A dream.'

'As she should be,' he hissed, his breathing hard from exertion. 'You could have hurt her by pulling a stunt like that!'

Hannah refused to accept the approbation. She might do many things, but she'd never hurt a horse. 'It was no stunt. I—'

'You said you couldn't ride!'

'I said I hadn't ridden in a long time.' Hannah glared at him, the excitement of the ride still coursing rich and hot through her veins. She stood straight and tall, holding her ground, hands planted on her hips, not caring if this broke every rule in his stupid handbook. Alessio didn't move, vibrating with a furious energy. It was as if both of them were sizing up the other for a fight. She took off her riding helmet and scrubbed her hands through her hair, damp with sweat. 'You told me she could jump and the quality of your horses is obvious. I would *never* have done anything beyond her capabilities. It's not as if I hopped on her back and threw her straight over the fence. We've ridden for an hour already. I had her measure.'

His sensual lips thinned. The merest of frowns creased his brow. 'You've been holding back on me. All morning.'

Something of a warning flashed in his eyes and she knew it was because she hadn't admitted the truth to him earlier in the day. And that was a problem because he'd been holding back for her too, when they both could have ridden like the wind together. But she hadn't wanted him to ask questions about her skills, rusty as they were in the beginning. Questions led to conversations, and conversations brought back memories now bubbling close to the surface, of things which had haunted too many of her days, and some of her nights even still.

'I said I thought we'd met—'

'We haven't…as adults.'

That was why she and her friend had been in the car together and she hadn't travelled with her parents. They'd been giggling and gossiping about *him*.

'I've seen you ride before. I recognise your style and I'll always remember a horse. Who was yours?'

It wasn't really a question but a command. He stood

there formidable, with the assurance of a person to whom no one would say no. The type of person who was never unsure. She'd remembered him like that, when she was only sixteen and unsure about everything. His confidence, the certainty about him. Part of her wanted to knock him down now, refuse to answer his questions. But she'd be damned if he thought she'd be reckless on horseback. All she needed to do was withstand the memories that would once again storm over her, leaving her wrung out for days. She couldn't do that here. There was nowhere to shut herself away and grieve unrestricted.

'His name was Beauchamp… Beau.'

'A palomino?'

She nodded, astounded Alessio could remember. Beau was so beautiful he had looked as if he'd been forged from gold. She might have had no siblings, but he was like her brother, her best friend. His loss in such a terrible way, with her parents, had almost broken her. He might have survived the accident, but he hadn't been able to survive the mortal injuries. She'd wanted everyone to try, because he was all she had left after her parents had died instantly, but the vet said no, and in the end others had made the decision she couldn't make for herself. She'd never shaken the feeling she'd let them both down that day, and in those moments any sliver of hope something might be left to her out of the horror had died with him.

She turned her head, not wanting Alessio to see the vulnerability, the tears that she couldn't prevent.

'You were good. You could make him fly like you

both had wings.' Hannah couldn't believe Alessio had noticed her, could remember her horse. She'd always thought he was the type of man who wouldn't notice anyone like her.

'Why did you stop?' he asked.

She couldn't answer that question, not now. 'Why did you?'

Her voice threatened to crack. She reined in the emotion.

'Always with the questions, yet no answers for me,' he said. 'How does someone so young have so much to hide?'

She shrugged. 'I could ask the same.'

He hesitated for a second, which was pronounced because he was a man who hesitated at nothing. 'My country needed me. And you?'

The desire to say it was like a poisoned thing bursting out of her chest and she couldn't contain it any longer.

'There was an accident. My parents. My horse. I lost everything.' Hannah let out a long, slow breath. Closed her eyes. Rested her forehead on Kestia's warm body.

'When I left England, my groom told me of a tragedy but there were few details. I had no idea it was you.' His voice was soft and kind, but it didn't really help. Nothing did. 'I'm sorry.'

'It was a long time ago now, and it's fine. Really.'

Those were the lies she told herself. So many lies. She'd wondered for years what was the purpose of her surviving, till she found she could document the moments of others so precious memories would never be lost. That was her calling now. Photos might fade, but she tried to paint those portraits capturing an essence a photo never could. Her pictures could hang on a wall, there for ever.

'No. It's not.' A brush of heat coursed through her from the soft touch of Alessio's fingers at her elbow. The gentle pressure somehow comforting. She turned around, looked into his darkly handsome face. The tightness of his eyes, the pinch to his mouth. Pain drawn across him, reflecting her own. 'I was called home after my mother fell ill. Then we lost her. The country might have shared the grief but in truth it was all mine, and nothing about that is fine, Hannah. It is as if nothing will ever be fine again.'

He'd moved forward. They stood so close now, the heat from his body warming her cold soul. She wanted to take it all for herself. Wrap herself in it like a blanket and let him comfort her for ever, because in some small way he understood.

'There were days when it was all too hard.'

'And yet here we are today.'

Their bodies were hidden behind the horses, where no one could see. She was so aware of the solidity of him, his broad shoulders holding the weight of grief. The burdens of a prince. How she wished some days she could share hers with another, let them carry the load for a while. Let someone with the strength of this man shoulder them. But that was a vulnerability she couldn't afford because it wouldn't last, a gateway to more pain, and she'd had enough in her twenty-five years to last her a lifetime.

Yet the moment seemed full, teeming with things unsaid, emotions repressed waiting to explode. Hovering between everything, and nothing at all. She could smell him this close, the seaside tang of fresh male sweat from their ride in the sun, and the undertone of something else dark and sweet like treacle she could drown in. One step closer and they'd touch. That was all it would take, a move from either of them.

Alessio cupped her cheek, his palm burning on her flesh. The look in his eyes soft. Sad, as if carrying the weight of the world. Then he slid his hand away, stroking her skin as if wanting to linger. Goosebumps drifted over her as he stepped back. It was as if a tension in the stables had snapped, the release a kind of let-down, almost a disappointment.

'You may come and ride Kestia at any time you wish whilst you're here. Simply let the groom know.'

'What about you?'

The corner of his mouth turned upwards in a wry smile. 'I have a country to rule.'

'Is it enough?'

'It's all I have, and all I was born for. It must be enough.' He called over the groom, who led away his two charges. 'Now I'll leave you. We have the dinner tonight, where you'll accompany Stefano. I have much to do before then.'

He turned and strode out of the stables, as if hell itself were chasing him.

CHAPTER FIVE

ALESSIO STOOD BEFORE a mirror, carefully adjusting the white silk bow tie till it sat stiff and perfect at his throat. He wanted to rip it off, the infernal fabric too tight, the top buttons of his pristine shirt choking him. Instead he turned away, breathing slowly, slipping gold cuff-links adorned with the royal crest into the holes of his turned-back cuffs. Sealing them, and him, into place. He shrugged on his jacket, checked again that the Prince of Lasserno had been buttoned, cuffed and tied into his costume. Trying not to think of the afternoon. Of a woman with dark hair the colour of melted chocolate, flying over a fence on a horse. Her grief that twinned his own. The thrill of her warm skin under his fingers.

In Alessio's experience, women were cool, per-fumed, and polished in all ways. Hannah had been none of those things today. Instead she'd been heat and fire and sweat and it was all he could do when the tears had gleamed in her eyes not to crush her to him and burn that grief away with a kiss. To see whether the skin of the rest of her was as soft as her cheek under his palm.

He flexed his fingers. Turned from the mirror and

began to pace, his energy restless tonight, even after the ride. He'd held back on Apollo today in deference to what he'd believed was Hannah's lack of skill. That knowledge now pricked at him like an irritation. They'd wasted the afternoon on a sedate ride, when instead they could have challenged each other and their horses. Perhaps he'd go out again tomorrow, alone. But like every day, tomorrow his calendar was full. He supposed if he asked Stefano to find time his friend might suggest dropping the hospital visit, but that was the one thing he'd never cancel. Lasserno's sick children needed him, and he would not give up on them. Alessio dropped his head. Scrubbed his hands over his face. There was no time to rid himself of this sensation of needing to move. Not wanting to stop lest creeping thoughts caught up with him.

He checked his watch as a light tap sounded at the door. Almost time to leave.

'Enter.'

He expected Stefano but as the door cracked open it was as if the breath had been punched from his chest. Hannah stood before him in a floor-length dress in the cool, silver-green of olive leaves, her hair up in some soft, loose style which fell about her face. Lips a perfect plum pout. Eyes a little smoky. She looked up at him and he couldn't breathe, his collar once again too tight, his bow tie choking him.

Alessio tugged at the neck of his shirt as her eyes widened. She was seated with Stefano at the dinner tonight, but, seeing her now, he wanted her with him in a way which defied rational thought. Better still, they could ignore the function and stay at the palace. Have a quiet candlelit dinner for two...

He shut down those errant thoughts. They had no place in his life.

'What are you doing here?' he asked, a little more harshly than he should have, but these were his private rooms. No woman had been in them before.

'Stefano told me to meet you here. Something about running late?'

That was unheard of. Stefano's views on punctuality were similar to his own. Alessio checked his phone and sure enough there was the message. He'd been so preoccupied he hadn't heard the alert.

Hannah stood, expectant. It wasn't quite time to leave and he couldn't have her waiting in the hall, so he stepped back, inviting her into the sitting room. Her long dress swished against the floor, sparkling at the hemline and part way up the skirt. Apart from that shine, the rest of her was unadorned. He couldn't shake the sense that she shouldn't go to the dinner without armour. Whilst the function was filled with more friends, such as they were, than enemies, even he knew how the worst of them could be. He could take care of himself. As he was Prince of Lasserno, people pandered to him. But any attack on Hannah he might not let go ignored. And he had to ignore her.

Except every fibre of his body rebelled at that knowledge.

'How were you after your ride?' Safer ground. He needed to make conversation rather than entertain thoughts of defending her like a prince from some fairy

tale. Life was not a fantasy. Though she didn't appear
to be faring much better, the way she looked at him in
his suit. There was a prickling in his skin whilst she
assessed him as if she were stripping him bare, breaking him down. Sometimes he wanted to know what she
saw when she did that. What she was looking for when
she cast her eyes over him. Did she find him lacking
in any way?

Why the answer to those questions was imperative,
he couldn't say.

'I'm a little stiff but that's no surprise, since I haven't
ridden for almost nine years. But I had a long bath,
which helped.'

Visions of her naked, lazing back in the large tub in
her room, flushed with the heat of the water, assailed
him and he couldn't get rid of them. What colour her
nipples would be. Whether she'd be natural or waxed
bare. And now those thoughts were planted in his head,
they took root like weeds. This was insanity. Usually
with women he had control. Around her his control
frayed and shredded like rope being hacked by a knife.

'Excellent.' He could make light conversation. It was
one of the things at which he excelled. 'You look…
beautiful tonight.'

Not exactly where he wished to head, but he was
being polite. Any man would say the same. Although
it wasn't mere politeness driving him. She looked like
some sprite or will-o'-the-wisp, intent on leading him
to his doom.

A soft flush of pink tinted her cheeks at the compliment. Who was there in her life to tell her she was

beautiful? Was there anyone at all? The thought that no one might have said this to her recently seemed somehow wrong.

'Thank you.' Her voice was soft. Always that tone which was slightly lower and huskier than he expected, causing a tremor right through him, like fingernails scoring down his spine. And the change in her voice suggested that she was affected too. He grabbed on to that thought as if it were a golden nugget of hope.

He'd never had that hope or insecurity before. Women found him attractive. He had a wealth of experience to back up that certainty. But right now he didn't care about anyone else. He only cared that *this* woman was attracted to him, and Alessio didn't know why it mattered. Certainty was his friend. This sensation, of standing on shifting sands, was not.

She began to move, walking around the room as if inspecting it, her glorious dress glittering under the lights as she did.

'Would you like a seat?' he asked. It was as if she were parading in front of him, and he couldn't take his thoughts from the way her bodice cinched at her slender waist. How her gauzy capped sleeves sat tantalisingly at her shoulders. Half on, half off, as if with the wrong shift they would fall and leave more of her glorious skin exposed, the cool, creamy sweep of her décolletage, which would no doubt haunt his dreams, naked and perfect. It should at least be adorned with some jewels, so they could distract him, rather than cause the near impossible-to-control desire to drop his gaze to the gentle swell of her cleavage.

'No. I'm a bit scared to sit down.' She brushed her hands across the fabric, which seemed to sit in multiple layers. When had the construction of a dress ever held such fascination for him? 'I don't usually wear things like this, and I don't want to crush it.'

His first thought was that she should wear dresses like this every night. The next thought was of him holding her in his arms, kissing her. Crushing her dress in the most satisfying of ways.

'You've no jewellery.'

Hannah cocked her head, as if what he'd said was a kind of slight, when really he was only making conversation to stop the itch in his fingers, which tempted him to reach out and touch, to see how much softer she'd feel after her bath.

'No, *Your Highness*.' Those words contained no deference at all. She wielded them as a weapon. 'I didn't want to outshine you.'

A slight smile touched the corner of her lips. He should be offended, but he liked the way she didn't pander to him.

'I'm afraid you already have. No one will be paying any attention to me with such beauty in the room.'

The colour still ran high on her cheeks, but apart from that blush she seemed unaffected. 'Oh, dear. How does it feel, the risk that the spotlight won't be on you?'

A blessed relief. But it was something he could never admit, for the spotlight would never be turned away. 'I'm sure my fragile ego can handle the assault for one night, especially since I'm accompanied by you. Beauty has a way of outshining the beast.'

She snorted, the sound more cute from her than disdainful. 'You're more Prince Charming tonight than Beast.'

'Perhaps I was a beast this afternoon.'

Her gaze dropped to his mouth and held. Was she recalling his touch in the stables, wishing he'd kissed her? The burn of that recollection, the desire...it ignited and began to flare almost out of control. But he'd had years of practice managing it. No matter how much he might want her right now, it would pass. It always did.

'You obviously love your horses and had no idea of my experience. It was understandable. Anyway, it's well known that a *real* princess can tame the beast, and you'll have one of those soon. Isn't that the way the story goes?'

It should be. His longlist was now slimmed to a shortlist. But Alessio wasn't sure. He didn't care for the map of his life right now, the journey relentless most days, unwelcome on others. Required every day. He had no choices, the needs of his country forgotten too long by his father. His own desire to do better, to repair the damage done to his people, overcame any personal sentiments. But tonight, perhaps *just* for tonight, he could engage in a small moment of folly. Those glimpses of sadness Hannah had exposed this afternoon, the shadows which haunted her face from the loss she'd suffered, they hadn't quite left her. Fleeting happiness was what he could provide, and in his experience, women loved jewels. Though he wasn't sure about anything with Hannah. She didn't fit the familiar moulds. Still, he wanted to make *her* feel like a princess tonight.

'A woman should always outshine the man.'

'That's not the way it is in the animal kingdom.'

'I say that's the way it should be.'

'Are you pulling the prince card here? I'm the ruler... my rules?' Her eyes glittered with mirth under the lights. He wanted her covered in jewels that shone as much as she did, to keep that smile on her face.

'Wait here.'

He walked through his bedroom, to the dressing room. Behind a panel in the wall, he opened a safe. Drew out a rich purple velvet box. People wanted diamonds, rubies, emeralds, sapphires. The gaudy gems. In his hands was a necklace which matched Hannah's dress to perfection. Matched her, with its understated elegance. It might not have seemed as precious as the crown jewels, but to him it was more beautiful because of how uncommon it was. The stones were awash with the same grey-green as her dress, with swirls of gold like the bleeding colour from the watercolour pencils she'd shown him. The surrounding diamonds were an old mine cut, designed to show their true beauty in candlelight.

He tried not to think too hard about what he was doing as he closed the safe and returned to Hannah. These jewels he'd inherited. They were not part of the crown jewels his father had begun to plunder when needing a bauble to give away or for a bribe. These had been locked in the safe in his room too long. They needed to shine again.

Hannah stood with her back to him, gazing out of the window. Staring at the view into Lasserno's capital, glittering like her in the darkened landscape. As he entered the room she turned, those all-seeing eyes fixed on the box in his hands.

'What's that?'

'Adornments. They match your dress.'

Her eyes widened a fraction, her mouth opened. Shut.

'I'm getting the feeling this is a bit like a movie moment. I'm not sure I like it.'

'I promise you will, and you can always say no. But please look.' He opened the box and turned it to her. The jewels lay on pristine white satin inside.

'Oh.' She reached out and then drew back her fingers. 'What's the stone? The colours... And it looks like there are tiny ferns in it.'

'Dendritic agate. Most people don't appreciate its beauty. But the pattern is made in nature and it would have taken years to put together the complementing pieces. Far harder than matching other gemstones.'

'It looks old.' Her voice was a breathy whisper. The kind you wanted in your ear when making love. The whole of him tensed.

'About two hundred years or so. Everyone seeks out the sparkle of new gemstones, the brilliant cuts, but I prefer this. And the greens match your dress.'

'I can't. It's—'

'Try it on.' It seemed imperative now that she wear it. A drive he couldn't ignore. 'Come here.'

She edged to where he stood, near a gilt mirror. He took the cool, heavy necklace from its box. Reached over Hannah's head and draped it round her neck, settling the gems at her throat and securing the clasp. His breath disturbed fine hairs curling at her nape as they escaped her hairstyle. Goosebumps peppered her skin. He craved to run his hands over them. Feel the evidence of her pleasure under his fingertips.

Alessio looked up at her in the mirror, the moment so profoundly intimate and domestic it zapped through him like an electric shock. Instead of giving in to the desire threatening to overwhelm him, he stepped back.

'Do you like it?'

She reached her hand up, and tentatively touched the central stone. She smelled of the final days of autumn, like apples and the last of the season's roses. Rich and intoxicating.

'It's almost like an underwater scene.'

'It's perfect.'

'I can't wear this.' She shook her head. The diamonds twinkled as she moved. 'They're crown jewels.'

'They're not officially in the royal collection. They're mine to do with what I wish, and my wish is that you leave them on. Every woman should have the opportunity to wear something like this, at least once in her life. To feel like a princess.'

'That might have been Mum's nickname for me, but I'm no princess.'

Alessio wondered whether they had talked of Hannah marrying a prince, and whether her dream had died in the accident. He wasn't sure why it mattered, if it had.

'You look like one.'

It was as though the moment froze, with them standing so close in the room, as if time had paused and was giving them this small slice to cherish before wrenching them back into reality. But Alessio knew reality always intruded.

An alert chimed and here the world caught up with them like some spell had been broken. Then a knock sounded at the door.

'Enter.'

Stefano walked in, gave a brief bow.

'Your car has arrived.' He turned to Hannah. His gaze held at her neck for a heartbeat, that hesitation saying more than words could. Her hand fluttered to touch the necklace again, as if afraid someone would take it away. Stefano gave her a brief smile. 'Signorina Barrington.'

To Alessio, he raised an eyebrow.

'Do you know what you're doing?' The words were spoken in Italian, so Hannah couldn't understand.

Alessio checked the time on his watch. Straightened his bow tie. It was the first time in a *long* time that his friend had questioned him. From the moment he had received the call to say his mother was unwell, he'd known. His course unwelcome but set. Ignoring his needs and desires for the good of the country. He straightened his spine like the prince he was.

'*Ovviamente.*' Of course.

Stefano responded with nothing more than a curt nod as they left for the cars. And all the while on the journey to the dinner, Alessio's lie stuck like a fish-bone in his throat.

They stood outside the doorway of a ballroom in a magnificent villa on the outskirts of the capital. Hannah had been told on the way here that this would be a more intimate function, but it didn't sound like it from the cacophony of voices drifting from the ballroom ahead. She touched the central stone of the magnificent necklace, sitting warm and heavy round her throat in a way that seemed comforting, the piece so beautiful she had almost wept when Alessio had shown it to her.

She'd loved the way he had looked at her tonight, after clasping the gems round her neck. As if she was someone precious. Special. Someone to be revered. The intensity of his gaze had left her tight and shivery, hot and cold all at once. It was how she felt about him, watching Alessio now in his black dinner suit, snowy white waistcoat and bow tie. Dressed so formally he looked…more. In control, in charge, masterful. For the tiniest of moments she allowed temptation to whisper that she'd love him to master her.

Hannah's cheeks heated with the illicit thought, but at least the lights were lower out here in the hall. She wouldn't look so much like a vividly toned root vegetable. No one paid her any attention anyway. Right now, Alessio and Stefano were in discussion with what appeared to be a master of ceremonies, who alternated between wringing his hands and bowing as if in apology as Stefano gesticulated.

Alessio stood back a little, his disapproval obvious in the way he held himself, his jaw hard as he checked his watch. Stiff, as if he were retreating into himself and rebuilding another persona by degrees. He glanced over at her, and she decided not to hang back as if this weren't her place. She'd been invited here. She had the dress, the heels, the jewels, and for one night she could be the princess in a story of her own making.

She walked over to the two men. 'Is there a problem?'

Alessio smiled, but the smile didn't touch his eyes. Fake. A mask and nothing more.

'There appears to have been an error. You've been seated next to me.'

She was supposed to sit with Stefano tonight, but a beat of something a lot like anticipation thrummed through her at the thought of being by Alessio's side. Still, she understood the impossibility of her desire and what was *not* being said. Alessio appearing with a woman would invite speculation which a deeply private man like him would despise.

Hannah pasted on her own fake smile. 'I'll change tables, then.'

'Changing tables means changing place cards and will invite more gossip.'

He turned and spoke in Italian to the worried-looking man still hovering in the doorway between the hall and where the dinner would be held. When Alessio finished, the man sagged a fraction and bowed a final time, before hurrying inside the ballroom.

'Come,' Alessio said to her. 'People know we're here. It's time to go in.'

'What did you say to him?'

'That wherever we're placed is suitable, but Stefano would miss your presence at his table.'

'Will he?'

There was something inscrutable about the way he looked at her.

'Any man would.'

The pleasure at those words slid through her with the potency of a shot of spirits. A sensation all too intoxicating to be good for her, so she tried to ignore it. Hannah moved into position and Stefano took her arm, given he'd walk her inside, but Alessio in front held all her attention. He was entirely changed, the metamorphosis into Lasserno's ruler complete. Strength and stability radiated from him like a beacon. Solid. Uncompromising. And yet behind the mask of his public persona, she still glimpsed the true man simmering underneath. He carried himself with an unnatural stiffness, and a tightness around the eyes suggested he wasn't entirely happy in this new skin.

The master of ceremonies announced something to the assembled guests she couldn't understand. The noise of chairs scraping back interrupted the murmurs from the room. A hush descended as everyone waited. Alessio's shoulders rose then fell as if he took a deep breath, then with a straightening of his spine he stepped forward through the doorway as she and Stefano followed. Her eyes adjusted to the brighter lights of the room and she gasped at the sparkling chandeliers, towering floral decorations and gleaming silver candelabras adorning the opulent ballroom. About fifty people stood round tables scattered through the space and every face was turned to Alessio as he waited at the top of the stairs, allowing the assembled guests to take their fill of him, their Crown Prince, and his most honoured guest. It was a dizzying sensation to realise there were a hundred eyes on them as he made his way down the sweeping marble staircase into the room, a leader of his nation in all ways. Arresting and intoxicating.

As they walked through the room Hannah touched her necklace again, almost as a reflex. The curdle of something like fear slithered in her belly but the jewels reminded her that she had a place here tonight. They moved through tables to their seat and people stared and whispered as she passed. When they reached their table, Stefano pulled out her chair.

'I'll see you later, Hannah,' he murmured. It was said quietly enough to seem private, loud enough to pique people's interest. The game of deflection had begun. She merely smiled. Ignored everyone's curious stares as she sat and accepted a glass of champagne from the waiter, thanking the man who poured it for her.

'Ladies, gentlemen.' The table descended into silence as Alessio spoke. 'I'm pleased to introduce Signorina Hannah Barrington. My portrait artist, who has taken two weeks from her hectic schedule to be here before returning to England.'

It was a statement of intent. One she understood, but something about it left her feeling deflated, like a leftover balloon from a long-forgotten party. Alessio named the people at the table for her benefit. Counts, countesses, the Prime Minister and his wife. Lasserno's aristocracy. The country's *Who's Who*.

A few people nodded with interest or stared as if in disbelief at the position she held, sitting to Alessio's left. She could understand why. He was a man in his prime. Available, a prince. Who wouldn't want to be her? They must know he was looking for a bride. Did they assume she was in the running? Her throat tightened and she took a sip of her champagne, the bright bubbles sparkling on her tongue and slipping too easily down her throat. Surely everyone here knew he was looking for a princess? And yet as she watched the other guests' open looks of avarice, she realised this dinner held all the danger of picking her way through a room filled with broken glass in bare feet.

She steeled her spine. Whatever these people might think, they were all wrong and she'd show them. Alessio had to deal with this every day and Hannah couldn't imagine how wearing it must be. She glanced at him now, making easy conversation with the Prime Minister.

'How do you find His Highness's hospitality?' asked a man in a uniform festooned with medals. She didn't like the supercilious way his brow rose when he spoke to her.

Still, her place at this table wasn't to make trouble but to smooth it over. Hannah smiled. 'His Highness is a gracious host, as one would expect.'

'Are you spending much time in his presence?' The corner of the man's mouth turned up in a smirk. 'For research purposes, of course.'

People near them began to watch the exchange, whilst Alessio seemed engrossed in his own conversation. Around the table the air vibrated with tension, a warning. This question was a kind of trap, but she wouldn't fall into it, because no matter how strong and uncompromising he seemed, Hannah realised that Alessio needed shielding. All these people were vultures waiting for others to hunt down their prey and then pick over the carcass left.

She refused to be their victim.

'He's managed to fit me into his hectic schedule.'

The man's smile in response appeared knowing, when he really had no clue. 'I'm *sure* he has.'

Those words carried a weight and meaning everyone sitting at the table would understand. She pretended to be oblivious. To rise above it, since innocence was her weapon.

'Enough to sketch and make the studies I need for the coronation portrait.'

'You're young to receive such an illustrious commission,' said a countess wearing a shimmering gold dress of liquid satin and diamonds round her neck the size of pigeon eggs. 'You must have quite prodigious…talents.'

Hannah swallowed. She couldn't stop the fire igniting in her belly at these insinuations. She knew her worth, the work and the sacrifice she put into her art. Her achievements. She didn't care what the guests here thought of her. Alessio was the one getting the portrait. She'd never paint any of these people, no matter how much they offered. Even if they *begged*, because she didn't want to know them.

Not the way she was coming to know Alessio.

'I'll leave that judgement to others. My job's to paint. To find the essence of a person.'

'And have you found the essence of His Highness?' Those words were delivered with a venomous smile. One which appeared friendly but carried a sting.

'Not yet. But I've never painted a prince before.'

A few people murmured at her response, but she couldn't understand what was being said. They seemed friendly enough, so she suspected it wasn't a criticism. She hardly cared. They could think what they wanted. She knew the truth. Then next to her, Alessio straightened. She could almost feel the electric crackle of him from his seat.

'I suggest, Contessa, that you do your research. Signorina Barrington has won some of the most prestigious portrait competitions in the world. She is the best. There is *no one* more qualified to paint my coronation portrait than her.'

His voice bristled with warning, sharp and cold. Now everyone at the table stared at them. Whilst his chill was meant to give a clear message, to her his voice was like being immersed in a warm bath. She basked in his defence, even though it would likely cost him. For a man whose private life was deliberately opaque, he'd allowed the door to crack open a chink, showing in the tiniest of ways that she mattered.

She couldn't thank him in public, so she smiled benevolently as if praise like this were given to her every day. But, since they sat next to each other, she moved her thigh towards his until their knees touched. A tiny gesture to say thank you in a way she couldn't immediately vocalise. Hannah applied the smallest amount of pressure, to let Alessio know her move wasn't accidental. The fingers of his left hand flexed on the tablecloth and he pressed back. The thrill of that secret acknowledgement bubbled through her like the sparkle of champagne. They sat knee to knee, calf to calf, ankle to ankle, and even through the layers of her dress it was as if she could sense the heat burning between them.

The conversation changed after his intervention, the flow of it around the table broken by the royal toast. Hannah stood with everyone else and the sense of loss she suffered at the lack of that supportive touch seemed almost visceral, as if something magical had been broken. She watched Alessio, who managed to look utterly alone even when surrounded by this host of people. There was a blankness about him which showed that any emotion had been well and truly shuttered and locked down. She didn't know how he managed to eat, other than out of politeness. She sampled the beautiful-looking food and, whilst delicious, it held no appeal. This crowd would likely poison your meal as anything else. It was almost a surprise that Alessio didn't have an official food taster, they were all so toxic.

'Have you ridden with His Highness?' the Countess asked, after they'd resumed their seats. She was surprised the woman hadn't accepted Alessio's put-down, but she was young enough to be interested in him for herself and there was a determined gleam in her eye. 'He's known as a passionate horseman.'

She decided to tell the truth because enough people had seen her ride with Alessio to make a lie far worse.

'Yes. Have you?'

Even though she wasn't looking at him, she was aware as Alessio stiffened, so attuned to him now that she could sense the slow freeze again. He shifted as she pressed her leg to his once more. Letting him know she had this. That he'd protected her, but it was okay for him to accept her help too.

The Countess's mouth thinned. If looks were daggers, Hannah would be properly skewered. 'No, I have never been invited to ride by His Highness, but it would be my *extreme* pleasure to do so.'

Hannah raised an eyebrow in a way she hoped looked imperious. 'Perhaps one day, if you're a good enough rider, you'll be lucky and get your chance.'

She didn't think the woman had the care, intuition or skill to be allowed anywhere near Alessio's beloved horses. Hannah only realised now the privilege she'd been afforded being allowed to ride Kestia whenever she wished.

The Countess turned her attention to Alessio. 'Your Highness, it's an uncommon honour you invited Signorina Barrington to sit at your table.'

He fixed the woman with a cold glare. 'It's you who should be honoured, to have such a prestigious artist in your company.'

'The sad truth,' Hannah said, no doubt breaking protocol with her interruption but not caring less, 'is there was a terrible mix-up in the beginning. I was meant to sit with Stefano.'

She was coming to realise gossip was the currency of value fuelling these people, so she'd give them something to talk about. She glanced over to where Stefano sat at a distant table and gave a little wave. He raised his champagne flute and toasted her in response.

'You were looking forward to sitting with His Highness's private secretary?'

'Oh, yes. Very much,' Hannah said. 'But there's always tomorrow.'

This could have been a pleasant evening in a magnificent room, with exquisite food and wine. Her fantasy for just one night. She resented the people here intent on ruining it. Some of them were trying to goad Alessio's responses, to play a game in which there could be no winners.

The thing was, they hadn't counted on her.

Alessio adjusted the napkin on his lap. As he did so his hand brushed hers, feather-light. So fleeting it could have been a mistake, but she knew it hadn't been. Her breathing hitched, a shiver of pleasure running through her, settling low and heavy.

Tonight, she and Alessio were a team. None of the people here could touch them. She ate some more food, sipped more champagne. All the time exquisitely aware of the man sitting next to her. And as their legs touched under the table once more, their secret, she prayed this dinner was over soon and that she'd done enough.

CHAPTER SIX

THE JOURNEY BACK to the palace had been in near silence. There was too much going through Alessio's head for him to say anything at all. The sly comments, the innuendos, all directed at one woman.

A woman who'd seen fit to defend him in the face of obvious attacks.

'Do you need to discuss this evening's events?' Stefano asked as they walked towards the royal suite. Hannah remained silent. Alessio wanted to know how she felt, given everything that had passed. 'And would you like me to take Signorina Barrington on a very public sightseeing tour tomorrow? A quiet word in the right news organisation's ear and—'

'No, and no press.'

'If we used them properly, it could be to your advantage. They fabricate news about you, since they get none. Why not feed the beast a different story?'

This old argument between them could wait for another day. He didn't want Hannah used to deflect attention from his own errors. Inviting her into the hornet's nest was his mistake. She'd done enough tonight by tolerating the dinner. For that alone he must thank her.

'I need to place the necklace in the safe,' he said. Hannah stood there with her head held high, looking more like royalty than he felt after tonight's efforts. Lasserno's aristocracy had not crowned themselves in glory.

Hannah reached behind her neck to undo the clasp and he shook his head.

'You can remove it in my room,' he said, then added to Stefano, 'We can speak tomorrow if there's a need.'

Stefano gave Hannah a lingering look, nodded, then left.

Alessio opened the door of his suite and walked inside with Hannah following. The burn in his gut overtook him now, raging close to the surface over the way she'd been treated. All the while his emotions mingled with something softer, more tempting. She'd defended him, worked to ensure there were no rumours about them. Pretended *for* him. That protectiveness was unfamiliar in his experience. Its allure potent. The memory of their knees pressing together, the hidden support... he couldn't put it out of his mind. In his role as Prince of Lasserno he was tasked as protector of a nation. The weight of all decisions fell on his shoulders. Tonight, Hannah had relieved some of his burden and he could never thank her enough.

'Would you like a drink?' He rarely resorted to alcohol, avoiding any kind of excess, but he needed something to dull the immediacy of his anger.

She shook her head. Standing under the soft lights,

glittering and perfect. As if this were her place. But it couldn't be, no matter the temptation.

'No, I think I've had more than enough wine. But feel free.'

He smiled at the audacity of her giving him permission in his own rooms. She was a constant challenge to his position, and he feared he was enjoying the challenge far too much.

'I will.' He poured a slug of amber fluid into a glass.

'You are the Prince and all. You can do what you like.'

The weight of responsibility sometimes threatened to crush him, and yet he couldn't yield to it. He took a swig of his drink, the burn of the spirit doing nothing to ease the emotions sliding through his veins. Anger, desire. A dangerous mix when coupled with a beautiful, uncompromising woman.

A woman who seemed to be shifting from foot to foot, as if she were in discomfort.

'Are you all right?'

She winced. 'Do you mind if I take off these heels? They're like a torture device.'

'Feel free.' He lifted his glass to take another swig of Scotch but stopped as Hannah grabbed on to the corner of a chair, kicked off the heels and wiggled her toes in the carpet, closing her eyes and sighing as she did so. 'Heaven.'

Alessio couldn't tear his gaze from her toes, peeking out from under the hem of her dress. Red. He swallowed. Bright. Vibrant. Red. For some reason that bold colour was unlike one he thought she might wear. It surprised him. As if he were being allowed to glimpse some secret about her. He didn't know why a need pounded through him now, his heart like an anvil being struck by the blacksmith's hammer. They were only feet. But that intimacy again almost undid him.

'I'm sorry,' Alessio said.

She shrugged. 'For formal occasions I know they're expected. Beauty is pain and all that. I just don't have any need to wear heels around the farm.'

'Not about the shoes.' Alessio couldn't look at her right now. Instead he turned to the mirror and tugged his bow tie undone. Wrenched the top button of his shirt open, crushing the perfectly pressed cotton under his fingers. Even then his clothes choked him. 'The people.'

She came into view, reflected behind him. Picked up a small porcelain figurine of a horse that decorated a side table, inspecting it, running her fingers over the smooth surface. What he wouldn't give right now to have those fingers running over his skin instead. He took another sip of his drink. No good would come of those thoughts. His responsibility was to look after her as an employee, not dream of Hannah undressing him with her gentle, stroking fingers.

Yet it was this last thought he couldn't get out of his head.

'I'm used to the mean girls,' she said. 'You meet a few.'

Alessio wheeled around. She was precious. She shouldn't have to deal with anyone cruel. 'Where would you meet people like *that*? Your clients?'

'No, my clients are nice…' she skewered him with

her insightful gaze and smiled sweetly '…in the main. I came across them at boarding school after my parents died. Girls could be cruel to an orphan like me.'

'Oh, *bella*.' Her eyes widened a fraction as the term of endearment slipped out unchecked. He started forward, wanting to comfort her, but that wasn't his role. It never could be. Though the reasons for that seemed to be getting a little hazy. 'Why were you at a boarding school?'

She walked to a portrait on the wall, another glowering ancestor, all a reminder of the job he had to do for Lasserno. He ensured they stared down on him from every private wall in the palace so he would never falter.

'My aunt and uncle were my guardians. They didn't have children of their own and said it would give me stability.'

'Did it?'

'No. It was awful. I didn't…cope. So they brought me home and sent me to the local school. Not prestigious, but small and familiar.'

He could barely imagine the pain she had suffered, both parents lost. Being sent away from everything she'd known. The unfairness tore at him. At least when his mother had died he'd had some sympathetic courtiers, given his father was of no use.

'I enjoyed boarding school. Away from the constraints of the palace. Away from my parents' cold war.' The open battles over his father's infidelity. 'It seemed like bliss in comparison, even though boys can be brutal.'

There was a softness in the way she looked at him

now, like sympathy, when he was owed none from her. 'Being a prince, you would have been top of the tree.'

He threw back the last of his drink. Tempting to have more, but not sensible in the circumstances. 'That's not always the best position to be in. It brings with it a certain entitlement which I needed to unlearn.'

She had an uncanny way of getting him to speak the truth of everything. He put his glass down on a side table. The *domesticity* of this scene assailed him once more. As if she should be here. As if this was her rightful place. A delectable sense of inevitability slid through him.

As if there was no other place she should *ever* be.

'You learned that at least. If you had one wish, what would it be?'

Her questions. Funny how she'd stopped asking the ones on her infernal list. However, this one seemed appropriate. He had so many wishes. That he had a sibling, so he was not all alone. That his parents had had a happy marriage like some of those he'd witnessed with his school friends. That his mother had not died. But there was one wish, above all. It came to the fore on nights like tonight, when he realised every choice was taken away by duty. *That* wish pricked at him like a dagger between the ribs, sliding true to his heart. His deepest secret, and some days his greatest shame.

'Not being the Prince of Lasserno.' Being an ordinary man with ordinary choices. He looked over at the decanter of Scotch sitting on the sideboard. He'd never drowned his regrets in alcohol before, but tonight he wanted to down the whole bottle. 'And you?'

Hannah paled, her skin translucent in the lights. The antique diamonds glittering at her throat. She should always be in diamonds, this woman. Draped in jewels to frame her beauty. Her head dropped. She scuffed at the carpet with her pretty painted toes.

'I wish I'd been in the car with my parents.' Her voice was so soft he almost didn't hear it, but the force of what she said struck him like a blow. His whole body rebelled at the thought she might not be here, that if she'd been in that car the world would be without her brilliance.

'No!' He cut through the air with his hand as her eyes widened. He was surprised by his own vehemence. The visceral horror that this was how she might feel. 'You do *not* wish that.'

He strode towards her, the hectic glitter in her eyes telling him tears were close. He wasn't good with tears. His mother had spilled enough of them in his presence, railing against his father. He'd been inured to most of them in the end, learning to comfort without feeling the pain himself.

The threat of Hannah's ripped at the fabric of his being.

'It's my wish. It can be what I want.'

'Survivor's guilt.' As if those two words could ease her dark thoughts. Had she had counselling after her parents had passed? Her aunt and uncle had sent her away to boarding school. Perhaps they'd expected her to get over things without the help a teenager might need after such a loss. 'If this is the way you feel then you should—'

'You don't understand.' She turned away from him,

wrapped her arms round her waist. 'If I hadn't travelled with my friend that afternoon, we'd have gone a different way home. We wouldn't have been on that road. The tractor wouldn't have been on the bend. They might…'

They might be alive.

Alessio went to her, placed his hands gently on her shoulders. Her skin was warm, soft as satin. He circled his thumbs on her exposed flesh. She leaned back into him. As if taking, for a moment, the meagre solace he could provide.

'We both want things we can't have,' he murmured.

'You could give up the throne. I can't turn back time.'

He let out a long, slow breath. Occasionally in his fantasies he'd allow himself to simply be a man, but he had the luxury of being able to think that way. 'No. I can't. I have a duty to my people and that duty is more important than anything. More important than a man's desires.'

She disengaged from him and he mourned the loss of his hands on her skin, the warmth of her. 'At least you can change things.'

'I'll always be the leader of Lasserno.'

'Not everything has to be for duty. You talk about finding the perfect princess. Is that duty as well?'

'All that I do is for my country.'

'Then what feeds the man's soul?'

He walked to the windows of the palace overlooking his capital. The city, glittering in the late evening like a bright jewel. One entirely in his care. 'The man doesn't exist in isolation from the Prince. They're one and the same.'

'What about love?'

'What about it?'

'You could marry for that. Love's not about duty.'

Alessio wheeled around. He knew this story, an age-old one. Love had no place in his life. He'd seen how it ate away, destroyed when one party stopped loving the other, or perhaps had never loved them in the first place. His parents' relationship had been the best evidence of that. It inured him to ever seeking anything more for himself. If duty it was to be, then that would extend to his princess, who'd understand the constraints of royalty, the expectations of her role.

Sure he'd had promises before…of love, of adoration…all so a woman could get a crown on her head too. He could never be sure of anyone, whether they wanted the man, the money or his family's name, especially after Allegra's efforts. Better he found someone who knew what this was, a dynastic endeavour. Protecting his country from a vacuum, nothing more. In many ways Hannah was the same as others, accepting the exorbitant fee he'd offered her to paint his portrait. The suspicion overran him, needy and unfamiliar. Had he not been the Prince of Lasserno, would she have agreed to paint him with no complaints? Probably. And that was something he should never forget. Even though tonight, she had seen fit to protect him at her own expense.

'And who would I find to love? You?'

Hannah's eyes widened, and then she laughed in a mocking kind of way, as if what he'd said was ridiculous. 'Me? That's absurd.'

Which was not the answer he'd been expecting. He'd expected a shy glance, some fluttering of eyelids. A woman playing coy at the hint something more might be on offer. Any reaction other than suggestions of foolishness on his part.

'Many women want to be a princess.'

'When they're little girls, perhaps. But I'm all grown up, and those kinds of dreams die when you realise that's all they are. Silly, glitter-covered fantasies which tarnish as soon as you expose them to reality. I'm an artist. A commoner. We don't marry princes.'

Had her dreams died with her parents? He wanted to rail against it. She should be allowed to have the fantasy she could be whatever she wanted. He couldn't have that dream, but that didn't mean the same was unavailable to her.

'What feeds the woman's soul?'

The flush ran over her cheeks. 'My art consumes me. When I paint, nothing else exists. It's all I've wanted for a long time. It's enough.'

It sounded like an excuse.

'You look like a princess. And tonight, at the table, you acted like a queen. No royalty I know would have done better.'

It was as if she'd protected one of her own, when no one apart from Stefano ever leapt to his defence, only tried to tear him down. The warm kernel of something lit in his chest. Bright, perfect. Overlaid with an intoxicating drumbeat down low. Desire that was dark, tempting and forbidden. Something to be taken care of by himself, on the rare occasion it afflicted him, or with a willing partner who knew what this was. A few hours of passion, nothing more.

Not with a woman he'd begun to crave with a kind of obsession. *Never* that.

A slow stain of colour crept up her throat. A gentle smile on her lips. The obvious pleasure in a compliment letting him know she was still a woman underneath all her talk otherwise.

'Thank you. I'll let you in on a secret. For a little while, I felt like one. The make-up, a pretty dress. Some exquisite jewellery that isn't mine. It's all smoke and mirrors really. But for one night, I'll admit it was fun.'

She didn't understand. It wasn't the trappings that had her competing with royalty, but her demeanour. The way she had stood up to those who tried to cut her down. The way she had stood up for him…

'What if for one night, it's what we could have?' The urgency of his need gripped him. The fantasy that he could have her for this moment. Every part of him began to prickle with anticipation, the hum of pleasure coursing through his blood. 'If we could pretend that I'm simply a man, and you're simply a woman.'

'That you're not the Prince of Lasserno? Are you asking me to grant your wish?'

A pulse beat at the base of her throat, an excited kind of fluttering that told him she wanted this too.

'And I'd treat you like the princess that you are.'

Her pupils expanded, drowning the rockpool green of her eyes till the colour was a mere sliver. Her lips parted, as if the oxygen had been sucked from the room, and he sensed it too. The tightening of his chest as if he couldn't fill his lungs.

She stood in front of him, glowing, beautiful in a way which evoked physical pain. He wanted her so badly he would drop to his knees and beg her like some supplicant so long as she granted him one evening, for both of them to lose themselves in the pretence they could be something other than who they were.

'Bella?' Her blood-red toes curled into the carpet. He clenched his hands to fists so he wouldn't reach out, touch. Take. 'I will do nothing unless you say yes. The choice, it is yours alone. Stay, or go.'

He had the power here. An imbalance she must never feel beholden to. He needed her to crave him as much as he craved her, to a kind of distraction.

She licked her lips. The mere peek of her tongue almost undid him. How he wanted to plunder that mouth. Tear the clothes from her body. Rip apart the fabric of both their lives for a night of pleasure, lost in her arms.

'If I'm a princess tonight, then who are you?'

The fantasy wove around him. Something which allowed them to forget who they were and what they were doing here.

'I'm the frog you're about to kiss.'

'But that means you'll turn into a prince.'

'I won't be Prince of Lasserno. I'll be *your* prince.'

Hers alone.

Hannah's lips curled into a wicked smile. 'For only one night.'

It wasn't a question, and in a strange way that gave him some comfort. But the thought laced him with a kind of pain, that when the sun rose in the morning this blissful, illicit fantasy would be over.

'That's all it can ever be. Sex has a way of changing things, but it can't change this,' he said, as much of a warning to him as it was to her. Though the fantasy wove into a reality, where she could turn him into someone else for a few hours, because they both willed it.

'And what about duty?'

'Tonight?' It could only be one night and nothing else. That was all he would allow himself. And for him, that would be enough. 'Duty can go to hell.'

Duty can go to hell.

The words rang through her like some clarion call. He stood there, jaw hard. Hands clenched to fists at his sides. His bow tie hanging loose, and the top of his shirt unbuttoned to show the dark hair at his throat. Yet he wouldn't come to her. She knew it. She saw it in the tense set of his body. He wanted her to decide. And she craved him, with a zeal that made little sense to her. She'd never been particularly interested in sex, or so she had always thought, the idea of getting too close to someone, letting anyone in, crushing the breath right out of her. Caring was dangerous. Loving, even more so. But around Alessio, there was no common sense. As if he were all the oxygen in the room, as if to breathe she had to have him.

She wanted to walk into his arms, into all that strength. Bury her nose to the hollow at the base of his throat. Let every part of him overwhelm her. She took a step. The first. It wasn't so hard because this was a moment of fantasy where they could pretend to be other people. Alessio flexed his fingers as she took another step, and another. And only when she stood so close that his warmth seeped into her, did he wrap his arms round her, as strong as she'd imagined them to be. He dropped his head as if in slow motion. She rose on her toes and their lips touched. The warm press of skin to skin. Gentle, strangely innocent in a way that almost broke her heart. She dropped back, looked into his all-dark eyes, the pupils drowning out the velvet brown.

'Look,' she whispered, her voice cracking. A hesitation between them as if everything was tentative and the universe waited. 'I've made a prince.'

And then it was as if the world exploded around them. Alessio groaned and took her face in his hands, crushing his lips to hers. She met him, her hands on his chest, fingers curling into the strong muscles there. She had no experience, but this seemed to lack all finesse, drawn from pure need. Their tongues touched, battled, as if each were trying to win over the other. Her body was all heat and fire, her exquisite dress of fine fabric a scraping interruption to his fingers on her overheated skin. She slipped her hands under his jacket, over the shoulders, tugging because every piece of clothing between them was a travesty. He let her face go, tore the jacket from his body. Tossed it to the floor.

'Your dress. I don't trust myself.'

She barely did her *own* self. But she reached round with trembling fingers and slid the zip down, slowly. As if this were a kind of performance, because she was transfixed by the hooded rapture in his eyes as he watched. There was no time for nerves, no time for doubts. Not here, not now. Tonight she *was* a princess, and she could do and have anything she wanted.

And how she wanted Alessio.

The dress slumped from her shoulders as she shrugged out of the bodice. The fabric slid over her body, fell to the floor. She stepped out of it, as if it were a sea of foam on the ground and she was leaving the ocean, reborn, in only the exquisite lace bra and panties which she'd purchased to match the dress. The single extravagance she'd allowed when preparing her trip to Lasserno. Her skin seemed too tight, as if she were a butterfly ready to burst from the chrysalis. It was as if for the past nine years she'd been in stasis, waiting. And now she'd been changed on a cellular level.

Hannah began to walk forward towards Alessio and he held up a hand.

'Wait. I want to look at you. To always remember your beauty.'

There were so many things that would be left unsaid tonight, but how precious these moments were would not be one of them. Now wasn't the time to be shy, but to be brave.

'I need to see you too,' she whispered, unsure as to whether her voice was loud enough with all the emotion trembling through it. Alessio's throat convulsed with a swallow which told her all she needed to know, that he'd heard her plea. He grabbed his bow tie, dragged it from round his neck and dropped it on the floor. Undid a button on his shirt, then another and another. Tugged the zinc-white fabric from the waist of his trousers, tossing it aside the way of his coat and bow tie. She inhaled sharply at the sight before her, his broad shoulders, the muscles of his arms all sculpted and bronzed. The hair at his chest, dusting the muscles there, trailing down, darkening and disappearing at his trouser waistband. Her fingers became restless to run them through the crisp hair. To touch. He undid his belt, drew it slowly from his trousers before tossing it aside. Her eyes dropped as he gripped the top of his trousers. Even though they were black, the evidence of his arousal was bold and obvious.

She'd done that to him.

'Like what you see?'

'I'd like to see more.'

He chuckled and the ripple of it rolled through her, like a promise for something she didn't know she'd been waiting for. Anticipation at its finest.

'Your wish is my command, *Principessa.*'

A thrill shivered through her, that she had any sway over this man. That he stood there, tense with his physical masculine beauty, waiting for her next word.

'Slowly.'

The corner of his mouth kicked up and he did exactly as she demanded. It was as if each notch on the zip took an age. Almost as if time were standing still. The leisurely, deliberate tease all for her as he hooked his hands into the waistband of his trousers and his underwear. The heat of this moment flamed in her cheeks. The boldness of it, all because of what she desired. It could career out of control at any second, but for now this was hers. Alessio bent at the waist as his trousers

passed his thighs, everything hidden, then they slipped
to the floor and he rose. Stepped out of the superfine
black wool and kicked them and his underwear away.

He stood straight, allowing her eyes to take their fill.
She might be inexperienced, but she'd seen naked men
before. In art, on the internet, in life-drawing classes.
This, however, was more than she had ever experienced.
A perfect man, drawn by the hand of angels. Too real to
be human, yet undoubtedly flesh and blood. His arousal,
because of her, intoxicating.

'I need to touch you. For you to touch me.' His voice
was tight, as if he were in pain, and she understood.
The ache inside her built and built. She felt she might
double over with need, self-combust if their hands were
not on one another soon.

'Yes. *Please.*'

He made it to her in a few strides, hands hot and
hard on her hips, slipping round to her buttocks, pulling her close and against him. Burying his face in her
neck and breathing her in. His lips kissing and skimming the sensitive skin there till she moaned. He slid
his hands up her back as she shivered and quaked under
his exquisite touch. Unhooked her bra. Slipped it over
her arms and let it fall to the floor. He moved his hands
to cup her breasts, stood back a mere fraction to look,
brushed his thumbs to her nipples and they tightened
with a burning pleasure. He looked down at her with
reverence, as if she were a kind of revelation.

'Touch me,' he groaned and released one breast, taking her hand in his. Guiding it between them. Clasping
it tight around his hard length. He hissed in a breath as

he thrust into her palm, dropping his head back, and the tendons on his neck stood out, tense and as if he were in agony. She marvelled at the feel of him, silk over steel, and at his size, which she knew on a biological level should fit her, yet on a pure female level an uncertain niggle like fear began to seed and grow.

Fear had no place here, not tonight on her one evening allowing herself to be the princess in this fantasy. A night to give, take, indulge, before going back to real life, or her new version of it.

His grip on her hand loosened. He left her to stroke him up and down in the rhythm he'd set, returning his attention to her nipples, which were tight and aching. She shifted under his ministrations, *needing* him. It would be easy to ignore the obvious, not tell him about her inexperience, but this would do a disservice to them both, and she'd allow *nothing* to interfere with tonight.

She let him go and he opened his eyes, his lips apart. Eyes glazed and unfocused with pleasure.

'Alessio, I…' She hesitated when this was not the time for it. Now was the time to be bold. To take what she wanted for herself. He stopped teasing her nipples, rested his hands gently on her hips. Looked down at her with the slightest of frowns, of concern, she thought, and the warmth of realisation flooded her. She traced her hands up his body, to rest on the firm swell of his pectoral muscles, as the dark hair on his chest pricked and teased under her fingertips.

'You have something to say, *bella*?'

'I—I've never done this before.'

His grip on her hips tightened and released. 'This?'

'Sex. Any of it.'

His eyes widened a fraction. Then he wrapped his strong arms round her and drew her close into his embrace. The tears pricked at her eyes. Her virginity wasn't something she'd ever thought much of. It simply *was*. A fact. A reality. She'd never believed it merited much thought, until now.

'I'm your first.' The words were muffled and hot, murmured into her hair.

In everything.

'Yes.'

He stroked a hand up and down her spine. Light, tender brushes, and goosebumps sprinkled over her skin, as soft and warm as a spring shower.

'A better man would send you to bed on your own.'

'A better man wouldn't leave me feeling like this.' She pulled back and his arms fell loose. Hannah looked up at him. His pupils were drowning out the colour of his eyes till they were almost black. He was still hard and hot against her belly.

'Like what?' he ground out, all gravel and darkness.

'Empty. Like I'm going to die if you're not inside me. I *hurt* for wanting you so badly.'

His nostrils flared, lips parted a fraction. 'I won't leave you. I'll make it good for you. I promise.'

He slipped his hand to her left nipple again. Toying with it. Harder now. A light pinch.

'Do you like that?' he murmured.

She arched her back into him with the bright spark of pleasure rushing straight between her legs. Not so gentle then, and the slow burn between them became hotter and hotter.

'Yes.' Her voice was a sigh, nothing more.

'I can take the pain away,' he said as he eased her panties from her body till they slipped down her legs. 'You'll be screaming tonight from pleasure.'

Alessio slipped his hand between their bodies, between her thighs. Gentle strokes where she needed him most. It was too much and not enough all at the same time. She moved against him, desperate for more. Desperate to be filled, to be overwhelmed by him. She couldn't look at him now. Closed her eyes as if to hold on to the sensation so it would never end.

Then he slowed. Slid a finger inside her. Her fingers clawed into the hard muscles of his chest as he stroked something deep in her body, making Hannah quiver and quake with a flood of heat between her legs. 'I'll take care of you,' he murmured gently into her ear, kissing feather-light where his breath had stroked at her skin.

She clung round his neck because she'd fall if she didn't. Riding his hand like a woman who was a stranger to her.

Her head tipped back, and his lips were on hers. Soft, passionate. She opened and let him in. Their tongues touched, tangled together. She craved for him to invade every part of her. His fingers brushing her nipple, the sense of him deep inside, thrusting with one finger, then another.

'Let go, *bella*.' He whispered the words against her lips before crushing them to his again, adding a thumb to brush over her clitoris in soft, insistent strokes. He was everywhere, her world. She was burning like the hottest flame, till she was sure her skin would blister with it.

Then she came, cracked in two as if Alessio had torn her apart with pleasure. Screaming as he'd promised, in a rush of perfect, blinding heat.

Alessio breathed in the scent of her, the brightness of her perfume, the dark musk of her arousal, as she clenched hot and wet round his fingers. Then the weight of her arms round his neck intensified, as if her knees were giving out underneath her. He swept Hannah into his arms, her body soft and limp, her eyes glazed with arousal, a flush of colour tinting her cheeks, her chest. So beautiful in that dying blush of pleasure it almost caused him physical pain. He dropped his mouth to hers, her lips soft and yielding like the rest of her. All slick and hot and wet.

The privilege of being granted her trust flared inside him. He silently vowed it would be good for her, *better* than good. He wanted these hours with her to transcend mere sex. Something to be remembered, treasured, especially given it was her first time.

There would be no disappointing Hannah tonight. On the contrary, he feared she would be a revelation to shake the foundations of his being. He laid her gently on the covers of his bed, his body trembling with the desire to be inside her, where his fingers had been. But he would make sure tonight was about her. Her pleasure first and foremost.

Her eyes lay closed, the beautiful lashes feathering

on her cheeks. He allowed her the bliss of the come-down from her orgasm. Perhaps her first at the hands of another. Marvelled at her body, splayed with abandon on the bed before him. Settled himself between her thighs where he could smell the sweet scent of arousal, the necklace at her throat like a jewelled symbol of his possession, making this all the more erotic. He dropped his head and licked, the taste of her like a drug shooting straight into his veins, and she groaned as he toyed with her. Worshipping her in the best way he knew how.

Her back arched from the bed as she gripped and released the covers.

'Alessio... I...it's too much.'

He ceased his ministrations. Stroked his thumbs gently on the insides of her thighs. As much as she said it was too much, her back arched, bringing her body closer to his mouth.

'Relax. You have no idea how much your body can take but I can show you. I can show you it all. Let me pleasure you,' he murmured against her, so close to where he wanted his mouth to be it almost watered.

'Yes.' The word came like the softest of exhales, the sweetest capitulation, and he began his gentle ministrations again, the light flicking of his tongue, till she thrashed on the bed, her words indecipherable. She thrust her hand into his hair and gripped tight, the bright needles of pain causing the heat of passion to roar through him like lava in his blood. He slipped his hands under her buttocks, the whole of her trembling. Held her in place as he sucked on the tight little nub at the centre of her and relished her second scream of the evening, this time his name sung to the room.

There was no time now for him to wait, every part of him frayed and overheating. He had to be inside her. He'd spill himself on the sheets like a teenager if he wasn't, and soon. He reached for his bedside drawer, the condoms there. Sheathed himself with difficulty because he was affected by it too, this thing between them. Climbed over her and she wrapped her arms round him tight.

'Do you want me inside you?'

'Never more than now.'

'I'll go slowly,' he said, a promise voiced so he'd be forced to keep it, because all he wanted was to take. Ease his own agony. But tonight was for her. He kissed her, their tongues twining together, hot, erotic, as he slid against the folds of her, testing her wetness to ensure his entry would be easy enough, even though he wished he could promise her no pain. He notched himself at Hannah's centre, slid a bit further, a little way inside, and shut his eyes at the overwhelming pleasure of her heat enveloping only the tip of him. Worked gentle thrusts, a little deeper, deeper still, till Hannah's kisses became harder, more insistent. Bruising. She tilted her hips and he slid all the way inside, the hitch of her breath catching as he did so. He pulled his head back to look at her, to breathe through the pleasure to ensure her own, almost losing himself to his own orgasm right there.

'Good?' Sentences were beyond him, but he needed to check on her, the desire to make sure she wasn't hurting, that she was enjoying this, clasping at something deep inside him.

She opened her eyes and stared deep into his. Alessio's muscles trembled as she clenched tight and hot round him. Gripping him like the warmest silken glove, so tight it was almost his undoing.

'Perfect.' Her voice was a sigh shivering right through him. The pleasure threaded in her voice, like a plea.

'Should I move?'

'Move? Yes.'

His arms rested either side of her head. He stroked his thumbs to her temples, the necklace glittering in the soft light of the room, winding the blissful fantasy of the night round him once more.

'It would be my greatest pleasure.'

He rocked into her again and her eyes fluttered shut for a moment before opening. Holding his gaze. He said it would be his greatest pleasure, but all he craved was hers. She wrapped her legs tight round him, moving with him. He lost himself in her gaze, the flush of her skin, her lips, parted as if she couldn't take in enough air. Head thrown back and eyes glazed and far away with ecstasy. The heat of her, the scent of her around him. The sound of their bodies coming together wound him tighter and tighter. And the words left his mouth in his own language. Murmurings of ecstasy, of thanks, of truth.

'I don't understand,' she whispered, her blinks long and slow, her body tightening even harder round his.

The tingle at the base of his spine heralded that he was close, so close.

And against all his better judgement he told her.

'You are so beautiful. It is too much. The privilege of being inside you.'

He changed his angle, went deeper. Ground his hips against her body. Her eyes widened as the bright spill of tears gleamed and threatened. Then her gaze became unfocused as she stiffened, gasped and cried out his name as she came. He plunged over the edge with her, the ecstasy tearing up his spine as if he were being struck by lightning. A blinding white flash in his head almost obliterated his consciousness. Then, as he came back to himself once the spasms subsided, all he could see was her. Tears now tracking from the corners of her eyes. The sparkling necklace at her throat. For tonight he'd allow them both the fantasy.

'La mia principessa.'

My princess.

Reality would come soon enough.

CHAPTER SEVEN

HANNAH SAT IN an armchair opposite Alessio's desk as he paced the rich crimson carpet of his office, checking his watch. He was dressed today in a crisp white shirt with a vibrant lemon-yellow tie. No jacket, which she suspected counted almost as casual with him. His body was tense, every part of him bristling as he almost wore a path through the plush flooring. She wanted to put her arm on him. To tell him it was okay to simply stop. She knew he could. That he could channel his restless energy elsewhere. How she craved a repeat performance. To spend her days and nights learning about him in every way. A slide of heat wound through her, hot and tempting. She didn't know how he could be so immune to it all, when she wanted to melt into a human-shaped puddle in her seat.

His gaze rested on her, cool and hard. So unlike the loose, relaxed, passionate man from the night before she was almost forced to wonder whether she'd dreamt what had happened between them. Today all she saw was the ruler of Lasserno, as if the man, Alessio Arcuri, had ceased to exist.

'The hospital visit is private. No press have been alerted. I hope you recognise the privilege of this invitation. The children—'

'*The children are not in some circus where you can watch them perform.* I'm aware how vulnerable children can be.'

She'd never use sick children as fodder, he had to realise that. Or perhaps he didn't really know her at all. But it wasn't about his comment. No, he was distancing himself from her. Pulling away from the night they'd shared. This morning, waking to a cold and empty bed. The loss something almost palpable, drawing tears to her eyes when she'd wanted to portray herself as a sophisticate who understood they'd had one night together and that was all it could ever be.

'*Sex has a way of changing things...*'

He'd warned her and he'd been right. She understood passion now, the bruising agony of it, whereas once it had been an abstract concept experienced by others. Now, to her, Alessio sprang to life in glorious colour. She knew how his body worked in ways more than the cold anatomy of him. How his muscles bunched as he moved over her. The way the cords of his neck tensed as he was close, the blissful lack of focus in his eyes as he lost himself in her body. His care *for* her and her pleasure. All these things she could see even now, as his back was to her. They ran through her head, causing the whole of her to run hot, as if on fire. Things which showed he was a human and not the myth he tried so hard to portray to the world.

Yet something about the way she was being dismissed slashed at her deep inside. Though she supposed Alessio could hardly ask *are you okay?* if he wanted to keep what they'd done secret, given Stefano was sitting in the corner with one eyebrow cocked, watching them both. Did he know what had happened? Was it painted all over her face in the heat rising there? How was she going to keep things together at the hospital?

She took a deep breath. She was an adult, a grown woman. Last night had been a blissful, incredible, earth-shattering experience which could never be repeated. *One night. One night.* She'd say that mantra till it sank in and wove itself into the fibre of her being.

Stefano announced the cars were ready and they left, Alessio travelling alone. He always seemed alone, she realised, and perhaps that was the way it had to be as a ruler, a solitary journey. The ache of that burned in her chest as they arrived at the hospital to a back entrance with no fanfare. Hannah was introduced and welcomed as the official portrait artist, reminding her that this was her *job*, so she pulled out her sketch pad and her pencils from a satchel, the familiar weight of them in her hands spreading a calm through her.

Most people at the hospital seemed to be nonplussed with a prince in their midst, as if he did this often. Maybe he did, though it surprised her that the children's ward was such a dour place. White walls, grey floors. A few faded pictures on the wall. All the children tucked neatly into the beds, though a few brightened up when Alessio arrived, grinning at him, waving as if he were an old friend. He grinned back, greeted some by name. She turned to the doctor who'd brought them here.

'They seem to know him.'

The doctor smiled. 'Yes. A few of the children have serious health problems and have been here for some time. His Highness is popular with them. He visits as often as his schedule allows. He's planning works on the children's ward soon and likes to hear their ideas.'

Alessio talked to a sad-looking little boy wearing a cast. The soft concern on his face made him seem unrecognisable from the stern Prince in the palace he'd shown to her earlier.

'Have you thought about art on the walls?'

'We have hopes for many things. A complete refurbishment. So little money has been spent for so long. But the children would benefit if this were a happier place.'

Alessio now seemed to be having an intense conversation with another child's bear. It could have been a political discussion the way he gesticulated, whilst the little girl who owned the bear giggled, brightening the mood of the room. Hannah's heart melted at the scene, a small shred of joy in this joyless place.

'The corridor on the way in would be a wonderful place for a mural. If the children were being brought into the ward, it could make them less fearful to have something fun to look at. And then in here—' Hannah gestured to another blank wall, the ideas flowing as to the scenes she'd like to paint, the cartoon characters, the animals '—even bright paint colours would be a simple solution. I could jot down some colour schemes and ideas that don't cost much money if murals won't fit into the budget.'

'Please do.' The doctor smiled. 'Now I should introduce His Highness to some of the newest patients here. *Scusi.*'

Hannah sat in a plastic chair, far enough away so she had a perfect view of the whole room. She opened her sketch pad, lingering for a few moments on the drawing of Alessio's hands. His questing fingers, the way they drifted across her skin. But those were thoughts she wasn't allowed to have because there'd be no repeat of the night before. She ignored the ember glowing deep inside, one she couldn't stoke to life again. Instead, she turned to a fresh page and began another drawing. This picture was of Alessio, holding an animated conversation with the little girl's bear.

As she sketched the scene she became aware of movement nearby. She turned to a young boy who'd crept up beside her as she drew. Hannah smiled.

'Hello. What's your name?'

The boy's eyes widened, and she realised he might not be able to speak English. She pulled out her phone and searched for a translation app. *'Come ti chiami?'*

He laughed, probably at her parlous pronunciation. 'Giulio.'

'Hello, Giulio. My name is Hannah.' She patted her chest.

He gave a tentative smile, then pointed to the page where she'd sketched Alessio. She didn't know what to say. Their barrier was language, but her art spoke a language all of its own. Hannah turned to another fresh page and considered the blank wall and what kind of mural she'd put there, then began sketching.

'Watch,' she said to the dark-eyed waif, who'd now pulled up a little plastic child's chair to sit beside her. And she drew a field of grass and flowers. A teddy bear's picnic, with all the kinds of fairy-tale foods the children might love. Ice cream, incredible towers of jelly, cakes. Not a vegetable to be seen. Bears playing, flying kites, including one which had been blown away on a strong gust of wind, and the bear holding it sailing into the sky with others trying to pull it down.

The little boy next to her laughed, and the sound spurred her on. She began mapping out a few ideas, losing herself in the fun of creating a joyous space, something better than this, something to make the children less fearful. Soon she had a small audience watching her. Children with wide eyes and wider smiles. What more could she draw for them? She didn't really watch television, didn't go to see movies, and had no nieces and nephews, being an only child, so wasn't sure what children liked. That sense of isolation pricked at her. Most of the time she didn't really feel lonely, not with her art. It was as if she were always in the presence of the person whose portrait she painted. Immersed in them, kept company by their picture and her understanding of them as a person. Today, she was overwhelmed by the knowledge there was only her. She looked up at Alessio, talking to some of the nurses. He was alone too. Did he ever have the sense of it, a kind of emptiness, or did duty fill the spaces?

He glanced over in her direction, almost like he knew she was watching him. As he took in the children surrounding her, a look crossed his face. Something intense, not implacable at all. The potency of that moment ignited those flickering embers deep inside. Then a child touched her arm and pointed at the page. She laughed because she knew they wanted her to keep drawing, so she turned her attention to the sketch pad once more. Alessio wasn't safe. The children were. Looking at the boy who'd first come to her, with his dark curls and eyes, Hannah began to sketch him, a little caricature. It was how she had first started with her art. Doodling in class, drawing friends, till her parents had died and the obsession overtook her, that her memory of their faces might fade. So she'd drawn them incessantly, etching them into her brain so she would never forget.

A shadow crossed her page as she was almost done. A shiver of awareness shimmied down her spine. There was only one person it could be.

'You have a crowd.' Alessio's voice was as warm as the summer's day outside, heating her as if she'd stepped into the midday sunshine.

She tore herself from her drawings and their gazes caught and held. Her pulse took off at a gallop, the wild beat only for him. 'Is your ego coping with the lack of attention?'

He did nothing for a heartbeat, then burst out laughing. It was as if happiness had exploded into the room. Everyone stared at him. The princely Alessio was a foreboding force. The passionate man in bed a study in absolute focus. But *this* man, laughing and real, showing his human side for the first time since she'd known him—this man was a danger. The type of man who could break a woman's heart.

Except there was nothing left to break. She'd lost her heart years ago on the day she'd lost everything. She'd encased it in a protective cage and now nothing could get through to harm it ever again. Hannah ignored those musings, and simply took in the man smiling at her in his own blinding way.

'You're a woman who's hard for my ego every day. But I'm sensible enough to know who the real talent is here. It's not me.'

'It's not me either—it's the health professionals.'

The burnt umber of his eyes smouldered like brown coal on fire as the look on his face softened, darkened. She knew it well, having seen it in his bedroom the night before. A shiver of longing coursed through her. Her cheeks heated as she remembered the pleasure, the delicious aches which remained. The memory of Alessio and his body over her. Inside her. Did it show on her face? Because naked desire was written all over his. But it had only been for one night. They'd agreed, and, as much as she craved more of him, she knew she'd only take what life gave her rather than ask for more. Since in the main, if she wanted more, life slapped her down in the cruellest possible ways.

'They are indeed. What are you doing there?' He nodded to the pages on which she'd drawn.

'I had some ideas to brighten up the ward, make it a more welcoming place for the children.'

The doctor who'd spoken to her earlier approached. 'Signorina Barrington suggested some murals. As you know, Your Highness, we talked of the ward becoming more welcoming. Less clinical.'

Alessio glanced at his watch, at Stefano, who began to approach. 'That's an excellent idea. I'll ensure there's a place in the budget. Anything for the children.'

He crouched down on his haunches. Said something to the children surrounding her. A slightly older boy answered back.

'Do you know any superheroes?' Alessio asked.

Hannah smiled. 'I'm sure I can think of a few. Does he want me to draw some?'

Alessio nodded. Even in this position, he ruled the room like the Prince he was. His gaze dropped to her mouth and lingered there. His lips parted as if he was going to say something more, but no words came. Those perfectly drawn lips of his had spent the night exploring her body in the most exquisite of ways, finding places she didn't know could give her pleasure. Yet Alessio had seemed to find them all.

'I—I should get started, then.'

She scribbled on the page with shaky fingers. The children seemed enthralled, and she was too, but by the man blazing in front of her. His nostrils flared. Did he know what she was thinking about? Was he thinking the same? It couldn't go anywhere, so better not to dwell on it at all.

They held each other like that for a few moments, their gazes clashing. Then Stefano approached and cleared his throat. Alessio stood, the break between them almost more painful than waking this morning to find herself alone.

'We should go. You have a meeting with the Health Minister.'

It was said in English for her benefit, she was sure. The children clamoured around Alessio as he moved to leave, making obvious noises of disappointment as they were ushered back to bed by the staff. All Hannah could do was watch his back as he walked away from her, as if she'd ceased to exist.

Alessio walked through the maze-like corridors of the hospital exquisitely aware of the woman trailing behind him, whom he could feel as if she were touching him. The flush on her cheeks. Her wide eyes. Those lips of hers a cherry blush. She had the look of a woman well-loved, as if she'd suddenly come into herself.

It had been all he could do to leave his bed this morning. To gather his clothes, the evidence they'd been together. To shower, scrub his body and try to wash her away. Yet he had failed. Nothing could wash away the memory of her sighs, her skin, so soft under his fingers.

Then with the children… How they'd flocked to her, her natural charm and grace drawing them in like the sunshine on a spring day, something beautiful and warm, welcoming. In a pretty blue dress with dark hair spilling unrestrained over her shoulders, she looked like every fantasy drawn to life. For those fleeting moments in her presence he didn't see problems, but possibilities, where his life only had one course. Right now he should let her join Stefano in the car behind his and travel to the palace by himself. Yet he was tired. Tired of the feeling his journey was one which should always be taken alone, with no one to share it with. For a moment he allowed himself to want without guilt.

'Signorina Barrington comes with me. I wish to know more about her ideas for the children's ward.'

'Do I need to ask again?' Stefano murmured.

Do you know what you're doing?

Alessio cut him off. 'No.'

The word left his mouth with barely a thought, and once uttered he would not take it back. He never did. Yet the truth screamed loud in his head. He didn't know what he was doing. He should be far away from her. Travelling with her was a breach of a self-imposed protocol.

And right now, he didn't care.

Stefano gave a small bow, the merest of smiles on his face. His eyebrow rose a fraction once more, the expression of amusement seeming to have become almost a permanent fixture Alessio had seen it so often over the past days. He wouldn't explain because none of this was explicable. His driver opened the door of the car and Hannah slipped into the back seat with him. Clipped on her seatbelt and looked out of the window. The car slid away from the rear of the hospital, starting the journey towards the palace.

'You were wonderful with the kids,' Hannah said, her voice soft and almost wistful.

'So were you.' They'd flocked to her, with her drawings of them, cartoon characters and everything in between. Those unwell children giggling with delight at the things she drew.

'They're an easy audience.'

Her smile lit up the interior of the car. Something in his chest clenched, the whole of him too hot and tight.

They'd agreed on one night, that it was enough, yet he hadn't realised one night with her could *never* be enough. There was nothing experienced about her, but Hannah's innocence and naked enthusiasm were like a drug that had him craving. He might never erase the memories from his room, which seemed ridiculous, yet no other woman had ever graced his bed at the palace. He dreaded the anticipation of lonely nights when she left. Craving to take his fill now, whilst he could.

His palms itched, wanting to touch, determined not to. Yet his resolve failed as she kept speaking. All he thought about was her natural beauty and how the children clambered over her as if she were a pied piper. As if she were some kind of saviour.

'There are so many ways you could help them. A mural would be a beautiful addition to the ward. It would brighten their lives, especially the little ones who need to stay there a long time. I have so many ideas.'

The cabin of the vehicle closed in on him, compressing to a pinpoint that was only them, as if the rest of the world didn't exist. He loosened his tie, now too tight round his neck. He needed to get out of this small space so he could breathe, so he could think. Even the journey back to the palace felt too long. And, since there was a driver up front, there was nothing he could do here. Yet he kept a small office in the capital, a well-guarded secret, and they were only minutes away from it.

'Manuel, please take us to the city office.'

'Of course, Your Highness.'

A few deviations and they arrived, driving through a gated archway and into an internal courtyard. The car stopped and Alessio didn't wait for his driver. He opened the door himself and stepped out into the baking summer's heat.

Hannah frowned. 'Are you leaving?'

He peered into the cabin where she sat, her teeth biting into her bottom lip. 'No. We have things to discuss. I have an office. It's private.'

Her mouth opened but she didn't reply. Merely nodded and followed him from the car. The few staff who ran the premises in his absence scrambled as he entered unannounced. He smiled at them, but it felt more rictus than genuine, each second not alone with Hannah a moment wasted. With introductions over he flung back the door of his office, and she followed him inside. He closed it behind her. Stood in the cool silence and could breathe again.

'What do you want to discuss, Your Highness?'

He wheeled around, hating that this formality had returned. He'd been wrong in the way he'd treated her this morning. Especially when the desire still ran rich and hot through his veins, calling him out as a liar for pretending what had happened between them was nothing. And, whilst he might lie to himself, he couldn't lie to her.

'Is once enough for you?'

Hannah's eyes darkened, pupils black in the oceanic green. He'd seen them look the same as she'd come apart underneath him in his bed, beautiful and wide with desire matching his own. Her lips parted as a flush crept from her throat. 'Never.'

'Good, because I want more.' His voice was a hiss

through clenched teeth at the agony of need unfulfilled. More a command than a request. Harsh and low. Clotted with desire.

Who stepped first, he couldn't have said. They fell into each other, his hands thrust into her silken locks of hair. Lips on hers, hard and fast. She clung to his shoulders, their tongues touching, and he moved back to a large sofa in the corner. Dropped into it with her straddling his hips, rocking forward on the hardness of him as he groaned into her mouth. He slid his hands to her buttocks, drawing her even closer, hiking up the skirt of her dress till he could grab at the soft, pale skin of her thighs. She quivered under his palms as he moved back in the seat a little and slid a finger between them, her underwear damp with evidence of her arousal. He rubbed over her most sensitive spot. Light touches that had her panting and squirming against him, holding her on a cruel edge. Tormenting her in the way she had unknowingly tormented him by merely existing, the noises she made increasingly desperate. He didn't care. He wanted her to beg for her pleasure, here in his office, where they could both lose their minds.

He was agonisingly hard now. Her heat was against him, relentless and brutal. He'd been unprepared. He had no protection. The pulse of need drove him on, but as much as he craved to release himself and slide into the wet heat of her, he wouldn't. The risk to her as much as to him was too great. This journey could lead nowhere permanent. But pleasure was something they could give one another. He had nothing on this afternoon he couldn't cancel. They could spend it in his rooms once back at the palace, or in hers. It didn't matter, so long as he was inside her.

Hannah let out a groan. A curse. A *plea*.

'Ah, *bella*. Am I neglecting you?' The words were said against her gasping mouth. He slid two fingers inside her, curled them to reach the sensitive spot he knew drove her wild. Worked his thumb over the tight bundle of nerves at the juncture of her thighs as her breath held, the whole of her drawn tight as a bow till she broke apart around him, her shuddering body letting him know she'd tumbled over the edge, moaning his name as her spasms went on and on, clenching round his fingers. With a final flutter she sagged into him. He withdrew from her, wrapped Hannah tight in his arms. His own body, so hard and aching, objected to the way she nestled into him, screaming for its own release. Yet he did nothing, giving her this time. After a few moments relaxed in his arms she stirred, rocked against him again. He gasped as a bright burst of pleasure exploded through him.

'What about you?' Her voice was a sigh against his neck, feathering over his skin. She pulled back, her eyes soft, dreamy. Skin flushed a delicate pink. Mouth plump and well-kissed.

What he wouldn't give to forget being a prince, forget the consequences, take for himself and be damned. But that would make him like his father, and he was not that man.

'I didn't come prepared for this.'

'You wouldn't make a very good boy scout, then, would you?'

He chuckled, even though the ache in his groin intensified as she voiced her need to give him pleasure as well. Too often people had been prepared to take from him. Someone considering his true desires seemed like hedonism at its finest.

'It's something I've never considered. Being Prince of Lasserno, others tend to prepare for me.'

The corners of her plush, kiss-reddened lips curled into a wicked smile. She leaned forward, her voice a whisper in his ear. 'Luckily I have a few ideas for how I can help, *Your Highness*.'

A quake ran through him at the sound of his title spoken with her low, intent voice. It was almost a taunt but he didn't care. She pulled back, and with trembling fingers Hannah worked at his belt buckle, the closure on his trousers, the zip. Then her cool hand reached into his underwear and took him out. He stifled a groan. Almost lost control in that moment, unable to tear his gaze away as she tightened her grip and worked him the way he'd shown her the night before. Damn, if they weren't going to make a mess here and right now, but he didn't care. Gone mad with a feverish desire that nothing bar her would satisfy. Then Hannah moved from his lap, dropped to her knees on the floor before him. Loosened the relentless grip and stroking which had him close to the edge and almost tumbling over.

'I don't really know what I'm doing—you'll have to guide me.'

Alessio frowned, not sure what she was talking about until she dropped her head, and the warmth of her breath caressed a sliver of flesh at his stomach. He jerked in her hand as the knowledge of what she was about to do coursed through him like an electric current.

'Devour me like you've never been hungrier in your life,' he groaned.

She looked up at him, eyes that intense rockpool green, dark and still. With depths he could never fathom. A wicked smile played at the corners of her perfect mouth. 'Just remember, I'm not going to stop.'

She took him into the heat of her mouth. His brain blanked with white noise roaring in his ears. Hannah was tentative till he moaned, and her efforts became intense. Determined. His hand tangled into her hair, guiding her, but there was no need. She followed his instructions to a perfection belying her inexperience. He was close, so close, feeling the tingling at the base of his spine, the heaviness, the tightening in his groin. He held on but the vision of her worshipping him like this, because that was how it seemed, drove him to the edge of control. She wanted him as much as he wanted her. Of that, he had no doubt. And her words, *'I'm not going to stop…'* ran on repeat. Like an endless loop in his head, winding him tighter and higher.

'Hannah… I'm going to… Hannah…'

He tugged at her hair in warning, but she didn't let up on the relentless rhythm. For once in his life he allowed the scorching fire of his orgasm tear through his body with no thought or care for the consequences.

Letting the burn set him free.

CHAPTER EIGHT

ALESSIO SAT BEHIND his desk, trying and failing to make sense of some financial reports. The numbers on the page swirled and blurred into one another. Yesterday had been an exercise in hedonism. Something he'd never indulged in. He and Hannah in his city office. Cancelling his appointments. Spending the afternoon in bed, repaying her a thousand-fold, making her scream. That filled his thoughts. Not these dry figures and graphs about tourism which should be holding his interest.

Yet he couldn't see what he and Hannah were doing as a mistake. Not now. It might be a glorious folly, like the pavilion on the palace grounds. Built to a love that was all an illusion. But they had set an end: the date Hannah left Lasserno. Then he could choose his princess, establish his throne. Renew the glory of his country.

Still, what had once driven him now held no excitement. He rubbed his hands over his face. Took another long draught of his coffee. Today it was as if his bones were made of lead. Strange that around Hannah he seemed…lighter. More energised, invigorated, as if plugged straight into a power source. Not bowed by this weight, as if the expectations of the world sat on his shoulders.

He checked the time, then his diary. More meetings. Soon Stefano would walk in and they'd go. Instead of preparing, all he could think about was another evening in bed with Hannah. Driving away his worries for Lasserno in the warmth of her body. The way her hands stroked tenderly over his skin. A shred of softness at the end of a hard day...

'Sir, His Highness is busy... Sir! You can't go—'

'My abdication does not mean this has ceased to be my palace. I go where I choose. I choose to see my son.'

Alessio's blood froze, then his repressed rage heated it till it was near boiling. That voice sent a jagged spear through the heart of him. His father. Since his abdication he'd barely been near the palace, holed up in his personal villa on the outskirts of the capital, where few people paid any attention to his exploits and greater excesses. The double doors of his office were flung open and the former Prince himself strode in as if he still owned the room. To some people in this country he still did, but that was a problem for another day. Stefano followed, fists clenched.

'I'm sorry—'

Alessio held up his hand. If he'd not been able to curb his father, then his best friend had no chance. 'It's okay. I'm sure he'll leave soon.'

The man in question looked around the room as Stefano backed out and closed the doors behind him. The corner of his father's top lip curled in a sneer. 'I don't favour what you've done with the place.'

'I don't care. Your taste isn't mine.' In *anything*. He'd happily rid the space of the more garish furniture and installed less frivolous antique pieces, more solid and befitting the future ruler of Lasserno.

Alessio gritted his teeth so hard he could almost taste blood. This was the man who'd left his wife and Lasserno's beloved Princess to die alone. The man who'd plundered the crown jewels as he'd seen fit, as if it wasn't bad enough in days long past that the royal family had lost the coronation ring present in so many portraits here, never to be recovered. A reminder to Alessio of responsibility and all he was tasked to protect.

'All your talk of austerity and yet you decide to re-decorate. I wonder, is this what hypocrisy looks like?'

'This furniture was already in the palace. None of it's new. At least I didn't raid the crown jewels, the *country's* treasures, to fund my lifestyle or provide baubles to sycophants.'

His father threw back his head and laughed. Dressed in a favoured Savile Row suit, he remained a handsome man, although his hair was greying, and he carried a little thickness around the middle. To Alessio's disgust, he looked more like this man than he did his beautiful mother, with her pale hair and eyes. His father's genes had erased everything of his mother from him…almost. Not her inherent goodness, he hoped. Alessio strove to carry that always.

'The country's? No. We're an absolute monarchy. Everything in Lasserno is *ours*, to take as we see fit.

Or have you forgotten? Next, you'll be talking constitutions and presidents. Save me from a straw crown. I want none of it.'

Alessio sat still in his seat, the lessons of his childhood coming to the fore, when all he wanted was to stand and rage. But he refused to give this man the satisfaction of showing any emotion. Anyhow, toddler tantrums were his father's specialty. He had more control. Alessio gripped the arms of his chair a little tighter, to prevent himself from leaping from it.

'A ruler can be absolute, and still do the right thing by the country and its people.'

'Doing what's right for oneself is much more entertaining. Yet, despite your efforts, *the people* don't seem to think you're doing a good job. What are the press saying again?'

That he was cold. Autocratic. Opaque. Those words might have stung if his path weren't clear. The people would see, once Lasserno took its rightful place on the world stage rather than being a forgotten backwater.

'I don't care, and that's where our core difference lies. Since I'm a busy man fixing the messes you left, get to the point. Why did you come here? I suspect it wasn't to criticise my decorating style.'

His father took a seat in the chair opposite Alessio's desk, lounging in an indolent kind of way that was the man's specialty.

'I've come to congratulate you.' His father's gloating tone sounded a warning. 'You're not a lost cause yet, when for some time I thought you were all work and no play. She really is a masterstroke.'

Alessio froze. It couldn't be. He *couldn't* know about Hannah. Everyone in the palace was faithful to him. No one would say a thing. He'd learned a hard lesson about misplaced trust and had rid himself of his father's cronies and hangers-on the minute the man had walked away from the throne. Any whispers could only be rumour because he'd been seen with a woman, whose presence had been well reported before she'd even arrived in Lasserno. It was one of the few things he'd allowed Stefano to tell the press, the coup of his coronation portrait being painted by the world's finest young artist, something to be celebrated rather than hidden.

'Who are you talking about?'

His father waved his hand theatrically, twisting that spear even harder. His disdain for his son and only child had seemed to increase over the years. Alessio had long ceased trying to impress the man. He'd given up around the time he'd been called home from England, leaving behind his dreams of riding for his country any more. Arriving home to find Lasserno in disarray.

'The artist. I should have done the same.'

Alessio's veins turned to ice. 'Stop talking in riddles.'

Yet even as he said the words his voice was like dust in his mouth, dry and lacking conviction. His father was a master of playing vicious, wicked games. He enjoyed them, and Alessio wondered whether the 'mistake' in Hannah's placement at his table for dinner hadn't been a mistake at all but a move designed to create gossip.

'Installed my mistress before marriage. What did that prim little English nanny of yours always say? Something about beginning as you mean to end things.'

Start as you mean to finish.

'I have no mistress.' That was not what was happening here. Hannah would be leaving soon. But the denial caught in his throat, threatening to throttle him.

His father was only guessing, assuming his son would debauch any beautiful young woman the same as he would. The bile rose in Alessio's throat. He tried not to think that was exactly what he was doing. This was different. He didn't have a wife; he didn't have a child. There was nothing currently tying him to any person. He was as free as he could be.

'You can keep telling that to your conscience. Marry the perfect ice-cold princess and have your passionate piece already installed. You're setting the expectations of your wife early. Perfect.'

'I have nothing to trouble my conscience. Unlike you, I'll be a faithful husband and I would never leave my wife to die alone.'

'Your mother wanted me nowhere near her, especially not at the end. If she had I might have spent more time with her. Let's say she was satisfied with having an heir. She was never going to give me a spare. Trust me when I say a lack of passion makes for a very cold bed to lie in for eternity.'

Alessio stood then, began pacing the carpet.

'Perhaps if you'd been faithful, she might have been inclined to like you rather than despise you. Take care. This is my *mother* whose memory you're disparaging.'

'Whose necklace you allowed your little artist to wear. Which was sensible. They form no part of the crown jewels. Sets the girl's expectations, wearing secondary gems. She'll always know her place.'

'She is not my anything.'

'Lie to yourself all you want but say it with more conviction next time. Or better, admit to your failings. You have me as a father after all. One day you'll awaken a lonely old man and only then, when it's too late, you'll see I was right.'

'Is that all you have to say?' Alessio gritted his teeth, tried to maintain his temper. Swept his hands over the paperwork sitting on the desk. 'Because I have work, and no time for your ravings. You chose to abdicate this responsibility. Now leave me be.'

'Of course, *Your Highness*.' His father's voice was a cold sneer. 'Just remember, the work is always there. As the English like to say, *All work and no play makes Alessio a dull boy*. My suggestion? Keep your artist and find your royal wife. What use is being a prince if you can't have what you want?'

His father rose with the presence of a ruler, stalked to the study doors and flung them back. They smacked into the walls on either side with unnecessary force as he left the room. Alessio couldn't stop moving, the anger burning in his gut as he paced. His father didn't really know what was going on—he was fishing for information. But this, the palace, all the intrigue…it would sully what he had with Hannah, their last precious days spent together. He wanted perfect memories for them both. Had to get her away from here, but everywhere was fraught. Any of the other royal homes, the royal yacht, had bigger problems. Whilst he'd rid the palace in the capital of his father's sycophants, he couldn't be sure of elsewhere.

Where to go? Somewhere close enough to the capital to be able to return easily, but far enough away to avoid prying eyes.

Stefano entered the room, brow furrowed in concern. 'All okay?'

In those days after his father's abdication, only his best friend knew the true extent of the trouble his father had caused. Alessio stilled. The solution stood in front of him. One he'd used a few times before when riding his horses had ceased to be enough. 'I need to escape for a few days. The usual way.'

Stefano nodded, yet his eyebrows rose again. 'Will Hannah be joining you?'

'Yes.' Alessio clenched his jaw. He would have no judgement on this, not from his friend. 'Are you going to ask whether I know what I'm doing?'

Stefano gave him a wry smile. This man was one of his closest supporters. Like a brother. He placed a hand on Alessio's shoulder and gave a brief squeeze of solidarity.

'I don't have to, my friend. I think you know exactly what you're doing. And for once it's what you want to do, rather than what you believe you should. That's a *good* thing.'

Stefano released him and left the room, phone to his ear. In his office, all alone with the weight of his ancestors' portraits around him, Alessio wasn't sure he could take any comfort from his friend's parting words.

CHAPTER NINE

HANNAH WALKED DOWN a gangplank to the harbour at dawn. The whole journey had been cloaked in secrecy. She had been told to pack for the beach for two days, and that was it. Not that she'd come to Lasserno prepared for needing beachwear. When she'd told Alessio, a host of bags had arrived in her room. Clothes with tags from designers who left her breathless, so she simply stuffed it all into a duffel bag she'd brought with her. In the pale morning light Alessio looked nothing like his usual self, unrecognisable in shorts showing off his strong calves, a T-shirt, cap jammed on his head, like a disguise. The whole episode was all subterfuge. He'd even driven them here through a back exit of the palace, with no entourage. Something cloak and dagger about it thrilled her.

They arrived at a magnificent yacht that looked as if it had come straight out of a classic movie, with three soaring masts and gleaming, honeyed wood. Alessio helped her aboard, where they were met by the crew. He shook their hands. Introduced her.

'Remember, the same rules as last time,' Alessio said.

The captain nodded. 'Of course, sir. We'll be underway immediately.'

'Thank you.'

No *Your Highness*…no bowing. Little ceremony at all, as someone spirited away their bags. Alessio slid a hand to the small of her back and they traversed the expansive deck to the bow. As they reached the rail, Alessio checked his watch. She placed her hand over his wrist.

'You do that constantly.'

'I want to see if we're leaving in good time.'

He'd told her this weekend was for them, to get away. It seemed as if he never could, always managing his day to the last second. She turned his wrist over, unclipped the burnished gold band and slid the timepiece from his wrist. Rubbed a thumb over his pulse-point. Over the mark the clasp had left. Relishing the feel of his smooth, golden skin under her fingers.

'You need to stop sometimes.' She clasped the watch in her fist as Alessio let out a slow breath, his shoulders relaxing as if some weight had been removed. 'I'd like to pitch it into the sea to make sure you do, but it's probably valuable.'

'My maternal grandfather gave it to me.'

'Did you like him?'

The corner of Alessio's mouth kicked up into a smile. 'I did.'

'Then I'll keep it safe.' She slipped it into the pocket of her skirt, its weight against her thigh. A reminder of how little time they had, which was something she shouldn't even be thinking about. She should be living in the now, because her time here had always had an end date. Hannah tipped her head back to look up into the complicated rigging.

'This is an amazing boat.'

'*Il Delfino*. A schooner built in 1910. One hundred and seventy feet long, if you're interested.'

'It's beautiful.'

'So are you.'

She smiled, breath catching in her throat. 'Thank you.'

Since her parents had died, there'd been no one to tell her she was beautiful. Her dad had said those words to her, to her mother, all the time. Back then her parents had made sure she felt as attractive as an awkward teen could, with pimples and hormones causing trouble. On the other hand, her aunt and uncle hadn't realised what she'd needed. Or hadn't cared. Maybe the only thing they'd ever been interested in was the money her parents had left.

Tears burned at her eyes. There was no time for them here. Instead she stared out over the horizon. Ribbons of pink and gold threaded through the sky. The cool breeze brushed her face.

Alessio moved behind her, wrapping strong arms round her body. She leaned into him, tried to relax. To make the most of every second here.

'This feels like another movie moment,' she said.

'Is that a bad thing this time?'

'Only if the boat sinks.'

'She's had a complete refit, if you're worried.'

Hannah wasn't. Around Alessio she almost felt more

secure than with anyone else, apart from the way she had as a child with her mother and father. 'I'm sure you'll keep me safe.'

His arms tightened a fraction. She closed her eyes to savour the moment. He'd keep her safe physically. Emotionally though…it was as if she stood in a crowded room, naked. But this, between them, was *all* physical. An attraction. Nothing more.

'You mentioned something to the crew about rules,' she said. 'What are they?'

'This is Stefano's yacht. Here, I'm not the Prince of Lasserno, I'm him.'

He played Stefano, so he could hide her. Part of that made sense. He was protecting them both from the press. Another part of it stung like a bee ruining a barefoot walk in the grass.

'Stefano? This isn't just any old boat. Where did he get it?'

'Family. Stefano's the Conte di Varno. The Moretti family and mine have a long history. Each count has served the royal family in their own way. Stefano's way is as my private secretary, since I trust him implicitly.'

'It's nice that you have so much trust in someone.'

Alessio loosened his arms and turned her, a slight frown forming on his brow, the look concerned and earnest. 'And you don't?'

It was as if she were standing on a precipice. This between them was supposed to be casual. That meant light banter and fun. But she was driven to unburden herself, as if telling Alessio might set herself free.

'My uncle was a financial advisor. He looked after

my inheritance. Six months ago, he ignored my wishes. Invested in something I didn't want. That investment failed. My parents didn't have much, but my dad had an insurance policy. It's all gone now. I'm hanging on to the cottage.'

Barely. Hannah didn't know if it felt any better, having told Alessio. It was a terrible admission, her failure to keep an eye on things.

Alessio's jaw hardened. His mouth a tight, thin line.

'Are the police involved? Surely by law, your uncle wasn't allowed to do such a thing?'

She hated this. Hated that the people who should have been looking after her interests had let her down so badly. Whilst they hadn't been her parents, they'd been her last link to one of them. But she'd learned a powerful lesson from the experience. All she really had was herself.

'He used a few people's money, and he shouldn't have.' He'd been so sure that everything would be okay, and that in the end she'd thank him for ignoring her wishes. The arrogance of it. 'And yes, the police are involved. But that won't get my funds back. Everything my parents left me, I lost.'

'Ah, *bella*. It's not your fault.' Alessio stepped forward and bundled her in his arms. She rested her head on his chest as he held her tight. As if he were holding her together. And all of it was dangerous. They weren't meant to share, not like this.

'Would you have taken this commission if your uncle hadn't done what he did?'

'No.' She pulled back. Shook her head, honesty all

she had left. 'You. Horse riding. The showjumping circuit. It brings back memories I'd do anything to avoid.
But now I'm here, I'm glad I agreed.'

'I'm…glad too.'

She noticed it, the slightest of hesitations in a man
she suspected hesitated over nothing. He tightened his
arms around her.

'Do you trust me?' he asked.

Hannah was lost in the deep, warm brown of his
eyes. She didn't know if she trusted anyone, and that
caused her gut to clench like a hard fist inside. She had
to remind herself what this truly was. It had an end date
marching up faster and faster. She'd pack her bags, her
art equipment and leave. Paint his portrait. Throw all
her emotion into it, then set it free and let him go. Alessio would find and marry his perfect princess, and all
would once again be right with the world.

'With my body? I trust you implicitly.'

Alessio's smile in answer to her comment was sultry and slow.

'I'll always look after you.'

That sounded as if this had a permanence to it, which
she knew to be untrue. But then, words were easy. It was
actions which were harder. And she knew he wouldn't
stop her winging away from here. He'd put her on the
plane himself. But it was fine. She'd known the day
her parents died that the picture of her own life would
be different from what she'd imagined it would be as a
child. In her wildest dreams, she'd never believed a fortnight like this could happen to her. And the memory of
it would be enough. Would carry her through the years.

It *would*.

Enough of this introspective mood. The glorious sun rose in the sky, filling her with a lazy warmth. The tang of salt hung invigoratingly in the air. They had time and she'd take her fill of every second. She needed to lighten the mood, since it had become far too serious.

'So, this is Stefano's yacht. Don't you have one of your own?'

'Of course. Mine's a modern yacht. Some might say…better,' Alessio said with a smirk.

'And I bet it has a crown embossed on the bow.' She gave him a smile of her own. She liked him like this, the man relaxed, unlike the Prince he showed to the world every day.

He held out his arms. Even in casual clothes he had an intoxicating presence. As if he owned the world. 'What's being a prince if one doesn't have the crown?'

'Is your ego taking a bit of a battering that I might like Stefano's better than yours?'

'My ego remains intact, despite your best and most constant efforts.' Those wide arms of his wrapped round her again. Pulled her close. Dropped his head to her ear. 'Let me show you.'

His body pressed into hers, his arousal, bold and obvious, stoking the fire of her own. She flexed her hips against his hardness. Ran her hands down his back, relishing the strength of his muscles as they flexed under her fingers.

'I think there are a few things I need to know whilst I'm here,' she said.

'Port is left. Starboard is right.'

'Thank you, Your Highness.' Hannah laughed. 'No. Your talk of the rules before. Are there any I should know?'

Alessio looked up at the golden sky, brow furrowed as if in thought. 'The first rule is that I'm always right.'

'Oh, really? Any others?'

'Hmm… The second…' He tapped at his chin then looked down at her, the colour of his eyes swallowed by his pupils, the dawn painting him golden as well. 'When we're alone together you should always be naked. Clothes are a travesty on you.'

Heat rose to her cheeks. 'And is that rule reciprocated?'

'*Ovviamente*. Now we're heading out on water, rule two is invoked. You're wearing too many clothes.'

'Are you sure about that?' she asked as Alessio inched his fingers under her shirt, stroking the sensitive skin of her side. A shiver of goosebumps skittered down her arms. He began unbuttoning the soft cotton shirt she wore, his eyes glowing and intent. Always fierce. Always in a hurry, or at least where she was concerned. He dropped his head and began kissing her shoulder, light brushes that made her liquid in his arms.

'I refer you to rule number one,' he murmured, the warmth of his breath tickling her neck.

She laughed again, something so different about him here, out of the palace. As if he could become a man, rather than being a ruler of all he surveyed. She gave a little push on his chest and he let her go. She stood back. Shrugged her top from her shoulders, slowly exposing the exquisite floral bikini top she wore underneath from the clothes she'd been given. His gaze raked over her, jaw tight, arousal straining at his zipper.

'Dio. Sei così bella.'

She didn't know what that meant but it sounded like a worship, a benediction. Yet he stood there, fully clothed, simply watching her set the pace.

'Where's the reciprocation?'

The corner of his mouth curled into a heated smile.

'Come here,' he said, the voice all command that sent a shiver of longing through her. She loved this of him, the demanding, passionate man. All the while knowing that if she said no, if she took a step back, he'd wait for her.

'Still rule number one?'

He raised an imperious eyebrow, but a smile teased his mouth. She walked forward into his embrace, his lips sinking onto her own. She never failed to be surprised at how such a seemingly hard man could be all softness when he held her. As if the fact he had a human side was their secret.

'I'm not being a good host. It's time I showed you the stateroom.'

Alessio swung her into his arms and strode down the deck like a man bent on completing a mission—that of making her cry his name to the room.

Alessio woke to the lull of slapping water on the side of the yacht. The gentle sway of the ocean. For the first time in an age, he was at some kind of peace. Sleepy, sated. Barely caring whether he moved all day. There was one reason for this newfound satisfaction—a person.

He reached to the side of the bed for Hannah and brushed only the warmth of empty sheets. Not long gone, then. He lay for a moment, listening for her, but there was no sound, so he rolled over and sat up, scraping his hand through his hair.

She was curled on a sofa opposite the bed at the other side of the room. Feet tucked under her. Drawing on a sketch pad on her lap with a stick of charcoal.

'You're naked,' he said. The sight of her perfect skin made the blood race down low. Would he ever get enough of her? He feared not.

She glanced up at him, the merest of smiles touching her well-kissed lips.

'Rule number two, remember?'

He lounged back on the bed. 'And you did what I said. Rule number one. It's a miracle.'

She snorted, such a cute sound, as she peered up at him again, then returned to the page before her. Sketching, rubbing at the paper with her fingers. 'I think I liked you better when you were asleep.'

'I don't believe you,' he said, his body heating each time her insightful gaze returned to him. Arousal, heavy and low, snaked through him again. This attraction, it overtook everything, an overwhelming need only Hannah could satisfy. 'You like me very much when I'm awake.'

He didn't hide how much she affected him. He'd not hold anything back from her. The freedom of such a short time frame meant he didn't have to. Yet the realisation of how little time they had left stung like a forgotten wound exposed to seawater. A surprising and unwelcome jolt. He ignored it. There were better ways of using their day than musing over things like that. He patted the bed next to him. 'Come here.'

'Does your ego need stroking?'

An insistent pulse of desire kept beating its demanding tempo. 'Something needs stroking.'

She didn't even look up at him, her focus all on the page, a slight frown creasing her brow. 'No. I haven't been doing enough sketching. You keep distracting me.'

Hannah being more interested in what was on the piece of paper in front of her than in the real man put him in his place, firmly rooted in a world where he was not the most desirable, sought-after person. It made him feel normal, feel *real*.

A blessed relief.

'Can I see what you're doing?'

'You get the final painting. Everything else is mine. Just lie back and enjoy it. Everyone needs to stop some time.' She looked up at him, that frown still present, her face a study of intensity, making him believe she saw all of him. His sins, his flaws. There was no hiding them with her. And it made him curious.

'What do you see when you look at me?'

'Do you really want to know?'

'I asked the question.'

She put down her charcoal. Placed her hand flat on the page in front of her so her drawing was hidden.

'You like to think you begin and end as Prince of Lasserno. That there's nothing else. But you're more.'

Inside of him, something clenched. Almost like a warning, but she'd piqued his interest now.

'Tell me.'

'Someone who works hard. Too hard.' A shaft of sunlight filtered through the cabin window, painting her pale skin in its warm glow. She looked a picture of perfection sitting there. Alessio didn't want the moment to end. He shrugged.

'It's all part of the job description. My father didn't work hard enough. Saw life as a prince for only what he could get from it. He almost drove Lasserno into ruin.' A tightness rose inside again. Of things unfinished, of work yet to do. It was relentless, exhausting. Never-ending. A needling sensation interrupted the moment. He raised his left wrist, but his watch wasn't there.

'I've put it away for a few days. You need to relax. You'll have plenty of time to save the country. Years of it, in fact.'

The certainty carried in her voice, as if there was no doubt. When, deep down, he doubted himself often. 'Thank you for your confidence. What else do you see?'

She smiled again, a beautiful thing which lit up the room better than the late-morning light.

'Fishing for compliments?'

'Wanting to know how well you know your subject.'

She brought her hand to her mouth. Tapped her lips with her index finger.

'You appear cold, aloof, but you're not. That's the Prince of Lasserno's costume, what you allow the world to see, but it's not real. You care, deeply, for your country and your people, but you refuse to show it to anyone. As if you're not the man, but you *are* the crown. Except there's a human heart beating in your chest.

But some days, I think you wish there wasn't. Because being human is messy and ugly and imperfect. It's about desire and need and feelings, and that's not who you want to be. The trouble is, that's exactly who you are.'

Each word hit him like an arrow shot straight, finding its truest and most damaging place. She saw him too well, and her insights caused his heart to race, his chest to constrict.

Others only saw what they assumed was the truth. He could control the narrative with them. Like acting, putting on a show. Right now, Hannah was all risk. Huge reward, but the risk terrified him most of all. She gave him the tantalising glimpse of a life without meticulous attention to duty, and that was a terrible temptation.

'I think that you're worried if you show people the real you, they won't love you. The thing is, they'd love you even more if you would be yourself. Because you're a good man.'

He didn't want to talk now, but he couldn't move. It was as though he was pinned to the bed, frozen in place. He couldn't take this attention on him. He didn't know why he had asked the question of her, because he should have known she'd see things he hadn't wanted others to see.

'Do you want to know what I see in you?' he asked, trying to deflect from himself because the spotlight burned too brightly when it focused on the truth.

'Not really.' She closed her notepad, sat up straighter. So perfect and relaxed in her nakedness.

'Why is that, Hannah?'

She hid herself as well. They both wore costumes, even now pretending to be something they weren't.

'I'm not that interesting.'

'I disagree. Rule number one, remember.'

She rolled her eyes. 'Yes, Your Highness.'

As he was a prince, people didn't mock or tease him. Or joke with him much at all. Stefano was the only person who did, but he'd been a friend for years. Alessio found himself enjoying it from her. The irreverence. The freedom for them both to...*be.*

'You talk about me hiding myself? You do it too. You're a passionate woman when it comes to your art. But you deny that part of yourself, forgetting what you're like in my arms. In bed.'

'And what about you?' Hannah said. 'Wanting to marry someone you barely know and don't love. Better not to marry at all.'

He didn't want to think of marriage, matchmakers, or perfect princesses right now, but they were the reality he couldn't escape. A shortlist of candidates was on his desk, whom he would meet...when Hannah left.

'I have a dynasty to preserve.'

'What if your precious yet-to-be-found princess falls in love with you and you don't love her? Where will you be then? You're condemning someone to a life that's unfair.'

'She'll know what to expect.'

'Or are you afraid of forming a real attachment? That's when you have most to lose.'

Her words hit sharp and true. He couldn't let them

go unanswered. He sat up, the sheet falling from his torso. Hannah's cheeks pinked, but she didn't look away.

'Says the woman who claims she's not interested in love. That her art is enough.'

'At least I'm not trying to draw anyone else into it. This is my life. I'll live it how I see fit.'

She stood and sauntered to him, beautifully naked, the rolling sway of her hips and tight nipples, the slight flush on her chest were telling him what she had in mind. Distraction. And he didn't care because her kind of distraction was the most delicious of all. Let them both drown in it, forgetting everything else.

'You're so perfect in everything you do. Even now, lying in this bed. As if you're artfully displayed. It makes me wonder if you know how to be anything less. Makes me want to mess you up.'

'I invite you to try.'

There was something about her that warned of danger. Like an impending storm, dark and brooding, hovering on the horizon. The bed dipped as she sat on the edge close to him, her fingers blackened from the charcoal she'd smudged across her page. Hannah reached out with one hand to his chest and smeared her fingers across his flesh, leaving dark stripes there. The smile on her face was pure wickedness. 'How does that feel, Your Highness?'

'Like you're not trying hard enough.'

Her pupils flared as she rose to his challenge and climbed over him, straddling his body. Rocking on the hardness between his thighs. He sat forward to wrap his arms around her but she planted her hands flat on his

chest and pushed. He fell back, enjoying her new asser-
tion far too much. Hannah took his face in her hands,
rubbed her thumbs over his cheeks. He didn't need to
see in the mirror to know that she was marking him
with the charcoal on her fingers. As if she were claiming ownership. His blood rang in a furious roar as he
enjoyed her possession, as if with each stroke she were
writing *mine* on his skin. She leaned forward, her lips
touching his. Her mouth open, lush. Claiming him. He
let her. In this fantasy, for these few days they could
be anything they desired. He took what she gave, his
hands at her hips as she moved against him. The sheet
between them an interruption, a distraction, but necessary. How he wanted to slide into her with no protection, forget they were the Prince and his artist.

She broke the kiss and he almost thrust his hands
into her hair and dragged her to him once more, but the
way she leaned back with a subtle smile on her lips suggested she was admiring her handiwork.

'Condom,' she said, as she cupped his jaw and traced
her thumb almost lovingly in another stripe along his
cheek.

He didn't need to be asked twice, reaching to the bedside table where he'd left a number rather than fumble
for a packet and interrupt these fleeting moments. Hannah sat back as he grabbed a sliver of foil, tore it open.

'You're going to have to move,' he said. His hands
trembled with the desire to be inside her. She shifted
back as he shoved down the sheet and rolled the protection in place. All the while she watched him, her

fascination with his body addictive, her attention on him complete.

She placed her hand on his chest again. 'Now lie back and relax.'

He almost laughed. How could he relax when he was wound so tight he wanted to snap? His thighs shook. The whole of him quivered with barely restrained desire. It was like nothing he had ever experienced. She positioned herself over him and lowered slowly. He watched her body take him, the shock of the feeling, coupled with the vision, electric. Her head thrown back, hair tumbling over her shoulders, nipples tight and beading with arousal. Such an erotic picture she painted for him. Hannah rode his body as he thrust up into her. Lost in her heat. The sounds she made. Her pure, erotic abandon had the tight, bright sting of arousal crack and shatter with one hard, sharp thrust and shout. Then Hannah tightened around him and broke as well, falling forward onto his heaving chest as he wrapped his arms round her.

'You're well messed-up now,' she said with a shaky laugh, which told him she was probably *well messed-up* herself. And there was nothing he could say or do because she was right. The problem was, he might never wish to go back to his tidy, perfect, righteous life, ever again.

CHAPTER TEN

TWO NIGHTS AND three days of bliss and it was now over.

Hannah sat in the front of an anonymous-looking grey car with Alessio at the wheel. They'd spent the early morning swimming in the deep, cobalt waters of the Mediterranean. Avoiding the inevitable. Pretending the world couldn't touch them. It touched them now. Everything tightening, tensing.

As they drove towards the outskirts of Lasserno's capital, where they would return to the palace, Alessio began to change the most. It was like watching the ground freeze over by degrees. As if the cold chill of winter were creeping up on them, slowly and relentlessly. Where once he'd been loose and relaxed, all of him seemed to be on high alert. Their easy conversation on the yacht dried away, his grip on the steering wheel almost white-knuckled.

She settled back and tried to relax into the seat. The fantasy of the weekend was well and truly over, those few days where they ate, slept, made love, soon to be but a precious memory. She'd thought this would be enough, that she'd be unaffected by it all. But what she hadn't banked on was how much changed when you got to see a real person. And Alessio had become real to her. Not a prince like he was on paper but a magnificent, kind, self-deprecating man who could make her laugh and would soon make her cry, of that she had no doubt.

She wanted to cry for him now. She didn't know how he'd marry some princess in a cold, practical relationship, when their own days had been full to the brim with passion. She couldn't see him as surviving with anything less than what they had had. She could barely take in any air at those thoughts. Of Alessio married, with children. Without her. The idea of him in any other woman's arms thrust through her with all the brutality of a sword to the heart. She looked over at him. His jaw was set, as though he was steeling himself for a life he didn't want.

As if he knew she was looking at him, Alessio turned his head a fraction. 'You've had a touch of the sun. Your skin's pink.'

She shrugged, blinking away the burn in her eyes. His concern and notice could undo her, and she wasn't sure there was thread enough in the world to stitch herself together again. 'I'll be fine. It's a little sunburn.'

'I should have paid more attention.' She couldn't see his eyes, hidden behind sunglasses as they were, but his voice was filled with care. 'Remembered the sunscreen. Your beautiful skin is so pale.'

'Too much time indoors, painting.' She'd never felt like that before, but there'd been a blissful sense of freedom to being in the sunshine, the breeze in her hair. Something other than standing in her studio surrounded by solvent and paints. The same way she'd forgotten the joy of being on horseback, not practising her showjumping, just the pleasure of the ride. All the small things she'd shoved away from herself over the years. Perhaps when she returned home, she could buy a little horse. Take some time to ride again. If she could afford to, because even with Alessio's commission, funds would still be tight. But there was a kernel of hope there, for something more, even if she couldn't have him.

Hannah let out a slow, even breath. She'd not be here much longer and time seemed to be speeding up and careening away.

'I'd like to do a bit of sightseeing in the capital before I leave. I should get a souvenir for Sue.'

She had many things to thank her agent for. Many things to curse her for as well, with this commission. It had shown her life had possibilities again, whilst also snatching them away.

'I'll arrange security for you. A list of places to go.'

It sounded as if he was making himself responsible for her, and that was something she didn't need when they should be pulling apart rather than meshing even further.

'I hardly think I'll have a problem buying a snow globe or something similar. Who'd be interested in me?'

His hands flexed on the steering wheel, though his focus remained resolutely on the road ahead.

'I want you to be safe. I want that for you.'

The words were loaded because she was sure he meant far more. Hannah squashed down the lick of heat running through her. He was a good man. He cared.

The way he did with the children at the hospital, that was all. It meant nothing more.

It couldn't.

He was not safe, not for her. Not ever. With him, she found herself wanting things she'd not contemplated for years, and those things could crack her in two. Because love meant leaving the door open to your own destruction and inviting the destroyer in. She could never give her whole heart because then she'd lose all over again, and she wasn't sure she'd survive it when she barely had last time.

'I'd like to go on my own. Having security would be strange and take the fun away from things. But I'll take a list of places to go. Thank you.'

'If I could have come with—'

'You're the Prince of Lasserno.' She put him back in that box where he should remain. Would even tie it with a tight, bright gold ribbon to keep him firmly back in place. 'You can't just go sightseeing with some random tourist.'

'You're not a random tourist, Hannah.' His voice was soft. The cabin of the car filled with the weight of things unsaid. Of how much more this, between them, had become.

'I'm sure you'll have too much to do.'

Alessio checked his watch, now firmly back on his wrist as if it had never left. 'Always. I may have a parliament for advice, but in the end, this is an absolute monarchy. There is only me.'

There is only me.

He'd never let anyone in, and it struck her as sad and exhausting.

The roads were busier as they approached the capital but the run to the palace seemed clear. As she sat staring at the castle looming on the horizon the roar of a motorcycle came from behind, louder, closing in. Then it was right there. At the passenger side. Two people, one driving, one pillion. Something in their hand. Camera. Trying to shove it against the window of the car. A flash.

She reflexively held up her hand against the tinted glass, her heart pounding a sickening tempo. Another flash. Alessio hissed something through his teeth. She didn't need to understand Italian to know he swore. He grabbed the brim of his cap and pulled it lower. Hannah wore nothing on her head but did have sunglasses. She pushed them up her nose, not that it would make much difference.

'In the glove compartment there's a cap. Put it on. Pull the sun visor down.'

She did as he said. The motorcycle sped ahead while the passenger turned, trying to get photos through the windscreen. A shrill tone rang out through the car. Alessio's phone. He answered hands-free and a terse voice filled the interior, speaking rapid Italian. Stefano.

She couldn't understand what they said, but the fury in Alessio's voice, the tight, cold rage, chilled the car by degrees. She wrapped her arms round herself as she took in the importance of what was happening. But what did the press know? It could be he'd taken her out sightseeing as he'd suggested, the Prince showing

a guest around his country. That was easily enough ex-
plained, wasn't it?

The call disconnected. Silence filled the car apart
from Alessio's hard, jagged breaths.

'I'm sorry,' she said, because what more was there
to say? 'It might not be that bad.'

'It is *that bad*.' His grip tightened on the wheel again,
his mouth a thin, hard line. 'They are at the palace.
Every entrance, though the western gate apparently
has fewer.'

'Can we—?'

'Not now.' He took one hand from the tight grip of
the wheel and dragged it over his face.

She'd been royally dismissed. Experienced it in the
sharp cut of his voice. In the way all of the warmth had
left him, and he'd turned into Lasserno's ruler once
more. Another motorcycle joined the first. Alessio
kept the speed steady and didn't try to outrun them,
for which she was thankful. She stopped looking at the
road in front and instead stared down at her lap, her
fingers twisting in the soft fabric of her dress. Maybe
no one would know who she was, but a sick feeling of
bile rose in her throat. Her quiet, anonymous life in
the country was likely to be shattered. The protection
of those walls she'd built around herself—her art, her
peace—all crumbling away. The palace loomed large
ahead, and she saw it now like a kind of prison. They
didn't approach from the front, or from the entrance
they'd sneaked out of only three blissful days earlier,
but a side entrance where palace guards stood, holding
back a throng of photographers jostling for position. If

this was the western gate, she'd hate to see what the others were like.

The car pushed through into a large courtyard. Alessio stopped, switched off the engine. Sat for a few moments then turned to her. She couldn't see his eyes behind the sunglasses but the whole atmosphere inside the car felt accusatory. As if somehow, she was to blame for this. Then he opened the door, thrusting it wide as he launched himself from the car and slammed it shut behind him.

Hannah took off her cap to put it back in the glove compartment and grabbed her handbag before following, running to keep up as Alessio barely broke his stride, his staff bowing as he passed, looking at her with some curiosity.

She didn't know how long they walked through what appeared to be service corridors, until they reached a vast, familiar hall and a door she immediately recognised. Alessio's office. Inside, Stefano stood by one of the mullioned windows, speaking rapid-fire on the phone. When they entered, he hung up. Alessio tore off his sunglasses and cap, tossed them on his desk. He and Stefano exchanged a look—Stefano's all sympathy, Alessio's barely concealed fury.

'What's being said?'

'They know about the hospital visits. That's been online already.'

'The families?'

'Are being protected. They won't talk. You know that.'

Alessio's head dropped. He stared at the carpet as if

a solution could be divined there. All the while, Hannah realised she was superfluous. And she didn't know what to do. Stand. Sit. Pace. Everyone in this room was still. Her, Alessio, Stefano. Like chess pieces waiting for the first move.

'They're using the sick children to make a story about me.'

'It's not a bad thing, since it's a good story. As I've said before.'

'What about this?' Alessio waved his hands between him and Hannah, as if she were nothing. His dismissal sliced sharp and fresh like a paper cut.

Stefano deigned to look at her then. Nice to know she existed. She couldn't tell what he was thinking, everything about him inscrutable in those moments. But he seemed paler, his eyes tight. No tie, the top button of his shirt undone.

'The speculation online is intense, but only in the less reputable media...for now. The photographs of you in the car will break soon enough. Who knows what they'll say? My staff won't talk, if that's your concern.'

'They never have before. I have *no* concerns there.'

'I have a team considering the problem.' Stefano looked at her again and in the deep pit of her stomach she knew *she* was the problem here. Something to be dealt with. Not a person with fears of her own. 'I'll see them now, on how we manage things going forward.'

He left the room and Alessio walked to the window, looked out over Lasserno. His country. The only thing he desired or needed, she was coming to realise.

'Never complain, never explain,' she said.

He wheeled round, all of him so hard and tense it was as if one more push and he might snap. She wanted to do something. Reach out. Comfort. Say it would all be okay. But she knew some things would never be okay again, for either of them.

'What?'

'The British Royal family. That's what they do.'

'Trust me.' He began to pace the room in that familiar way of his, as if he needed to expend energy. 'I won't be giving statements.'

'How did the press find out?'

He raised one coal-dark eyebrow at her, the burnt umber gaze of his so heated only hours ago, now cold and forbidding like some bottomless, muddy pool. 'How, indeed?'

'You think…me?'

He looked so out of place in this moment, in his disarray. Wearing casual clothes and not the suit he donned as his usual armour. Surrounded by his ancestors glaring down from their lofty height on the walls, as if the weekend of humanity he'd stolen was some kind of disgrace.

'I trust everyone else around me. But this story is a familiar one.'

It dawned on her then, what he wouldn't say out loud. He didn't trust *her*. 'It might be an annoyance for your private life, but have you ever thought how this debacle could affect me?'

He stopped his pacing. Dead.

'You?'

Said as if he'd only just realised she was a person

who might have thoughts and feelings about this too. She threw up her hands and began pacing then. As if Alessio's will to constantly be on the move had infected her.

'No, clearly you haven't thought about me at all. Other than to accuse me.'

'I've accused you of nothing.'

The *yet* hung unsaid.

'I sign non-disclosure agreements with all of my clients. My word about what I discover is absolute. Would any of them trust me if they thought I would spill my secrets to the press? No. Sure, I could paint people, but it would never be the same. It would destroy my process. Ruin *everything*.'

The corner of his mouth rose in something like a sneer. Not quite contempt, but close enough.

'You're financially distressed. Your uncle mismanaged your inheritance. A tell-all about me would fill your bank account,' Alessio hissed, cold, cruel and furious.

She stopped then, as if those words had stripped the will to move right out of her. There was such accusation in his gaze. It was as though he was a brittle shell filled with nothing but disdain.

'You honestly believe I would talk about this, us...' she waved between them as he had done, only this had meant something to her '...to the press? What kind of world do you live in?'

'Look around you.' He spread his arms wide, like some sacrifice. 'I live in the real world! Where people want what they can't have and take what they can.'

His words cracked her, cleaving her in two. She grabbed on to the back of an armchair and gripped the silken fabric tight in case the halves of her fell to the floor. 'If this is the real world then I don't want any part of it.'

'Luckily for you, you shall have none.'

A reminder once again she was being firmly put in her place. A place she'd never sought to leave, until the weekend just past. 'I know.'

'Do you? I'm glad to hear it, since you'll leave today. Within the hour. I'll have your things sent to you. My jet—'

She shook her head. Let go of the armchair's support. She needed none. She'd lived on her own terms almost since the day her parents had died. She'd do it again. As for now, she needed to get away from him, from his life and the trappings of it. Get back to the comfort and safety of her home and her relative anonymity. She didn't want sorrowful looks from royal flight attendants as she wept into a cup of tea.

Because she'd cry, but not in front of him.

'I'll fly on some airline.'

He shook his head. 'You think the press in Lasserno are bad? They're kittens compared to what you're walking into. How will you drive home, on narrow country roads being chased by motorcycles? Cars? I think not.'

If he were concerned he might have looked stricken, but that wasn't what was happening here. He didn't care about her. He never really had. His reputation was his only interest and everything else was peripheral. But there was one thing they needed to address: what she was being paid to do, since she was just an employee now.

'Your portrait.'

Something about him changed then. Alessio seemed to straighten, stand taller. Even if you didn't know it, seeing him in this moment you'd realise he was ruler of all he surveyed. Uncompromising and absolute.

'I want no portrait. Every time anyone looks at the painting, they'll speculate about what *you* saw and exactly how much. It can *never* be what I wanted it to be, a statement of intent. I'll find someone else. But don't fear. You'll be paid for your time.'

There was the final blow, his words like a kick to the stomach. It was as if for a second time her world had been taken from her. All of this, here, had been for nothing.

If she weren't made of stronger stuff, she might bend in two. But she'd survived the death of her parents and her horse, the rejection of her boyfriend, the dishonesty of her uncle. She could survive Alessio Arcuri. And she'd show him.

'You'll pay me…for my *time*. My…services rendered. What a fine way to make a woman feel cheap.' She took a deep breath, looked him straight in the eye so he could see how strong she really was, and just how much he'd meant to her until this. 'I don't want to be paid. I want nothing from you. So go and find your perfect princess. I hear royal weddings and babies are big news. They'll erase any rumours about me from your life.'

She turned her back on him, needing to get out and

get away. Wanting to run but carrying herself with all the dignity she deserved, because she wasn't at fault, even though this whole place seemed intent on blaming her. Instead, she injected steel into her spine and walked to the door with her head held high. Walked away from him. As she reached out for the door handle, she hesitated. Not turning, because she didn't want to see Alessio ever again. Seeing him might remind her of what she'd lost. What she never really had in the first place.

'Thank you, Your Highness, for making our parting so much easier.'

CHAPTER ELEVEN

ALESSIO STARED AT the broken-apart travelling crate. The wood was scattered about the floor of his office after he'd cracked it apart with the crowbar he'd asked his staff to deliver here. That infernal wooden case had taunted him from the moment it had been delivered a few days before. No note, no explanation. A return address for Ms Hannah Barrington the only suggestion of what it contained.

A portrait. One he didn't want, but one he got anyway.

And *this* portrait. He stood back. This wasn't a painting to be hung in a throne room. It was deeply, achingly personal and he had no idea what to do with it. Because as he looked at the picture, what he saw was not the man he stared at in the mirror every morning but another self. Real. A better version of him.

There was no elegant quality to the brushstrokes. They slashed across the canvas with a terrifying brutality. *He* was the sole focus of the artist's gaze. Sitting side-on, with his head turned to the painter. White shirt slightly unkempt, open at the neck. Hair unruly as if he'd rolled out of bed and raked his hands through it, sat in a chair and looked at the person holding the brush. Hannah. His fingers were steepled, contemplating her. Eyes intense and focused, fixed on one woman, as if he would never look away. Corners of his lips tilted in the merest of smiles in a moment where it seemed some secret had been told, which only the painter and the subject knew.

This was a picture for a private space, for a bedroom, where the intimacies it spoke of could be understood only by the people who saw it each day.

From the packing had also fallen two small spiral sketchbooks, those she'd carried around with her. He flicked through them. There was the small landscape in watercolour pencil she'd done when she'd first arrived. The view from her window. The rest were sketches of him. His hands, his eyes. Lips. Rough outlines of him stalking the floor. Smiling. Naked in bed on Stefano's yacht. His life, the man, in black, white and grey. In the beginning, he recognised the person in those pictures. Cold, aloof. Remote from everything around him. As they progressed, Hannah had seen him in ways he no longer saw himself, seen the tiny glimpses of happiness. And then those when they were together, alone. In them, he was unrecognisable.

A man changed.

He glanced at the desk, where a folder lay: his short-list of princesses. They were everything he'd asked for. Bright, beautiful, intelligent women from royalty who understood the job they'd be asked to do. He'd been to dinner with a few and each time he had, every part of him rebelled. Spending even a second with a woman who was not Hannah felt like a betrayal.

Because no matter how he'd tried to forget her, he couldn't. Work didn't help. Riding Apollo didn't help. Nothing did. Her touch, her laugh, the scent of her like autumn apples...all embedded in his memory. And now he had the portrait, which hinted at something he dared not name because of what he'd done to her.

He loathed how she'd looked at him on her last day here. As if he'd warped something perfect, to make it ugly. Taking his fears and frustrations out on her, when she was the victim. Because she wasn't the perpetrator, of that he was sure. He had all the power. She was the one with everything to lose. A rumoured affair with his artist had risen as a moment of brief interest in a world of many such events and faded away. All the while she'd maintained a dignified silence. His father might have laughed at the evidence of his son's human failings, though to Alessio those taunts were now meaningless. All he'd been obsessed by was its effect on her, trawling her name in the daily international press, but she was a secondary character in a story already forgotten by everyone except him.

The door of his palace office opened, and Stefano walked in. Hesitated beside the picture still half in its packing case. Nudged the crowbar discarded on the carpet beside it with the toe of his shoe.

'I thought you'd send it back or put it away without looking at it.'

He'd wanted to. The sheer terror of what Hannah might have painted had stopped him breaking open the picture for days. But he'd needed to exorcise her, and he thought, by finally confronting the portrait, that he would. He hadn't, and in fact it had made things worse.

'It's only a painting.' The lie stuck in his throat. It was more than that. So much more. A mirror to possibilities he'd rejected in a way that couldn't easily be repaired.

'If you say so.'

His friend looked drawn and tired. As if he carried a burden too heavy for one man. No enthusiasm left in him. Stefano hadn't been the same since Hannah had left the palace. Alessio thought it was managing the press fallout, the work since. He began to realise how much he missed, and how this might be something more.

'What do you say?' Alessio asked.

'I say we've both made terrible mistakes, and now it's time to face them.'

Something about the weight of those words carried a warning that things might never be the same again. 'I don't know what you mean.'

'You're not a stupid man, my friend. I don't need to point out your grave error. As for mine...' Stefano handed Alessio an envelope. 'My resignation.'

A terrible cold settled over Alessio, even in the middle of Lasserno's glorious summer. As if everything were changing and he would be the ultimate loser. Stefano stood back. Formal. Aloof. An employee and nothing more. Alessio wouldn't accept it. Right now, things needed to stay the same.

'No. Whatever the problem is, I'll fix it. Do you need a holiday? A pay rise?'

Stefano laughed. There was no humour in the tone. It sounded like a mockery of all things happy. 'Ever the Prince. There are some things you can't repair with money or power.'

'Why are you doing this?'

Stefano didn't answer. He turned, walked towards Hannah's painting. Alessio wanted to hide it. Keep it to himself. Such a deeply private piece left him vulnerable, as though everything about him was set to be exposed, his darkest hopes and dreams, which only Hannah knew.

'She's in love with you,' Stefano said.

'What?' A bright burst of something perfect, like hope, tore through him. A cruel sensation when he had nothing to hope for after what he'd done.

'As I said, you're not a stupid man. *Look* at the picture.' Stefano pointed at it, his finger stabbing the air. 'What you need in your life, Alessio, is someone to see you like *that*. The man behind the mask of the prince. You also need someone in your life you can look at as you looked at Hannah in that very moment.'

Inside he *knew*. This was a picture painted by someone who saw the soul of another person. That didn't come simply by fine observation. It was more. Hannah had quietly given him her heart somewhere in the two weeks they'd been together. He'd selfishly taken it, and cruelly rejected it when she'd asked for nothing in return but his respect.

The problem was, he'd given her his heart as well,

which was why everything seemed broken. Because she'd taken it back to England when she'd gone, and now he was left only half a man.

'Is *this* why you're resigning?'

Stefano slowly shook his head, as if the movement was too wearying to bear.

'I'm resigning because, whilst you *might* be able to repair your great error, I can't repair mine. You want to know who leaked to the press? I did.'

Alessio dropped into the chair behind his desk. He had no power to move, like a child's toy whose batteries had gone dead.

'You threw Hannah and me to those leeches?' A wicked fire lit inside, the burn threatening to overwhelm him. He clenched his fists. If he hadn't known Stefano his whole life he might have thrown punches in this moment. But there was so much he'd missed with Hannah, what hadn't he seen with his oldest friend?

Stefano shoved his hands in the pockets of his trousers. Dropped his head. 'Only about your visit to the hospital. What I failed to recognise is that small piece of information would start press interest about what else you might be doing in secret. *That's* what led to them discovering about you and Hannah. And I'll never forgive myself for it.'

It was as if the floor fell out beneath him. Alessio gripped the arms of his chair to hold himself stable when nothing in his life was any more.

'*Dio!* Stefano. Why?'

'You hide all of yourself. What you present to the world is a version of who you think everyone should see.

Yet that image didn't comfort the people of Lasserno. It made them fear they were getting someone who didn't care for them at all, and that opinion was bleeding into the press. I thought a small glimpse of the private man would help show people who you truly are. And that it would allow you to see past the constraints you impose upon yourself, to the *possibilities*. Instead I caused greater harm.'

Alessio nodded. What more could he do? He'd lost everything. Hannah. His best friend. He couldn't fathom Stefano's betrayal. He couldn't forgive himself for what he'd done to Hannah, driven by fear of finding something real.

'You need a person you can trust in this position. I've arranged for someone temporary to take my place. There were a few good candidates in the palace.'

'That's…acceptable.' Alessio didn't know what more to say. His world crumbled around him with Stefano the last brick to fall.

His friend walked towards the door of the office for the last time. Just as Hannah had walked away only months before.

'My family has served yours for centuries. But you must believe this has never been work for me. It's been my pleasure as your friend.'

He then stopped…hesitated with his hand still resting on the doorknob.

'I have some advice. From Machiavelli. *"Any man who tries to be good all the time is bound to come to ruin among the great number who are not good."*

Allow yourself some imperfections. You have a chance to make things right. I've run out of mine.'

Stefano gave a final bow and shut the door. And for the first time in his life Alessio felt completely alone.

Hannah stood in her studio, the window opening wide onto the sunny garden beyond. This place had once been her oasis of peace, where she could lose herself. Now it seemed more like a prison. She flopped into the threadbare sofa in a dusty corner, cup of tea in hand, body sluggish with a tiredness that hadn't seemed to have left her since she'd returned home. Self-inflicted to be sure, but it was as though she'd never feel awake again, this pressing lassitude which had stolen over her.

From the moment she'd walked into this space on returning from Lasserno she'd begun to work, grabbing a canvas and painting with a ferocity which shut everything out. She'd worked all day and through the nights. Barely sleeping or eating till she'd finished Alessio's portrait. Pouring all her heart and most of her soul into the picture to get one man out of her life. The tears and the pain worked through her fingers onto the canvas, then she'd let it go.

Or that was what was supposed to have happened. In the past, each time she'd finished a portrait had been like a great cleansing. She'd send the picture on its way and leave its subject behind as a fond memory whilst she started afresh.

Not this time. The ache of loss remained like a wound unhealed, as if the bleeding out would never stop. Hannah realised what it was now. All that time she'd spent shielding herself from the pain of love and her heart had gone and fallen in love anyway. At least she'd learned something. Suffering this kind of pain wouldn't break her. Even though the colours of the world didn't seem right, as if everything were sepia-toned, she was still standing. One day she might even be able to look back to a time when for a few fantasy moments she was made to believe she could be a princess.

She hadn't been treated like a princess in the end, though. That Alessio believed she might betray what they'd shared had shredded what remained of her heart. It told Hannah that, whilst what had happened was of great moment to her, to Alessio it meant nothing. It can't have, or he would never have thought she'd talk to the press.

Sure, they'd sniffed around when she returned to the UK, offering large sums for an exclusive. It would have solved all her financial woes, just as he'd accused. But the idea of betraying those precious moments with Alessio made her sick to the stomach.

And yet, some money had arrived in her account. Whilst she'd refused it back in Lasserno, Sue had been more circumspect when contacted by the palace. Now there were funds enough to keep the sharks at bay. It might not refill the coffers her uncle had raided, but it would do. Her uncle's assets were being sold to help pay his debts, and that would help too. She could rebuild. She had her art. Things would be fine. Truly fine.

If only she could plug the Alessio-sized hole in her heart.

She stared at the blank canvas on her easel, one she

had no inspiration for. At least, not for the intended subject. Another consumed all her interest. A man with black hair and umber eyes and a glance which could set her aflame. If she picked up a pencil now she'd be able to perfectly reproduce the crinkles at the corners of his eyes when he smiled, the sensual curve of his lips when he looked at her. It was as if she would always be able to draw him. He was embedded inside her. Yet a prince had no part in her life. She went to the window. Breathed the warm air. Tried reminding herself that these simple things were what made her happy. One day her heart *would* believe her head, but not today.

The tinkle of the doorbell woke Hannah from her inertia. She'd had a few visitors since she'd returned here. Kind people in the village bringing jams, biscuits and sympathy. Probably seeking gossip, but she gave them none and the small tokens had helped.

She made her way to the front door. Pulled a band from the pocket of her jeans and raked her hair into an untidy knot on her head. Steeled herself for a visitor she didn't really want. She'd had a spyhole installed at the suggestion of the local constable when some of the press had become more insistent. Out of caution she peeked through.

Alessio.

She grabbed on to the door jamb to hold herself upright, her heart rate spiking at the thrill of seeing him again, even through the dim fisheye glass. She'd tried telling herself over and over he didn't matter but her heart now called her out as a liar. Hannah froze. Open the door? Ignore it? Tell him to go away? She stood back, trying to steady her rapid breathing, and jumped when the bell gave another short, sharp burst. In that moment she acted on impulse, turning the key and wrenching at the door.

He came into view in a dizzying rush, like the swoop of a roller coaster. More beautiful than she remembered, but then Alessio had always seemed hyper-real to her. He wore an immaculate blue suit, pristine white shirt, bold viridian tie. Nothing at all conciliatory about him, clothed in his armour of choice, as if ready for battle. The only thing about him that wasn't perfect was the stubble on his jaw of a day or two unshaven. The contrast between that casual aberration and the rest of him made her treacherous little heart flutter like the butterflies around the hollyhocks in her garden.

'Hannah.'

The way he said her name… It tumbled from his lips as if the syllables hurt to speak them. As if it had so much meaning. She wanted to mean something to him, but it was a fool's game she had no time to play. She knew her place, and needed to remind herself of it, so she dropped herself into a deep curtsey. 'Your Highness.'

He winced. 'There's no need. Not after—'

'Of course there's a need. What did your dossier say? *"The first time you meet His Royal Highness in the day, you shall curtsey."'*

'We're not in the palace.'

'No, we're definitely not.' She gripped the door, focused on the cut of the wood into her palm. Better that than focusing on the pain in what remained of her heart.

'Did you come looking for more horses? Because there are none here.'

'I'm looking for something, but not horses.'

'And no private secretary to act as a shield between you and me. What a risk-taker you are. How people might talk.'

He dropped his head, looking at the doorstep. To the worn doormat, the faded "Welcome" she'd meant to replace but never seemed to find the time.

'Any risk to me here is deserved. May I come inside?'

She didn't want him here and craved him all the same, the emotions confused and jumbled in a way she couldn't sort out. Curdling in her stomach like an ill-chosen meal.

'What are you doing here?'

'I need to…talk.'

'I'm not sure I need to listen.'

He shoved his hands in the pockets of his trousers. 'I deserve that. But I'd still like you to hear what I have to say. Please.'

She studied him now, in a way she hadn't allowed herself only moments before. Part curiosity, part need. Those lines around his eyes that creased when he smiled appeared more pronounced, though the look wasn't a happy one. There were dark smudges underneath his eyes as if she'd run her charcoal-covered fingers there. That thought was a reminder of a blissful afternoon on Stefano's yacht when everything had seemed so perfect. But she shouldn't reminisce about those few days—they were long gone. Still, listening didn't cost her much and might give them both some closure, far enough away from their tortured last day. She stepped back and allowed him in. He crowded out the small entry foyer.

'Come to the studio.'

That was her war room, where she usually felt competent and safe. Though everything seemed a risk to her right now. Once again, Alessio was her greatest danger, and yet she still wanted to poke her fingers into the fire and be burned. But she'd remind them both of her place in his life.

'I should thank you for the payment, even though you went against my wishes.'

'I took two weeks of your time. It was the least I could do.'

The least he could do... The pain of that morning roared back in a rush and she couldn't hold it in. She didn't care any more, striding right up to him, invading his space. Wanting to push him away and hold on tight, all at the same time. The burn of tears pricked at her eyes, but she was *done* crying. Too many tears had been shed over him already.

She planted her hands on her hips. Better than reaching out to touch.

'I would have walked away, at the end of it all. After those two weeks, I would have stepped onto a plane and you would never have heard from me again.' As much as her heart had rebelled at the time, it was what she would have done because he was looking for someone other than her. Because she loved him and that was what you were supposed to do when you loved something:

you set it free. 'But you cheapened *everything*. Turned something beautiful into something dirty.'

'I know. Only one of us was acting like an adult that day. I hurt you intentionally.'

She bit on her lower lip, hoping the sting might take her mind off the pain his admission caused.

'Is that what this is, a kind of sorry? You didn't need to fly all the way here. You could have sent a card. *My deepest apologies for being a jerk.* Maybe some flowers as a final kind of blow-off.'

Alessio stood there. Immaculate. Impassive. Taking what she gave. Even though he appeared a little careworn, it only added to his underlying appeal.

'I'll never forgive myself for how I treated you. I was afraid of what I felt but the coward in me chose to believe I meant no more to you than the money I could provide. That's *my* issue. I shouldn't have cheapened the most treasured time of my life because of fear, when the perpetrator of the press leak was closer to home.'

'Who talked?' Alessio trusted everyone in the palace. He had assured her that what they had could be kept secret. And yet someone had betrayed him. It had to hurt for a man like Alessio, that misplaced confidence. She saw the cracks in his façade then, not only the two-day growth and tired eyes, but also his slightly paler skin. The tightness around his mouth. All of him looking older and more deeply etched than before.

'Stefano.'

It was as if a rock had settled in the pit of her stomach. She almost reached out to him, to comfort. But Alessio hadn't wanted her before, and if he pushed her away again she might never recover. There were some memories she wouldn't allow to become any more tainted.

'I'm sorry.' She meant it. She understood betrayal from someone she should have been able to trust too. 'Did he say why?'

Alessio might have been cruel to her but she wouldn't be the same to him. She was better than that. He walked over to the battered table holding her paint, brushes and palette.

'His intentions were good, but misplaced. And yet I can't find it in my heart to blame him.' He mindlessly sorted through the tubes of paint. Picked one up. 'Alizarin Crimson. The colour of righteous anger.'

He might have smiled then. Something about him seemed to lighten for a moment, the hint of his lips turning up at the corners. It softened him, like a dry brush smudging over the sharp edges of a painted line.

'You remembered,' she said. A door inside her that should have been locked tight opened a fraction. But they wanted different things, didn't they? He'd told her from the beginning. Yet her silly heart simply craved to beat to a singular rhythm.

Alessio's.

'I remember everything. I can't forget. But I'm not good at the words for this.' He took off his coat, tossed it on the worn couch. Loosened his tie, as if he was going into a battle of another kind. An emotional one. 'I don't know how to be anything other than the Prince of Lasserno. It's all I was trained for. Then I received the portrait and drawings. And I finally saw myself through your eyes. I want to be *that* man. The one in the picture. I want to be that man, for you.'

Everything stopped. The silence, as if the universe waited and yet she couldn't quite fathom the words.

'What are you saying?'

'Do I have a chance to make this right?'

All colour in the world flooded back in a rush, as though things were too bright, too real. But the threat of his words crept up like some choking vine round her throat. That this couldn't work, that dreams didn't come true. Yet when she looked at him, all she saw on his face was hope. And her choice became clear. Saying no meant fear had won. Hannah was tired of losing that battle. She'd been afraid for long enough. It meant there was only one answer to give. So she let that hope fill her and overflow as she prepared to say one simple word.

'Yes.'

Yes. That single syllable went off like a bomb in Alessio's head, shattering everything. A chance. A fragile chance to repair what he'd broken. Build anew. She stood before him like a warrior. Tall. Proud. Putting him to shame. In her worn jeans with rips at the knees that perhaps hung a bit more loosely than the last time he'd seen her in them. Her hair in a messy topknot, strands falling about her face. Her green eyes flashing bright and vibrant, a warning to him that nothing here was certain. And yet he knew today was about laying his soul bare for her to trample on as she saw fit, even if it meant he lost the precious chance she'd granted him. Now was the time to be brave. As brave as her.

'I love you, Hannah.' Those words ground out of him, though easier than expected because they were his deepest truth. The root of all things good in his life. Her eyes widened a fraction, her hands clenched. He didn't know what those things meant, but he carried on regardless. She deserved these words; she should have nothing less. 'From the moment I saw you here I knew you were a danger to me, so to ruin any chance with you I was unspeakably cruel. But that doesn't change the *real* truth. There is only you.'

Her eyes gleamed a little brighter. Tears? What he wouldn't give to hold her, to tell her it would all be okay, but he couldn't, because he was the cause of her suffering.

'What about your perfect princess?'

'I've spent too long setting standards of perfection that were impossible for me to meet. I don't want some perfect princess. I need the woman who captured my heart.'

She turned and walked to the window, staring outside into the rambling cottage garden, bright and beautiful in the English summer. Her hand reached up to her face, swiping at it.

'You hurt me. Claiming you now love me isn't a free pass.' Her voice was almost a whisper. The ache in it clawed at him, his own pain at what he'd done to her well deserved. His cross to bear. Alessio walked towards her, close enough to comfort if she eventually accepted it, far enough to give her the space she obviously needed.

'I know. All I've ever seen of love is that it brings

pain. It seemed to be a poisoned thing. What I failed to realise is the great joy it can bring as well. I want to repair what I've done here, even if you can't love me back.'

Her shoulders hunched. She wrapped her arms round herself, as if she were trying to hold all the pain in. He hated that he'd done this. Failed the person he cared for the most.

'The problem is I can't *stop* loving you.'

He shut his eyes, giving a quiet thank-you to the heavens. It was as if everything that had been knotted up tight began to loosen. She loved him. She *still* loved him. His responsibility now was even greater than before. To honour her the way he should have from the beginning.

'I want to take the pain away by loving you back. Fiercely and for ever.'

Hannah turned, her eyes pink-rimmed. It was all he could do not to reach out and hold her, but he didn't have permission for that, not yet. She held out her hands in front of her, looked down at them. Splayed her fingers. The light from the window behind bathed her in an ethereal glow. She looked like a beautifully flawed angel.

'I'm pretty sure princesses don't have paint-stained hands.'

He feared he'd been the one to make her unsure about this, about herself, when he'd witnessed her being more regal than most royalty he'd ever met. Being a mere princess was beneath her. If he could make her a queen, he would.

'A princess can have whatever she wants. What *I*

want is the artist who painted the portrait of the man now hanging in my bedroom. The man I should have aspired to be all these years. Not a prince, but a man in love. That love is what makes me a better person. There is no one other than you, Hannah. There never will be. The question is whether you want me for ever in return. And I'm prepared to wait. However long it takes.'

She looked up at him, eyes wide and sad and yet still tinged with hope, because it was all either of them had left. Hope that each would take a chance on the other, to build something towering and great, that could withstand anything life threw at them.

'What if however long is right now?'

He couldn't help the smile that broke out on his face, the fire of blazing happiness that lit inside. That she wanted him, that he was enough. The weight of the world rose from his shoulders. A lightening in his soul.

'Then I'll immediately accept whatever you allow. I don't expect your trust, perhaps not for years. But I'll fight for it each day. For you to be by my side. As my wife, my princess, my artist, my *everything*. You already own all my heart. Let me give you my whole world.'

She took a step towards him. 'You have my trust now. I'm not risking my heart for just anyone.'

Alessio opened his arms and Hannah walked right into them. He tightened them round her, soaking in her warmth, relishing in the feel of her body against his. His love. His heart. His home. She tilted her head up, her lips parted. He dropped his mouth to hers, the kiss coaxing, loving, saying in his gentle way what he had trouble verbalising. That he loved her more than words could ever express.

'It's no risk, *bella*.' That was his vow and promise, from this moment forward. 'I will cherish and care for your precious heart for ever.'

EPILOGUE

ALESSIO STROLLED THROUGH the doorway of the pavilion where Hannah now had her studio. The afternoon sun filtered like a patchwork through the windows, warming the space. She didn't look up at him as he entered. He loved that about her...her absolute focus when absorbed by her art.

No words were necessary to describe the love they shared, even in those moments. As she'd begun painting his coronation portrait he'd sat for her, stretches of blissful silence where he could watch her work. The concentration. She had it now, a tiny frown plaguing her forehead, as if something about the canvas troubled her. Something about him, since she was still working on his picture.

'I worry about you down here—it's too far from the palace.'

Her frown melted away. She looked up at him and smiled. The joy in it, seeing him, could light up his darkest places. When fear threatened, that he wouldn't be enough to guide the country through what was ahead of it, she could chase it away with the tilt of her perfect lips. With Hannah, there was no room for anything other than courage, love and trust.

'Don't be ridiculous. It's only a short stroll and the light's perfect.' She rose from the stool on which she'd been sitting and placed her hands on the small of her back, arching in a stretch. The soft fabric of her dress moulded to show off her rounded belly. Four months along and the pregnancy news in his country had reached fever pitch, with speculation over whether the baby would be a boy or a girl and bets being taken. Not even he and Hannah knew. Not yet. They wanted to keep some surprises, and to them it didn't matter. Either a little prince or princess would fill them with even more happiness, if that were possible.

He welcomed every moment of the bliss Hannah had brought to his life. A flood of warmth coursed over him. Love, pride. A whole mix that filled every day. He walked towards her, slowly, because she'd banned him from seeing his portrait until she was satisfied with it. He wondered if she ever would be.

'May I look now?' he asked.

'I think it's done.' That little frown was back again. He wanted to wipe it away, but at least the only time she ever seemed uncertain now was with her art. Not about his love, or her role. Never those things. He adored her; his people adored her. The murals she had designed and helped paint at the children's hospital had cemented Lasserno's love for its new Princess.

Even his father had given public praise for Alessio's choice of bride. Not that Alessio cared, but Hannah and her pregnancy had opened a door to communication that months ago would have seemed insurmountable. Perhaps miracles could happen. Alessio hadn't put any faith in them till Hannah's presence in his life made him believe anything was possible, including a truce with his father.

'What are you waiting for?' Hannah asked. Alessio shook himself out of his introspection. He walked round the canvas on the easel in the middle of the room and saw himself. It was like looking in a mirror. In this picture he sat in his office, surrounded by his ancestors. A magnificent representation of the Prince he'd once striven to be. His honours and regalia pinned to his military jacket. He didn't care for any of it.

The only honours he craved now were Hannah's.

'He seems almost forbidding. Unlike your other portrait.'

Strange how his perceptions of what his country needed from him had changed with Hannah's presence in his life, all the hard edges of himself burnished smooth by the love she brought to him. Love he wasn't afraid of any more. Her love made him strong, not weak.

'The first portrait is of the private man. The one only I'm privileged to see. I'll keep him all for myself. This one is the Prince your country needs. Strong. Eternal. The greatest prince Lasserno will ever have.'

That praise filled him. Her love, and how freely she gave it, was boundless. He swooped her up, swung her into his arms. She shrieked, and then started giggling.

'What are you doing?'

'Taking this somewhere more comfortable.'

He moved to the seating area he'd installed in this

place. Nothing wanting, for her at least. Every comfort available to her. If this was to be her studio, it had to be perfect. Given the time she spent down here, he hoped it was.

He placed her gently on the large, soft sofa in the corner. Knelt in front of her. Kissed her pregnant belly. Her hand moved to his head, stroked through his hair. He shut his eyes and savoured her touch. One quiet moment of perfection in an otherwise long day. There had been so many small moments like this and Alessio relished each one.

When he opened his eyes Hannah's head tilted to the side, as if she were trying to peer inside him. He could hold no secrets. She owned them all.

'Have you spoken to Stefano?'

Ah. The one wound that remained unhealed. The only ache that hadn't gone away. Being more open with the media now, Alessio saw what Stefano had tried to do. Lasserno *was* happier when shown their leader openly caring. In that way, he'd been right.

'I've tried.'

'You're writing him missives, aren't you?'

Hannah knew him too well. In some things, change came slowly. 'He may not want to speak to the man, but he *will* answer to his Prince. His family always has. It's treasonous to do otherwise.'

'Allow him his pride. He'll answer when the time's right. Anyway, I don't answer you a lot of the time. Am I committing treason too?' Her lips curled into a sultry smile.

'That's to my benefit. You remind me I'm only human, and that's all I have to be.'

Hannah's hand drifted to her belly and all he could see was their future, bright and brilliant.

'I love the human side,' she said.

Alessio trailed his fingers up her legs and she shivered under his touch, goosebumps peppering her skin. 'I love it when you're wearing a skirt.'

'I know.' Her legs parted and his hands drifted higher, his thumbs circling on her inner thighs, her body pliant as it sank into the softness of the sofa.

'I love it even better when you're wearing nothing at all,' he said.

'Rule number two, I seem to remember.'

'What about rule number one?'

She rolled her eyes. 'I didn't promise to obey you when we married. But I did promise to love you.'

Alessio laughed. There was so much laughter in his life now. Hannah brought it into every day. Yes, there was plenty of work too, but there was still play. She could infuse even the difficult times with a sense of fun.

'I love *you*,' he said. Those three words never seemed enough for the bone-deep sentiment they carried. He was aware of the privilege and the trust she'd shown him by saying *yes*. Alessio ensured she knew it every day, so there could be no doubt she'd made the right choice in choosing him.

She cupped his face and the look she gave him could have cut him off at the knees, so it was good that he was kneeling right now. Her eyes were soft, brimming with emotion. So much emotion. He could constantly worship her…it was no trial at all.

'I love you even more.'

He took her hand, running his thumb over her wedding ring and her engagement ring. The ring, which he'd had made especially for her. Their love was so bright and new he wanted gems to reflect that truth. Reflect her. A large emerald the colour of her eyes, flanked by two rubies, the colour of his endless love.

'Never doubt my feelings.'

'I never do.'

He smiled again, slipped his hands into the warm silk of her hair. Alessio relished the lifetime of these moments ahead of them. A future which held her in it was one to anticipate and cherish. Then he dropped his mouth to hers. Kissed her welcoming lips. And spent the afternoon in this pavilion, once built to love, proving their words to be true.

* * * * *

Stealing The Promised Princess

Millie Adams

MILLS & BOON

Books by Millie Adams

Harlequin Modern

The Kings of California

The Scandal Behind the Italian's Wedding

Visit the Author Profile page
at millsandboon.com.au.

Millie Adams has always loved books. She considers herself a mix of Anne Shirley (loquacious but charming and willing to break a slate over a boy's head if need be) and Charlotte Doyle (a lady at heart, but with the spirit to become a mutineer should the occasion arise). Millie lives in a small house on the edge of the woods, which she finds allows her to escape in the way she loves best—in the pages of a book. She loves intense alpha heroes and the women who dare to go toe-to-toe with them (or break a slate over their heads).

DEDICATION

For all the Harlequin Modern novels that came
before this one. It is the other books, and the
other authors, that brought me my love of
romance. And it is why I'm writing them now.

CHAPTER ONE

"I HAVE A debt to collect, Violet King."

Violet stared out the windows of her office, glass all around, providing a wonderful view of the Pacific Ocean directly across her desk, with a view of her staff behind her. There were no private walls in her office space. She preferred for the team to work collaboratively. Creatively.

Her forward-thinking approach to business, makeup and fashion was part of why she had become one of the youngest self-made billionaires in the world.

Though, self-made might be a bit of a stretch considering that her father, Robert King, had given her the initial injection of cash that she needed to get her business off the ground. Everyone worked with investors, she supposed. That hers was genetically related to her was not unheard-of nor, she supposed, did it fully exclude her from that self-made title. But she was conscious of it. Still, she had made that money back and then some.

And she did *not* have debt.

Which meant this man had nothing to say to her.

"You must have the wrong number," she said.

"No. I don't."

The voice on the other end of the phone was rich and dark, faintly accented, though she couldn't quite nail down what accent it was. Different to her family friend, now her sister's husband, Dante, who was from Italy and had spent many years in the States since then. Spanish, perhaps, but with a hint of Brit that seemed to elongate his vowels.

"Very confident," she said. "But I am in debt to no man."

"Oh, perhaps I misspoke then. You are not in debt. You are the payment."

Ice settled in her stomach. "How did you get this number?"

In this social media age where she was seemingly accessible at all hours, she guarded her private line with all the ferocity of a small mammal guarding its burrow. She—or her assistants—might be available twenty-four hours a day on the internet, but she could only be reached at this line by business associates, family or personal friends. This man was none of those, and yet somehow he was calling her. And saying the most outlandish things.

"How I got this number is not important to the conversation."

She huffed. "To the contrary, it is extremely important."

Suddenly, she felt the hairs on the back of her neck

stand on end and she turned around. The office building was empty, just as she thought it was. It was late in the day and everyone had gone home. Her employees often worked from home, or at the beach, wherever creativity struck them.

Her team wanted to be there, and she didn't need to enforce long office hours for them to do their work. The glass walls of the building made it possible for her to see who was in residence at all times, again, not so she could check up on them, but so there was a sense of collaboration.

It also made it easy to see now that she was alone here.

Of course she was. A person couldn't simply walk into this building. Security was tight, and anyone wanting entrance would have to be buzzed in.

But then suddenly she saw a ripple of movement through the outermost layer of glass, motion as a door opened. A dark shape moved through each clear barrier, from room to room, like a shark gliding beneath the surface of clear water. As each door opened, the shape moved closer, revealing itself to be the figure of a man.

Her chest began to get tight. Fear gripped her, her heart beating faster, her palms damp.

"Are you here?" she whispered.

But the line went dead, and she was left standing frozen in her office, her eyes glued to the man steadily making his way deeper and deeper into the office building. The glass, however transparent, was bulletproof, so there was that.

There were so many weirdos in the world that an abundance of caution never went amiss. She had learned about that at a fairly early age. Her father being one of the wealthiest businessmen in California had put her in the public eye very young. The media had always been fascinated with their family; with her brother, who was incredibly successful in his own right; her mother, who was a great beauty. And then, with her for the same reason.

It had always felt so...unearned to her. This great and intense attention for doing nothing at all. It had never sat well with her.

Her father had told her to simply enjoy it. That she was under no obligation to do anything, considering he'd done all the work already.

He'd always been bemused by her desire to get into business, but he'd helped her get started. He'd been humoring her, that much had been clear. But she'd been determined to prove to him that she was smart. That she could make it on her own.

Even now she had the feeling he regarded her billion-dollar empire as a hobby.

The only one of them who had seemingly escaped without massive amounts of attention was her younger sister, Minerva, who Violet had always thought might have been the smartest of them all. Minerva had made herself into the shape of something unremarkable so that she could live life on her own terms.

Violet had taken a different approach, and there

were times when the lack of privacy grated and she regretted living the life that she had.

Sometimes she felt an ache for what might have been. She wondered why she had this life. Why she was blessed with money and a certain amount of success instead of being anonymous or impoverished.

Some of that was eased by the charity she ran with her sister, which made it feel like all of it did mean something. That she had been granted this for a reason. And it made the invasions of privacy bearable.

Though not so much now. She felt vulnerable, and far too visible, trapped in a glass bowl of her own making, only able to watch as a predator approached her, and she was unable to do anything but wait.

She tried to call the police, her fingers fumbling on the old-fashioned landline buttons. It wasn't working. She had that landline for security. For privacy. And it was failing her on every level.

Of course she had her cell phone, but it was…

Sitting on the table just outside the office door.

And then suddenly he was *there*. Standing right on the other side of her office door. Tall, broad, clad all in black, wearing a suit that molded to his exquisitely hard-looking body, following every cut line from the breadth of his shoulders to his tapered waist, on down his long muscular legs. He turned around, and how he saw she was thinking of him in those terms she didn't know. Only that he was a force. Like looking at a sheer rock face with no footholds.

Hard and imposing, looming before her.

His face was…

Like a fallen Angel. Beautiful, and a sharp, strange contrast to the rest of him.

There was one imperfection on that face. A slashed scar that ran from the top of his high cheekbone down to the corner of his mouth. A warning.

This man was dangerous.

Lethal.

"Shall we have a chat?"

The barrier of the glass between them made that deep, rich voice echo across the surface of it, and she could feel it reverberating inside of her.

She hated it.

"How did you get in here?"

"My darling, I have a key."

She shrank back. "I'm not your darling."

"True," he said. "You are not. But you are my quarry. And I have found you."

"I'm not very hard to find," she said. She lifted her chin, trying to appear confident. "I'm one of the most famous women in the world."

"So you are. And that has me questioning my brother's sanity. But I am not here to do anything but follow orders."

"If you're here to follow orders, then perhaps you should follow one of mine. Leave."

"I answer to only one man. To only one person. And it is not you."

"A true regret," she said tightly.

"Not for me."

"What do you want?"

"I told you. I am here to collect payment. And that payment is you."

She was beautiful. But he had been prepared for that. When his brother had told him that it was finally time for him to make good on a promise given to him by Robert King ten years ago, Prince Javier de la Cruz had held back a litany of questions for his lord and master. He wondered why his brother wished to collect the debt now. And why he wished to collect it at all, at least in the form of this woman.

She was conspicuous. And she was everything his brother was not. Modern. Painfully so in contrast with the near medieval landscape of Monte Blanco. Yes, the kingdom had come a long way under his brother's rule during the last two years, but there was still a long way to go to bring it out of the Dark Ages their father had preferred. If a woman such as Violet King would be something so foreign to their people, then imagining her his queen was impossible.

But then, on some level, Javier imagined that was his brother's aim. Still, it was not Javier's position to question. Javier was as he had ever been. The greatest weapon Monte Blanco possessed. For years, he had undermined his father, kept the nation from going to war, kept his people safe. Had freed prisoners when they were wrongfully withheld. Had done all that he could to ensure that his father's impact on their people was as minimal as possible. And he had done so all under the oversight of his older brother, who—when he had taken control—had immediately begun to revive the country, using the money that he had earned with his business acumen. The Tycoon King, he was called.

And this—this deal with Robert King—had been one of those bargains he'd struck in secret. Apparently this deal had been made long ago, over drinks in a casino in Monte Carlo. A bet the other man had lost.

Javier was surprised his brother would hold a man to a drunken bargain.

And yet, here he was.

But Matteo was not a thoroughly modern man, whatever moves he was making to reform the country, and this sort of medieval bargain was just the type he knew his brother might favor.

Still…

Looking at her now, Javier could not imagine it.

She was wearing a white suit. A crisp jacket and loose-fitting pants. Her makeup was like a mask in his estimation. Eyelashes that seemed impossibly long, full lips played up by the gloss that she wore on her mouth. A severe sort of contour created in her cheeks by whatever color she had brushed onto them.

Her dark hair was in a low ponytail, sleek and held back away from her face.

She was stunningly beautiful. And very young. The direct opposite of their poor mother, who had been so pale and defeated by the end of her life. And perhaps that was the point.

Still, forcing a woman into marriage was possibly not the best way to go about proving your modernity.

But again. He was not in a position to argue.

What mattered most was his brother's vision for the country, and he would see it done.

He was a blunt instrument. Not a strategist.

Something he was comfortable with. There was an honesty to it. His brother had to feign diplomacy. Had to hide his agenda to make the world comfortable.

Javier had to do no such thing.

"I don't know who you are. And I don't know what you're talking about," she said.

He made his way over to the door, entered in the code and it unlocked.

Her father had given him all that information. Because he knew that there was no other choice.

She backed against her desk, her eyes wide with fear.

"What are you doing?"

"This is growing tiresome. I'm Prince Javier de la Cruz, of Monte Blanco. And you, Violet King, are my brother's chosen bride."

"What?" She did something he did not expect at all. She guffawed. It was the most unladylike sound he had ever heard. "I am *nobody's* chosen bride."

"You are. Your father owes my brother a debt. Apparently, he ran out of capital at a gambling table and was quite…in his cups, so to speak. He offered you. And I have come to collect you."

"My father would not do such a thing. He would

not…gamble me away. My brother, on the other hand, might play a prank on me that was this ridiculous. Are there cameras somewhere? Am I on camera?"

"You are not on camera," he said.

She laughed again. "I must be. If this is your attempt to get a viral video or something, you better try again. My father is one of the most modern men that I have ever known. He would never, ever sell one of his daughters into marriage. You know my sister came home from studying abroad with a baby, and he didn't even ask where the baby came from. He just kind of let her bring it into his house. He does not treat his daughters like commodities, and he does not act like he can sell us to the highest bidder."

"Well, then perhaps you need to speak to him."

"I don't need to speak to him, because this is ridiculous."

"If you say so."

And so he closed the distance between them, lifted her up off the ground and threw her over his shoulder. He was running low on time and patience, and he didn't have time to stand around being laughed at by some silly girl. That earned him a yelp and a sharp kick to his chest. Followed by another one, and then another.

Pain was only pain. It did not bother him.

He ignored her.

He ignored her until he had successfully transported her out of the building, which was conveniently empty, and down to the parking lot where his limo was waiting. Only then, when he had her inside with the doors

closed and locked, did she actually stare at him with
fear. Did she actually look like she might believe him?

"Violet King, I am taking you back to my country.
Where you are to be Queen."

CHAPTER TWO

SHE DIDN'T HAVE her phone. She might as well have had her right hand amputated. She had no way to reach anybody. She was an undisputed queen of social media. And here she was, sentenced to silence, told she was going to be Queen of a nation, which was something else entirely.

But this guy was clearly sick in the head, so whatever was happening…

She looked around the limousine. He might be sick in the head, but he also had someone bankrolling his crazy fantasy.

"Is this your limousine?"

He looked around and rolled his shoulders back, settling into the soft leather. "No."

"Who are you working for?"

"I told you. My brother. The King of Monte Blanco."

"I don't even know where that is."

She searched her brain, trying to think if she had ever heard of the place. Geography wasn't her strong suit, but she was fairly well traveled, considering her job required it. Also, she loved it. Loved seeing new places and meeting new people. But Monte Blanco was not on her radar.

"It's not exactly a hot tourist destination," he said.

"Well."

"It's not my brother's limousine either, if you are curious. Neither of us would own something so…" His lip curled. "Ostentatious."

Old money. She was familiar enough with old money and the disdain that came with it. She was new money. And often, the disdain spilled over onto her. She was flashy. And she was obvious. But her fortune was made by selling beauty. By selling flash. Asking women to draw attention to themselves, telling them that it was all right. To dress for themselves. To put makeup on to please themselves, not necessarily to please men.

So yes, of course Violet herself was flashy. And if he had an issue with it, he could go… Well, jump out of the limo and onto the busy San Diego Freeway. She would not mourn him.

"Right. So you're a snob. A snob who's somehow involved in a kidnapping plot?" She supposed, again, he could be an actor. Not someone wealthy at all. Somebody hired to play a prank on her.

Somebody hired to hurt her.

That thought sent a sliver of dread through her body. She wouldn't show it. After all, what good were layers of makeup if you couldn't use them to hide your true face?

"I'm not a snob. I'm a prince."

"Right. Of a country I've never heard of."

"Your American centric viewpoint is hardly my problem, is it, Ms. King? It seems to me that your lack of education does not speak to my authenticity."

"Yes. Well. That is something you would say." The car was still moving, farther and farther away from where they had originated. And she supposed that she had to face the fact that this might not be a joke. That this man really thought she was going to go back to his country with him. If that country existed. Really, she had nothing but his word for it, and considering that he seemed to think that she was going to marry his brother, he might be delusional on multiple levels.

"I want to call my dad."

"You're welcome to," he said, handing her the phone.

She snatched it from him and dialed her father's personal number as quickly as possible. Robert King picked up on the second ring.

"Dad," she said, launching into her proclamation without preamble. "A madman has bundled me up and put me in his limousine, and he's claiming that you made a deal with him some decade ago, and I'm supposed to marry his brother?"

"I didn't make a deal with your dad," Javier said. "My brother did."

"It doesn't matter," she hissed. And then she sat there, waiting for her father to respond. With shock, she assumed. Yes, she assumed that he would respond with shock. Because of course this was insane. And of course it was the first time her father was hearing such a thing. Because there was no way he had anything to do with this. "So anyway, if you could just tell him that he's crazy…"

She realized how stupid it was the minute she said that. Because of course her father telling Javier he was crazy wouldn't likely reinforce it if the act of flinging her into his limousine hadn't done it.

"Violet…" Her father's voice was suddenly rough, completely uncharacteristic of the smooth, confident man that she had always looked up to.

Her father was imperfect. She wasn't blind to that. The fact that he was completely uninvested in her success was obvious to her. When it came to her brother, he was always happy to talk business. But because her business centered around female things, and she herself was a woman, she could never escape the feeling that her father thought it was some kind of hobby. Something insubstantial and less somehow.

But surely he wouldn't… Surely that didn't mean he saw her as currency.

"He's crazy, right?"

"I never thought that he would follow up on this," her father said. "And when you reached your twenties and he didn't… I assumed that there would be no recourse."

"You promised me to a king?"

"It could've been worse. I could have promised you to the used car salesman."

"You can't just promise *someone else* to *someone else*. I'm a person, not a… A cow."

"I'm sorry," he said. "Violet, I honestly didn't think that…"

"I won't stand for it. I will not do it. What's to stop me from jumping out of the car right now—" she looked out the window and saw the scenery flying by at an alarming clip, and she knew that that would keep her from jumping out of the car, but her father didn't need to know that "—and running for freedom?"

"The businesses. They will go to him."

"The businesses?"

"Yours and mine. Remember we sheltered yours under mine for taxes and…"

"Maximus's too?"

Because if he had sheltered her business, surely he had sheltered her brothers as well…

"No," her father said slowly.

"What's the real reason you kept mine underneath your corporation? Was it for this?"

"No. Just that I worried about you. And I thought that perhaps…"

"Because you don't think anything of me. You don't think that I'm equal to Maximus. If you did, then you wouldn't have done this to me. I can't believe… I can't believe you."

She could keep on arguing with her father, or she could accept the fact that he had sold her as chattel to a stranger. And with that realization, she knew that she needed to simply get off the phone. There was no redeeming this. Nothing at all that would fix it.

She had come face-to-face with how little she meant to her father, how little he thought of her.

She had taken his reaction to Minerva coming home with the baby to mean that he was enlightened, but that wasn't it at all. Minerva was being traditional, even if she hadn't had a husband initially when she had brought the baby home.

Still, he would rather have seen Minerva, in all her quirky glory, with a baby, than see Violet as a serious businesswoman.

There was no talking to him. She stared across the limo at the man who had taken her captive, and she realized...

That he was a saner option than arguing with her father.

She hung up the phone.

"So you are telling the truth."

"I have no investment in lying to you," Javier said. "I also have no investment in this deal as a whole. My brother has asked that I retrieve you, and so I have done it."

"So, you're a Saint Bernard, then?"

A flash of icy amusement shot through his dark eyes, the corner of his mouth curving up in a humorless smile. "You will find that I am not so easily brought to heel, I think."

"And yet here you are," she said. "Doing the bidding of someone else."

"Of my king. For my country. My brother and I have been the stronghold standing between Monte Blanco and total destruction for over a decade. My father was always a dictator, but his behavior spiraled out of control toward the end of his life. We were the only thing that kept his iron fist from crushing our people. And now we seek to rebuild. Who my brother wants as his choice of bride is his business. And if you'll excuse me… I don't care one bit for your American sensibilities. For your money. For your achievements. I care only that he has asked for you, and so I will bring you to him."

"Good boy," she said.

His movements were like liquid fury. One minute he was sitting across from her in the limousine, and the other he was beside her. He gripped her chin and held her fast, forcing her to look into his eyes. But there was no anger there. It was black, and it was cold. And it was the absence of all feeling that truly terrified her.

She did not think he would hurt her.

There was too much control in his hold. He was not causing her any pain. She could feel the leashed strength at the point where his thumb and forefinger met her chin.

"I am loyal," he said. "But I am not good. The cost of keeping my country going, the cost of my subterfuge has been great. Do not ever make the mistake of thinking that I'm good."

And then he withdrew from her. It was like she had imagined it. Except she shivered with the cold from those eyes, so she knew she hadn't.

"How are you going to make me get on the plane?"

"I will carry you," he said. "Or you could get on with your own two feet. Your father won't harbor you. I assume that he told you as much. So there's no use you running back home, is there?"

She was faced then with a very difficult decision. Because he was right—she could try to run away. But he would overpower her. And she had a feeling that no one would pay much attention to what would look like a screaming match between two rich people, culminating with her being carried onto a private plane. They were far too adjacent to Hollywood for anybody to consider that out of the ordinary.

And even if she did escape... Her father had verified what he'd said. Her father saw nothing wrong with using her to get out of a bad situation. He had sacrificed not only her, but her livelihood.

"You're not going to hurt me," she said. And she searched those eyes for something. All right, he'd said that he wasn't good. But she had a feeling that he was honest. Otherwise, there would have been no reason for him to tell her he wasn't good, except to hit back at her, and she had a feeling that wasn't it. That wasn't why.

There was more to it than that.

Somehow she knew that if she asked this question, he would answer. Even if the answer was yes, he was going to hurt her. He had no reason to lie to her, that was the thing. She was at his mercy and he knew it.

"No," he said. "I swear to you that no harm will come to you. My brother intends to make you his bride, not his slave. And as far as I go... I'm your protector, Violet, not your enemy. I have been charged with transporting you back to Monte Blanco and if I were to allow any harm to come to you, you can rest assured that my brother would see me rotting in my father's favorite dungeon."

"Your father had a favorite dungeon?"

"More than one, actually."

"Wow."

She didn't know why she felt mollified by his assurance that he wouldn't hurt her. Especially not considering he had just said his father had a favorite dungeon. But he made it clear that he and his brother weren't like their father. So if she could believe that...

It was insane that she believed him. But the thing was, he hadn't lied to her. Not once. Her father had tricked her. Had made her believe that the life she was living was different than the one she actually had. That their relationship was different.

But this man had never lied.

Her world felt turned upside down, and suddenly, her kidnapper seemed about the most trustworthy person.

A sad state of affairs.

The car halted on the tarmac, and there was a plane. It didn't look like a private charter, because it was the size of a commercial jet.

But the royal crest on the side seemed to indicate that it was in fact his jet.

Or his brother's. However that worked.

"This way," he said, getting out of the limousine and holding the door for her.

The driver had gotten out and stood there feebly. "I think he was going to hold the door," she said, looking up at Javier.

Her heart scampered up into her throat as her eyes connected with his again. Looking at him was like getting hit with a force. She had never experienced anything quite like it.

It wasn't simply that he was beautiful—though he was—it was the hardness to him. The overwhelming feeling of rampant masculinity coming at her like a testosterone-fueled train.

Admittedly, she was not exposed to men like him all that often. Not in her line of work.

She actually hadn't been certain that men like him existed.

Well, there was her brother-in-law, Dante, who was a hard man indeed, but still, he looked approachable in comparison to Javier.

This man was like a throwback from a medieval era. The circumstances of her meeting him—the ones where she was being sold into marriage pit debt—certainly contributing to this feeling.

"Too bad for him," Javier shot back. "I don't wait."

And that, she concluded, was her signal to get out of the limo. She decided to take her time. Because he might not wait, but she did not take orders.

And if she was going to retain any kind of power in the situation, she had better do it now. Hoard little pieces of it as best she could, because he wasn't going to give her any. No. So she would not surrender what she might be able to claim.

"Good to know." She made small micromovements, sliding across the seat and then flexing her ankles before her feet made contact with the ground. Then she scooted forward a bit more, put her hands on her knees.

And he stood there, not saying anything.

She stood, and as she did so, he bent down, and her face came within scant inches of his. She forgot to breathe. But she did not forget to move. She pitched herself forward and nearly came into contact with the asphalt. He wrapped his arm around her waist and pulled her back against him. Her shoulder blades came into stark contact with his hard chest. It all lasted only a moment, because he released her and allowed her to stand on her own feet as soon as she was steady. But she could still feel him. The impression of him. Burning her.

"If I walk on my own two feet to the airplane, it is not a kidnapping, is it?"

"I'm certainly not married to the narrative of it being a kidnapping. Call it whatever you need to."

She straightened her shoulders and began to walk toward the plane.

Toward her doom.

Violet didn't know which it was.

But she did know that she was going to have to find her control in this, one way or another.

Even if it were only in the simple act of carrying *herself* aboard the plane.

CHAPTER THREE

JAVIER STUDIED THE woman sitting across from him. Her rage had shrunk slightly and was now emanating off her in small waves rather than whole tsunamis.

She had not accepted a drink, and he had made a show of drinking in front of her, to prove that no one was attempting to poison her, or whatever she seemed to imagine.

He was going to have to have words with Matteo once he arrived in Monte Blanco. "You might want to lower your shields," he said.

"Sure," she said. "Allow me to relax. In front of the man who is holding me against my will."

"Remember, you walked on your own two feet to the airplane, which you felt was the difference between a kidnapping and an impromptu vacation."

"It's a kidnapping," she said. "And I'll have some champagne."

"Now that you've watched me drink a glass and a half and are satisfied that I'm not going to fall down dead?"

"Something like that."

"Why are you in a temper now when you were fine before?"

"This is absurd. I haven't been able to check my social media for hours."

"Is that a problem for you?"

"It's my entire business," she said. "It's built off that. Off connectivity. And viral posts. If I can't make posts, I can't go viral."

"That sounds like something you would want to avoid."

"You're being obtuse. Surely you know what *going viral* means."

"I've heard it," he said. "I can't say that I cared to look too deeply into it. The internet is the least of our concerns in Monte Blanco."

"Well, it's one of my primary concerns, considering it's how I make my living. All fine for you to be able to ignore it, but I can't."

"Also not going to allow you to post from the plane. Anyway. We don't have Wi-Fi up here."

"How do you not have Wi-Fi? Every airplane has that."

"My father didn't have it installed. And my brother has not seen the use for it."

"I find that hard to believe. He's running a country."

"Again. That is not a primary concern in my country. You may find that we have different priorities than you."

"Do you have electricity?" she asked, in what he assumed was mock horror.

"We have electricity."

"Do you live in a moldering castle?"

"It's quite a bit less moldering than when my brother took the throne. But it is a bit medieval, I'm not going to lie."

"Well. All of this is a bit medieval, isn't it?"

"I felt it was quite modern, given you weren't traded for a pair of sheep."

"No. Just my father's gambling debt, extracted from him when he was drunk. What kind of man is your brother that he would do that?"

"I would say honorable. But his primary concern is the country, and while I don't know what his ultimate plans are for you, or why he wants you specifically, I do know there is a reason. One thing I know about him is that he has his reasons."

"Woof," she said.

In spite of himself, amusement tightened his stomach. And that was the last thing he expected to feel at her insolence. She had no idea who he was. He was a weapon. A human blade.

And she… She taunted him.

He was used to women reacting to him with awe. Sometimes they trembled with fear, but in a way that they seemed to enjoy. He was not blind to the effect he had on women. No indeed. He was a powerful man. A man with a title. A man with wealth.

He commanded a military.

Violet King did not tremble with fear when she looked at him.

He took a champagne glass from the table next to him and poured her a measure of liquid, reaching across the space and handing it to her. She didn't move.

"You'll have to come and get it. Contrary to what you may have heard, I don't fetch or deliver."

She scowled and leaned forward, grabbing hold of the glass and clutching it to her chest as she settled back in her chair.

She looked around the expansive airplane. "Do you think this thing is a little bit big?"

"I've never had any complaints."

Color mounted in her cheeks. "Well. Indeed." She downed half the glass of champagne without taking a breath. "I really do wish there was an internet connection."

"But there isn't. Anyway, we left your phone back in your office."

She looked truly panicked at that. "What if somebody else gets a hold of it? I can't have anybody posting on my social media who wasn't approved."

"Such strange concerns you have. Websites. You know, I've been fighting for the life and health of my people for the last several years. I can't imagine being concerned that somebody might post something on a website in my name."

"Optics," she snapped.

"Optics are no concern of mine. I'm concerned with reality. That which you can touch and see. Smell. Feel. That is my concern. Reality."

"It's no less real. It changes people's lives. It affects them profoundly. I built an entire business off of influence."

"You make a product. I did a cursory amount of research on you, Violet. You don't simply post air."

"No. But for want of that air my products wouldn't sell. It's what exposes me to all those people. It's what makes me relevant."

"I should hope that more than a piece of code floating out in cyberspace would make you relevant."

Her lips twitched and she took another sip of champagne. "I'm not going to argue about this with a man who thinks it's perfectly reasonable to bundle me up and take me back to his country."

"I didn't say it was reasonable," he said. "Only that it was going to be done."

After that, they didn't speak.

Upon arrival in Monte Blanco, Javier parted with Violet and made a straight path for his brother's office.

"I've returned," he said.

"Good," Matteo said, barely looking up from his desk. "I assume you have brought the woman with you?"

"Yes. As promised."

"I knew I could count on you. Did she come quietly?"

He thought of the constant barbs that he had been subjected to on the trip.

"No. She is *never* quiet."

Matteo grimaced. "That could be a problem."

"Your Highness."

Javier turned around at the sound of the breathy voice. Matteo's assistant, Livia, had come into the room. She was a small, drab creature, and he had no idea why his brother kept her on. But Matteo was ridiculously attached to her.

"Yes," Matteo said, his voice gentling slightly.

"It's only that the United Council chief called, and he is requesting the presence of Monte Blanco at a meeting. It's about your inclusion."

This was something his brother had been waiting for. His father had stayed out of international affairs, but it was important to both Matteo and Javier that Monte Blanco have a voice in worldwide matters.

"Then I shall call him."

"I don't know that that will be necessary. He only wishes to know if you will accept his invitation to come to the summit this week."

"Well, I'm a bit busy," Matteo said, gesturing toward Javier.

"Oh?" she asked.

"Yes," he responded. "Javier has brought my bride to me."

Livia's eyes widened, but only for a moment. "Of course." That slight widening was the only emotional reaction given by the assistant. But Javier knew how to read people, and he could see that she was disturbed.

He could also see that his brother did not notice. "It is of no consequence," he said. "We must attend. Javier, you will make sure that Violet acclimates while I'm gone."

"Of course," he said. What he did not say was that he was not a trained babysitter for spoiled socialites, but a soldier. Still, he thought it.

"See that my things are collected immediately," Matteo said, addressing Livia. "All the details handled."

He spoke in such incomplete sentences to the woman, and yet she scurried to do his bidding, asking for no clarification at all.

"Don't you think this is a bit outlandish, even for you?"

"My mouse will have no trouble taking care of things," he said, using his nickname for Livia.

"Yes. I forgot. She is your mouse, living only to do as you ask. Though your appalling treatment of your assistant was not actually what I was referring to. That you had me drag this woman across the world, and you will not be in residence."

"It's perfect," he said. "A more traditional sort of relationship, yes? Hearkening back to the days of old. We won't meet until the wedding."

"You forget, she's an American. A thoroughly modern one."

"*You* forget: she has no choice."

"Why exactly do you want Violet King? That's something that I don't understand."

"Because we need to modernize. Because we need

to change the way that the world perceives Monte Blanco."

"I was told by your fiancée that the world does not perceive it at all."

"A blessing," Matteo said. "Because if the world did have a perception of us before now, it would not be a good one."

"And you want to change that." He thought of everything Violet had said to him regarding the internet. "Why don't you have Wi-Fi on your plane?"

Matteo blinked. "What does that have to do with anything?"

"Violet seemed to find it odd that you didn't. I told her you weren't concerned with such things. But it appears that you are."

"Well, I've never needed it in the air."

"Your future bride would want it. Otherwise I think she will find traveling with you onerous."

"I didn't realize you would be so concerned for her comfort."

"Well, you put her comfort in my charge."

"And I leave it to you now." Matteo stood from behind the desk. "I understand that it's not ideal, but I know that you'll also trust me when I tell you this is necessary."

"I know," Javier said. "You never do anything that isn't."

"I'm not our father," Matteo said, and not for the first time Javier wondered if he was telling him or telling himself.

He was well familiar with that internal refrain. He knew his brother walked a hard road, but a different one than Javier did.

Javier had been part of his father's army.

Under Javier's oversight, missions had been carried out that had caused harm. He had believed, fully and completely, that he was in the right.

Until one day he'd seen the truth. Seen what love and loyalty had blinded him to.

And he had learned.

That a man could be a villain and not even know.

That with the right lie, a man could commit endless atrocities and call it justice.

"I know," Javier repeated. "You have spent all these past years defying him. I hardly thought that a little bit of power was going to corrupt you entirely."

"But I must be on guard against it. I understand that you may think it medieval for me to force the girl into marriage…"

Javier shrugged. "I have no thoughts on it one way or the other." And it was true. He knew that Violet was unhappy with the situation, but her happiness was not his concern.

Swaths of unhappiness had been cut through his country for decades, and he and his brother were working as hard as they could to undo it. If Matteo thought that making Violet his queen would help with the situation, then it was collateral damage Javier was willing to accept.

"You say that," Matteo said. "But I have a feeling that you always have thoughts."

"Are they relevant, My King?"

"I told you, I am not our father. But for the fact that I'm a few years older than you, you would be King. Or, if I were dead."

"Stay alive," Javier said. "I have no desire to bear the burden of the crown."

"And yet, the burden is heavy enough that I daresay you can feel the weight of it. It is not like you are immune to the responsibilities we face."

"What is the point of sharing blood with our father if we don't do everything, to the point of spilling it, to correct his wrongs?"

"No point at all," Matteo said, nodding. "I must go check on my mouse's progress."

"You call her that to her face?"

"Yes. She finds it endearing."

He thought back to the stricken look on Livia's face when Matteo had mentioned his fiancée. But Javier also thought of the slight note of warmth in his brother's voice when he said it. *Mouse.* He didn't say it as if she were small or gray, though in Javier's opinion she was both. No, he said it as if she were fragile. His to care for.

"She may."

"No. It is because of how I found her. Shivering and gray, and far too small. Like a mouse."

Javier was not certain that Livia liked to be reminded of her origins. However much Matteo might find his name for her affectionate. He meant what he had said to Violet. Javier was not a good man. Matteo might be, but for the two of them it was more honor than it was anything quite so human as goodness.

In fact, the only real evidence Javier had ever seen of softness in his brother was the presence of Livia in the palace. He didn't know the full story of how he had come into... Possession of her, only that he had found her in quite an unfortunate situation and for some reason had decided it was his responsibility to fix that situation.

"You will keep things running while I'm gone," Matteo said, a command and not a question.

"Of course I will."

"And I will endeavor to make sure these meetings go well. You remember what I told you."

"Of course. If ever you were to exhibit character-istics of our father, it would be better that you were dead."

"I meant that."

"And I would kill you myself."

His brother smiled and walked forward clasping his forearm, and Javier clasped his in return. "And that is why I trust you. Because I believe you would."

They were blood brothers. Bonded by blood they hated. The blood of their father. But their bond was unshakable and had always been. Because they had known early on that if they were ever going to over-come the evil of their line, they would have to tran-scend it.

And they could only do that together.

Their relationship was the most important thing in Javier's life. Because it was the moral ballast for them both. Because Javier knew how easy it was to upset morality. How emotion could cloud it.

How it could cause pain.

Whether he understood Matteo's being so intent to marry Violet or not, he would support it. All that mattered was Monte Blanco. Violet's feelings were a nonissue.

All that mattered was the kingdom.

CHAPTER FOUR

VIOLET HAD BEEN essentially born into money. So she was used to grandeur. She was used to the glittering opulence of sparkling shows of wealth. But the palace and Monte Blanco were something else entirely.

It wasn't that the walls were gilded—they were entirely made of gold. The floor, obsidian inlaid with precious metals, rubies and emeralds. The doorframes were gold, shot through with panels of diamond.

Given what Javier had said about the limo, she was somewhat surprised to see such a glaring display of wealth, but then she imagined the palace had been standing for centuries. She could feel it. As if it were built down into the mountain.

And it was indeed on a mountain. Made of white granite, likely the namesake of the country.

It reminded her of Javier himself. Imposing, commanding, and entirely made of rock. The view down below was… Spectacular.

A carpet of deep, dense pines swooping down before climbing back upward to yet more mountains. She could barely make out what she thought might be a city buried somewhere in there, but if it was, it was very small. The mountains loomed large, fading to blue and purple the farther away they were. Until they nearly turned to mist against the sky. A completely different color than she had ever seen before. As if it were more ice than sky.

She had not thought it would be cold, given that she didn't think of cold when she thought of this region, but nestled as it was between France and Spain at such a high elevation, it was shockingly frigid and much more rugged than she had thought.

Queen of the wilderness. He had brought her out here to be Queen of the wilderness.

The thought made her shiver.

Then she turned away from the view and back toward the bedroom she had been installed in by a helpful member of staff, and she couldn't think of wilderness at all. It was ornate to the point of ridiculousness.

The bed was made of gold. The canopy was comprised of layers of fabric, a glittering and a gauzy layer, with heavy brocade beneath. The covers were velvet, rich purple and gold.

It made the clean, modern lines of her all-white apartment stark in her memory.

She wasn't going to waste time pondering the room, though. What she needed to do was figure out how to talk the King out of this ridiculous idea that they needed to get married. First, she needed to figure out what his motives were. Obviously if he were crazed by lust where she was concerned, there wasn't much she could offer him. At least, nothing much that she was willing to offer.

Violet knew that no one would believe it if she told them, but she had no physical experience with men. She had never been carried away on a tide of passion, and she fully intended to be carried away on a tide of passion when she allowed a man to... Do any of that.

The problem was, she had met so many kinds of men in her life. Hazard of being well connected and well traveled. She had met rich men. Talented men. Actors, chefs, rock stars. CEOs.

Javier is the first prince you ever met...

Well. That didn't matter. The point was, she'd been exposed to a variety of powerful men early on, and inevitably she found them to be... Disappointments.

They either revealed themselves to be arrogant jerks with overinflated opinions of themselves, secret perverts who had only been pretending to listen to her while they contemplated making a move on her, or aggressive nightmares with more hands than a centipede and less sense.

And she had just always thought there could be more than that. More than shrugging and giving in to a wet kiss that she hadn't wanted anyway.

The richer she had become, the more men had seemed to find her a challenge. Whether she was actually issuing one or not.

And that had made her even more disenchanted with them.

And she hadn't held out for passion for all this time to just…

To just be taken by some king that she didn't even know.

She could Google him if she had any devices. But there was no damned internet in this place.

The first active business would be to find out what he wanted. Because she had a lot. She was a billionaire, after all. And, she was well connected. He could break off a chunk of this castle, and it would probably equal her net worth, so there was that. But there had to be something. There had to be. Otherwise, it wouldn't matter if it was her.

Which brought her back to sexually obsessed. Which really creeped her out.

There was a knock on the chamber door, and she jumped. "Come in."

She expected it to be the same woman who had led her to her room, but it wasn't. It was Javier. And when he came in he brought with him all of the tension that she'd felt in her chest the entire time they were together on the plane ride over.

"I wasn't expecting you," she said.

"What were you expecting exactly?"

She realized there was no point in being difficult. Because Javier might be the key to this. "Where is your brother?"

"Eager to see him?"

"No," she said, and she found that was honest. Better the devil she knew, after all. Even if said devil was as unyielding as a rock face. "Did he tell you why he wants to marry me?"

She needed to know. Because she needed to formulate a plan. She needed to get some power back. Or, rather than getting it back, needed to get some of it in the first place.

"Yes," Javier said.

He just stood there. Broad, tall and imposing.

"Would you care to share with the class?"

"I don't think it matters."

"You don't get that it matters to me why this stranger wants to marry me? I would like to know if it has to do with him harboring some sort of obsession for my body."

That made him laugh. And it offended her. "No. My brother has no designs on your body. He thinks that you will be useful in improving the world's view of Monte Blanco. It is in fact his sole focus. Which is what I came to tell you. He is not here."

"He's not here?"

"No. He has gone to the United Council summit. It is very important to him that Monte Blanco be granted inclusion into the Council. For too long, we have been without the benefit of allies. For too long, we have not had a say in how the world works. And it is something my brother feels is key to bringing us into the twenty-first century."

"So he wants my... Influencer reach?"

That was ridiculous. But she could work with that. "He wants me to make the country look better."

"Yes," Javier said.

"Well. That's easy. I can do that without marrying him."

"I'm not sure that's on his agenda."

"Well, then I'll just have to convince him that it's a better agenda. I'm very convincing. I entered a very crowded market, and I managed to essentially dominate it. You know that I'm the youngest self-made billionaire in the world?"

"Yes," Javier said. "We did in fact look at the basic headlines about you."

"Then he should know that I'll be of much more use to him as a business consultant."

"You sell makeup," he said.

She bristled. "Yes. And I sell it well. Enough that he seems to have taken notice of the impact that I've made on the world. So don't belittle it." She huffed a breath. "Anyway. All I need is a chance to get to know the country."

"Excellent. I'm glad that you think so. Because I believe that my brother's mouse is making an agenda for while they are away."

"His what?"

"His assistant. We have assignments for while he is away. And I am to oversee."

"Are you *babysitting* me?"

"In a sense."

"You know," she said, keeping her voice carefully deadpan. "I seem to recall a Saint Bernard that acted as Nana in a classic cartoon…"

"Don't push it. I can always tell him you met with an unfortunate accident."

"You said you wouldn't hurt me," she said, meeting his gaze, keeping her eyes as stern as possible.

He inclined his head. "So I did."

"Are you a man of your word, Javier?"

"I am."

The simple confidence in those words made her stomach tighten. "Somehow I knew that."

His eyes narrowed. "How?"

She shrugged. "I don't know. I'm a good judge of character, I think. I was born into wealth, and I will tell you that it's an easier life than most. But I had access to... Anything. Any excess that I wanted. Any sort of mischief that I might want to get into. Drugs and older men and parties. People were always after me to do favors for them. And I had to learn very quickly who my real friends might be. Because let me tell you... What people say and what they do are two very different things. Words don't mean anything if they're not backed up by actions."

"Well, I've kidnapped you. What does that action tell you?"

"I didn't think we were going with *kidnap*?"

"That was your call, not mine."

"Well, you're loyal to your brother. I also think you're loyal to... Your own sense of honor. You might say that you aren't good. But you have a moral code. And even if it does extend to allowing you to kidnap me if your brother says it's the right thing to do, I do not think it would ever extend to hurting someone who couldn't defend themselves against you."

He inclined his head. "Fair enough. My father enjoyed inflicting pain upon the weak. He enjoyed exploiting his power. I have no desire to ever involve myself in such a thing. It is an act of cowardice."

"And you're not a coward," she said confidently. "And I think that you might even want to help me prove to your brother that I don't need to marry him so that I can get back to my real life."

"That's where you're wrong. I genuinely don't care about your plan. Not one way or the other. Happiness, in that fleeting immediate sense, is quite immaterial to me. What matters is the greater good. If my brother feels the greater good is served by marrying you, then that is the goal I will help him accomplish. Not what will make you... Happier. As you said, you had a happier life than most. Drugs, parties and rich men, from the sounds of things."

"But I had none of those things," she said, not sure where she had lost the conversation. "It's just that I had access to them. I haven't experienced them. I have too much to live for. Too much experience to explore."

"It seems to me that you had ample opportunity to do so prior to your engagement to my brother."

"I am not engaged. I am *kidnapped*, as you just stated."

"Walked onto the plane with your own two feet, I think you mean."

"You were the one that introduced *kidnap* again."

"You're the one who seems hung up on the terminology."

"I'll prove it. I'll prove that we don't need marriage."

"Fantastic. Feel free. In the meantime, I will set about to fulfill the items on my brother's list. Because that is all I care about."

He turned and began to walk away from her. "Do you have any feelings about anything?"

When he turned back to face her, his eyes were blank. "No."

"You must be a great time in bed," she shot back, not sure where that came from. Except she knew it made men angry when you called their prowess into question, and if she couldn't elicit sympathy from him, then she would be happy to elicit some rage.

"Thankfully for you," he said, his tone hard, "my bedroom skills will never be a concern of yours. You are not meant for me."

And then he was gone. Leaving her in the oppressive silence created by those thick, wealth-laden walls.

And she had a feeling that for the first time in her life she might have bitten off more than she could chew.

Except, it wasn't even her bite. It was her father's. And she was the one left dealing with it.

CHAPTER FIVE

HER WORDS ECHOED in his head all through the next day, and when he finally received the memo from his brother's assistant, his irritation was at an all-time high. Because what Violet King thought about him in bed was none of his concern. She had an acerbic tongue, and she was irritating. Beautiful, certainly, but annoying.

Had he been the sort of man given to marriage, she would not be the woman that he would choose. But then, marriage would never have to be for him. He didn't have to produce heirs.

He charged down the hall, making his way to her room, where he knocked sharply.

"Don't come in!"

"Why not?"

"I'm not decent."

"Are you undressed?" The image of Violet in some state of undress caused his stomach to tighten, and he cursed himself for acting like an untried boy. She was just a woman.

"No," she said.

He opened the door without waiting for further explanation. And there she sat, at the center of the massive bed looking…

Scrubbed clean.

She looked younger than when he had first seen her yesterday, than she did in any picture he had ever seen.

Her lashes were not so noticeable now, shorter, he thought. Her face looked rounder, her skin softer. Her lips were no longer shiny, but plump and soft looking. Her dark hair fell around her shoulders in riotous waves.

"I don't have my makeup," she said.

He couldn't help it. He laughed. He couldn't remember the last time he had felt actual humor. Until now. The woman was concerned because she did not have her makeup.

"And that concerns me why?"

"It's my… It's my trade. I don't go out without it. It would be a bad advertisement."

"Surely you don't think you need all of that layered onto your face to make you presentable?"

"That's not the point. It's not about being presentable, or whatever. It's just… It's not who I am."

"Your makeup is who you are?"

"I built my empire on it. On my look."

"Well. No one is here to see your look. And we have assignments."

"Assignments?"

"Yes. First, time to give you a tour of the palace. Then we are to discuss your… Appearance."

She waved a hand in front of her face. "I have been discussing my appearance this entire time."

"Well. I don't mean that, precisely. Your role as Queen will require a different sort of… A different sort of approach."

"I'm sorry. I've made it very clear that I'm not on board with this whole Queen thing, and you're talking about how you're going to change my appearance?"

"I'm only telling you what's on the list. We also need to go over customs, expectations. Ballroom etiquette."

"Don't tell me that I'm going to have to take dancing lessons."

"Precisely that."

"This is… *Medieval*."

"Tell me what it is you need from home, and I will accommodate you." Looking at the stubborn set of her face, he realized that he could drag her kicking and screaming into completing these tasks, or he could try to meet her in the middle. Compromise was not exactly second nature to him, but sometimes different tactics were required for dealing with different enemies.

He and his brother had been covert by necessity when dealing with their father. He could certainly manage a bit of finesse with one small makeup mogul.

"I… Well, I need all my beauty supplies. I might be able to come up with a queen-level look using my makeup, but nobody's doing it but me."

"We'll see."

"I can't wear someone else's products." She was verging on melodrama and he would not indulge it in the least if it weren't for his brother.

That was all.

"My concern is not centered on your business. And anyway, yours shouldn't be at this point either."

"Untrue. My primary concern is my business, because I think it's what I have to offer here."

"Why don't we discuss this over breakfast."

"I told you. I can't go out looking like this."

He pushed a button on the intercom by the door. Moments later the door opened, and in came breakfast for two.

"Oh," Violet said.

"You keep introducing issues that are not issues for me."

She looked deflated. "Fine. I don't actually care about my makeup."

"Then why exactly are you protesting?"

"Because. I want to win. And I figured if you thought I was this ridiculous and unable to function without a full face of makeup, you might send me back."

"Again. Whether or not you become the next Queen of Monte Blanco is not my decision. So you can go ahead and try to make me believe that you are the silliest creature on planet Earth, but it still won't change what's happening."

He moved the cart closer to her bed. She peered down at the contents. "Is that avocado toast?"

"It is," he said. "Of course, I'm told that it's quite trendy the world over. It has always been eaten here."

"Fascinating," she said. "I didn't realize that you were trendsetters."

He picked up his own plate of breakfast and sat in the chair next to her bed. Then he poured two cups of coffee. Her interest became yet more keen.

"I'm not going to poison you," he said. "You keep staring at me as if I might."

She scrabbled to the edge of the bed and reached down, grabbing hold of the plate of avocado toast, bringing it onto the comforter.

Her eyes met his and held. A shift started, somewhere deep in his gut. She didn't move. Or maybe it only felt like she didn't. Like the moment hung suspended.

Then her fingers brushed his as she took the cup, color mounting in her face as she settled back in the bed, away from him.

The distance, he found, helped with the tightening in his stomach.

She took a sip and smiled. "Perfect," she said. "Strong."

"Did you sleep well?"

"I slept about as well as a prisoner in a foreign land can expect to sleep."

"Good to know."

"The pea under the mattress was a bit uncomfortable." A smile tugged the edge of her lips.

She was a strange sort of being, this woman. She

had spirit, because God knew in this situation, many other people would have fallen apart completely. But she hadn't. She was attempting to needle him. To manipulate him. From calling him a Saint Bernard to pretending she was devastated by her bare face.

And now she was drinking coffee like a perfectly contented cat.

"Why don't you go ahead and say what's on your mind. I can tell you're dying to."

"I will complete your list," she said. "Down to the dancing lessons. But I want you to show me around the country. Not just the palace."

"To what end?"

"I've been thinking. Your brother wants to bring this country into the modern era. Well. I am the poster child for success in the modern era. And I believe that I can bring some of that to you. I can do it without marrying your brother."

"As far as I'm concerned it's not up for negotiation."

"Fine. We'll table that. But I want you to give me the tools to make it a negotiation with him."

"Perhaps," he said, taking a long drag of his own coffee.

"Look. Even if I do marry your brother, you're going to want me to do this."

"He didn't leave orders to do it. I have no personal feelings on the matter."

"If you get your way, I'm going to live here for the rest of my life," she said, her voice finally overtaken by emotion. "You don't even want me to see the place?

Don't you think that I should be able to… Envision what my life will be?"

This was not a business negotiation. Finally. She wasn't playing at being sharp and witty, or shallow and vapid. Not holding a board meeting curled up in her canopy bed. This, finally, was something real.

And he was not immune to it, he found.

"I'll see what I can accomplish."

She picked up her toast and took a bite of it with ferocity. "Well. At least I approve of your food." She set the toast back down on the plate and brushed some crumbs away from her lips.

She managed to look imperious and ridiculous all at once.

He could not imagine his brother wrangling this creature. She was as mercurial as she was mystifying, and Javier had never been in a position where he had to deal with a woman on this level.

When it came to his personal relationships with women, they weren't all that personal. They were physical. Suddenly, he was in an entanglement with a beautiful woman that was all… All too much to do with her feelings.

"Finish your toast," he said briskly. "I will send a member of staff to escort you downstairs in roughly an hour. And then, it is time we begin your training."

Violet muttered to herself as she made her way down the vast corridor and toward the ballroom. "Begin your training… Wax on. Wax off."

This was ludicrous. And she was beginning to get severely anxious. She had been in Monte Blanco for more than twelve hours. She had not seen the mysterious King—who had vanished off on some errand, if Javier was to be believed—and she didn't seem to be making any headway when it came to talking herself out of her engagement.

But she was the one who had decided she was better off trying to take the bull by the horns, rather than running and hiding in California. She supposed she had to own the consequences of that rash decision, made in anger.

The castle was vast, and even though she had received rather explicit instructions on how to get to the ballroom, she was a bit concerned that she might just end up lost forever in these winding, glittering halls. Like being at the center of a troll's mountain horde. All gems and glitter and danger.

And as she walked into the vast ballroom and saw Javier standing there at the center, she felt certain she was staring at the Mountain King. She knew he wasn't the King. Javier was acting on his brother's behest; he had said so many times. Except it was impossible for her to imagine that this man took orders from anyone.

It took her a moment to realize there was someone else in the room. A small round woman with an asymmetrical blond haircut and a dress comprised of layers of chiffon draped over her body like petals.

"The future Queen is here," she said excitedly. "We

can begin. My name is Sophie. I will be instructing you in basic Monte Blancan ballroom dance techniques."

"They could be anyone's ballroom dance techniques," Violet said. "They would still be completely new to me."

"You say that like it should frighten me," Sophie said. "It doesn't. Especially not with the Prince acting as your partner."

Violet froze. "He dances?" She pointed at him.

"I have been part of the royal family all of my life," he said. "That necessitated learning various customs. Including, of course, ballroom dancing. There is nothing that you will be subjected to over the course of this training that I was not. And a great many things you will be spared."

There was a darkness to that statement that made a tremor resonate inside of her. But before she could respond to it, he had reached his hand out and taken hold of hers, drawing her up against the hardness of his chest.

He was hot.

And her heart stuttered.

And she felt…

She felt the beginnings of something she had read about. Heard about… But never, ever experienced before.

When he looked down at her, for a moment at least, it wasn't nice what she saw there in his dark eyes. No. It was something else entirely.

She looked down at the floor.

"I will start the music. Javier is a very good dancer, and he will make it easy by providing a solid lead."

He was solid all right. And hot. Like a human furnace.

His hand down low on her back was firm, and the one that grasped hers was surprisingly rough. She would have thought that a prince wouldn't have calluses. But he did.

She wondered what sort of physical work he did. Or if it was from grueling workouts. He certainly had the body of somebody who liked to exact punishment on himself in the gym.

Music began to play in the room, an exacting instrumental piece with clear timing. And then she was moving.

Sophie gave instructions, but Violet felt as if her feet were flying, as if she had no control over the movements herself at all. It felt like magic. And she would have said she had no desire to dance like this, in an empty ballroom in a palace that she was being held in, by the man who was essentially her captor, but it was exhilarating.

She hadn't lied to him when she said she had been given the opportunity to indulge in a great many things in life. She had turned away from most of them. They just hadn't appealed.

But this…

Was this the evidence of being so spoiled that it took some sort of bizarre, singular experience to make her feel? No. She didn't think that was it.

She looked up slightly and could see his mouth. There was something so enticing about the curve of it. Something fascinating about it. She spent a lot of time looking at people's features. Using the natural planes and angles, dips and curves on people's faces to think about ways that makeup might enhance them.

But she had never been entranced by a mouth in quite the way she was now.

She licked her own lips in response to the feeling created inside her when she looked up at him. And she felt him tense. The lines in his body going taut. And when she found the courage inside of herself to look all the way up to his eyes, the ice was completely burned away. And only fire remained.

But she didn't feel threatened. And it wasn't fear that tightened her insides. Wasn't fear that made her feel like she might be burned, scorched from the inside out.

She took a breath and hoped that somehow the quick, decisive movement might cover up the intensity of her reaction to him. But the breath got hung up on a catch in her throat, and her chest locked, as she leaned forward. Her breasts brushed against the hardness of his chest and she felt like she was melting.

She swayed, and he seemed to think she was unsteady, because he locked his arm around her waist and braced her against his body. She felt weightless.

And she had the strangest sense of security. Of protection. She shouldn't. This man was her enemy. After the way he had dismissed her suggestions for finding ways of not being forced into marriage, he was her sworn enemy.

But in his arms she was certain that he would never hurt her. And when she looked up into those eyes, she could easily see an image of him in her mind, holding a sword aloft and pressing her against his body, threatening anyone who might try to claim her. Anyone who might try to take her from him.

She was insane.

She had lost her mind.

She never reacted to men like this. Much less men who were just holding her in captivity until they could marry her off to their brothers.

But looking up into his eyes now, looking at that sculpted, handsome face, made it impossible for her to think of that. It made it impossible for her to think of anything. How isolated she was here. How her friends weren't here, her family wasn't here. She didn't even have her phone. She hadn't thought about her phone from the moment she had woken up this morning.

She had gotten up, scrubbed the makeup off her face, discarded her fake eyelashes and seized on the idea to play a ridiculous damsel in distress. Over eyeliner. And see where that got her. She hadn't been able to stomach it. Because it was too ridiculous.

He might have believed it, but she found that her pride had to come into play somewhere.

So that had been her first waking thought. And then he had appeared.

There had been toast.

He had been handsome.

Now he was touching her.

And somewhere in there logic was turned upside down, twisted, then torn in half.

Because somehow she felt more connected, more present with this man, here in isolation, than she could remember feeling at home for a very long time.

But he's not why you're here.

The thought sent such a cold sliver of dread through her, and it acted like a bucket of icy water dropped over her head.

She was being ridiculous however you sliced it. But feeling... Physical responses to him were ludicrous. Not just because he had brought her here against her will, but because he wasn't even the reason she had been brought here.

It was his brother. His brother who she hadn't even met. She hadn't even googled anything about him, because she didn't have the means to do it.

She extricated herself from Javier's hold, her heart thundering rapidly. "I think I got the hang of it," she said.

"You are doing okay," Sophie said. "I wouldn't call it masterful."

"Well, I'm jet-lagged," Violet said. "Or did you not hear that I was forced onto a plane yesterday afternoon and flown from San Diego."

Sophie looked from Violet to Javier. "I admit I didn't know the whole story."

"Forced," Violet said. "I am being forced to marry King Whatever-his-name-is."

"King Matteo," Javier said.

"Are you?" Sophie's face turned sharp.

"She's fine," Javier said. "Cold feet."

"Oh yes, prewedding jitters are a real issue for kidnapped brides."

"You're clearly terrified for your life," Javier said dryly. "You definitely treat me like I might kill you via lack of Wi-Fi at any moment."

"I'm in withdrawal."

"Leave us," Javier said to Sophie.

"Should I?" Sophie asked Violet.

"I'm not afraid of him," Violet said, tilting her chin upward.

Sophie inclined her head and left the room, doing what Javier told her. "You have my employees questioning me."

"Good. Maybe we'll start a revolution."

"I would advise against that."

"If you hear the people sing, you might want to make a run for it. And make sure you don't have any guillotines lying around."

"If revolution were that simple, I would have engaged in one a long time ago."

"The history books make it look simple enough."

"And full of casualties. My brother and I did our best to work behind the scenes to keep this country from falling apart. We prevented civil war."

"Good for you," Violet said, but she felt somewhat

shamefaced now for making light of something that was apparently a very real issue here. And she shouldn't feel guilty, because she was being held here against her will. There was no place for her to be feeling guilty. He should feel guilty. But of course he wouldn't.

"I have work to do," he said.

"I thought you were going to take me into the city," she called after him.

"I have no desire to spend any more time with a spoiled brat."

"Oh, how awful of me. Do I have a bad attitude about being your prisoner?"

"This is bigger than you. Can't you understand that?"

He really thought that she should be able to take that on board. That she should just be willing to throw her life away because he was convinced that his brother thought she would be the best Queen for the country.

The longer she stood there staring at him, the longer she felt the burn of his conviction going through her skin, the more she realized they might as well be from different planets.

It wasn't a language barrier. It was... An *everything* barrier.

He had sacrificed all his life for the greater good. He could not understand why it didn't make sense to her. Why it wasn't the easiest thing in the world to abandon her expectations about her life and simply throw herself on the pyre of the good of many.

"Javier," she said.

His expression became haughty. "You know people don't simply address me by my first name."

"What do they call you?"

"His Royal Highness, Prince Javier of Monte Blanco."

"That's a mouthful. I'm going to stick with Javier."

"Did I give you permission?"

Tension rolled between them, but it was an irritation. She had a terrible feeling she knew what it was. That maybe he had felt the same thing she had when they had been close earlier.

She chose to ignore it.

She chose to poke at him.

"No. But then, did you ask me if I cared to get it?"

"What is it you want, Violet?"

Her throat went dry, and she almost lost her nerve to ask him what she had intended to.

"Do you do anything for yourself?" She decided that since she was already acting against what would be most people's better judgment, she might as well go ahead and keep doing it.

"No," he said. Then a smile curved the edges of his lips. "One thing. But I keep it separate. In general, no. Because that kind of selfishness leads to the sort of disaster my brother and I just saved our nation from."

"But you know that's not the way the rest of the world works."

"The rest of the world is not responsible for the fates of millions of people. I am. My brother is."

"We just don't expect that, growing up in Southern California."

"That isn't true. Because you're here."

"Because of my business," she said.

"And your father," he said. "Because whatever you think, you feel an obligation toward something other than yourself. Toward your father. Your family. You know what it is to live for those that you love more than you love your own self. Magnify that. That is having a country to protect."

Then he turned and left her standing there, and she found that she had been holding her breath. She hadn't even been aware of that.

She looked around the room. She was now left to her own devices. And that meant... That she would be able to find a computer. She was sure of that. And once she had the internet at her disposal, she would be able to figure out some things that she needed to know.

It occurred to her that she could contact home. If her brother had any idea what had happened to her...

She could also contact the media.

But something had her pushing that thought out of her mind. If she needed to. If she needed to, she could make an international incident. But for some reason she believed everything that Javier told her. And since she did, she truly believed that things in their country had been dire, and that he and his brother were working to make them better.

She didn't want to undo that.

So she supposed he was right. She did have some sense of broader responsibility.

But that was why she needed a better idea of what she was dealing with. Of who she was dealing with. And that meant she was going exploring.

CHAPTER SIX

JAVIER IMMEDIATELY WENT to the gym. He needed to punish his body. Needed to destroy the fire that had ignited in his veins when he had touched Violet King. It was an aberration. He knew he had to turn his desires on and off like a switch.

In his life, it had been a necessity. Sometimes he had to go months without the touch of a woman, when he and Matteo were deep in trying to redirect one of his father's plans from behind the scenes, or when they were actively harboring refugees, helping wrongly convicted citizens escape from prison... Well, sometimes there was no time for sex. When he wanted a woman, he went and found one.

Weekends in Monaco. Paris. Women who had appetites that matched his own. Voracious. Experience to match the darkness that lived inside of him.

And never, ever a woman who was meant for his brother.

He had far too much self-control for this.

Perhaps the issue was he had been too long without a woman.

It had been several months while he and Matteo worked to right the balance of Monte Blanco. And though he did not think they had been entirely celibate— either of them—since his brother had taken the throne, it had left little time for them to pursue personal pleasure.

Javier was feeling it now.

He growled and did another pull-up before dropping down to the floor, his breath coming hard and fast.

And he could still feel the impression of her softness in his arms. He had been in the gym for hours now, and it had not dissipated.

He would find a woman. He would have one flown in.

At this point, he felt deeply uncomfortable finding his pleasure with women in his own country. The power imbalance was too great.

And he was wary of being like his father.

So you're more comfortable lusting after the woman you're holding captive?

No, he was not comfortable with it. It was why he was here.

Because she was in his care, if one could say that of a captive. And he could so easily... Crush her.

He had harmed people before in the service of his father. A blot on his soul he would never scrub out.

"Oh."

He whirled around and he saw the object of his torment standing there, her mouth dropped open, her eyes wide.

"What the hell are you doing in here?"

"I asked around. They said that you might be in the gym. And I had found a computer, so I found an internal schematic for the palace and… Anyway. I found my way down here."

"A computer?"

"Yes," she said. "You see, conveniently, your staff doesn't know that I'm a prisoner. They all think that I'm here of my own accord. So of course there is nothing wrong setting me up with a computer that has internet. Really. You need to watch me more closely."

He crossed his arms over his bare chest. "I hear no helicopters. So I assume you did not call in the cavalry?"

"No. I figured I would wait for that."

Her eyes skittered down from his face, landed on his chest and held. Color mounted in her face.

He gritted his teeth. It was a dangerous game she was playing. Whether she knew it or not.

"If you have something to say," he said, his temper coming to an end point, "say it. I'm busy."

"I can see that," she said. "Do you suppose you could find a… You don't have a shirt on hand, do you?"

He didn't particularly care if she was uncomfortable. Not given the state of his own physical comfort over the last several hours. "No. And I'm in the middle of a workout. So I won't be needing a shirt after you leave. It would be wasted effort. Continue."

It was only then that he noticed she was clutching a portfolio in her hand.

She was still wearing the simple outfit that had been provided for her by the staff earlier in the day. Her hair was still loose, her face still free of makeup.

It was unconscionable, how attractive he found that.

He was a busy man. And consequently, his needs were simple. When he pursued a woman for a physical relationship, he liked her to be clearly sophisticated.

A very specific, sleek sort of look with glossy makeup, tight dresses and high-heeled shoes.

Obvious.

Because when you were short on time, *obvious* was the easiest thing.

Violet was anything but, particularly now, and yet she still made his blood boil.

Perhaps this was it. The taint of his father's blood coming to the fore. Bubbling up the moment there was a woman in proximity who was forbidden. Who was forbidden to him? No one and nothing. And so what had he done?

What had he done? He had made the forbidden the most attractive thing.

And that was it. It had to be his body creating this situation. Because there was nothing truly special about her.

Except that tongue of hers.

Razor-sharp and quick.

Her bravery in the face of an uncertain future.

He gritted his teeth again. None of those things mattered to him. A woman's personality meant nothing. She would serve his brother well when it came to a choice of bride, provided Matteo could handle the sharper edges of her, that was. But those things, Javier presumed, would make her a good queen.

When it came to a bedmate... No. It wasn't desirable at all. A construct. A fabrication.

Brought to him by the less desirable parts of him.

He and his brother had always known those things lurked inside of them.

How could they be of their father and consider themselves immune to such things? They didn't. They couldn't.

And so, Javier had to be realistic about it now.

"I have put together a portfolio. Everything I learned about your country. And the ways in which I think I could help by bringing my business here."

"What do you mean?"

"You used to have manufacturing here. You don't anymore. I do most of my manufacturing in the United States, but with products coming to Europe... I don't see why I couldn't have some of it manufactured here. In fact, I think it would be a good thing. It would allow me to keep costs down. And it would bring a substantial amount of employment to your country."

"We are not impoverished."

"No. But particularly the women here are underemployed. Child marriages are still happening in the more rural villages. I know your father looked the other way..."

"Yes," he said, his teeth gritted. "We fought to stop that. We did not look the other way."

"I know. And I know you're still fighting for it. Again. I did a lot of reading today. I feel like I understand… More of what you're trying to do here. Well. I believe in it. And you're right. It doesn't do us any good to live a life to serve only ourselves. And that has never been my goal. Don't you know I have a charity with my sister, for women who are abused?"

He shook his head. "I regret that I do not."

"My sister… She ended up raising her best friend's baby after her friend's ex-lover murdered her. My sister has always been so regretful that she couldn't do more. And so the two of us established a foundation in her honor. I've been looking for more ways to help vulnerable women. Minerva inspired me." She blinked. "I did work only for myself for a while. To try and make my father…" She shook her head. "It doesn't matter. Working on this charity has made me feel better about myself than anything else ever has. Making Monte Blanco my European base will bring an entirely new light to the country."

"You think very highly of yourself."

She shook her head. "No. But I do know a lot about public perception. And I'm very good with it. Gauging it, manipulating it, I suppose. If you want to call it that. I can help."

"Well. I don't think Matteo would be opposed to that."

"I know he wouldn't. And what does he think, anyway? That he could just put me on ice here until he gets back?"

Javier laughed. "I guarantee you he thinks exactly that."

"I'm to believe that he is the softest, most compassionate ruler this country has ever known?"

Javier nodded. "He is. You may find that hard to believe, but it's true."

"I have a question for you."

"Why bother to let me know? You don't seem to have any issue saying exactly what you think or asking for exactly what you want to know."

"All right. So tell me this. How did you know that what your father was doing was wrong? And what inspired you to try to fix it? How did you see outside of the way you were raised? Because a few hours ago when you were facing me down, I realized something. We were not speaking the same language. We expect different things. Because of our realities. For you... Caring about this entire nation of people is part of you the same as breathing. But it wasn't for your father. You weren't taught this... How did you know it?"

It was something he would have wondered, had the memory not been so emblazoned in his mind.

"The answer is the same as it always is. The moment you see the world outside of the little bubble you're raised in, is the moment you stop believing that your perspective is infallible. It is the moment that you begin to question whether or not your reality is in fact the true reality of the world. It was a child marriage. I was newly in the military. Sixteen years old. I happened upon a village. A six-year-old girl was being married off, and she was terrified."

Even now the memory made his teeth set on edge. Made him burn for blood.

"I put a stop to it. Rallied the military, ordered them to hold her father and the groom captive. I remember picking the child up. She was terrified. When I went to my father and told him I was appalled to see that these things were still happening in our country... He scolded me. He said it was not up to me to impose my beliefs on our citizens. My father was no great believer in liberty, Violet. His motivations were related to money. Peace, border protection. Not freedom." He stared hard against the back wall of the gym. "The minute I knew that was the minute that I stopped believing what I saw. It didn't take me long to realize my brother was in a similar crisis of faith. And that was when the two of us began to work to affect change."

"It's amazing," she said. And somehow, he truly believed her. He had never felt particularly amazing. Only like a grim soldier carrying out marching orders that he had never received. But the ones that should have existed. If their leader had had any integrity.

"Most people look away, you know," she said.

"Not me," he said.

"No. Will you please take me out into town?"

"Yes," he agreed.

Because he saw her purpose now. Saw her intent. And because she was correct. It wasn't reasonable for Matteo to keep her here on ice, so to speak.

Anyway, he did not have to check with his brother on every last thing. They had to trust each other. With the way things had been for the past decade and a half, they had no choice. And so, Matteo would have to trust him in this as well.

"Perfect. But I need… I need a phone."

"Your phone, along with your makeup, is making its way here. You will have it tomorrow. And then I promise you, we will go on your field trip."

"Thank you," she said.

It occurred to him then, the ludicrousness of it all. Of her thanking him when she hated him. Of him standing there, desire coursing through his veins when she was off-limits.

But it didn't matter. Nothing mattered more than Monte Blanco. Nothing mattered more than the good of the nation.

Certainly not his own errant lust.

But tomorrow everything would be as it should be.

He was a man of control. A man of honor.

And he would not forget.

CHAPTER SEVEN

IT HAD TAKEN her several hours to regain her breath after seeing him without his shirt. There it was. She was that basic.

She had known that he was spectacular. Had known that he was muscular and well-built. Because she wasn't blind, and it didn't take a physique detective to know that he was in very good shape underneath those clothes.

But then she had seen it.

His body. All that golden, perfect skin, the dark hair that covered his chest—she would have said that she didn't like chest hair, but apparently she did—and created an enticing line that ran through the center of his abdominal muscles.

He was hot.

Her captor was hot.

She did not have time to ponder that. She had a mission.

She steeled herself and took one last look in the mirror before leaving her room. She had told him they could meet in the antechamber. She was pretty sure she knew which room the antechamber was. She had made it her business to figure out the layout of the palace. It was difficult. But she had done it.

And she had her phone back.

She had been feeling gleeful about that since the moment it had been deposited into her hand this morning.

And yet... And yet.

She hadn't been able to think of a single thing to update her account with.

If she still didn't want to call home.

Because she was mad.

Because she didn't even know what to say.

She tucked her phone in her purse and made her way to the appointed meeting place. He was already there. She tried to force her eyes to skim over him, not to cling to the hard lines and angles of his body. To the terrifying symmetry of his face.

Terrifying and beautiful.

Saved only by that scar along his cheekbone.

She wanted to know how he got it.

She shouldn't want to know how he got it. She shouldn't want to know anything about him.

"Good morning. As you can see," she said, waving her hand over her face, "I'm restored to my former glory."

His eyes moved over her dispassionately. And she felt thoroughly dismissed. Insulted.

She shouldn't care.

"All right. Where are we going to first?"

"The capital city. I thought that would be the perfect place to start. It's about thirty minutes away. Down the mountain."

"Excellent."

Her stomach tightened, her hand shaking. And she didn't know if it was because of the idea of being in close proximity with him in a car for that long or if it was stepping outside of this palace for the first time in several days.

The lack of reality in the situation was underlined here. By her containment. In this glittering palace of jewels it was easy to believe it was all a dream. Some kind of childhood fantasy hallucination with the very adult inclusion of a massive, muscular male.

But once they left the palace, the world would expand. And the fantasy that it was a dream would dissolve. Completely.

There was no limousine waiting for them. Instead, there was a sleek black car that was somehow both intensely expensive looking and understated. She didn't know how it accomplished both of those things. But it did.

And it seemed right, somehow, because the car's owner was not understated and could not be if he tried.

Looking at him now in his exquisitely cut dark suit, she had a feeling that he was trying.

That this was the most inconspicuous he could possibly be. But he was six and a half feet tall, arrestingly beautiful and looked like he could kill a hundred people using only his thumb. So. Blending wasn't exactly an option for him.

He opened the door for her, and she got inside.

When he went to the driver's seat, her tension wound up a notch.

It was even smaller than she had imagined. She had thought they might have a driver. Someone to help defuse this thing between them.

Between them. He probably felt nothing.

Why would he?

He was carved out of rock.

Well. One thing.

She thought of his response to her question yesterday. The way that his lips had curved up into a smile.

One thing.

The idea of this rock as a sexual being just about made her combust. She did not need those thoughts. No, she did not.

He was not the kind of man for her. Even in fantasy. She needed a sexual fantasy with training wheels. An accountant, maybe. Soft. One who wore pleated-front khakis and emanated concern. A nice man named Stephen.

The kind of man that would bring her cinnamon rolls in bed.

After… Making tender love to her.

Nothing about that appealed.

She had no idea why her sexuality was being so specific. She had never intended to make it to twenty-six a virgin.

And she had certainly never intended for this man to awaken her desire.

No. It was just exacerbated by the fact that this felt like a dream. That was all. She wasn't connected to reality. And she was… Stockholm syndrome. That was it. She was suffering from sexual Stockholm syndrome.

When the car started moving, she unrolled the window and stuck her head out of it. Breathed in the crystal mountain air and hoped that it would inject her with some sense.

It didn't.

It did nothing to alleviate the bigness of his presence in the tiny vehicle.

"Are you going to roll the window up? Because you know I don't make a habit of driving to public spaces with women hanging out my car."

She shot him a look and rolled the window up. It really did her no good to oppose him now. She was on a mission. Trying to prove something. "I was enjoying the air."

"Now which one of us is a Saint Bernard?"

"Did you just make a joke?" She looked at his stern profile and saw the corner of his lip tip upward. "You did. You made a joke. That's incredible."

"Don't get used to it."

It felt like a deeper warning of something else. But she went ahead and ignored it. Along with the shiver of sensation that went through her body.

They were silent after that. And she watched as the

trees thinned, gave way to civilization. The dirt becoming loose rocks, and then cobblestone.

The town itself was not modern. And she would have been disappointed if it was. The streets were made of interlocking stones, the sidewalks the same, only in a different pattern. Tight spirals and sunbursts, some of them bleeding up the sides of the buildings that seemed somehow rooted to the earth.

The streets were narrow, the businesses packed tightly together. There were little cafés and a surprising number of appealing-looking designer shops that Violet suddenly felt eager to explore.

"This is beautiful," she said. "If people knew… Well, if people knew, this would be a huge tourist spot."

"It was not encouraged under the rule of my father. And in these past years businesses have rebounded. But still…"

"There is ground to gain. Understood. Pull over."

"What?"

"Pull over."

She saw a bright yellow bicycle leaned against a wall. And right next to it was a window planter with bright red geraniums bursting over the top of it.

All backed by that charming gray stone.

"We need to take a photo."

He obeyed her, but was clearly skeptical about her intent.

She got out of the car quickly and raced over to the bike. Then she looked over into the courtyard of the neighboring café. People were sitting outside drinking coffee. "Excuse me? Is this your bike?" She asked the young woman sitting there working on her computer.

The woman looked at her warily and then saw Javier, standing behind her. Her eyes widened.

"It's fine," Violet said. "He's harmless. I just want to take a picture with your bike."

"Of course," the woman said.

She still looked completely frazzled, but Violet scampered to where it was, positioning herself right next to it and putting her hand over the handlebars. "A picture," she said. She reached into her purse and pulled her phone out, handing it to him.

"That's what all this is about? Also. I am not harmless."

"Yes. Very ferocious. Take my picture."

She looked straight ahead, offering him her profile, and tousled her hair lightly before positioning her hand delicately at her hip.

"There," he said. "Satisfied?"

"Let me verify." She snatched the phone from his hand and looked at the photo.

It had done exactly what she wanted to do, and with some tweaking, the colors would look beautiful against the simple gray stone.

"Yes," she confirmed. "I am."

She pulled up her account, touched the picture up quickly and typed:

Exploring new places is one of my favorite things. Stay tuned for more information on your next favorite vacation spot.

"There," she said. "That's bound to create speculation. Excitement."

He looked down at the picture with great skepticism. "That?"

"Yes."

"I do not understand people."

"Maybe they don't understand you," she said.

He looked completely unamused by that.

"Sorry. Joke. I thought you were getting to where you understood those sometimes."

The look he gave her was inscrutable.

"Show me the rest of this place," she said. "I'm curious."

He looked at her as if she had grown a second head. "You realize that I'm slightly conspicuous?"

"Usually I am too," she said. "I guess… I just figure you ignore it."

"You're not conspicuous here."

"No," she said. "But that won't last long, will it? I mean, if I'm going to be the Queen…"

"You're not going to be inconspicuous as long as you're walking around with me. That's a pretty decent indicator that you might be important."

"Wow. No points for humility."

"Do you have false humility about the degree to which you're recognized? Or what your status means? You've been throwing all sorts of statistics at me about your wealth and importance ever since we first met."

"All right," she said. "Fair enough."

They walked on in silence for a moment. She paid

attention to the way her feet connected to the cobble-
stones. It was therapeutic in a way. There was something so quaint about this. It was more village than
city, but it contained a lot more places of interest than
she would normally think you would find in a village.

"What is the chief export here?"

"There isn't any. We are quite self-contained. What
we make tends to stay here, tends to fuel the citizens."

"That's very unusual."

"Yes. It also feels precarious."

"So… If we were to manufacture my products here,
I would be your chief export."

"In point of fact, yes."

"Though, if your other products became desirable
because of tourism…"

"Yes. I understand it would mean a great deal of
cash injection for the country. Though, thanks to my
brother's personal fortune, the coffers of the country
have been boosted as it is."

"Yes, I did some research on him. He's quite a successful businessman."

"You would like him. Other than the fact that he's
a bit of a tyrant."

"More than you?"

"Different than me." He relented. "Perhaps not
more."

"A family of softies."

The sound he made was somewhere between a huff
of indignation and a growl. "I have never been called
soft."

She looked at him. The wall of muscle that was his chest. The granite set of his jaw. She meant her response to be light. Funny. But looking at him took her breath. "No. I don't suppose you have."

There was a small ice-cream parlor up the way, and she was more than grateful for the distraction. "I want ice cream," she said.

"*Ice cream?* Are you a child?"

"Ice cream is not just for children," she said gravely. "Surely you know that, Javier."

"I don't eat ice cream."

"Nonsense. Everyone needs ice cream. Well, unless they're lactose intolerant. In which case, they just need to find a good nondairy replacement. And let me tell you, in Southern California they're plentiful."

"I'm not intolerant of anything."

She tried, and failed, to hold back a laugh. "Well, that just isn't true. I've only spent a few days in your company, but I can tell you that you're clearly intolerant of a whole host of things. But, it's good to know that dairy isn't among them."

"You are incredibly irritating."

"*Not* the first time I've heard that."

"And who told you that?"

"My older brother, for a start. Also, my surrogate older brother, Dante. He's now my brother-in-law, incidentally."

"That seems convoluted."

"It's not really. Not at all. Just the way things ended up. My father quite literally found him on a business trip and brought him home. Took care of him. I think my sister was in love with him for most of her life."

"But you weren't."

She laughed. "I remember very clearly telling Minerva that I didn't like men who were quite as hard as Dante."

A tense silence settled between the two of them. She hadn't meant to say that. Because of course that implied that perhaps it had changed. And perhaps there was a hard man that she might find appealing after all.

She gritted her teeth.

"And I still don't," she said. "So. Just so we're both clear."

"Very clear," he said.

"Now. Ice cream." She increased her pace and breezed straight into the shop. And she did not miss the look of absolute shock on the faces of the proprietors inside. It wasn't to do with her. It was to do with Javier.

"I saw that there was ice cream," she said cheerily. She approached the counter and looked at all the flavors.

"We make them all here," the woman behind the counter said, her voice somewhat timid. "The milk comes from our own cows."

"Well, that's wonderful," Violet said. "And makes me even more excited to try it." There was one called Spanish chocolate, and she elected to get a cone with two scoops of that. She kept her eyes on Javier the entire time.

"You don't want anything?"

"No," he said, his voice uncompromising.

"You're missing out," she said.

She went to pay for the treat, and he stepped in, taking his wallet from his pocket.

"Of course we cannot ask Your Royal Highness to pay," the woman said.

"On the contrary," Javier said, his voice decisive. "You should be asking me to pay double. Consider it repayment."

The woman did not charge Javier double, but she did allow him to pay.

"I didn't need you to buy my ice cream," she said when they were out on the street.

"It's not about need. It is about... What feels right."

"You're that kind of man, huh? The kind that holds open doors and pays for dinner?"

He laughed, a dark, short sound. "You make me sound quite a bit more conventional than I am."

"A regular gentleman."

"I would not say that."

"Well, what would you say, then? You're single-handedly setting out to save the country, and you saved a little girl from child marriage. You worked for years to undo the rule of your father." She took a short lick of her ice cream. It was amazing. "I would say that runs toward gentlemanly behavior, don't you?"

"I think that's overstating human decency. I would like to think that any man with a spine would do what I did in my position. Inaction in my position would be complicity. And I refused to be complicit in my father's actions."

"Well. Many people would be, for their comfort."

She looked down the alleyway and saw a lovely hand-painted mural. She darted there, and he followed. It was secluded, ivy growing over the walls, creeping between the brick.

"I just need a picture of this."

She held out her hand, extending her ice-cream cone to him. "Can you hold this?"

He took it gingerly from her grasp, looking at it like it might bite him. She lifted her brows, then turned away from him, snapping a quick picture and then another for good measure.

He was still holding the ice-cream cone and looking aggrieved, so when she returned, she leaned in, licking the ice-cream cone while he held it still.

His posture went stiff.

He was reacting to her, she realized. The same way that she reacted to him. And she didn't like how it made her feel. Giddy and jittery and excited in a way she couldn't remember feeling before.

And she should pull away. She should.

But instead, she wrapped her hand around his, and sent electric sensation shooting through her body.

"You should taste it," she said.

"I told you, I didn't want any."

"But I think you do," she insisted. "You should have some."

She pushed his hand, moving the cone in his direction, and she could see the moment that he realized it was better to take the path of least resistance. He licked the ice cream slowly, his dark eyes connecting with hers.

She realized she had miscalculated.

Because he had his mouth where hers had been.

Because she was touching him and he was looking at her.

Because something in his dark eyes told her that he would be just as happy licking her as he was this ice cream.

And all of it was wrong.

Why couldn't she hate him? She should.

Why couldn't she get it into her head that this was real? That it was insane. That she should want to kick him in the shins and run as far and fast as she could. Call for help at the nearest business, rather than lingering here in an alley with him.

"It's good," she said, her throat dry.

"Yes," he agreed, his voice rough.

Then he thrust it back into her hand. "I think I've had enough."

"Right."

Her heart clenched, sank. And she didn't know what was happening inside of her. Didn't know why her body was reacting this way, now, to him. Didn't know why she felt like crying, and not for any of the reasons that she should.

"I'm not done exploring the city, though. And I

wouldn't want to take my ice cream back in your car. I might make a mess."

But the rest of the outing was completely muted. Not at all what it had been before.

And that it disappointed her confused her even more than anything else.

When she was back at the palace, back in her room, she lay down and covered her head. And only then did she allow herself to think the truth.

She was attracted to the man who was holding her captive.

She was attracted to the brother of the man she was being forced to marry.

But more important, he was attracted to her. She had seen it.

She had very nearly tasted it.

Thankfully, they had come to their senses.

She spent the rest of the night trying fitfully to be thankful when all she felt was frustrated.

And she knew that she had come up with a plan, no matter how it made her stomach churn to think of putting it into action.

She had no choice.

CHAPTER EIGHT

HIS BROTHER STILL hadn't returned.

Javier was tired of being tested. He had been avoiding Violet since they had come back from the city the other day. The temptation that she had presented to him was unacceptable.

That he had the capacity to be tempted was not something that he had first seen. But Violet King had tested him at every turn, and the true issue was that he feared he might fail a test if she continued.

He curled his fingers into fists. No. He was not a weak man.

Even before he had turned on his father, he had not had an easy life. He had faithfully served in his father's army. And that had required work guarding the borders in the forests, camping out for long periods of time. His father's paranoia meant that he was certain that enemies were lurking behind every tree.

And Javier had found that to be so. His father had had many enemies. And Javier had done his job in arresting them.

He wasn't sure what he wished to avoid thinking about more. That period of time in his life, or his current attraction to Violet.

"Of course, the architecture is nothing compared to the natural beauty. You got a little peek outside the window, but more to come later on this beautiful vacation spot."

He heard Violet's voice drifting down the corridor, coming from the expansive dining room where his brother often held dinner parties.

It was a massive room with a view that stretched on for miles, a large balcony connecting it and the ballroom and making the most of those views.

Violet was standing right next to the window, her cell phone in her hand. She waved—not at him, but at her screen—then put the phone down at her side. "I was filming a live video. Doing more to tease my location."

"Of course you were," he said.

She gave him a bland look. "Just because you don't understand it doesn't mean it's not valid."

"Oh, I would never think that."

"Liar. If you don't understand it, you think it's beneath you."

"I didn't say I didn't understand it."

"But you do think it's beneath you."

"That was implied in my statement, I think."

"You're impossible."

She walked nearer to him, and he tried to keep his focus on the view outside. But he found himself looking at her. She had most definitely regained her precious makeup. She looked much as she did that first day he had seen her, which he assumed was a signature look for her.

"So you must go to all this trouble," he said, indicating her makeup, "to talk to people who aren't even in the room with you."

She winked. "That's how you know I like you. If I talk to you in the same room, and I don't bother to put my eyelashes on."

"Your eyelashes are fake?"

"A lot of people have fake eyelashes," she said sagely. "I used to have them individually glued on every week or so, but I prefer the flexibility of the strips so I can just take them off myself at the end of the day."

"I have to say I vastly don't care about your eyelashes."

He looked down at her, at the dramatic sweep of those coal black lashes they were discussing. And he found that he did care, more than he would like. Not about the application, but that he wished he could see them naturally as they had been the other morning. Dark close to her eyes, lighter at the tips. He appreciated now the intimacy of that sight.

And he should not want more.

"You know what I do care about?" she asked. "Outside. I would like to go outside."

"Well, the garden is fenced in, feel free to wander around. Just don't dig underneath it."

"Very cute. Another joke. We could write that in your baby book. However, I would like a tour."

"A tour of the grounds?"

"Yes."

"Of the garden, or of the entire grounds? Because I warn you, they are quite wild."

"I find I'm in the mood for wild."

She smiled slightly and enigmatically. He could not tell whether she intended for the statement to be a double entendre.

But the moment passed, and he found himself agreeing to take her out of the palace.

One path led to the carefully manicured gardens that had been tamed and kept for generations. A testament to the might of the royal family, he had always thought. And as a result, he had never liked them.

"This way," he said. "This is where Matteo and I used to play when we were boys."

The rocky path led down to a grove of trees. Heavily shaded, and next to a deep, fathomless swimming hole.

A waterfall poured down black, craggy rocks into the depths.

The water was a crystalline blue, utterly and completely clear. The bottom of the river was visible, making it seem like it might not be as deep as it was. But he knew that you could sink and sink and not find the end of it.

He and Matteo had always loved it here. It had seemed like another world. Somewhere separate from the strictures of the palace. Though, at that point he had not yet come to hate it.

Still. He had appreciated the time spent outdoors with his brother. His brother had been most serious at that age.

Perhaps because he had always known that the burden of the crown would be his.

"This is beautiful," she said. He expected her to reach for her phone immediately, but she didn't. Instead, she simply turned in a circle, looking at the unspoiled splendor around them.

"Yes. You know something? I know that my father never set foot down here." He stared at the pool. "And now he's dead."

"That's a tragedy," Violet said. "To live right next to something so beautiful and to never see it."

"There were a great many things my father didn't see. Or care about. He cared about his own power. He cared about his own comfort. This is just one of the many things he never truly looked at. Including the pain that he caused his own people."

"But you did. You do," she said.

"For better or worse."

"You used to swim down here?"

"Yes."

"Did you laugh and have fun?"

"Of course I did."

"I can't imagine you having fun."

"I can assure you I did."

"It's safe?" she asked.

"Yes."

She took her phone out of her pocket and set it on the shore. Then she looked back at him and kicked her shoes off, putting her toe in the water. "It's freezing," she said.

"I said it was safe. I didn't say it wasn't frigid water coming down from an ice melt."

She stared at him, a strange sort of challenge lighting her eyes.

"What?"

"Let's swim."

"No," he said.

He realized right then that the outright denial was a mistake. Because her chin tilted upward in total, stubborn defiance. And the next thing he knew she had gone and done it. Gone in, clothes and all, her dark head disappearing beneath the clear surface. And she swam.

Her hair streaming around her like silken ribbon, her limbs elegant, her dress billowing around her. And he was sure that he could see white cotton panties there beneath the surface. He felt punched in the gut by that. Hard.

"Swim with me," she said.

"No."

She swam up to the edge, giving him an impish grin. "Please."

He remembered her words from the other day. *Don't you do anything for yourself?*

He didn't. He didn't, because there was no point.

But swimming wasn't a betrayal.

He could feel his body's response to that in his teeth. A twist in his gut. Because he knew what he was doing. Knew that he was pushing at that which was acceptable.

But the water would be cold.

And he would not touch her. Tension rolled from his shoulders, and he unbuttoned his shirt, leaving it on the banks of the river. His shoes, his pants. And leaving himself in only the dark shorts that he wore beneath his clothes.

Then he dived, clearing her completely, sliding beneath the surface of the water at the center of the pool, letting the icy water numb his skin like pinpricks over the surface of it. Maybe it would knock the desire that he felt for her out of his body.

Maybe.

He swam toward her, and he saw something flash in the depths of her eyes. Surprise. Maybe even fear.

He stopped just short of her.

"Is this what you had in mind?"

"I didn't expect the strip show."

The characterization of what had occurred made his stomach tighten. Or the cold water had no effect on his desire.

He couldn't understand why. Why this woman, at this moment, tested him so.

Any retort she might have made, any continuation of the conversation seemed to die on her lips.

And he knew. He knew that he had just gone straight

into temptation. Had literally dived right in. Whatever he had told himself in that moment on the shore was a lie. All he had wanted to do was to be closer to her.

He had never experienced anything like this. Had never experienced this kind of draw to a woman before. To anyone.

She had nothing in common with him. A spoiled, sheltered girl from the United States. But when she looked at him, he felt something. And he had not felt anything for a long time.

She began to draw closer to him.

"Don't," he said.

"I just…" A droplet of water slid down her face, and her tongue darted out. She licked it off. She reached out and dragged her thumb over the scar on his cheek. "How did you get this?"

Her touch sent a lightning bolt of desire straight down to his groin. "It's not a good story."

"I don't care."

"You think you don't care, but you haven't heard it."

Her hand was still on him.

"Tell me," she insisted.

"You know you should be afraid of me," he said. "And here you are, pushing me."

"You said you wouldn't hurt me."

"And I wouldn't. Intentionally. But you are here touching me as if I cannot be tempted into anything that we would both regret."

"Who says I would regret it?"

He gritted his teeth. "You would."

"Javier…"

"I was helping a man escape from prison. Wrongfully arrested by my father. One of his guards attempted to put a stop to it. It was war, Violet, and I did what had to be done."

She said nothing. She only looked at him, her eyes wide.

"Yes. It is what you think."

"You did what you had to," she said softly.

"But that's what I am. A man who does what he has to. A man who is barely a man anymore."

She slid her thumb across his skin, and he shuddered beneath her touch. "You feel like a man to me," she whispered.

"You are not for me."

He pushed away from her and swam back to the shore. She watched him dress, the attention that she paid him disconcerting. Then she got out of the water, the thin fabric of her dress molded to her curves. He could see her nipples, clearly visible, and his arousal roared.

"You are not for me."

Then he turned, leaving her there. She would find her way back. Follow the path.

But he had to do them both a favor and remove himself from her. Because if he did not, he would do something that they would both come to bitterly regret.

He was familiar with the sting of failure. The process of deprogramming himself from his father's rule had been a difficult one when he had been sixteen years old and he had wanted to believe with intensity that his father was a benevolent ruler. And he had seen otherwise. The way that it had hurt his soul, torn him in two, to begin to look differently at the world, at his life and at himself, had been the last time he had truly felt pain. Because after that it was over. After that, the numbness had sunk in, had pervaded all that he was.

It was Matteo who had seen him through it. Matteo, who had been struggling with the exact same thing, who made Javier feel like he wasn't losing his mind.

His brother had been his anchor in the most difficult moment of his life.

And now there was another wrenching happening in his soul. It was all because of the luminous, dark eyes of Violet King.

In that alleyway, when she had put her hand over his, when she had tempted him with a bite of ice cream like she was Eve in the garden offering him an apple, he had not been able to think of anything but casting the frozen treat aside and claiming her mouth with his own.

In the water he had longed to drag her to the shore, cover her body with his own. Claim her.

And that was a violation of all that he had become.

He was a man of honor because he had chosen it.

None of it was bred into him. None of it was part of his blood.

He and Matteo knew that, so they were always on guard.

And this woman… This woman enticed him to betray that.

To betray his brother.

The one man to whom he owed his absolute loyalty.

The man he had promised to destroy should that man ever abuse his power. Such was their bond.

Such was his dedication.

But now… Lusting after his brother's fiancée made him compromised.

It compromised that promise. Compromised what he was. What he claimed to be.

His phone rang.

It was Matteo. As if his brother could feel his betrayal from across the continent.

"Yes?"

"We have been successful," Matteo said. "Monte Blanco will now be included in the United Council. My mouse has proven herself indispensable yet again."

"Is she in the room with you?"

"Of course she is."

Javier didn't even have the right to scold his brother for that. Not at this point. He had lost his right to a moral high ground of any kind.

"When do you return?" he said, his voice heavy.

"Two days. We have to make a stop in Paris for a diplomatic meeting."

"I suppose, then, that it is good you spent all those years studying business."

"Yes. Not the way our father did it, but there are similarities to diplomacy in business and when it comes to running a country. Of course, the bottom line is not filling your own pockets in the situation."

"No indeed."

The bottom line was not about satisfying themselves at all.

It stung particularly now. As he thought of Violet. As he thought of the deep, gut-wrenching longing to touch her.

And the anger that crept in beneath his skin. Anger that was not at himself, though it should have been. Anger at the cruelty of fate. That he should want this woman above all others when she was perhaps the only woman in the world who was truly off-limits to him.

He was a prince. He could snap his fingers and demand that which he wished.

Except her.

The insidious doubt inside of him asked the question. Was that why he wanted her? Was that why she presented a particular appeal? Because she was forbidden.

Because she was forbidden to him and no matter how hard he tried to pretend otherwise, he was born a man with a massive ego who didn't feel that a single thing on the earth should be barred from him should he take to it.

No. He would not allow it.

He would not allow that to be true.

"I look forward to your return."

"How is my fiancée?"

"Not exactly amenable to the idea of being your fi-ancée," he said.

It was the truth. Everything else could be ignored. For now.

"I must say, the connection between myself and her is one of the things that made our meetings the most interesting. She is well liked, world-renowned for her business mind. Such a fantastic asset to me she will be."

"You don't know her."

"And I suppose you do now. I will look forward to hearing how you think I might best manage her."

His brother hung up then. And left Javier standing there with his hand curled so tightly around the phone he thought he might break. Either his bones or the de-vice, he didn't know. Neither did he care.

He gritted his teeth and walked out of his office. Something compelled him down to the ballroom where he had the dance lesson with Violet. Where he held her in his arms and first began to question all that he was. It was unconscionable. That this woman he had known for a scant number of days could undo twenty years' worth of restraint.

And when he flung open the doors to the ballroom... There she was.

Curled up in one of the tufted chairs that sat in the corner of the room, next to the floor-to-ceiling win-dows, sunlight bathing her beauty in gold.

Her legs were tucked up underneath her, and he could see the edges of her bare toes peeking out from beneath her shapely rear. She was wearing simple, soft-looking clothes, nothing fancy. Neither did she have on any of her makeup. She was reading.

Not on her phone.

And it made him want to dig deeper. To question all that she presented of herself to the world, all that she tried to tell him about who she was and who she actually might be.

She looked up when she heard his footsteps. "Oh," she said. "I didn't expect you to be lurking around the ballroom."

"I didn't expect you to be lurking around at all. Much less away from the computer."

"I found this book in the library," she said. "And the library's beautiful, but it doesn't have the natural lighting of this room."

"Protecting the books," he said.

"Makes sense."

"What is it you're reading?"

"It's a book of fairy tales. Monte Blancan fairy tales. It's very interesting. We all have our versions of these same stories. I guess because they speak to something human inside of us. I think my favorite one that I've read so far is about the Princess who was taken captive by a beast."

"Is that what you think me? A beast?"

She closed the book slowly and set it down on the table beside the chair. "Possibly. Are you under some kind of enchantment?"

"No."

"That's something I found interesting in your version of the story. The Prince was not a beast because of his own sins. He was transformed into one as punishment for something his father had done. And then, much like the story I'm familiar with, the woman is taken captive because of the sins of her father. It feels shockingly close to home, doesn't it?"

"Except I believe in the story my brother would be that enchanted Prince."

Her gaze was too frank. Too direct. "If you say so."

"You were shocked by your father's deal?"

She nodded slowly. "I was. Because I thought that we... I knew he wasn't perfect. I did. But it's not like he was a raving villain like your father."

"You know, I didn't realize my father was a raving villain until I started to see, really see the things that he had done to our country. And I don't know that your father is a villain so much as he was made a desperate man in a desperate moment. And my brother took advantage of that. My brother does his best to act with honor. But like me, he is not afraid to be ruthless when he must be. I do not envy the man who had to go up against his will."

"He should have protected me. He should never have used me as currency. I can't get over that. I won't."

"Is that why you came? To teach him a lesson?"

Her lips twitched. "Maybe. And I won't lie, I did think that perhaps my notoriety would keep me safe. You know, because people will miss me if I'm not around. But I sort of like not being around. It's been an interesting vacation."

"Except you're going to marry my brother."

"Yes. I know you think so."

"You can take it up with him when he returns. He tells me he'll be back in two days."

Shock flared in the depths of her eyes. "Two days?"

"Yes. Don't look so dismayed."

"I can't help it. I am dismayed."

"Why exactly?"

"I just thought there was more time."

There was something wild in the depths of her eyes then, and he wanted to move closer to it. But he knew that would be a mistake. Still, when she stood, it was to draw closer to him.

"I know that you feel it," she said. "It's crazy, isn't it? I shouldn't feel anything for you. But you… I mean, look, I know it's chemistry, or whatever, I know it's not feelings. But…" She bit her full lower lip and looked up at him from beneath her lashes, the expression both innocent and coquettish. "Don't you think that maybe we should have a chance to taste it before I'm sold into marriage?"

"I thought you were intent on resisting that," he said, his voice rough.

"With everything I have in me."

"I cannot. I owe my brother my undying loyalty. And I will not compromise that over something as basic as sex. You mistake me, *querida*, if you think that I can be so easily shaken."

"I know that you're a man of honor. A man of loyalty. But I feel no such loyalty to your brother. And it is nothing to me to violate it."

She planted her hand on his chest. And he knew that she could feel it then. Feel his heart raging against the muscle and blood and bone there. Feel it raging against everything that was good and right and real, that which he had placed his faith in all these years.

She let out a shaking breath, and he could feel the heat of it brush his mouth, so close was she. So close was his destruction.

He was iron. He was rock. He had been forced to become so. A man of no emotion. A man of nothing more than allegiance to an ideal. Knowing with absolute certainty that if he should ever turn away from that, he might become lost. That corruption might take hold of him in the way that it had done his father. Because he considered himself immune to nothing.

And so, he had made himself immune to everything.

Except for this. Except for her.

So small and fragile, delicate.

Powerful.

Not because of her success or her money. But because of the light contained in her beauty. A storm wrapped in soft, exquisite skin that he ached to put his hands on.

And when she stretched up on her toes and pressed her mouth to his, no finesse or skill present in the motion at all, he broke.

He wrapped his arms around her, cupping her head

in one of his hands, shifting things, taking control. And he consumed her.

What she had intended to be a tasting, a test, he turned into a feast. If he was going to be destroyed, then he would bring the palace down with him. Then he would crack the very foundations of where they stood. Of all that he had built his life upon. Of all that he was. If he would be a ruined man, then the world would be ruined as a result. As would she.

He nipped her lower lip, slid his tongue against hers, kissed her deep and hard and long until she whimpered with it. Until she had arched against him, going soft and pliant. Until there was no question now who was in charge. Until there was no question now who was driving them to the brink of calamity. It was him.

He had made his choice. He had not fallen into temptation; he had wrapped his arms around it. He had not slid into sin; he had gathered it against his body and made it his air. His oxygen.

And she surrendered to it. Surrendered to him.

The white flag of her desire was present in the way her body molded against his, in the way that she opened for him, the small, sweet sounds of pleasure that she made as he allowed his hands to move, skimming over her curves, then going still, holding her against him so that she could feel the insistence of his desire pressing against her stomach.

He was a man of extremes.

And if she wanted a storm, he would give her a hurricane.

If he could not be a man of honor, then he would be a man of the basest betrayal.

It was the sight of that book sitting on the side table that brought him back to himself. Just a flash of normality. A familiarity. A reminder of who he was supposed to be, that caused him to release his hold on her and set her back on her feet.

She looked dazed. Her lips were swollen. Utterly wrecked.

Just like he was.

"Never," he said. "It will never happen between us."

"But... It already did."

He chuckled, dark and without humor just like the very center of his soul. "If you think that was an example of what could be between us, then you are much more inexperienced than I would have given you credit for."

"I..."

"The things I could do to you. The things I could do to us both. I could ruin you not just for other men, but for sleep. Wearing clothes. Walking down the street. Everything would remind you of me. The slide of fabric against your skin. The warmth of the sun on your body. All of it would make you think of my hands on you. My mouth. And you would try... You would try to use your own hand to bring yourself the kind of satisfaction that I could show you, but you would fail."

"And what about your brother? Would he fail?"

"It is why I won't do it. Because yes. After me. After this... Even he would fail to satisfy you."

And he turned and walked out of the room, leaving her behind. Leaving his broken honor behind, held in her delicate hands. And he knew it. He only hoped that she did not.

The sooner Matteo returned, the sooner Javier could leave this place. Could leave her. Matteo needed to do what he thought was best for the country.

But Javier would not stand by and see it done.

CHAPTER NINE

SHE HAD FAILED. It kept her awake that night. The sting of that failure. She was supposed to seduce him. It had been her one job. Granted, it had all gotten taken out of her hands, and she had a feeling that her own inexperience had been played against her.

Her heart hadn't stopped thundering like it might gallop out of her chest since.

She hadn't expected him to find her in the ballroom. That was the real reason she had been in there. Who hung out in an empty ballroom? But then he had appeared. And she had realized it was her chance.

She hadn't actually been sitting there scheming. She had been avoiding her scheme.

After her failure at the waterfall, and after...

The problem was, he had shared something of his past with her there, and she felt like she knew him better. Felt guilty for her seduction plan even though it felt like the perfect solution to her problem.

Because she knew on some level that if Javier were to sleep with her, Matteo would not want her anymore.

And she had been… She had been excited about it, perversely, because for the first time in her life she was attracted to a man, so why not take advantage of it? She didn't want to marry him. He was… He was an unyielding rock face, and she had no desire to be stuck with a man like that for any length of time.

But then she had been sitting there reading that fairy tale. And not only had she—through those stories—come into a greater understanding of his culture, there was something about the particular story of the beast she'd been reading that had made her understand him.

Transformed into something due to the sins of his father and so convinced that the transformation was a necessity.

That he had to sit in the sins, in the consequence, to avoid becoming a monster on the inside as well as a monster on the outside.

She had been so caught up in that line of thinking that when he had appeared, she had clumsily made an effort at seduction, and she had been carried away in it.

That was the problem with all of this.

She was a reasonable girl. A practical one. A businesswoman. Thoroughly modern and independent in so many ways, but she had been swept up in a fairy tale, and nothing that she knew, nothing that she had ever achieved, had prepared her for the effect that it was having on her.

For the effect that he was having on her.

She had been kissed before.

Every single time it had been easy to turn away.

Every single time she had been relieved that it was over. When she could extricate herself from the man's hold and go on with her day, untouched below the neck and very happy about it thank you.

But she wanted Javier to touch her. And she feared very much that the vow he had made to her before he had stormed out of the ballroom was true.

That if it were to become more, she would never, ever be able to forget. That she would be ruined. That she would be altered for all time.

"That's ridiculous," she scolded herself. *It's the kind of ridiculous thing that men think about themselves, but it's never true. You know that. It can't be.*

The idea that she might fail in her objective to avoid marrying Matteo terrified her. But somehow, even more, the idea that she might leave here without... Without knowing what it was like to be with Javier was even more terrifying. And she despised herself for that. For that weakness. Because it was a weakness. It had to be.

Without thinking, she slipped out of bed. She knew where his room was. She had studied the plans to the palace, and she was familiar with it now. Had it committed to memory. She had a great memory; it was one of the things that made her good at business. And, it was going to help her out now.

With shaking hands, she opened up the door to her bedroom and slipped down the corridor. It wasn't close, his chamber.

But suddenly she realized. That wasn't where he would be. She didn't know how she knew it, she just knew.

Where would he be?

His gym. That made sense. She had found him there that day, and the way that he was committed to the physical activity he was doing was like a punishment, and she had a feeling he would be punishing himself after today.

No. She stopped.

He wouldn't be there.

The library.

He would be in the library. Somehow she knew it. He would be looking at the same book that she had been earlier. She could feel it.

It defied reason that she could. And if she was wrong... If she was wrong, she would go straight back to her room. She would abandon this as folly. All of it.

She would leave it behind, and she would find another solution to her predicament. She would use her brain. Her business acumen.

Right. And you're still pretending that this is all about avoiding the marriage?

She pushed that to the side. And she went to the library.

She pushed the door open, and the first thing she saw was the fire in the hearth.

But she didn't see him.

Disappointment rose up to strangle her, warring with relief that filled her lungs.

But then she saw him, standing in the corner next

to the bookshelf, a book held open in his palm. The orange glow of the flames illuminated him. The hollows of his face, his sharp cheekbones.

But his eyes remained black. Unreadable.

"What are you doing here?"

"I was looking for you," she said. "And somehow I knew I would find you here."

"How?"

"Because you wanted to read the story. You wanted to see how it ended."

"Happy endings are not real."

"They must be. People have them every day."

"Happy endings are not for beasts who spirit young maidens away to their castle. How about that?"

"I don't know. We all have that story. Every culture. Some version of it. We must want to believe it. That no matter how much of a beast you feel you might be, you can always find a happy ending."

"Simplistic."

"What's wrong with being simplistic? What is the benefit of cynicism? And anyway, what makes cynicism more complex?"

"It's not cynicism. It is a life lived seeing very difficult things. Seeing tragedy unfold all around you. Knowing there is no happy ending possible for some people. Understanding for the first time that when you have power, you must find ways to keep it from corrupting you or you will destroy the world around you. Great power gives life or takes it, it's not neutral."

"All right. But in here... In the library, it's just us,

isn't it? What does anyone have to know outside this room? It doesn't have to touch anything. It never has to go beyond here."

That wasn't the point of what she was doing. She should want Matteo to know. She should want there to be consequences.

But she wasn't lying to Javier.

Because suddenly, she just wanted to take that heaviness from his shoulders. For just one moment. She wanted to soften those hard lines on his face. Wanted to ease the suffering she knew he carried around in his soul.

Because he truly thought that he was a monster.

And he believed that he had to be above reproach in order to keep that monster from gaining hold.

She had intended to taunt him. To ask why he was so loyal to a brother who left him behind to be a baby-sitter.

But she didn't want to. Not now.

She didn't want this moment to have anything to do with the world beyond the two of them.

Beyond these walls.

Beyond this ring of warmth provided by the fire.

The heat created by the desire between them.

She had never wanted a man before.

And whatever the circumstances behind her coming to be in this country, in this castle, she wanted this man.

She had waited for desire, and she had found it here.

But it was somehow more, something deeper than

she had imagined attraction might be. But maybe that was just her ignorance. Maybe this was always what desire was supposed to be. Something that went beyond the mere physical need to be touched.

A bone-deep desire to be seen. To be touched deeper than hands ever could.

There was something inside of her that responded to that bleakness in him, and she didn't even know what it was.

Her life had been a whirlwind. Her loud, wonderful family, who she loved, including her father, even though he had wounded her as he had done. Parties. Vacations. Things.

The triumph in her business. The constant roar of social media.

But now all of it had faded away, and for the first time in her life...

For the first time in her life Violet King was truly self-made.

Was truly standing on her own feet.

Was making decisions for herself, and for no other reason at all.

This moment wasn't about proving herself to anyone.

It wasn't a reaction to anyone or anything but the need inside of her.

And she suddenly felt more powerful than she had ever felt before.

As a prisoner in a palace in a faraway land. Stand-

was over, she couldn't help but admire his golden physique, illuminated in the firelight.

"I didn't mind it," she said quietly.

"Why didn't you tell me?"

"Tell you what?"

"You were a virgin."

"Oh. That. Well, if it helps, I didn't really plan to be."

"You realize that makes this worse."

"How?"

"Because I have… I have spoiled you."

"I thought you said that was a promise," she said quietly. "A vow, if I didn't mistake you. That you would ruin me for other men."

"That is not what I mean now," he said, his tone feral. He stood up, and she went dry mouthed at the sight of his naked body.

"No. What do you mean? Perhaps I need clarification?"

"If you were a virgin, then it was meant for him."

"It was meant for who I gave it to."

"Did you give it to me? Or did you fling it away knowing what you were doing."

"No." She winced internally, not because she'd been thinking of her virginity, but she had considered the fact that this would make the marriage to Matteo difficult. But in the end, it wasn't why she had done it. "We don't all live in the Dark Ages, Javier, and you know that. I don't come from this world. Who I decide to sleep with is my choice and my business, and it is not a medieval bargaining tool, however my father treated me and my body. I do not owe you an explanation."

"But I owed my brother my loyalty."

"Then the failure is yours," she spat, feeling defensive and angry, all the beautiful feelings that she had felt only moments before melting away. "It was my first time, and you're ruining it. It was really quite nice before you started talking."

"But it is a reality we must deal with," he said. "You are to marry my brother."

"You can't possibly think that I will go through with it after this."

He stared at her, his eyes dark, bleak.

"You do. You honestly think that whatever this greater good is that your brother plans… You honestly think that it's more important than what I want. Than what passed between us here. You know that I don't want to marry him. Putting aside the fact that we just made love… You know that I want to go home."

Fury filled her. Impotent and fiery. She just wanted to rage. Wanted to turn things over. Because she felt utterly and completely altered, and he remained stone.

"How can nothing have changed for you?"

"Because the world around me did not change. My obligations did not change."

"This was a mistake," she said. "It was a huge mistake."

She began to collect her clothes, and she dressed as quickly as possible. Then she ran out of the library without looking back. Pain lashed at her chest. Her heart felt raw and bloodied.

How could he have devastated her like this? It had been her plan. Her seduction plan to try to gain a bid for freedom, and it had ended...

She felt heartbroken.

Because this thing between them had felt singular and new, and so had she. Because it had felt like maybe it was something worth fighting for.

But not for him.

When she closed the bedroom door behind her, for the first time she truly did feel like a prisoner.

But not a prisoner of this palace, a prisoner of the demons that lurked inside of Javier.

And she didn't know if there would be any escaping them.

When Matteo returned two days later, Javier had only one goal in mind.

He knew that what he was doing was an utter violation of his position. But he had already done that.

But things had become clearer and clearer to him over the past couple of days. And while he knew that his actions had been unforgivable, there was only one course of action to take.

"You need to set her free," he said when he walked into his brother's office.

"Would you excuse us, Livia?"

Like the mouse he often called her, Livia scurried from the room.

"You must be very happy with her performance on the business trip to address her by her first name."

"I am. Now, who exactly do I have to set free?"

"Violet King. You cannot hold her. You cannot possibly be enforcing her father's medieval bargaining."

"I instigated the medieval bargain. So obviously I'm interested in preserving it."

"She will be willing to offer her business services. But she does not wish to marry you."

"Why exactly do you care?" Matteo asked, his brother always too insightful.

"I slept with her," Javier said. "Obviously you can see why it would be problematic for her to remain here."

Matteo appraised him with eyes that were impossible to read. "You know I don't actually care if you've slept with her. As long as you don't sleep with her after I marry her."

"You aren't angry about it?" The idea of Matteo touching Violet filled him with fury. That his brother could feel nothing…

Well, he didn't know her. He didn't deserve her.

Matteo waved a hand. "I have no stronger feelings about her than I do for my assistant. She's a useful potential tool. Nothing more. What she does with her body is her business."

"I betrayed you," Javier said.

"How? She has made no vows to me. And I don't love her."

For the first time, Javier found his brother's complete lack of emotion infuriating. Because he had wasted time having far too many emotions about the entire thing, and apparently it didn't matter after all.

"Let her go."

"Now see, that does bother me, Javier. Because my word is law."

"And you wanted to know when you were overstepping. And it is now. She doesn't wish to marry you. She wishes to leave."

"And her wishes override mine?"

"You would force a woman down the aisle?"

"I told you what I wanted."

"And I'm here to tell you it isn't going to happen. She is mine."

"Then you marry her."

He jerked backward. "What?"

"You marry her."

"Why the hell does anyone have to marry her?"

"Because I made a bargain with her father. And I don't like to go back on a bargain. It was what he promised me in exchange for his freedom. I didn't ask, if you were wondering."

"He simply... Offered her?"

"Yes. I think he liked the idea of a connection with royalty."

"She doesn't want it."

"But you see, I made a business deal with Robert King. He gave me some very tactical business advice that was needed at the time. In exchange I promised that I would make his daughter royalty. Make him a real king, so to speak."

"In exchange for?"

"Manufacturing rights."

"Violet is prepared to offer those for her makeup line."

"Great. I'm glad to hear it. I would like both. Either I marry her or you do it, younger brother, but someone has to."

Javier stared at his brother, more a brick wall than even Javier was. And for the first time he truly resented that his brother was the leader of the nation and he owed him loyalty. Because he would like to tell him exactly where he could shove his edict. Because they were two alpha males with an equal amount of physical strength and a definite lack of a desire to be ruled by anyone.

But his brother was the oldest. So he was the only one that actually got to give that free rein.

But Javier thought of Violet. Violet.

And he could send her away, or he could keep her. The beast in the castle.

He could have her. Always. Could keep her for his own and not have to apologize for it.

"Why did you make it sound like her father didn't have any power? Like he'd lost a bet?"

"That's what he told me. He didn't want her to know that he had traded her for a business deal. He instructed me that when the time was right… I should embellish a little bit."

"That bastard."

"Honestly. He's decent enough compared to our father."

"Our father should not be a metric for good parenting in comparison to anyone."

"Perhaps not. So, what's it to be?"

"Even if I marry her, you will still have to marry."

"I'm aware," Matteo said. "I'm sure my mouse can help with that."

"I'm sure she shall be delighted to."

"She is ever delighted to serve my every whim. After all, I am her Savior, am I not?"

"I cannot imagine a worse possible man to serve as Savior. To owe you a debt must be a truly miserable thing. I will marry Violet."

"Interesting," Matteo said. "I did not expect you to accept."

"If you touch her," Javier said, "I will make good on my promise and find an excuse to kill you."

"So you have feelings for her?"

He had, for many years, looked into his soul and seen only darkness. But she had somehow traversed into that darkness and left the tiniest shard of hope in him. A small sliver of light. But it wasn't his. It was hers. He feared that the laughter she'd placed in him, the smile she'd put on his lips…he feared in the end his darkness would consume it.

But like any starving creature, hungry for warmth, he could not turn away either.

Though he knew he should.

Though it went against all he knew he should do, all he knew he should be. "She's mine. I'm not sure why it took this long for me to accept it. I'm the one who went and claimed her. You've kept your hands clean of it the entire time. If I'm going to go to all the trouble of kidnapping a woman, she ought to belong in my bed, don't you think?"

"As you wish."

"I do."

"Congratulations, then. On your upcoming marriage."

CHAPTER TEN

VIOLET'S ANXIETY WAS steadily mounting. Everything had come crashing down on her that moment in the library. The reality of it all. And then in the crushing silence Javier had delivered in the days since, it had all become more and more frightening.

She knew that Matteo was back.

But she still hadn't seen him. Everything was beginning to feel…

Well, it was all beginning to feel far too real.

When she had gone back to her room after they'd made love, her body had ached. Been sore and tender in places she had never been overly conscious of.

And her heart had burned. The sting of his rejection, of pain that she hadn't anticipated.

And she couldn't decide exactly what manner of pain it was.

That he had still been willing to give her to his brother, that he didn't seem to care what she wanted.

That he didn't seem to want her in the way that she

wanted him, because if he did then the idea of her being with another man would…

Well, it was unthinkable to her, and on some level she wished it were unthinkable to him.

That he didn't care that she wanted her freedom, because didn't the beast always let the beauty go?

But maybe this was the real lesson.

Because how many times had her female friends been distraught over one-night stands that had ended with silence? How often had they been certain that there was some sort of connection only to discover it was all inside of them? Violet had been certain that what was passing between herself and Javier had been magical. That it had been real, and that it had been real for both of them.

But that had been a virgin's folly. She was certain of that now.

And she was trapped here. Trapped.

For the first time, she knew that she needed to call home.

But not her father. Not her mother.

Instead, she took her phone out and dialed her sister, Minerva.

"Violet," Minerva said as soon as she answered. "Where are you?"

"Monte Blanco," she said, looking out her bedroom window at the mountains below.

Even the view had lost some of its magic. But then it was difficult to enjoy the view when you were finally coming to accept that you were in fact in prison.

"Why?"

It wasn't any surprise to her that her bookish younger sister had heard of the country.

"Well. It's a long story. But it involves Dad making a marriage bargain for me. With a king that I still haven't met."

"I'm sorry, what?"

"I'm serious. I got kidnapped by a prince."

"I… What is your life like?" she asked incredulously.

"Currently or in general?"

"I just don't know very many people who can say they've been kidnapped by a prince. At least not with such flat affect."

"Well, I have been. And it isn't a joke. Anyway. You lied and told the world that you had our brother's billionaire best friend's baby."

"Sure," Minerva said. "But Dante never kidnapped me."

"He did take you off to his private island."

"To protect me. That's different."

"Sure," Violet said. "Look. I don't know if I'm going to be able to get out of this. I'm trying… But I'm here now. I'm in the palace. Then… The worst part is… I… He's not the one that I want."

The door to her bedroom opened, and she turned around, the phone still clutched in her hand, and there Javier was, standing there looking like a forbidding Angel.

"I'm going to have to call you back."

"No. You can't say something cryptic like that and then go away."

"I have to. Sorry."

"Should I call the police?"

"I'm the captive of a king, Minerva. As in an actual king, not our last name. The police can't help me."

She hung the phone up then and stared at Javier. "Have you come to deliver me to my bridegroom?"

They hadn't been face-to-face since that night. The last time she'd seen him he had been naked. And so had she. Her skin burned with the memory.

"Who are you talking to?"

"My sister. Oddly, I have a lot on my mind."

"I spoke to Matteo."

She took a deep breath and braced herself. "And?"

"You are not marrying him."

A roar of relief filled her ears, and suddenly she felt like she might faint.

"You mean I'm free to go?"

"No," he said gravely.

"But you just said that I don't have to marry him."

"No. But you do have to marry me."

"I'm sorry, what?"

"It turns out that neither my brother nor your father were honest about the particulars of the situation. You may want to call him and speak to him. But my brother made a commandment. He said one of us had to marry you. But that sending you home was not an option."

"Except, what's to stop you from letting me go?"

"I refuse," Javier said. "He has turned your charge

over to me completely. And that means you're staying here. With me."

"But I have a life, and you know that. We… We know each other."

"And you wanted me to be something other than what I am. You want to believe that I am a man made into a beast. But you never gave space to the idea that I might simply be a beast. Given free rein to keep you, I think that I will. We are very compatible, are we not?"

"You…"

And she realized that the strange, leaping, twisting in her heart was because she was as terrified about this new development as she was exhilarated.

This man, this beautiful man, was demanding she become his wife.

And he was the man that she wanted.

If his words had been filled with happiness. If there had been any indication that he felt emotion for her, then she would have been… She would have only been happy. But there wasn't. Not at all. He was hard and stoic as ever, presenting this as nothing more than another edict as impersonal as the one that came before it, as if they had not been skin to skin. As if he had not rearranged unseen places inside of her. As if he had not been the scene of her greatest act of liberation, and her greatest downfall.

"Just like that. You expect me to marry you."

"Yes," he said.

"I don't understand."

"There is nothing to understand. You will simply

do as you're commanded. As you are in Monte Blanco now. And the law here is the law you are beholden to."

"But you don't care at all what I want."

"To be free. To go back to your life. To pretend as if none of this had ever happened. But it has. And you're mine now."

"Why? Why are you marrying me instead of him? I don't seem to matter to you. Not one bit."

That was when he closed the distance between them. He wrapped his arm around her waist and pulled her up against his body. "Because you are mine. No other man will ever touch you. I am the first. I will be the last."

She was angry then that she hadn't had the presence of mind to lie to him when they'd made love. Because it would have been much more satisfying in the end. To take that from him, when it clearly mattered.

"I will be the only one. Didn't I promise you? That no other man would ever satisfy you as I did?"

"Yes," she said, her throat dry.

"I know no man will ever have the chance to try."

"That's all you want. To own me?"

"It's all I can do."

There was a bleakness to that statement that touched something inside of her. This, for him, was as close to emotion as he could come. It was also bound up in his control. In that deep belief that he was a monster of some kind. He had told her he was not good, but that he had honor.

And she could see now that he was willing to leave her behind, embrace greed.

And on some level she had no one to blame but herself. Because hadn't she appealed to that part of him when she had seduced him in the library? Hadn't it been on the tip of her tongue to ask him why he was so content to let his brother have what he so clearly wanted?

But he didn't need her goading him to embrace those things now. He emanated with them. With raw, masculine intent. With a deep, dark claim that she could see he was intent to stamp upon her body.

Unknowing he had already put one on her soul.

It wasn't that he didn't feel it, she realized. It was that he didn't understand it.

Perhaps she had not felt the depth of those emotions alone. It was only that he did not know how to name them. Only that he did not understand them.

"And what will it mean for me? To be your wife?"

He stared at her, his dark eyes unreadable. "You did not ask me that. About my brother."

"Because I wasn't going to marry him."

She let the implied truth in those words sit there between them. Expand. Let him bring his own meaning to them.

"There will be less responsibility as my wife. I do not have the public face that he does."

"And if I should wish to?"

"Whatever you wish," he said. "It can be accommodated."

"What about charities?"

"You know that we would actively seek to establish

them. We must improve the view of our country with the rest of the world."

"My charity in particular," she said.

"Supported. However much you would like."

"The control of my money?"

He shrugged. "Remains with you."

"And if I refuse…"

"Everything you have will belong to my brother. And you will be bound to us either way."

"Then I suppose there is no choice."

There was. They both knew it. It was just a choice with a consequence she wasn't willing to take on.

And there was a still, small voice inside of her that asked if she still thought she was lost in the fairy tale.

If she was still convinced that she was the maiden sent to tame a beast.

Whatever the reason, she found herself nodding in agreement. Whatever the reason, she knew what her course would be.

"All right. I'll marry you. I will be a princess."

The announcement happened the very next day. Media splashed it all over the world. And she was compelled to put up a post with a photograph of the view outside of her bedchamber and an assortment of vague gushing comments.

"Will I be expected to give up all forms of social media?"

"No," Javier said. "Your visibility is appreciated. An asset."

"Indeed," she mused, looking at the glorious meal spread out before her.

"I will need a ring," she said. "It will have to be spectacular. Don't mistake me. It's not because I have any great need of a massive diamond. Simply that you want me to make some kind of a spectacle. Getting engaged to a prince will require that I have a very strong jewelry game."

"I will bring the Crown Jewels out of the vault for your examination, My Princess."

"Are you teasing me or not?"

"I am not."

The problem was, she couldn't really tell. And the other problem was, in the days since the engagement announcement, there had been no further intimacy between them.

The sense that she had known him had dissipated with their thwarted afterglow, and now she simply felt... Numb.

"Well. I guess... I guess that would be acceptable."

It was more than acceptable to him, apparently, because as soon as they were finished with the meal, he ushered her into the library, which felt pointed, and told her that the jewels would appear.

And appear they did. Members of his staff came in with box after box and laid them all out on the various pieces of furniture throughout the room. On the settee, the different end tables, a coffee table.

She blushed furiously when her eyes fell on the

place by the fire, where she had given herself to Javier and cemented her fate.

"This is maybe a little bit much…"

"You said you wanted spectacular. And so I have determined that I won't disappoint you." His dark eyes seemed to glow with black fire. She wondered how she had ever thought them cold. Now she felt the heat in them like a living flame inside her chest.

He moved to one of the end tables and opened the first box. Inside was a ring, ornate, laden with jewels that glittered in the firelight. And she would never be able to see firelight without thinking of his skin. Without thinking of his strong body searching inside of her. It was impossible.

She blushed, focusing on the jewel. Then, those large, capable hands moved to the next box. He opened it, revealing a ring filled with emeralds. The next, champagne diamonds. Citrine, rubies, every gem in every cut and color was revealed.

"There are the rings," he said.

"I…"

"Would you like me to choose for you?"

At first, she bucked against the idea. But what did it matter? Their marriage wasn't going to be a real one anyway. So what did it matter what she wore.

The idea made her eyes feel dry, made her throat feel raw. Because something about this felt real to her. More real than the diamonds that were laid before her. More real than the stones around them. This entire palace was made of gems; why she should be surprised and awed at the splendor laid before her she didn't know. But they were not real. Not in the way that the conviction and need that burned in her heart was.

This man was.

A man. Not a mountain. Not a beast. No matter how much he might want to believe that he was either of the latter.

The ring didn't matter, on that level. But it would matter what he chose for her. In the same way that it mattered the first night they had been together that she had known that he would be in the library. Known that he would be holding that book. Known that whatever he said, he was seeking a connection between the two of them. To deepen it. Because it was real. It was there.

She had spent her life seeking connections. Using connections. She had spent her life trying to show her father that she was worthy. That she was just as good as her brother, Maximus. Just as charming and delightful as her sister, Minerva.

But with Javier it was just there.

Whether they wanted it to be or not. And she had to cling to the fact that something in that was real.

"You can choose," she said.

"Very well."

It was the ruby that he picked up between his thumb and forefinger. He didn't even have to pause to think. With his dark eyes glowing with a black flame, he took her hand in his and he slipped that ring onto her finger.

"Mine," he said.

"Mine," she returned, curling her fingers around his. "If I am yours, then you must be mine."

There was something stark and shocked on his face as she said those words. "I'm a modern woman," she returned. "I believe in equality. If you expect that you will own my body, then I will own yours."

He inclined his head slowly. "As you wish."

"I like it," she said, looking down at the gem.

"Good. Because there is more."

He went to the coffee table, where wider, flatter jewelry boxes were set. He opened first one, then another. Necklaces. Spectacular and glittering with an intensity that mocked the fire.

There was one made of rubies, one that matched the ring. He pulled it out, held it aloft. All of her words were stolen from her. Lost completely in the moment.

And for her, it wasn't about the value of the gems, but about the care of the selection. About the fact that he knew what he wanted to see her wear. That he had chosen them for her. The necklace settled heavily across her breastbone, and he clasped it gently behind her neck.

The metal was cold against her skin and felt erotic somehow. She shivered. Of course, agreeing to be his wife meant more of this. This touching. This need.

This need satisfied and sated when they needed it.

He looked up at her, slid his thumb along her lower lip. And she shivered.

"Last time I had you here you belonged to him."

She shook her head. "No. I never did."

The corner of his mouth curved upward, and she recognized it for what it was: triumph.

"The tradition of what royal marriage means has been lost in my family," he said, his voice rough. "Have you read any of the other books on these shelves?"

She nodded. "A few."

"Did you happen to read about marriage customs?"

"No."

"Then I will explain. Because service is to be given, first to the country. Those who are royal do not belong to themselves. They belong to Monte Blanco. The woman who marries into the family surrenders in the same way."

"What about a man who marries into the family?" she asked.

"Women cannot sit on the throne here."

"That seems…unfair."

"I have seen how heavy the weight of the position is for my brother. I would call it a blessing."

"But it's gender bias either way."

"You may lobby for a change when we are wed."

He didn't even sound all that irritated with her.

It made her want to smile.

"A marriage into the royal family is a surrender of self," he said. "Except…except between the husband and wife there is a bond considered sacred. Nearly supernatural."

He moved his hand behind her back, and on an indrawing of her breath he undid the zipper on her dress with one fluid motion. It fell down her body, pooling onto the floor. Leaving her in her shoes, her underwear, the necklace and that ring.

Her nipples went tight in the cold air, her lack of a bra not a consideration before this moment, but now, with his hungry eyes on her...

She shivered.

"They have surrendered themselves to the greater good. To the nation. But in the walls of their bedchamber they surrender to each other. They belong only to each other. And it is ownership, *querida*. Not a partnership the way you think of it in your modern world."

"But they own each other," she pressed.

He nodded slowly, then he moved to the couch, and picked up another box. He opened it up and revealed two thick, heavy-looking bracelets. Gold and ruby, matching the rest of the jewels.

He moved close to her body and she responded. Being bare as she was with him so near made it impossible for her to breathe. To think.

He took the first bracelet out and clasped it tightly on her wrist. Then he took the second and put it around the other.

She felt the weight of them, heavy in a way that went beyond the materials they were forged from.

He moved again. "Surely there isn't more," she said breathlessly.

"Surely there is," he murmured.

The next box contained cuffs that looked much like the ones on her wrists.

"Do you know what these are?"

"No," she said, the word a whisper.

"These are very ancient. They have been in my family for hundreds of years."

"Oh."

"Out of use for generations. They are deeply symbolic. And they are never worn in public."

"Where are they worn?"

He looked at her with meaning.

"Oh."

"They speak of this ownership that I feel. The ownership I told you about, in these royal marriages."

"Oh," she said again, her throat dry, her heart fluttering in her chest like a trapped bird.

"Permit me."

And she didn't even consider refusing.

He knelt before her. With great care, he removed her shoes and set them aside. Then he lifted his hands, hooked his fingers in the waistband of her underwear and drew them slowly down her legs. A pulse beat hard at the apex of her thighs, and she closed her eyes tight for a moment, trying to find her balance.

She was embarrassed, to be naked with him kneeling down before her like this. And she didn't want to look. But also… She couldn't bear to not watch what he might do next.

So she opened her eyes, looked at him, his dark head bent, his position one of seeming submission.

But she knew better.

He clasped the first cuff to her ankle. Then the second. Then, nestled in those jewelry boxes she spotted something she hadn't seen before. Gold chains. Without taking his eyes from her, he clasped one end of the first chain to her ring on the left ankle cuff, then attached it to the one on the right.

After that, he rose up, taking the other gold chain in his hand, sliding it between his fingers and looking at her with intent. Then he repeated the same motion he had completed on her ankles with her wrists.

She blinked several times, trying to gather herself. She took a fortifying breath. "I don't understand," she whispered. "Surely these wouldn't actually keep anyone captive. They're far too fine."

"They're not intended to keep anyone captive. Not really. This captivity is a choice," he said, curling his forefinger around the chain that connected her hands. He tugged gently, and she responded to the pressure, taking two steps toward him. "It is a choice," he said again.

Understanding filled her.

Because he was giving her a moment now. To make the choice. Or to run.

It fully hit her now that it was a choice she had made. To stay here. To say yes to him.

She stood, and she didn't move.

She tilted her face upward, the motion her clear and obvious consent. He wrapped his hand more tightly around the chain, bringing her yet closer, and he claimed her mouth with his.

The gold was fine, delicate and such a soft metal. She could break free if she chose. But she didn't. Instead, she let him hold her as a captive, kissing her deep and hard. His one hand remained around the chain, and his other came up to cup her face, guiding her as he took the kiss deep, his tongue sliding against hers, slick and wonderful.

Hot.

Possessive.

He released his hold on her, taking a step back and beginning to unbutton his shirt, revealing hard-cut muscles that never failed to make her feel weak. To make her feel strong. Because wasn't the woman who enticed such a man to pleasure, to a betrayal of all that he was, even more powerful than he in many ways?

Maybe, maybe not. But she felt it.

This, this thing between them, was something that was hers and hers alone.

His.

Theirs.

Two people who belonged to a nation. But belonged to each other first.

She understood it.

He shrugged his shirt off his powerful shoulders and cast it onto the ground. Then, he wrapped his hand around the chain again and began to tug downward. "Kneel before royalty," he said, his voice rough.

And she did. Going down to her knees, the cuffs pressing against her ankles, the chain from her wrists pooling in her lap.

She looked up at him and watched, her mouth going dry as he undid his belt, slid it through the loops on his pants. She was captivated as the leather slid over his palm before he unclasped his pants, lowered the zipper.

And revealed himself, hot and hard and masculine. Hard for her.

A choice.

This was her choice. No matter the position of submission.

Just as when he had knelt before her, fastening the cuffs, it had appeared that he was the one submitting, but he had been in power. It was the same for her.

She reached up and circled her fingers around his length, stroked him up and down.

It was amazing to her that she had never been overcome by desire for a man in her life before, but everything about him filled her with need. He was beautiful. Every masculine inch of him. She stretched up, still on her knees, and took him into her mouth. He growled, the beast coming forward, and she reveled in that.

Because here was the power. Here was the mutual submission. That belonging that he had spoken of. She in chains, on her knees, but with the most vulnerable part of him to do with as she pleased. His pleasure at her command. His body at her mercy.

She was lost in this. In the magic created between the two of them. Even more powerful than it had been the first time.

Because she had all these physical markers of who she belonged to. And everything about his surrender proved that he belonged to her.

She kept on pleasuring him until he shook. Until his

muscles, the very foundation of all that he was began to tremble. Until his hands went to her hair and tugged tightly, moving her away from his body.

"That is not how we will finish," he growled.

He lifted her up from the ground, setting her on the edge of the settee. Then he kissed her, claiming her mouth with ferocity. He moved his hand to her thigh and lifted it to his shoulders, looping the chain so that it was around the back of his neck. Then he did the same with the other, so that he was between her legs, secured there.

Holding her tightly, he lowered his head, placing his mouth between her legs and lapping at her with the flat of his tongue. Giving her everything she had given to him, and then some. He feasted on her until she was shivering. Until she was screaming with her desire for release. Begging.

Until she no longer felt strong, but she didn't need to. Because she felt safe. Because she felt like his, and that was every bit as good.

When she found her release, she was undone by it. The walls inside of her crumbling, every resistance destroyed. Defeated. And then, the blunt head of his arousal was pressing against the entrance to her body, and she received him willingly.

He thrust hard inside of her, her legs still draped over his shoulders, the angle making it impossibly deep. Taking her breath away.

Their coming together was a storm. And she didn't seek shelter from it. Instead, she flung her arms wide and let the rain pour down on her. Let it all overtake her. Consume her.

She held on to his shoulders, dug her fingernails into his skin as her pleasure built inside of her again. Impossibly so.

And when they broke, they broke together. But when they came back to earth, they were together as well.

And she realized that he was circled by the chains as well. As bound to her as she was to him.

And they lay there in the library, neither of them moving.

Neither of them seeking escape.

And whatever he had said about his brother mandating the marriage, whatever she had said about not being able to surrender to his country, she looked into his eyes then, and she saw it. Clearly for them both.

It was a choice.

She was choosing him. The same as he was choosing her.

And the only sharp part of the moment was wishing that he might have chosen her for the same reason that she was choosing him.

She had fallen in love.

As she looked into those fathomless black eyes, she knew that it was not the same for him.

CHAPTER ELEVEN

HE DIDN'T SHARE her bed that night.

It wounded her more than a little. She had hoped that…that she tested his control a little more than that. Especially considering he had reshaped her into a person she didn't recognize.

One who had agreed to stay here.

Who had agreed to marry a man she barely knew.

Except…

Didn't she know him? On a soul-deep level? It was terrifying how real it all felt. She loved him. He had taken such a large piece of who she was in such a small amount of time.

And with the same certainty that she loved him, she knew he didn't feel the same.

She wasn't even sure he could.

It didn't change her heart, though.

Maybe she could change his. She hoped.

First, though, she had to take care of her life.

She took a deep breath and fortified herself. Then looked down at her phone.

Violet knew that it was time to speak to her father. She had been avoiding it for weeks now.

And it wasn't that she hadn't received calls from her family in the time since her engagement to Javier had been announced. She had. The only calls she had been at home to were from her brother and from her sister.

Maximus had been stern, and she had waved off his concerns. Minerva had been... Well, Minerva. Thoughtful, practical and a bit overly romantic. But then, Violet herself was being a bit romantic.

And anyway, she had talked Minerva through her situation with Dante, when the two of them had been having issues, and so of course Minerva had been supportive of whatever Violet wanted.

But her parents... She had avoided them. Completely. Not today. Today she was ready to have the discussion.

Today she was ready to hear whatever the answers might be.

That was the real issue.

If she was going to ask her father for an explanation, she had to be prepared to hear the explanation.

But something had shifted in her last night. That decisiveness.

She was no longer hiding from the fact that she had chosen this. That Javier was her choice.

That being in Monte Blanco was her choice.

She took a fortifying breath, and she selected her father's number.

"Violet," he said, his tone rough.

"Hi," she said, not exactly sure what to feel. A sense of relief at hearing his voice, because she had missed him even while she had been angry at him.

At least, missed the way that she had felt about him before.

"Are you all right?"

"It's a little bit late for you to be concerned about that."

"Why? I didn't expect that you would be cut off from communication with me."

"I haven't been. I've been perfectly able to call and communicate with whoever I wished."

"You haven't come back to California. You haven't been at work. From what I've heard you've only given minimal instruction to your team. It's not like you."

"Well. You'll have to forgive me. I've never been kidnapped before. Neither have I been engaged to be married to two different men in the space of a few weeks. Strangers, at that."

"I meant to speak to you about this," he said.

"You meant to speak to me about it?"

"It was never intended to be a surprise. But I lost my nerve when it came to speaking to you after I struck the deal."

"I can't imagine why. Were you afraid that I would be angry that you sold me like I was a prized heifer?"

"I figured that if I could position it the right way, you would see why it was a good thing. Being a business-woman is one thing, Violet, but a princess? A queen?"

"Well, I'm not going to be Queen now. I got knocked down to the spare, rather than the heir."

"What happened?"

Her father sounded genuinely distressed by that. "Do you really care?"

"It would've been better for you to marry Matteo. He is the King."

"No," she said, "it wouldn't be better for me to marry Matteo, because I don't have any feelings for him."

"Are you telling me you have feelings for… The other one?"

"Why do you care? You let him take me. You let me be kidnapped and held for reasons of marriage without explaining to me why. Without… Dad, I thought that I was worth more to you than just another card to be dealt from your businessman hand. You would never have done this to Maximus."

"Well, quite apart from the fact that neither of them would have wanted to marry Maximus…"

"Why not Minerva?"

"It was clear to me from the beginning that Minerva would not have made a good princess. But you…"

"I went on to build my own business. To build my own fortune. You didn't know that I would do that when you promised me to him at sixteen. And in the last decade you didn't have the courage to speak to me even one time about it."

"It won't impact your ability to run your business.

I mean, certainly you'll have to farm out some of the day-to-day, but you're mostly a figurehead anyway."

"I'm not," she said. "I brainstorm most of the new products. I'm in charge of implementation. I'm not just a figurehead." Her stomach sank. "But that's what you think, isn't it? You think that I've only accomplished any of this because of my connection with you."

It hit her then that her father genuinely thought he had been giving her a gift on some level. That there was nothing of substance that she had accomplished on her own, and nothing that she could.

And he couldn't even see that. It didn't even feel like a lack of love to him. And maybe it wasn't.

It was a deeply rooted way that he seemed to see his girls versus the way he saw his son. Perhaps the way he saw women versus the way he saw men.

"It was a good thing that you did," she said, "when you took Dante in from the streets of Rome. You thought he was smart. You sent him to school. If he had been a woman, would you have just tried to make a marriage for him?"

"I know what you're thinking," her father said. "That I don't think you're smart. I do. I think you're brilliant, Violet. And I think you're wonderful with people. Women have a different sort of power in this world. I don't see the harm in acknowledging that. I don't see the harm in allowing you to use that in a way that is easier. You can try to compete with men in the business world, but you'll always be at a disadvantage."

"I want to be very clear," Violet said. "I am choosing

this. Not for you. Your views are not only antiquated, they're morally wrong. That you see me as secondary to you, as incapable, is one of the most hurtful things I've ever had to face."

"I'm protecting you. No matter what happens with commerce, you'll always be a princess once you marry..."

"Javier. I want you to know that I'm choosing to marry him. Because I care about him. I'm not afraid of losing everything, Dad. Not the way that you are."

"That's because you don't know what it's like to have nothing," her father said. "I do. I didn't have any-thing when I started out. And I built my empire from nothing. You built yours off mine. Easy enough for you to say that you're not afraid to lose it."

"Maybe so," she said. "And I've always felt that, you know. That I built this off something that you started. And I suppose you could say that my marriage here is built off something that you started. But I'm the one that's choosing this. I'm the one that's choosing to make all that I can from it."

"Violet, I know that you're not happy with me about this, but clearly it worked out for the best."

She thought of last night. Of the passion that had erupted between her and Javier. Of the way that she felt for him.

It didn't feel like the best. It felt necessary. It felt real and raw and closer to who she was than anything else ever had. But it wasn't easy. And it wouldn't be.

Ever. Because Javier wasn't easy. And she wouldn't want him to be, not really.

She wished that he might love her.

The strength of their connection was so powerful she had to believe... He was wounded. She knew that. He was scarred by his past.

He would fight against his feelings.

But he had accepted the marriage. He wanted them to choose each other, own each other.

She was certain of nothing, but she trusted that commitment.

She had to hope that someday it could become more.

"It didn't work out for the best because of you," Violet said. "You can't take credit for what I felt. And believe me, the relationship I have with Javier I built."

She hung up the phone then.

She didn't know what she was going to do about her relationship with her father going forward. Though living half a world away was certainly helpful.

The kind of distance required for her to get her head on straight. That was for sure.

And now she had to clear her mind. Because tonight there was going to be a dinner with foreign dignitaries. And Javier had told her that in light of the fact he had no people skills, she was going to have to do the heavy lifting for him.

Conviction burned in her chest.

He needed her to be his other half.

And so she would be.

She would choose to be.

Perhaps if she went first, if she forged that path with love, he would be able to find his way into loving her back.

An impromptu dinner with foreign dignitaries was not Javier's idea of fun. But then, few things were his idea of fun. And if he had his way, he would simply walk out of the dining room and take Violet straight back to bed. But tonight was not about having his way. Unfortunately.

She looked radiant. She had sent one of the members of the palace staff to town and instructed them to return with a golden gown from a local shop. And they had delivered. She was wearing something filmy and gauzy that clung to her curves while still looking sedate.

Her hair was slick, captured in a low bun, and her makeup was similar to how it had been the first day they'd met. More elaborate than anything she had done during their time together here at the palace.

He found he liked something about that as well.

That this was her public face. And that the soft, scrubbed-fresh woman with edible pink lips and wild dark hair was his and his alone.

She was standing there, talking to a woman from Nigeria, both of their hand gestures becoming animated, and he could only guess about what.

But Violet was passionate about her charities. About businesses that centered around women, and he imagined it had something to do with that.

"She is quite something," his brother said, moving to stand beside him.

"Yes," Javier agreed. "She is."

Not for the first time he thought that she would be better suited to the position of Queen than being married to him.

"Come," Matteo said. "Let us speak for a moment."

"Are you going to have me arrested and executed?" Javier asked as they walked out of the dining room and onto the balcony that overlooked the back garden.

"No," Matteo said. "Had I done that, I would have made a much larger spectacle."

"Good to know."

"I wanted to thank you for following through with the marriage."

"You don't have to thank me."

"I can tell that you have feelings for her."

Javier gritted his teeth. "She's beautiful."

"Yes," Matteo agreed. "She is. But many women are beautiful."

Not like Violet. "Certainly."

"Without you, I never could have done this," Matteo said. "All the years of it. Making sure that the damage that our father was intent on inflicting on the country was not as severe as it might have been. You have been loyal to me. Even in this."

Loyalty? Was that what he called this? He had been a fox curled around a hen. Waiting, just waiting for her to be left alone. Vulnerable and beautiful and his to devour.

It had taken nothing for him to abandon his promise. His honor.

To prove that he was morally corrupt in his soul. Incapable of doing right if he led with his heart.

"You consider it loyalty?" Javier chuckled. "I slept with your fiancée."

"It does not matter which of us marries her. Only that it's done. I told you that. And I meant it."

"I didn't know it at the time."

"I brought you out here to say that you must not think our bond is damaged by this. And it must not become damaged by this. I don't want your woman."

"I didn't think you did."

"I would ensure that you do not labor under the impression that I might. Which I feel could drive a wedge between us. As I can see that you are… Distracted by her."

"Now we come down to the real truth of it," Javier said. "Do you have concerns about what you consider to be my state of distraction?"

"Not too many. But you must remember that we have a mission here. A goal."

"I am very conscious of it. In service of that goal, she might have been a better queen than anyone else you could choose."

"She will do well in her position as your wife. As for me… I will keep looking."

"You will never be him," Javier said, looking at his brother's profile. "Don't ever doubt that."

"I doubt it often," Matteo said. "But isn't that what

we must do? Question ourselves at every turn. I often wonder how I can ever be truly confident in anything I believe in. Because once I believed in him whole-heartedly. Once I thought that he had the nation's best interests at heart. Once I thought our father was the hero. And it turned out that he was only the villain."

Matteo gave voice to every demon that had ever lurked inside of Javier. When you had believed so wrongly, how could you ever trust that what you believed now was correct?

"We have to remember. An allegiance to honor before all else. Because if you can memorize a code, then you can know with your head what is right. Hearts lie."

Javier nodded slowly. "Yes. You know I believe that as well as you do."

"Good."

He turned around and looked through the window, saw Violet now standing in the center of a group talking and laughing.

"It's made easier by the fact that I have no feelings." He shot his brother a forced grin.

"Good."

Matteo turned and walked back into the party, leaving Javier standing there looking inside. Whether he had meant to or not, his brother had reminded him of what truly mattered. Not the heat that existed between himself and Violet. But progressing their country. Righting the wrongs of their father.

Javier had his own debt to pay his country. He had, under the orders of his father, used the military against its people. Had arrested innocent men who had spent time in prison, away from their families.

Who he knew his father had tortured.

He had been a weapon in the hands of the wrong man, with the wrong view on the world.

He was dangerous, and he couldn't afford to forget it.

Nor could he afford to do any more than atone for all that he'd been.

Nothing, nothing at all, must distract him from that mission.

Not even his fiancée.

"Someone else can go with me."

Violet was becoming irritated by the stormy countenance of her fiancé. He was driving the car carrying them down to town, wearing a white shirt and dark pants, the sleeves pushed up past his forearms. His black hair was disheveled. Possibly because earlier today they had begun kissing in his office, and she had ended up on his lap, riding the ridge of his arousal, gasping with pleasure until she realized that she was going to be late for her appointment at the bridal store in town.

"No," he said.

"You're not allowed to see the wedding dress that I choose anyway."

"It doesn't matter. I will wait outside."

"You're ridiculous," she said. "If you're going to go

wedding dress shopping with me, you have to at least look a little bit like you don't want to die."

A mischievous thought entered her brain, and she set her fingers on his thigh, then let them drift over to an even harder part of him. "Are you frustrated because we didn't get to finish?"

"Obviously I would rather continue with that."

His tone was so exasperated and dry that she couldn't help but laugh.

"If it doesn't impact your driving…" She brushed her fingertips over him.

"It does," he said.

She felt even more gratified by the admission that she affected him than she could have anticipated. She let that carry her the rest of the way down the mountain and into town. It was important to her that she get a dress from a local designer. It was part of an initiative that she was working on with King Matteo's assistant.

Livia was a lovely young woman, with large, serious eyes and a surprisingly dry sense of humor. She was extremely organized and efficient, and Violet could see that Matteo took her for granted in the extreme.

But between the two of them they had begun to figure out ways to naturally raise the profile of the country, coinciding with her marriage to Javier.

Acquiring everything from Monte Blanco that they would need for the wedding was part of that.

When Violet and Javier pulled up to the shop, he parked and got out, leaning against the car.

She made her way toward the shop and looked back

at him. He was a dashing figure. And she wanted to take his picture.

"I'm putting you on the internet."

His expression went hard, but he didn't say anything. And she snapped the shot, him with his arms crossed over his broad chest, a sharp contrast against the sleek black car and the quaint cobbled streets and stone buildings behind him.

And he was beautiful.

"Thank you." She smiled and then went into the shop.

Immediately she was swept into a current of movement. She was given champagne and several beautiful dresses. It would be difficult to choose. But the dress that she decided on was simple, with floating sheer cape sleeves and a skirt that floated around her legs as she walked.

She took a photo of a detail of the dress on a hanger and took all the information for the bridal store.

Because when all this was over, anyone with a big wedding coming up this year would want a gown from this shop, from this designer.

When she reappeared, Javier was still standing where she had left him. Looking like a particularly sexy statue.

"All right. Now you have to come with me for the rest of this."

They went through the rest of the city finding items for the wedding. They created a crowd wherever they went. People were in awe to see Javier walking around with the citizens like a regular person. Not that any-thing about him could be called regular.

"They love you," she said as they walked into a flower shop.

He looked improbable standing next to displays of baby's breath, hyacinth and other similarly soft and pastel-colored things.

"They shouldn't," he said.

"Why not?"

"Nobody should love a person in a position of power. They should demand respect of him."

"You have some very hard opinions," she said, reach-ing out and brushing her fingertips over the baby's breath.

"I have to have hard opinions."

He touched the edge of one of the hyacinth blos-soms and she snapped a quick picture. She enjoyed the sight of his masculine hand against that feminin-ity. It made her think of a hot evening spent with him. It made her think of sex. Of the way he touched her between her legs.

As if he were thinking the exact same thing, he looked at her, their eyes clashing. And she felt the im-pact of it low in her stomach.

"I'm definitely feeling a bit of frustration over hav-ing not gotten to finish what we started earlier," he murmured.

"Me too," she whispered. "But we are out doing our duty. And isn't that the entire point of this marriage?"

The question felt like it was balanced on the edge of a knife. And her right along with it.

"It is," he said, taking his hand away from the flower.

"Right. Well. I think I found the flowers that I want."

She spoke to the shop owner, placing her order. And then the two of them carried on.

"I think we ought to have ice cream for the wedding," she said, standing outside the store. She was searching for something. For that connection with him that they'd had earlier. That they'd had back when it was forbidden.

"I don't want any," he said.

"I… Well. I mean, we can order some for the wedding."

"I think you can handle that on your own," he said.

Her heart faltered for a beat. It felt too close to a metaphor for all that they were right now. She could also love him alone. She was doing it. But it hurt, and she didn't know if she was ever going to be able to close this gap between them.

"Of course," she responded. "I… I'll go and order it."

She did. Then she ordered an ice-cream cone for herself and ignored the pain in her chest. She ignored it all the way through the rest of the shopping, and when they arrived back at the palace and he did not continue where they had left off in his office.

And she tried not to wonder if she had chosen wrong.

She had to cling to the story.

Because eventually the beast would be transformed by love.

The problem was that her beast seemed particularly resistant to it.

And she wasn't entirely sure she understood why.

CHAPTER TWELVE

THE DAY OF the wedding dawned bright and clear. Violet was determined to be optimistic.

It has been a difficult few days. Javier's moods had been unpredictable. Some days he had been attentive, and others, she hadn't seen him at all.

He hadn't made love to her since the day he had given her the jewels.

They hadn't even come close since the day in his office, where they had been thwarted by her schedule. Something she bitterly resented now.

This distance made her feel brittle. Made her feelings hard and spiky, cutting her like glass each time her heart beat.

What would it mean to be with him like this, if it were this way forever?

When she'd imagined marriage to him, she'd imagined more nights like the ones they'd shared in bed together. With passion ruling, not duty.

But if their marriage would be like this...

She didn't know if she'd survive it.

She had bought a beautiful dress, a beautiful dress to be the most suitable bride she could be. What else could she do?

She knew that she couldn't wear the cuffs the way that she had done the day he had given them to her. But she did put two of them on one wrist and attached the gold chain, wrapping it artfully between the cuffs to make it look like an edgy piece of jewelry, rather than an intentional statement of bondage.

The day was made better and easier by the fact that her family was present. Minerva would be Violet's only bridesmaid.

Minerva looked radiant and beautiful in a green dress that skimmed over the baby bump she was currently sporting. She and Dante had taken to parenthood with zeal. They had been instant parents, given that it was a vulnerable baby that had brought the two of them together. They had adopted her shortly after they'd married, and then had their second child quickly after.

This third one had only waited a year.

"You look beautiful," Minerva said, smiling broadly.

"So do you," Violet said.

Falling in love with Dante looked good on her younger sister. Violet would have never matched her sister with her brother's brooding friend. She would have thought that somebody with such an intense personality would crush her sister's more sunny nature. But that wasn't true at all. If anything, Minerva was even sunnier, and Dante had lost some of the darkness that had always hung over him.

He had maintained his intensity; that was for sure.

Of course, when he held their children protectively, when he looked at Minerva like he would kill an entire army to protect her, Violet could certainly see the appeal.

Really, what could she say? She had fallen in love with a beast of a man who was as unknowable as he was feral. She could no longer say that the appeal of an intense partner was lost on her.

"You really are happy to marry him?" Minerva asked gently.

"Yes. It's complicated, but I think you understand how that can be."

Minerva laughed. "Definitely."

"How did you manage it? Loving him, knowing he might never love you back?"

The corners of Minerva's mouth tipped down. "Well. Mostly I managed it by asking myself if I would be any happier without him. The answer was no. I really wouldn't have been any happier without him. And the time I did spend without Dante was so... It was so difficult. I loved him so much, and I had to wait for him to realize that what he felt for me was love. He couldn't recognize it right away because... He didn't know what it felt like. More than that, he was terrified of it. And after everything he had been through, I could hardly blame him."

"Javier is like that," Violet said softly. "He's so fierce. A warrior at heart. And he believes that he isn't good. But that he has honor, and that's enough. He doesn't seem to realize that the reason honor matters to him is that he is good. And I think he's afraid to feel anything for me."

"Have you said that to him?"

Violet shook her head. "No. I don't want him to… I don't want him to reject me." It was one thing to be uncertain. In uncertainty, hope still blossomed inside her, fragile and small though it was.

But if she did say the words… If he rejected her definitively… Well, then she would not even have hope left.

"I understand that. But you know, it might be something he needs to hear. Because until he hears it, he's not going to know. Because he won't recognize it."

"I'm thankful for you," Violet said, wrapping her arm around her sister's shoulder. "I don't know very many other people who would understand this."

"My love was definitely a hard one," she said. "But I don't think it was wrong to fight for it. I feel like sometimes people think… If it doesn't just come together it isn't worth it. But the kind of love I have with Dante… There's nothing else like it. There's no one else for me. He was wounded. He needed time to heal. And it was worth it."

Minerva put her hand on her rounded stomach and smiled. "It was so worth it."

Violet smiled, determination filling her. This would be worth it too.

The love that she felt for him was so intense, it had to be.

It had to be enough.

* * *

Javier waited at the head of the aisle. The church was filled with people. Some who were from Violet's world, and many from his. Though he realized he didn't actually know any of the people in attendance.

He was disconnected from this. From the social part of his job. A figurehead.

It had been interesting going out into town with her. She drew people to them like a bright, warm flame drawing in moths. He had never experienced such a thing, because he was the sort of man who typically kept people at a distance simply by standing there.

But not Violet.

Everyone seemed to want to be around her. To be near her. He could understand why she had managed to build an empire over the internet. With people who wanted to look like her, be like her. People who wanted to experience a slice of what she was.

She was compelling.

And after today she would be his.

He gritted his teeth, curling his hands into fists and waiting.

She would come.

And the momentary hitch of doubt that he had was assuaged by the appearance of her sister, who walked down the aisle with a small bouquet of flowers.

He had met her sister for the first time this morning. The other woman had seemed cautious around him, and a bit wary. Her husband had been more menacing. As had her brother.

Her father had seemed shamefaced, and Javier felt that was deserved. Her mother had simply seemed excited to be in a palace.

Javier had no concept of a family like this. Large and together, even though they disagreed on things, and it was clear that they did.

Though, he imagined that most families that appeared dysfunctional disagreed on small things, and not whether it was appropriate that one of them sold another into marriage. But at this point, what was done was done.

And she would be here.

She wanted him.

And she seemed committed to serving her role for the country.

That was her primary motivation. She had made that clear in the flower shop.

And it was a good thing. Because he could not afford distractions. He could not afford to start thinking in terms of emotion.

The music changed and he turned his focus again to the doorway. Watching with great attention.

And then, there she was.

The sight of her stole his breath.

She was…

She looked like she did for him. Only for him. Her dark hair was long and loose, the veil that she had soft and flowing down her back. She looked almost as if she didn't have makeup on at all. Rather, she glowed.

Her lips looked shiny and soft, her cheeks catching the light. It was magic. And so was she.

He had held himself back these weeks, because it had felt like something he should do until it was done. But now, here she was. Now she was his.

There would be no turning back.

When she reached the head of the aisle, she took his hand. And he pulled her to him. It was all he could do not to claim her mouth then and there. Not to make a spectacle of them both in front of the congregation.

And that was when he noticed the bracelets.

She had them both on one wrist. But the chain was there as well.

And when she looked into his eyes, he felt the impact of it all the way down to his gut.

She nodded slowly.

An affirmation.

She was choosing to give herself to him. And she was saying that she understood. The bond, the loyalty that traditionally existed here in this country between a royal husband and wife.

But he did not know where ownership fit into that. He did not know where duty and responsibility fit in.

He had told her about it. Mostly because he had wanted to see her wear those for him. Those rubies and nothing more. But also he had... He hadn't understood. But suddenly, here, with those bracelets on her wrist, in a church, where they were about to make vows... Where she had brought the carnal into the sacred and blended them together, made them one, he could not understand how this bond could remain just another promise he decided to keep.

Because as she spoke her vows, low and grave in a voice that only he could hear, he felt them imprint beneath his skin. Down to his soul. And when he spoke his in return, they were like that gold chain on her wrist. But they wrapped around them both, binding them in a way that he had not anticipated.

He had thought he knew what this meant.

Because that day he had discovered the sorts of treachery his father protected. That day that he had realized that the orders he had taken for years had been in service of an insidious plan, and nothing that protected or bettered his people, he had sworn that he would uphold a set of principles. That he would not be led by his heart.

That he would not be led by anything other than a code of honor.

But now he had made vows to another person, and not an ideal.

When it came time to kiss her, it took all of his self-control not to claim her utterly and completely right there in front of the roomful of people. He touched her face, and he exercised restraint he did not feel, kissing her slowly but firmly, making sure that she knew it was a promise of more. A promise for later.

He had been restrained these past weeks.

But it was over now.

The vows were made. His course was set.

There was no turning back. Not now.

Whatever would become of this. Of them… It was too late.

You chose this.

He gritted his teeth against the truth of it.

It had been easy to say that he had done it for Matteo. That he was doing it to atone for the sin of taking her in the first place. But the fact of the matter was he was far too selfish to turn away from her.

The idea of giving her to another man had been anathema to him. An impossibility. Had his brother insisted on marrying her, he would have…

He would have betrayed him. He would have stolen her. Secreted her out of the country. Abandoned his post. Abandoned all that they had built.

The truth of that roared in his blood.

Like the beast that he was.

But there was nothing to be done about that now. She was his, so it didn't matter. She was his, so it couldn't matter.

He pushed it all away as he continued to kiss her, and when he was through, the congregation was clapping, and they were introduced.

But he didn't hear any of it.

There was nothing.

Nothing but the pounding of his blood in his veins, the demand that burned through his body like molten lava.

He would endure the reception for as long as he had to. For as long as he had to pretend to care about flowers and ice cream and all manner of things that were only stand-ins for what he had truly wanted all along.

He didn't care to touch the petals of an alarmingly soft purple flower. He wanted Violet. Her skin beneath his hands. He didn't wish to lick an ice-cream cone. He wished to lick her.

And he would play the game if he had to, but that was all it was to him. A game. A game until he could get to her. Because that was all that mattered.

She talked to her family, and he knew that he could not rush her away from them. She was speaking, even to her father, and though there was cautiousness between them, he wondered if she might make amends with him. Javier didn't know how.

He asked her that very question once they got back to their room. In spite of the fact that his blood roared with desire, he had to know.

"I don't know if it will ever be the same as it was," she said. "But it was never easy. It was never perfect. I can always see those sorts of tendencies in him. Those beliefs."

"But you will forgive him."

"Yes. I think sometimes… If you value your relationship with another person enough, you have to be willing to accept that they are flawed. I don't know that I'll ever be able to make my father see the world, or me, the way that I want him to. I can keep showing him, though. And in the meantime I can live my life. But cutting him out of it completely wouldn't fix the wound. It wouldn't heal anything."

"It might teach him a lesson," Javier said.

"I think having to watch me join with you might have begun to teach him a lesson," she said.

"What does that mean?" he growled.

"Only that you are a bit more feral and frightening than I think he imagined my royal husband might be."

"The beast, remember?"

"Yes. I think… We are husband and wife now. And I would like to know… Why?"

"Why what?"

"Why did you become the beast? The sins of your father. We talked about that. But it's deeper than that. I know it is. Because you changed when you found that little girl…"

"What do you think I was doing all those years before? I was seeing to his orders. Arresting men when he demanded that I arrest them. And women. Separating families as he commanded. And he would tell me it was for a reason. Because they were traitors. Because it was upholding the health of the country. But I realize now they were freedom fighters. People who wanted to escape his oppressive regime, and it was oppressive. That innocent people were put behind bars, tried and… I helped. I upheld his rule of law, and I regret it."

"You didn't know."

"Maybe not. But when you have believed so wholeheartedly in a lie, you can never trust yourself again. You can never trust in the clarity of your own judgment because you have been so fooled. Because you were a villain and all the while imagined yourself a hero.

And you will never, ever be able to walk through life without wondering which side you're on again. You will never be able to take it for granted."

"It takes such courage to admit that. You are brave. And I can see that you'll never take the easy way. You can trust yourself."

He shook his head. "No. I can't. I love my father and I allowed those feelings to blind myself to his faults."

"Well. So did I with mine."

"Your father is not a maniacal dictator. As challenging as he might be."

"No. I suppose not." She put her hand on his face, and he closed his eyes, relishing the feel of her delicate fingers against him. "You saved that girl, Javier."

"But so many more I did not save. So many I harmed myself. Arrested. Sent to a prison run by my father, where they were undoubtedly tortured. There is no salvation for such sins. My hands will not wash clean. But I can use them to serve."

"I'm sorry, but I know you, Javier. You're not a monster."

"I must assume that I am," he said, moving away. "The better to protect the world from any harm that I might do."

"I don't think you are," she said.

"This is not a fairy tale. The things that I have done cannot be undone. I can only move forward trying to do right now that I understand. Now that I have the power. It is not about being transformed by magic. Such a thing is not possible."

She moved to him and she bracketed his face with her hands.

He had no chance to respond to that, because she kissed his mouth, and he was dragged into the swirling undertow of desire by the softness of her lips, the slow, sweet sweep of her tongue against his. She was inexperienced, his beautiful goddess, but she had a sort of witchcraft about her that ensnared him and entranced him.

That made him fall utterly and completely under her spell.

How could the magic fail here? Because of him. That had to be it.

She was made entirely of magic. Glorious soft skin and otherworldly beauty wrapped around galaxies of light. She was something other than beauty. Something more.

Something that made his heart beat new and made him want to defy a lifetime of commitment to honor.

He had devoted himself to believing only in a code. A list of principles that helped him determine what was right and wrong because he knew full well that his own blood, his own heart could lead him in the direction of that which would destroy him and all those around him.

His belief in that had been unwavering.

When he looked at her, his Violet, his wife, he knew that he could believe entirely in her. In her magic. In the way her soft mouth rained kisses down over his skin, in the way her delicate fingertips brushed over his body. The way that she undid the buttons on his shirt and tackled the buckle on his belt. Yes. He could believe in that.

He could drop to his knees and pledge his loyalty to her and her alone, seal his utter and total devotion by losing himself in her womanly flavor. By drowning in the desire that rose up between them like a wave, threatening to decimate everything that he had built.

And he didn't care.

Just like he hadn't cared that first time they had kissed in the ballroom those weeks ago, when she had belonged to another man and his loyalty should have stood the test of time but crumbled beneath all that she was.

She was magic. And she was deadly.

And now, just now, he did not have the strength to deny her. To deny them.

And so, why not surrender? Why not drown in it? She was his, after all. He had gone down this path weeks ago, and it was too late to turn back. He had made her his.

His.

And tonight he would make that matter. He would revel in it.

He stole the power of the kiss from her, taking control, growling as he wrapped his arms around her and walked her back against the wall, pinning her there, devouring her, claiming her as his own.

He had spoken vows, but they were not enough; he needed to seal them with his body. He needed her to know.

He needed her to understand.

The way that she destroyed him. The way that he was broken inside. So that she would know. And he didn't know why he needed her to know, just like he didn't know why he had been in the library that night they had first made love. Why he had been looking through that same book that she was, trying to read the same story and find some meaning in it.

To try to see through her eyes the way that she might see him.

And it shouldn't matter. It never should have. Because she had been his brother's and he had been toying with betrayal even then.

But she's yours now.

Yes, she was his. For better or worse.

He feared very much it might be worse. Because he hurt people. It felt like a natural part of what he was. That monster.

But perhaps if it was only this, if it was only lust, he could control it.

He wrenched that beautiful dress off her body. She was an Angel in it, far too pure for him, and it nearly hurt to look at her. Burned his hands to pull the filmy fabric away from her. But it left her standing there in white, angelic underthings. Garments that spoke of purity, and he knew that he was unequal to the task of touching them. Just as he had been unworthy of touching her in the first place.

But he had.

And he would.

He tore them away from her body, leaving her naked before him. Except for those jewels. The necklace glittering at the base of her throat, the cuffs heavy on her wrist, the chain wound around them. And the ring, his ring, glittering on her finger, telling the world that she belonged to him.

He had never had her in a bed.

He hadn't realized that until this moment. And tonight he would have her in his bed. Their bed.

She would not have her own room, not after this.

It was often customary for royal couples to keep their own spaces, but they would not.

She would be here. Under the covers, in his bed with him. Her naked body wrapped around his. Yes. That was what he required. It was what he would demand.

He picked her up and carried her there, set her down at the center of the mattress and looked at her. He leaned over, spreading her hair out around her like a dark halo, and then he stood, looking at the beautiful picture that she made. Her soft, bare skin pale against the deep crimson red of the quilt. She took a sharp breath, her breasts rising with the motion, her nipples beading.

"Such a lovely picture you make, My Princess."

"I didn't think my official title was Princess."

"It doesn't matter. You are *my* princess. *Mine.*"

He bent down, cupping her breast with his hand, letting it fill his palm.

She was soft, so delicate and exquisite, and it amazed him that something half so fragile could put such a deep crack in the foundation of what he was. But she had.

He lowered his head and took one perfect, puckered nipple between his lips and sucked all her glory into his mouth. She arched beneath him, crying out in soft, sweet pleasure, and it spurred him on. He growled, lavishing her with attention, licking and sucking, stroking her between her thighs.

His wife. His beautiful, perfect wife, who threatened to destroy all that he was.

How had he ever thought that it was possible to maintain superior connections to this country. To duty and honor when the marriage bed presented shackles that could not be seen with the human eye. Perhaps that was why the cuffs existed. Not to create a sense that they were bound to each other, but to turn them physical. All the better to remove them when one chose to.

Because the ties that existed in his heart he could not see, he could not touch and he did not know how to unleash.

It was supernatural in a way that he would have said he did not believe in.

It was strong in a way he would have told anyone such a thing could not be.

And he was linked to her in a way he would have said he could not be to another human being.

Because he had given those things away so long ago. Because he had pledged loyalty to Matteo and not love. Because he had pledged his blood to Monte Blanco, but not love.

And what he wanted to give to Violet was deeper, and he was afraid that she was right. That magic had always only ever been love, and that it could turn and twist into something dark and evil, just like magic.

All that magic that she was.

All that… He did not wish to give the word a place, not even in his mind.

And so he covered his thoughts with a blanket of pleasure, wrapping them both in the dark velvet of his desire, lapping his way down her body, her stomach, down to that sweet place between her legs. He buried himself there. Lost himself in giving her pleasure.

Got drunk on it.

Because there was nothing to do now but revel in it. Afterward… Afterward there would be time for reckonings and for fixing all of this. But not now.

Now was the time to embrace it.

The only time.

Here in the bedroom.

And maybe that was what the cuffs were for.

To create a space where the world didn't matter. Where there could be an escape.

And maybe for other men that would have worked. But not for him.

Because he didn't know how to create space.

He only knew how to be all or nothing.

How to be an agent of his father, or a war machine acting against him.

How to be a man, vulnerable and useless. Or how to be a beast.

But he had the freedom to be that beast with her. And somehow, with that freedom he became both. Wholly a man and wholly an animal in her arms, and she seemed to accept him no matter what. She shouldn't.

She should push him away. She always should have pushed him away.

But she had gone with him, from the beginning.

She had chosen to be with him.

And when he rose up and positioned himself between her thighs, when he thrust into her body, and when her beautiful eyes opened, connected with his, he felt a shudder of something crack through his entire body like a bolt of lightning.

She lifted her head, pressed her soft mouth to his, and he felt words vibrating against his lips. He couldn't understand them. Couldn't do anything but feel them, as the sweet, tight heat of her body closed around his.

She clung to his shoulders as he drove them both to the pinnacle of pleasure. And when she released, he went with her. Pleasure pounding through him like a relentless rain.

And then, he heard her speaking again, her lips moving against the side of his neck, and this time, the words crystallized in his mind.

The words that he had been trying, trying and failing, not to hear. Not to understand.

"I love you," she whispered. Her lips moved against his skin, tattooing the words there, making it impossible for him not to feel them. He was branded with them.

"I love you. I love you."

"No," he said, the denial bursting forth from him.

He moved away from her, pushing his hands through his hair. Panic clawed at him and he couldn't say why. He was not a man who panicked. Ever. He was not a man acquainted with fear. Because what did he care for his own life? The only thing he feared was the darkness in himself, and maybe that was the problem now. Maybe it called to the weakness that he had inside of his chest.

The desire to sink into her. To drop to his knees and pledge loyalty to her no matter what.

Even if she asked him to mobilize against his brother. Against his people.

And it didn't matter that she wouldn't.

What mattered was losing the anchor that kept him from harming those around him.

What mattered was losing the only moral compass he knew how to read.

What mattered was Monte Blanco and it was becoming impossible for him to hold on to that.

"I'm sorry," she said. "You don't get to tell me that I don't love you."

"I cannot," he said.

"Why not?"

"Haven't you been listening? Haven't you heard anything that I've told you? Love is the enemy. You're right. Magic. And magic can be dark as easily as it can work for good."

"So why can't you trust that between us it will be good?"

"Because I cannot trust myself," he said.

She put her hand on his chest and he wrapped his fingers around her wrist and ripped it away. She stared at him, the hurt in her eyes far too intense to bear.

Because he did not have the freedom to be himself with her. It was far too dangerous. And he had been lying. Evidence of his own weakness if it ever existed.

That he had wanted to pretend that what he knew to be true wasn't. That he wanted to give himself freedom when he knew that he could not afford it. This woman was a gift that some men could have. But not him.

Yet he had been weak, far too weak from the beginning to turn away from her. He'd been given every chance. Every roadblock in his personal arsenal had been set up. She had been intended for his brother, and if that could not keep him away from her, then nothing could.

She was dangerous. Deadly.

A threat to his own personal code in ways that he should have seen from the beginning.

Because she had been eroding the foundation that he had built from the beginning. Just a touch. A kiss. And then he had stormed into his brother's office to tell him that Matteo could not marry her. To tell him that he could not see through the plan that he had to make their country better, because Javier had wanted Violet for himself. He had never wanted to let her go. He would have gone after her. That much he knew.

But his brother had given him options that he had liked, and so he had taken them. Made it easy to keep on going down that slippery slope.

So he had done.

And now... Now he was sitting here in the consequences of it. She loved him. He could not give her that love in return.

He had broken not only his own sacred vows, but in the end he would break her too. And that was unacceptable.

But he had married her. And that was done. Consummated. Presented before the entire world.

But they did not have to live together as man and wife. He could give her the freedom that she had wanted. But he could not give her this.

"Love is not to be," he said. "Not for me."

"I know that you don't trust it," she said. "And I understand why. But you have to understand that what I feel for you has nothing to do with the way you were manipulated into caring for your father."

"Was I manipulated? Or did I simply want to accept the easiest thing. The easiest reality."

"Do you think that I'm going to trick you into doing something wrong? Do you think that I'm secretly here to destroy your country?"

"No," he growled. "No," he said again. "It's not that. It has nothing to do with that. But a man cannot serve two masters. And my master must be my people. It must be my country. It must be to duty, and to honor.

That is where I must pledge my allegiance, and I cannot be split between a wife and a nation."

"Then make me part of your people. Make me one of those that you have a responsibility to. Surely that can't be so difficult."

Except that he knew it would destroy her. It was not what she wanted. It was not what she deserved. And without it she truly would be in captivity for all of his life. And he would be her jailer. And so he was trapped. Between violating all that he needed to be for his country and destroying the life of the woman who had married him.

He reached over to her and unclasped the first bracelet from her wrist. He unwound the chain that she had wrapped there, and then unclipped the second bracelet.

Her eyes filled with tears as she stared at him, but he knew that it would be a kindness. It was a kindness whether she saw it that way or not.

"What are you doing?"

"You are not my prisoner," he said. "And I will not make you a prisoner."

"Now you say this? Now, after we've been married? After I told you that I love you? That's when you decide to give me freedom?"

"We must remain married," he said. "That much is obvious. My brother would take a dim view on there being a divorce so quickly. It would cause scandal. And... I do not wish to undo all that you have done for my country. But you may go back to California. To

your life. There is no reason that you must stay here.
You do not need to be under my thumb."

"What if I choose to stay?"

"What you choose is up to you. But that will not
alter my behavior. That will not change the fact that
this place is my priority. That it is where my duty lies."

"I love you," she said.

She got out of bed, standing there, naked and radiant in the center of the room. "I love you, and you
can't make it so that I don't. I love you," she said, like a
spell, like an incantation, like she was trying to cast it
over him, like she was trying to change the very fabric
of what he was. Destroy him, then remake him using
those words to stitch him back together.

As if she might be able to use them to take the beast
and turn him back into a man.

"And I cannot love," he said. "It is that simple."

"You can," she said. "You can. But you're not a
beast to protect the world from you, you have to be a
beast to protect yourself from the world. You're afraid,
Javier. You're afraid of being hurt again, and I understand that."

Her words lashed against something inside of him
that felt tender and bruised. And he hadn't thought that
he had the capacity to feel such a thing.

"You don't know what you speak of," he said. "You
are protected. Even the betrayal that your father meted
out to you was not one that might put you in peril or
threaten your comfort in any way. He sold you to a
king. That you might be exalted. You have no idea what

I am fighting against. You have no idea what real suffering is. I have seen it. I have caused it. And I have to guard against ever causing it again. Do not give me your quick and easy sound bites, Violet King. I am not one of your internet followers. I am not impressed by quick, condensed versions of truth that are easy to digest. I have seen human suffering on a level that you cannot possibly understand. And I am related to the cause of it. If my life must be devoted to the undoing of it so that those in the future can simply live, then it must be. But don't you ever accuse me of being afraid."

And for the first time he saw her crumple. For the first time, he saw her bravery falter, and he hated himself for being the cause of that. He had plucked the woman from her office some weeks ago and taken her off to a land that she had never even heard of, and she had remained strong. She had remained stoic. She had an answer back for everything he had said. But not now. He had finally taken that from her. He had finally destroyed some of what she was.

And there was no joy to be had in that.

It was confirmation. Of what he was.

That spark of light she had placed in him was now extinguished in her.

She had said he was not a monster, but he knew that he was.

That he would destroy her only more as the years wore on.

He hurt people.

He had caused pain under the rule of his father, and

under the rule of his own heart, he would cause Violet pain as well.

"If you think that's what I meant, if you think that's who I am, then you haven't been paying attention at all. I thought that we knew each other. I thought that our souls recognized each other," she said, her voice breaking. "You saw me reading the book… And I knew that you would be reading it too. I knew it. You know the library was the first place that I looked for you that night we first made love. Because somehow I knew you would be looking at the same story I was, trying to see if you saw us in there."

"You misunderstand. I wasn't looking for answers because I already have them. I understand that this was significant to you. That this was a first for you. But I have lived life. I have already had all the revelations I will have. Perhaps you can think of me as a lesson learned."

"What an expensive lesson," she said, her tone full of venom. "Wedding vows seem a little bit extreme."

"As I told you, the wedding vows can remain."

"Why would I stay married to you? If you don't want to have a real marriage?"

He gritted his teeth, fought against the terror that clouded his chest at the idea of losing her. He liked much more the idea of being able to keep her while keeping her separate.

"Do what you must."

He gathered his clothes and began to dress.

"Where are you going?"

"Out."

"I would never have thought that you would transform yourself into a basic sort of man. But that is very basic. Just out. No explanation."

"Because I don't owe you an explanation. Because you got the explanation that you were going to get already. That you thought there was more is your problem, not mine."

He gritted his teeth against the burning sensation in his chest and he walked out of the room, closing the door behind him.

Closing the door on them. On temptation.

Whatever she did now was her choice.

But he had done his duty, for honor.

Whatever she said, that was why.

He ignored the kick in his chest that told him otherwise.

He ignored everything.

Because that was the real gift of having transformed himself into a beast.

When he had done that, he had taken his feelings away as well.

So why did his chest hurt so much?

CHAPTER THIRTEEN

VIOLET WAS STUNNED. All she could do was sit there in the center of their marriage bed, alone. She had known that he would have an issue with her loving him. She had. But she hadn't known that he would do this.

Why now? Why had it come to this now?

All this time he could have set her free. He could have made this bargain with her.

And suddenly she felt very alone. Her whole family had been here for the wedding today, but she hadn't had enough time to speak to them. Would she have found strength from them?

She could call her sister. Her mother. Her father even.

She knew what Minerva would say, actually. Minerva would want her to do what made her happy. But Minerva would also say that sometimes difficult men needed you to believe in them until they could believe in themselves. Because that was what had happened with Dante.

But no one had helped Violet up until this point. This had been the most independent she had ever been.

Yes, it was somewhat enforced by the entire situation, but it was still true. She had to stand on her own two feet since she had been brought here. It had been difficult.

Difficult to face the fact that her relationship with her family hadn't been what she thought. Difficult to be thrown in the deep end of independence, when she had been so surrounded by the people that she'd loved for so long. The people that she had depended on for her entire life.

But all of this had been about choice. A lesson in it.

Ironic that she'd had to be kidnapped and dragged across the world to really face the fact that she wasn't her own person. Not that what she had built wasn't hers to some extent.

But she had been propped up for so long by her father, and then was angry about the fact that he had been controlling things from behind the scenes when she had…

She had been fine with it as long as it had benefited her.

Allowing him to invest money when she had needed it.

Knowing that he was there as a safety net.

But nobody was a safety net for her in this. Because her heart was involved, her emotions. And there was no one who could fix it but her.

Her and Javier.

But he had broken it, because he was afraid. Whatever he said, he was afraid.

She understood what he thought. Understood why he felt the need to protect himself so fiercely.

There might not be real curses in this life, but there was pain that could feel like a curse. Betrayal that could make you feel changed.

And there might not be magic spells or incantations, but there was something even more powerful.

Love was the magic.

And she was going to have to figure out how to make it work.

She didn't have a spell. Didn't have anything to make the fairy tale literal.

But then, the beast wasn't on the outside. It was inside of him.

And it wasn't made of the sins of his father, wasn't made of tainted blood. It was made of fear.

And love couldn't exist alongside fear. Because they would always fight with one another. Love demanded bravery, and fear demanded that you hide.

He was hiding.

He was the strongest, bravest man she had ever known, but in the face of love, he was hiding.

If she could understand that.

Because he had just taken her heart and flayed it open. And she had already known that love could hurt, because the betrayal of her father had wounded her so badly, and she had to make the decision to forgive him in spite of that.

Was that what she had to do here? Forgive and love until he could do the same?

She didn't know.

She found herself wandering to the library, because it was where she had found him before. It was where she had found some of the answers she had been looking for. Maybe... Maybe she would find them again here.

Because she wanted to understand. Because she had so many questions.

Why had he done this now? Why had he turned away from her now? Told her she could live a wholly separate life from him, go back to California...

He didn't do it until he was sure that you loved him.

That truth sat there, like a rock in her chest. He hadn't done it until he was certain of her love.

He had not done it until part of him was certain that she would stay.

And so that meant she had to, she supposed. Even if it was the hardest thing she had ever faced in her entire life.

The idea of staying with a man who didn't love her.

She went straight to the back shelf, but she couldn't find it. The book with their story.

The book was gone.

And that, above all else, gave her hope.

"What are you doing down here?"

Javier looked up from the book and at his brother.

"Where else would I be?" He asked the question somewhat dryly, and yet to him, it made perfect sense that he was here. To him, it made all the sense in the world.

"Not Dad's favorite dungeon," Matteo said. "But still, definitely a logical choice for somebody who is punishing themselves."

"Is she still here?"

"Who?"

"My wife."

"As far as I know."

"Are you certain?"

"Honestly, I didn't consider the whereabouts of your woman to be my responsibility. I thought that was one of the perks of flopping her off on you. What has happened?"

"She's in love with me."

"Obviously," Matteo said.

"It's obvious to you?"

"Well. Not necessarily to me. But my mouse may have said something to the effect."

"Livia said something about it?"

"Only that she thought Violet seemed quite taken with you. And that it was probably a good thing she hadn't married me, all things considered."

"She's a fool."

"*Livia?* She's the least foolish woman I have ever known."

"No. Violet. She's a fool to love me. Anyone would be a fool to love either of us."

"It's true," Matteo said. "I don't disagree with you."

"So you understand that I told her I could not esteem her over the fate of the country."

"Is it a choice that must be made?"

"Yes. Because if the choice for Monte Blanco's well-being is not my ultimate motivation, then something else will replace it. And that makes me vulnerable."

"Vulnerable to what?"

He spread his arms wide. "To this," Javier said. "This. To being just like our father. A man with a favorite dungeon. A man who harms others."

"Is that what you think? That a mere distraction could turn you from the man that you are into the man that he was?"

"Haven't we always said that we must be careful to turn away from anything that might make us like him?"

"We must. I agree. But I suspect that you loving this woman will not bring it about. I think it is loving yourself above all else that opens you up to such concerns. Do you think that sounds right? Because our father never loved anybody. None of his corruption came from loving us so much. Or our mother, who we never even knew because she was dead before you ever took your first steps. No. Love did not cause what our father did."

"But I have to be vigilant…"

"Against what?"

"As we discussed, it would be far too easy to fall into another life. After all, wasn't it so easy to believe that our father was good because we thought we loved him?"

"What's the book?"

"Something that Violet was reading. A beauty and the beast story."

"What do you suppose you'll find in there?"

"An answer. Magic. I don't know. Some way to change myself, because I don't know how else I might. To be a man for her rather than a beast."

"Maybe you don't need to change it all. Doesn't the Princess in the story love him without changing?"

"But she deserves better. She deserves more."

"What did she ask for?"

"Nothing," he said, his voice rough.

"Then why not offer nothing but yourself?"

"Because that is something our father would do."

"No, our father would take the choice away from her. Which is what... Well, that's what I did, in the beginning, isn't it? Our father would do whatever he wanted regardless of what she asked for. So why don't you go back to her? And find out what it is she truly wants. Listen. Don't simply follow your own heart. That's what men like our father did. Consider another person. See where it gets you."

"Maybe to disaster. Maybe to hell."

"How does it feel where you are now?"

"Like *hell*," he responded. "Like I'm a foolish man staring at a fairy tale asking it for answers."

"Sounds to me like you don't have any further to fall. And I need you to be functional. So sort yourself out."

"Are you advocating for love and happy endings now?"

Matteo laughed, shaking his head. "Hell no. The opiate of the masses in my opinion. But if you wish to join the masses, Javier, then I won't stop you. And if it is what Violet wants, then all the better that she didn't marry me. Because I would never be able to give it to her."

"Are you such a hypocrite that you would advocate for me what you don't believe you can have for yourself?"

"Not a hypocrite. Just a king. A word of advice. Javier, you were not born to be the King so don't take on the responsibilities that I carry. Take on your own. You're a warrior. And you were born to be. That is your position in this country. And the difference between you and our father was always compassion. It was the sight of that little girl being married off that changed you. That made you see. It was always compassion that made you better. It was always caring. Because a man who is in and of himself a weapon ought to have that sort of counterbalance, don't you think? In my estimation, love will make you stronger at what you do."

"And for kings?" Javier asked.

"A king should not be vulnerable." Matteo turned, then paused for a moment. "But it might be the only thing that keeps a beast from being dangerous. If you are so worried about hurting others, perhaps you should think about that."

And with that, his brother left Javier there, sitting

in the bottom of the dungeon holding on to the book. And he knew that he would find no answers there. None at all. No. The only answers for who he was, who he might become, who he needed to become, lay with Violet.

If only he could find the strength in himself.

But perhaps, until then, he could borrow strength from Violet.

Suddenly the fairy tale made sense in a way that it had not before. His fingertips burned, and he opened up to a page with an illustration of the giant, hulking beast having his wounds tended by the delicate maiden.

Perhaps he was too focused on the transformation.

Perhaps he had not looked enough at what the story was really about.

As she said, almost every culture had a version of this tale. And in it, the beauty was seen by the reader to be the weak one. Put up against a dangerous beast.

But he was the one who changed. He was the one who transformed, because of the power of her love.

In the end, it was the beauty who held all the power.

In the end, it was her love that made the difference.

And so, he would have to trust in her power. Trust that, like in the story, she was more than able to stand up to the challenge of loving him.

He was the one who had to find his strength.

She had already proven that she had more than enough for the two of them.

CHAPTER FOURTEEN

SHE HADN'T GONE back to California.

Her social media efforts had begun to create more tourism in Monte Blanco, and she was working with the tourism bureau and local business owners on strengthening the market. She was still involved in her own company, with her VP holding down the fort on the local level back in San Diego.

She had begun spending more time in the city. She had rented office space and had begun working in earnest on her project to bring work to Monte Blanco. Specifically for women. She was in talks to figure out manufacturing, something that she was arranging with Livia, and she had already hired a few women that she had met at a local shelter to work on data entry.

She was having to do some training, and she had hired people to do that as well.

And all of it was helping distract from the pain in her chest, though it didn't make it go away.

She was still living in the palace. It was just that it

was so big it was easy to not see Javier at all. And he had allowed that to be the case. He hadn't come to her.

She wouldn't go to him. But she was there.

Because part of her was convinced, absolutely, that she needed to stay. That he needed to know she was choosing not to run. That he needed to know that she was choosing this life. That it was not a kidnapping, not anymore. It was just a marriage.

And she wasn't the one not participating in it. That was him. He was the one who was going to have to figure out exactly what he wanted and exactly how to proceed. She couldn't do it for him. And that, she supposed, was the most difficult lesson of all. That no matter how much she wanted to, she couldn't force a transformation if he didn't want it.

He had to accept her love.

And right now he didn't seem to be able to do that.

She looked around the small office space, up in the top of the small, cobbled building. Above the ice-cream shop. It was so very different from all that modern glass she had left behind in San Diego. But she wasn't sure she even remembered that woman. The one who wanted things sleek and bright. The one who had been so confident and set in her achievements.

She still felt accomplished. It wasn't that she didn't know that she had done impressive and difficult things. It was only that she had found something she cared about even more. She had been so focused for so long. And it hadn't allowed for her to want much else. That had been a protection. She could see now. Because caring this much about something else, about someone else, was extremely painful. But it had also pushed her to find a strength inside of herself that she hadn't known was there. And so for that she was somewhat grateful.

Grateful, if heartbroken.

Because no man would ever be Javier.

She knew that she would never find another man she wanted in the same way. That she would never feel this way for another man. Because she hadn't. Not for twenty-six years. She had had chance after chance to find another man, and she had never even been tempted. And she wouldn't be. Not like this. Not again. But that didn't mean she couldn't thrive. It was just that she would never fall in love again.

Tears pricked her eyes. She didn't want to fall in love again anyway. She just wanted to love him. And she wanted him to love her back. Even facing the fact that it was impossible now didn't make it seem real. Because she hoped... She just hoped.

She wanted to believe in the fairy tale. But she was afraid that the real world loomed far too large. That the damage inflicted on him by his father would be the ultimate winner.

And she didn't want to believe in a world like that. But she had to face the fact that it might be all she got.

She went downstairs, stopping in the ice-cream parlor and getting herself an ice-cream cone, trying not to cry when the flavor reminded her of Javier. The owners of the shop hadn't asked her any questions about why they hadn't seen Javier. Why it seemed that she was always alone, the Prince nowhere to be found after the two of them had been so inseparable at first.

Plus, she had a feeling she just looked heartbroken. She was trying her best to get on with things, but it was not easy at all. She was strong. But strength didn't mean not shedding tears. Strength didn't mean you didn't mourn lost love. Or in her case… Love that could have been if it weren't for a maniacal dictator who had taken the love of a young boy and used it so badly. Made him think that he was the monster, rather than his father.

When she went back out onto the street, she stopped. Because there, down one of the roads, she saw a silhouette that looked familiar. And she flashed back to that moment she had been standing in her office. But she had imagined then that he was dangerous. And now… Now the sight of him made her heart leap into her throat.

"Livia told me I might find you here," he said.

"Livia is a turncoat," Violet said.

"She works for my brother. Her loyalty is always going to lie there."

"Well. *Well.*"

"I need to speak to you."

"Why?"

"I need to know… I looked for answers. I looked for answers that didn't have an enchantment or a spell. I don't know how to change."

"You don't know?"

"No," he said. His voice rough.

Her heart went tight, and she looked at his sculpted, haunted face. "Javier, it was never about the right spell. In all the stories, in all the lands, in all the world. It was never magic that changed the beast. It was love."

He shuddered beneath her touch. "I know. But I looked and looked at that book. At this story." He held the book up. "The beast isn't the strong one. It's the beauty. It's her love. And still I'm not... I'm not fixed."

"Yes," she said, moving toward him, her heart pounding hard. "But don't you know what changes him? It's not just her loving him. It's him loving her back. Love is the magic, Javier. We might not have sorceresses and spells, but we have love. And that's... That's what makes people change."

Hope washed through her as she saw a change come over his face, his body. As he moved into action, swept her into his arms and pulled her up against his body. "Is that all I have to do? Just love you? Because I do. Because I have."

"Yes," she whispered.

"What if I hurt you? I am afraid... I have caused so much pain, Violet. All the years since don't make it go away."

"You have to forgive yourself. Because you're right, some things can't be undone. But people do change, Javier. You have. It doesn't wipe the past clean. But neither does a life of torturing yourself."

"If I hurt you... I am so afraid I will hurt you. More than I fear any other thing, more than I fear losing you, I fear hurting you. And that is what I could not accept."

"You won't," she said.

"You are so sure?"

"Yes," she said. "Because I saw the Prince beneath the beast the moment we first met. Even when I didn't know you, I trusted your word. You know the cost of selfishness, and you will never ask others to pay it. If you were your father, we would all know it by now. You simply have to believe it."

"What if I don't change?" he asked, the question sharp and rough. "What if love is not enough to change me?"

"I love you already. You're the only one who thinks you're a beast, Javier." She took a step back, putting her palm on his face. "*You* need to see the change. Not me."

"I love you," he said. "And I... You're right. I was afraid of what that might mean. Because I did love my father. Very much. But he was a monster. And I couldn't understand how I had been so blind to that. How I had seen only what I wanted to see. Because of how much I loved him. And I never wanted to be that way again. I never wanted to be vulnerable to making such mistakes. But I think... I think it is time for me to accept that I am a man, and no matter what, I will be vulnerable to mistakes. But with you by my side... You have a compassionate heart, Violet. And perhaps the secret is loving other people. Valuing their opinions. Not shutting yourself up in an echo chamber of your own desires so that nobody ever reaches you. So that no one can hold you accountable for what you do. Our love will make me better. Loving you... Matteo said something to me today. He reminded me that our father never loved anyone. That it wasn't love that made our father behave the way he did. It was the love of himself. The love of power above people. I trust that we will find right. Good. That you will help me."

The plea was so raw. So real. Straight from his heart.

"Of course," she said, resting her head on his chest. "Of course I will do whatever you want. I will be whatever you need."

"But what do you get from this? What do you get from me? I need you. I need you to be a moral compass. I need you to love me. I need you to change me. What I do, I do for you."

"You showed me my strength. You gave me the fairy tale I didn't even know I was looking for. And I became the heroine of my story in a way that I didn't know I could be. You are my prince. And you always were. Even when you were a beast."

A smile tugged at the corners of her mouth, and she kissed him. Deep and long. And when they parted she looked into his eyes. "And if am being honest. I quite like you as a beast. With cuffs and chains and the lack of civility. Because you've always held me afterward. Because you've always treated me with care. Because you know when to be both. A man and a beast. And I think that's better than just having one. It makes you perfect."

"I thought... I thought that my father had doomed me."

"No. The sins of our fathers might have brought us together. But they don't define us. It's about us. And it's about what we choose. It always has been.

"That's the real magic. That no matter where you end up in life… You can always choose love."

"I choose love," he said. "I choose you."

"So do I." She bracketed his face with her hands. "But I must warn you. I have a debt to collect, Prince Javier."

"A debt?"

"Yes. You owe me for the rest of my life."

"What is it that I owe you?"

"Only all of you. And I intend to collect some every day forever."

"Then you're in luck. Because I intend to give myself, all that I am, even the broken parts, forever."

"Excellent. I might still take you prisoner, though."

"I would happily be your prisoner."

"I shall have to figure out which of the dungeons is my favorite."

"Whichever one has a bed."

"Well. That I most definitely agree with. Did we break the curse?" she asked.

"I believe that we did."

"Magic," she whispered.

"Or just love."

EPILOGUE

"PRINCESS VIOLET," CAME a rich, deep voice from behind her. "I believe I have a debt to collect."

A smile touched her lips, and she looked down into the crib at her sleeping baby, a girl they had named Jacinta, then back at her husband, who was prowling toward her, a wicked smile on his face. Man and beast become one.

That was how he loved her. And it was how she liked it.

Fierce and tender. Dangerous but utterly trustworthy.

"Do you?" she asked. "Because last I checked I was still the richest woman in the world, and a princess on top of it. I doubt I owe anyone a debt." She had continued to run her company successfully from Monte Blanco, and with the country having become the most photographed tourist destination in the world, a phenomenon and a craze in the last five years, her brand— now primarily manufactured there—had only become more in demand.

"This is not a debt that can be paid with money.

Only with your body." A shiver ran down her spine. "And with your heart."

Javier was the best husband. The best father. He loved her even more now that they'd been married half a decade than he had in the beginning, and she never doubted it.

"I wanted a kiss earlier," he said, gruffly, nuzzling her ear. "You were too busy with Jacinta and Carlos."

"Carlos was eating paper," she said, in a voice of mock despair over their three-year-old son's taste.

"And I find I am still in need of my kiss."

So she kissed him.

"I find that is not enough," he said, and from behind his back he produced the jeweled cuffs. Anticipation fired in her blood.

"This is one debt I'm eager to pay," she said.

When she had paid—enthusiastically, and repeatedly—she lay sated against his body.

"You are right," he said finally. "You are magic. You have transformed me multiple times, you know."

"Have I?"

"Yes. From beast to man. Heartless to a man with more love than he can contain. You made me a husband. You made me a father. You made me love. You made me whole."

"Oh, Javier," she breathed. "This is the very best magic."

"Yes, My Princess," he agreed. "It is."

* * * * *

Keep reading for an excerpt of a new title
from the Romantic Suspense series,
CHRISTMAS BODYGUARD by Kathrine Garbera

Chapter 1

Daphne Amana was a leading attorney in international rights and criminal law. The company directory at Mitchell and Partners law firm described her as a brilliant mind who handled cases of real international importance. She was pretty sure her boss wouldn't see this as her most brilliant move. But she was out of options, so meeting an informant in a dark alley…well… might not be the safest decision, but it was the only play she had in this case. She was trying to return contested artifacts back to the village of Amba Mariam, the modern home of the Gondar tribe from Ethiopia.

The collection was part of items taken during the 1867 expedition of British and Indian soldiers with the stated aim of freeing British hostages and punishing Emperor Tewodros II and his people. The military assault was a success. Hundreds of items were pillaged by the soldiers, and many were sold at an auction where most of the collection that was housed at the British Museum was acquired. The only rival for its significance was the collection at the Los Angeles Museum of Foreign Cultures, which was donated by the grandson of one of the British soldiers and contained gold and silver regalia, jewelry, weapons and liturgical vessels and crosses from the Ethiopian Orthodox Church.

Daphne became aware of the collection at the Los Angeles Museum of Foreign Cultures when a cultural minister for Ethiopia, Marjorie Wyman, hired her law firm to petition to have the items returned when her discussions with the museum director stalled. Working in international rights gave Daphne a background that made this case one she wanted—no, needed—and she'd asked to be assigned to it. But the director of the Los Angeles Museum of Foreign Cultures, Pierce Lauder, was being difficult, and his attorneys kept asking for postponements of the actual trial that were making the discovery of the items still in the museum's collection difficult.

Daphne had taken the museum to court, gaining a motion to compel them to allow her access to their museum and storerooms, but still they were coming up with excuses for why she couldn't get in to inventory the items. Sure, it was the holiday season. Thanksgiving had been last week, so a lot of people had taken extra time off, herself included, but she could see through the flimsy excuse that Mr. Lauder kept providing.

Especially when the list of items he'd sent over marked several as *missing*. Not stolen or lost, simply missing. She'd gone on a local news show to make the public aware of the contested collection, which had stirred up interest and spawned several public protests, but still, Lauder wasn't returning her calls.

History had always been a passion of hers—the fact that many of the exhibits she'd enjoyed at places like the British Museum were taken as spoils of war had never seemed fair to her. It was part of the reason she'd become an international rights attorney.

The collection was a small one that had come to the Los Angeles Museum of Foreign Cultures by way of Jonathon Hazelton-Measham, who'd been part of the 1867 expeditionary force of British and Indian soldiers led by Sir Robert Napier into Maqdala, an almost impenetrable mountain fortress in northern Ethiopia that was the seat of power for Emperor Tewodros II. Tewodros had established a library and a treasury and dedicated a new church as part of his plan to unite the tribes of Ethiopia and create one united country.

The British had been helping Tewodros, including educating and training his son, when they had a falling out, which resulted in a massive assault on the fortress in 1868. It caused the deaths of hundreds of Tewodros's army with only limited British casualties. After the invasion, there was widespread looting of the fortress and church by soldiers.

Many of the pillaged objects were subsequently reassembled and auctioned. But Jonathon Hazelton-Measham kept the objects he'd collected, which included many items from the new church that had been constructed. The items, or tabots, included a silver censer used to burn incense during mass, a ceremonial cross, two chalices, and processional umbrella tops. He also had several weapons and regalia that were rumored to have come from the fortress. The thirty-nine items that Jonathon looted and brought home with him to England were sold via his descendants to the museum in 1985.

Of the thirty-nine items, the museum claimed that roughly twenty-five were still in their possession. Fourteen items either dropped off their inventory or were currently marked missing.

Her client represented the department of culture for Amba Mariam, the modern day name for Maqdala. The items weren't just in the Los Angeles Museum of Foreign Cultures but also in the British Museum. The bulk of the items still accounted for remained in England at different museums and libraries as well as a museum in Canada, all of which were holding ongoing discussions about their return to Amba Mariam.

Which didn't help Daphne's case. There was no precedent stating that the items should be returned. If the items had been returned in London, that would go a long way to swaying the judge to rule in her client's favor.

However, the recent theft of items by a complicit staff member at the British Museum was helping her with this case. There were only so many places to sell rare antiquities without raising suspicion.

The missing items included one chalice, the silver censer—apparently the brass censer was still in the museum's possession—a piece of regalia not named, two other tabots, and a diptych in a silver case that may have come from a private collection in France, which suggested to Daphne that the thief knew the value of what they were taking. Then there were two manuscripts that were described in the late Hazelton-Measham's will as part of his donation but had been dropped from the museum's inventory in the 2010s before the current director was in place.

It wasn't the monetary value that was at the heart of this case as far as Daphne was concerned. It was the cultural value. Emperor Tewodros II had collected these items from all of the tribes of Ethiopia to unite them into one kingdom.

Apparently there had been flooding at the museum, and some of the pieces had been lost during the evacuation of items. Which wasn't a suitable response as far as Daphne was concerned. Museums were sticklers for cataloging their priceless antiquities. She'd been going round and round with Pierce Lauder and his lawyer, Ben Cross, ever since, trying to figure out what happened to the mysterious missing pieces.

Which was didn't explain why she was sitting in her car at nine p.m., trying to get up the courage to go and meet an anonymous person who had messaged her on WhatsApp, saying that they had information on the missing items.

She'd tried to convince them to come to her office, but they'd been insistent they would only meet her away from both the museum and her offices. She'd suggested a twenty-four-hour coffee shop that she frequented, Zara's Brew on North Hollywood Boulevard. Her informant had agreed to her request, but they wanted to meet behind the shop so they wouldn't be observed.

She was a single woman who could protect herself, but still, this had *bad idea* written all over it. She knew Carl would have forbidden her to do it and probably would have removed her from the case entirely, so she hadn't let anyone know she was here. Which now seemed…well, not like her best idea. So she texted her assistant just to say she was meeting an informant and gave her location. She also held her phone in her hand with 911 ready in case things got dicey.

She left her car and hit the lock button as she walked

toward the coffee shop. The barista on duty had their head down scrolling on their phone, and there were only two diners in the café area. She took a deep breath as she headed around the back of the shop and saw that the alleyway was empty and dimly lit.

Because of course it was. Right?

Pulling the strap of her purse higher on her shoulder, she moved into the alley.

"Hello?" she called.

Stepping further into the alleyway, Daphne cautiously scanned the area. A shot rang out, and she felt the impact of the bullet in her shoulder. There was a sharp burning pain and she bit her lip to keep from crying out. God. That hurt. She hit 911 as she fell to the ground, trying blend with the shadows near the dumpster. She felt woozy and scared, and started the deep breathing exercises she'd learned to keep from passing out because she had a low blood pressure condition that gave her dizzy spells.

"911, what's your emergency?"

She heard the sound of footsteps running away and a thud. Glancing toward the sound, she didn't see anyone.

"I've been shot. I'm behind Zara's Brew. I got hit in the shoulder and am bleeding. I can't see who shot me."

"Stay on the line. I'm dispatching police and ambulance to your location."

Daphne leaned against the dumpster, keeping her legs close to her body, her head tipped back as she held the line. The 911 operator kept talking to her, and Daphne always responded, but she knew she was close to losing the battle to stay conscious. She reached for her purse to get a tissue to apply pressure to her shoulder.

She fumbled when opening it, and some of the contents spilled out on the dirty pavement. After a moment, she found the tissues and pressed one against her shoulder, then put her phone on speaker, setting it on her lap. She glanced around, realizing that her wallet had fallen out.

Placing the bloody tissue on her lap, she reached for the wallet and other items, and she noticed something that looked like a burlap bag with the museum logo on it. She pulled it toward her just as the cops parked at the end of the alley. She shoved the bag into her purse along with her wallet.

"I'm over here," she said.

Two cops came toward her location. One of them was on alert, gun drawn.

"I'm unarmed and injured," she said.

"Don't worry, ma'am, the ambulance will be here in a moment. Where are you hurt?"

"Shoulder," she said. She was starting to slur her words as the pain became too much. Her last conscious thought before she passed out was to draw her purse to her body. "Don't…leave…my…bag…behind."

"I won't. We've got you."

The world faded to black. She was semiconscious of being loaded onto stretcher and transported to the hospital. She was still in pain and still scared, but she knew that whatever was in that burlap museum bag was worth it. After all this time, she might have finally gotten a break in the case that would help her figure out why the museum had stopped talking with her and the cultural minister. What really happened to the missing artifacts?

* * *

Working for Price Security gave Kenji Wada a chance to use the skills he'd honed for nearly a decade in the CIA as a field operative. The job had been exciting, and there had been a few life-and-death moments, which suited Kenji's need for adrenaline rushes. But he'd retired after a case had gone sour. And when Giovanni "Van" Price had offered him a job working as a bodyguard at his elite company, Kenji had said yes.

He was Japanese American, raised by his single American mother. He didn't know much about his Japanese heritage except that his father's family was from a highly traditional background of wealth and status and hadn't approved of her. They hadn't been allowed to marry, so his mom had said deuces to his old man and came back to LA, where she'd raised him. He had been close to his mom from the beginning and had nothing but love and respect for her. But he always had questions about half of his lineage and no one to ask since his mom had died several years ago when he'd been overseas on an assignment. He still missed her.

Something he didn't like to dwell on.

As he waited for the latest briefing at Price to start, he knew that he was going to volunteer for whatever new assignment came up. Didn't matter that it was the start of December. Christmas wasn't his favorite time of year. It had always been a struggle for his mom to buy him presents, pay the bills and keep food on the table. She'd always made the holiday special and since he'd lost her… Christmas just felt empty. If Kenji had his way, he'd work through the holidays. He needed to stay busy and focused on the job. Not his personal life.

The others on the team arrived for the meeting. The Price Security team was small and tight. Van liked to say they were a family, and Kenji did view the other members like siblings. They all got along for the most part but also got on each other's nerves at times.

There were two women on the team. Luna Urban-DeVere was a former MMA fighter, wickedly smart and tough as nails. She was married to multimillionaire Nicholas DeVere, who she met while protecting him. Lee Oscar was the tech genius of their team, and though she had skills with weapons and hand-to-hand combat, most of the time she stayed here in the Price Tower, keeping tabs on the team and providing information to them.

Next was Rick Stone, a former DEA agent who always looked like he was about to fall asleep until there was danger—and then he turned lethal. Then Xander Quentin, a big British bloke who was former SAS and Kenji's best friend. Xander had recently fallen in love with a woman in Florida and was now splitting his time between the East and West Coasts. He had just finished an assignment in New York and was taking time off over the holidays to spend with Obie, his girlfriend.

Last, but certainly not least, there was Van Price. He wasn't that tall, but he was solid. All muscle from the tip of his bald head to his broad shoulders with the tattooed angel wings that peeked out from under his collar.

"We've got a new client. Should be a nine-to-five gig and will be running through the holidays and into January," Van said as he came in. "I know I promised some of you time off, so…"

"I'll do it," Kenji said.

"Mate, I thought you were coming to Florida with me," Xander said as he turned to him. His best friend looked hurt.

Kenji clapped him on the shoulder. "It's more important you go."

Xander bro-hugged him. "Yeah. Thanks for that."

"Depending on where it is, I could do it. Nicholas will be working until Christmas Eve," Luna said.

"I've got this," Kenji said. He needed to be busy, more than anyone else. "Unless I'm not right for the job?"

He looked over at Van, who just gave him that slow smile of his. "You're perfect for it. A local attorney was shot while meeting an informant about a case of potential art theft they're investigating, and her firm wants a bodyguard."

Cakewalk.

"Who is it?"

"Lee? You got the presentation ready?" Van asked.

Lee's fingers moved over the keyboard of the laptop she took everywhere with her, and the presentation flashed up on the screen at the end of the boardroom. But he wasn't listening or paying attention once the photo of the client was shown.

Daphne Amana.

Well, screw him. Of course he'd volunteer to protect the one woman he was pretty damned sure didn't want to see him again. He couldn't tear his eyes away from the screen. She'd matured, of course. It had been nearly twelve years since he'd told her *see ya* and broken up with her.

Her deep brown eyes sparkled with intelligence, and her face was still gorgeous, with high cheekbones and a full mouth. She had long black hair and tanned skin. In the corporate photo, she wore a suit that had been tailored to fit her shape in a way that immediately stirred regrets in him about how he'd walked away from her.

He'd done it because family hadn't been in his plans at twenty-three. He'd known that he wanted the most dangerous assignments the CIA had to offer, and having Daphne in his life would have been a liability. So he'd ended it, never expecting to see her again.

But here she was. Doing the good work she'd always wanted to do and putting herself in danger.

"Kenji?"

"Huh?"

"Mate, you okay?" Xander asked.

No way was he bringing up Daphne. He was the best man to keep her safe. Something Van might not agree with if he was aware of their past.

"Yeah," he said, shaking his head. "I'm good. When does the gig start?"

"Today. Head over to their offices, where you'll meet her and assess the situation," Van said.

"Cool."

The meeting went on with everyone updating the team on their current assignments or being briefed for the next one, but his attention was on his phone, where Lee had sent the case file. Daphne Amana. He wasn't sure this assignment was going to be the distraction he'd wanted. But he couldn't step away now.

Kenji walked back to the elevator to get ready for his assignment. Like there was a way to get ready to see the one woman he'd never really forgotten. He'd had moments when he'd thought of her. Had googled her late at night when he wasn't working or playing *Halo* against Xander online. Despite that, he'd never reached out.

When he walked down the hall, he noticed someone had put Christmas wreaths on his and Xander's doors. Kenji stood there staring at the display of holiday cheer. Christmas was going to be all around him. There was no way around it. At this time of year, he had to just grit his teeth and get through it. Normally work was a good distraction, and one time when X had been off the same time as he was, they'd gone to Aruba, rented a house, and gotten drunk and laid by some gorgeous women at their resort for ten days.

It had been perfect. No sign of Christmas or thoughts of exes or parents—the ones who were around and the one who hadn't ever tried to see him.

He rubbed back of his neck and used the security app on his phone to open the door as he heard the elevator opening. As close as he and X were, he didn't want to talk about Daphne or Christmas.

"Hold up, Kenji," Xander called as he got off the elevator.

"Yeah?"

"Hmm, well, I don't want to overstep, but is something up with you?"

They normally didn't do the intense emotional shit unless they'd both been drinking, when they could pretend that neither of them would remember it. So Kenji knew he must be showing signs of weakness. This was the one time when he shouldn't be.

"Dude," he said. Then realized that he was about to open up big-time, and neither of them wanted that. Also he didn't want to burst X's love bubble. He shook his head and opened his apartment door. He and Xander were the only two with apartments on this floor.

Xander put his hand on Kenji's shoulder and squeezed it. "I'm here if you need anything. Obie's working hard studying for finals, so I'm sort of at loose ends because Van didn't want me to get stuck out on assignment. But…"

Kenji turned and looked at the man who was more like a brother to him than just a friend. Xander was a lot like him. Work kept them grounded. True, Xander had his fiancée now, but that hadn't changed who he was at his core.

"I will. But like Van said, it should be a breeze," Kenji said. Hoping Xander bought it.

His friend just raised both eyebrows. "'Kay, but if it's not, I'm here."

"Thanks."

 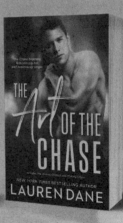